SOULCATCHER

WILLIAM SKELTON

ISBN: 978-1-66780-252-7 (printed)

ISBN: 978-1-66780-253-4 (eBook)

Table of Contents

Chapter 1

The bell sounded, announcing the end of lunch period on a beautiful day in mid-June. Most kids were already in their classes, but a few stragglers rushed off the playground and into the school.

"No running in the hall!" Principal Phillip Conner bellowed in his usual way to the usual suspects. Yet he still wanted them in their classes on time.

Other teachers noticed Laura Hanson lingering in the staff room. They headed off to their afternoon classes, leaving her to herself. She had been unusually quiet over lunch. Soon she emerged and made her way down the hall. Principal Conner, bald and lanky with a short stubbly beard threaded with white, had also noticed her delay. He peeked out from the office, watching her slow pace, and winced a little. He left and followed at some distance. As he peered up the stairwell she was ascending, he was appalled to see her stumble near the top of the second flight. She gripped the handrail with both hands for a few seconds. She looked up at the second-floor doorway as if summoning the strength to carry on. Her eyes widened, and she inhaled deeply and forced herself up the last few stairs, down the hallway, and into the bustling class.

Phil Conner quietly sprinted up the stairs. He went to the door of Laura's class. He stood back so as not to be noticed and peered through the wire mesh in the narrow vertical window in the door. Laura didn't acknowledge the bedlam in the Grade 5 class. She weaved her way to her desk, sat down, and stared blankly at the students for a few seconds. Then she closed her eyes. Two girls approached her desk as she laid her head down as though there was no one else in the room. The girls looked at each other and seemed concerned for their teacher. The rest of the class proceeded to celebrate the lack of supervision. The kids seemed to be anticipating it; maybe this was a regular event.

Phil took a step back and hung his head. "Damn it," he said under his breath. He pivoted on his heels and quickly returned to the school office. The only person there was the school secretary.

"Mary, I need you. Laura is drunk again. I gotta get her out of that class. I need you to take over the lesson."

Mary was visibly apprehensive. Laura's trials and tribulations were well known among the school faculty, but she had been stable since the fall. "I-I'm not a teacher, Phil. I don't know where she's at—"

"Neither does she! Please just do your best. We have to get up there right away. I'll get her out and you watch the kids, please. I'll see if Glen can take over after his class. I'll ask him to cancel volleyball."

Phil and Mary went up to Laura's class and Phil gestured for Mary to look in through the narrow window. Laura's head was still down on the desk. Mary was shocked but knew what she had to do.

"Okay." Phil went into game plan mode. "I'll go in and get the kids in their seats. You grab her purse—it should be in a drawer. I'll tell them she's ill and help her out of the class. You . . . I don't know . . . ask them what they're working on and get them reading their textbooks. I need to take care of this, but I'll check back with you as soon as I can."

Phil took a deep breath, exhaled through his nose, and opened the door. He walked in with a feigned confidence and spoke loudly, locking his eyes on as many kids as he could. "Class . . . everyone

. . . everybody back in their seats. Back in your seats, please." The class moved rapidly in response to this new authority figure. "Mrs. Hanson is ill. We're going to help her to the nurse's station. Secretary Mary will supervise the class for the time being. Be on your best behaviour! I'll be back!"

Then Phil gently held Laura by the shoulders, roused her, and spoke in her ear. Mary opened the deepest desk drawer and discovered her purse. The principal coaxed the teacher to her feet. She seemed surprised but suddenly lucid. Phil kept an arm around her shoulders as she shuffled to the door. Mary gave him the purse once they were in the hall, and then she returned to the class.

"Let's get to my office," Phil said quietly to Laura. She started to speak, but Phil interrupted, saying, "Let's just wait till we get to my office." They made their way down the stairs, and when they got to the office, Phil closed the door and sat Laura down. He went around his desk and sat down also, then let out a big sigh, blowing his cheeks out.

"Laura, I'm super disappointed. This is *it* this time. We have bent over backwards for you, sent you to rehab—twice! I'm done. I'm calling the superintendent, and I'll get Mary to call the union. When you came back *last time*, I thought you were finally in the clear, but this is *bad*."

"I haven't been drinking," Laura said in a low voice, slightly slurring her words. "I mean it. I haven't touched . . . I haven't been drinking."

"That's what you said last time. Laura, we are done. Done! I'm calling you a cab and sending you home."

"No! I mean it—I haven't been myself for a while, and in the past few days it's gotten worse. I can't put my finger on it. I've been down. I'm messed up for some reason, but I haven't been drinking!"

"You're messed up, all right." He inhaled deeply and exhaled. "Okay, okay. I need to do this anyway. I'll get the cab to take you to Island Occupational Testing Lab for a blood test." He shook his head. "It's a foregone conclusion, but we'll make it official and then that's it. Are you on any medication?"

"No." She shook her head and stared vacantly.

This confirmed his suspicions. "Okay," he said in exasperation. "I'll call you a cab, then start the process with the superintendent."

Phil walked her out to the cab and gave the driver the address to IOTL without giving him the company name. When Laura arrived, they already had her slotted in and knew the protocol to process her. She was in and out in twenty minutes. They called a cab to get her home.

* * *

A yellow Prius quietly rolled into the cul-de-sac of a mature neighbourhood. Laura stared at the screen on the back of the front seat, punched some buttons, and tapped her credit card. She carefully got out of the cab and scanned the adjacent houses for neighbours. Arriving incognito would be best right about now. As the hybrid vehicle crept away in stealth mode, she opened the gate of the white picket fence and mindfully walked down the path. Their neighbours Lazlo and Marta might be sitting on their porch swing— they often were. She opted not to look over and verify their presence. Lazlo and his wife had been the Hanson's neighbours for over ten years, and were aware of Laura's troubles—not in detail, but enough that they'd be concerned at her appearance. She knew they'd be wondering why she was home at this time, and why she'd come in a cab. Did she have car trouble? They would be friendly and help if they could. She couldn't completely conceal the two bottles of wine in her purse. Her ankle buckled about halfway to the house, causing her to stumble slightly.

Rosie, the Hanson's golden retriever, came around the side of the house to greet Laura. Ordinarily, Rosie would have been already there, anticipating her mistress's homecoming, but today Laura was early. Since their older home had a fully fenced yard, and Rosie was getting on in years and was so well behaved, they kept the dog door in the back porch accessible through the day; Rosie and Muss, their calico cat, could get in and out. Originally, the cat's name was Colonel Mustard, but that always seemed too formal and too much work to say. "Muss" was more fitting for the lazy feline. Rosie was moving slowly these days, not running up to Laura but walking as briskly as she could, wagging her tail and limping slightly until her back leg started working again—it was stiff from lying down.

Laura gently lowered her purse to the sidewalk and bent down on one knee "You look like I feel, girl," she said to the dog. She scratched Rosie around the neck for a few seconds, then rose, grabbed her purse and, with a clank of the glass bottles, continued toward the house. She opened the screen door, holding it with her leg as she unlocked the main door and pushed it. The cat joined them, quickly scrambling inside through her legs.

Laura put her bag on the kitchen table and extracted the wine bottles. One was already a quarter gone; she had partaken of it while in the back of the cab. She took another swig, then went to the main-floor bathroom and splashed some warm water on her face. Not satisfied with the results, she grabbed the soap and washed off her makeup. Dripping with water, she looked at herself in the mirror, less than happy with her fifty-year-old self. She felt a wooziness again; it was becoming more common. She gripped the sink and held on. Fatigue and dreary shame descended over her shoulders like a weighted blanket, making it hard to step away from the sink.

"Why do I feel this way? What the hell is going on?"

Her reflection didn't reply. How to cope? In the classic fashion of a binger, of course. If a wagon's going fast enough down a rough, unknown road, you're bound to fall off—that's just physics. She returned to the kitchen and poured herself a large goblet of wine, almost draining the first bottle. She busied herself feeding Rosie and Muss, then returned to her thoughts, and the table and the wine. How did she get caught up in drinking, anyway? It was a gradual, insidious thing. Stress. Availability. Heredity. Pain. Loss. The odds were stacked against her. When the drinking kicked in, feeling sorry for herself became a hobby. Mostly, Laura missed her mother—now more than ever, in spite of her passing almost ten years ago.

It was the anticipation of the decline that got to her the most. Watching her closest loved one go through that illness, then worrying the same damn thing was going to happen to her.

The memories of her times with her mother were vivid. She would visit her in the nursing home after every school day. About halfway through the forty-five-minute visit, finally it would come to her mother and she would say, "Laura! You're Laura!" Then laughter. Laura was happy and sad at the same time. Happy that her mum remembered. Sad that it took her so long to get there. It was taking longer and longer. Soon it didn't come at all. They couldn't play cards anymore. They couldn't discuss their daily lives, or the family's latest challenges. They couldn't even watch TV together. There was no sense of interaction. Laura resorted to sitting with her mum, flipping through old photo albums, and pointing out faces and places as if it was a memory test. It was flashcards for the demented.

Her beloved mother's expression soon became more and more blank as the plaque in her brain slowly betrayed her, robbing her of what little she had left. Zero memories. Not even knowing there was love around her—that was the worst.

A glass of wine when she got home from the care home. Then another. A few years of old folks' home visits took their toll. Finally, her mother was out of her misery, and Laura could start hers in earnest. Was that how it started for her mother? Depressed and saddled with a spouse who had a low score on the empathy scale, and a zero on the sympathy scale?

* * *

A few hours later, Ryan, Laura's husband of twenty-five years, got home. He entered the kitchen with a bag of groceries. He took one look at Laura holding a large glass or red wine and was crestfallen and in disbelief. "What's going on?"

"Had some trouble at school today," Laura said with some trepidation.

"What kind of trouble? Why are you drinking?" Ryan said calmly.

"They accused me of drinking at school. I'm suspended again."

"Accused you? But you *are* drinking! You're drinking right now! What the heck did you think was going to happen?"

"I wasn't drinking—I swear I wasn't drinking. Not then. I've been feeling funny—awful, really. Phil saw me and assumed I was drunk. They sent me for a test, sent me home."

"Great, Laura, just great. I thought this was all behind us. What a . . . You were doing so well! Your school year was going great. You were just about through it. Goddammit. You've really taken a giant leap backwards here. Jesus. I said the last time you got out of rehab that it was three strikes—or ten friggin' strikes, whatever it was—and I'd be gone. I can't believe this."

"Well, this is different," Laura said. "I wasn't drinking, I—"

"Then what's going on right now? What the hell do you call this?"

"If something's going to set me off, this would be it! I've had a trying day, and I . . . Yes, I fell off the wagon. I'll be fine tomorrow."

Ryan was indignant. "You're full of shit, you know that? You are just full of shit. You know the school and the union—and it's the same with us—three strikes and you're out. Over. Done. No recourse. You knew that! And here you are. Jesus, this is so disappointing." Ryan shook his head and rubbed his eyes with the heels of his hands. "I gotta think about this. This is a game changer."

"Ryan, honestly, I am . . . This is so temporary." Laura was mumbling. "Tomorrow I'll be on the straight and narrow. I'll call the union, call the school, call the superintendent, call Phil. Fix it all up. Bingo bango bongo."

"Listen, Laura. Look at me." He lowered his voice and bent down with his hands flat on the table, as if he was bargaining with a child. "Remember the last time, last term? *That* time was the *last* time they'd be offering you rehab. Do you remember? *The last time.* They made it real clear—the school board was done with you, and the union wouldn't help you anymore either. You've run out of options."

"I'm an excellent teacher—they know that. And I contribute tons of extracurricular activities. They can't just replace me just like that."

"They can, and they will. They probably already have." Ryan turned away from his wife and went up the stairs to the small bathroom. After a few minutes he returned to the kitchen.

He started back up. "What you do to yourself is no longer my concern. I'm moving on. I've made up my mind. I told you myself, along with everybody else, that the last time would be the last time. This is it—I'm gone." Ryan was firm.

"I have a disease! I'm going to relapse from time to time," Laura said, trying to justify her behaviour.

"I don't buy that disease bullshit! A person who has cancer or diabetes can't wake up tomorrow and decide not to have cancer or diabetes affect their lives. But you *can* wake up tomorrow and say you won't let this affect your life anymore. Disease, my ass."

Ryan was still speaking as he left the kitchen. He sought some alone time again, at least a few minutes to gather his thoughts. He looked through some mail stacked on the stand near the front door, but he was just going through the motions. His mind was still churning through his confrontation with Laura. He went back into the kitchen.

"You know, our relationship hasn't been perfect, but we have— we *had*—a marriage that was working again. The last six months, things were clicking, right? You were doing so well. Work was going good, and you liked your class. When you're good, you're great. A great mother, a great wife, a good friend. And when you're drinking, it's bad. Real bad. There's no happy medium. How goddam long is it going to take you to learn that? You missed out on half of Emily's teenage years! She loves you so much, and you just squandered so much time you could have had with her. You were absent for months on end. We've raised a lovely daughter and gotten her into university, almost paid off this house. We're close to getting that cabin for summer vacations, or maybe for our retirement. That's pretty good in anybody's book. Now you piss it all away in one fell swoop. We could see the finish line. It was all coming together, but for some reason you just couldn't stand to see it happen, so you did this."

"That's not true! I'm working for this marriage just as much as you are!" She was obviously under the influence.

Ryan rubbed his temples and ran his hands through his hair. He paused for a long time, deep in thought and squinting as if in pain. "I've lost count of how many times we've had this argument. Déjà vu all over again. We only argue when you're drinking. Have you noticed that? Probably not. Anyway, I'm not waiting around to watch you descend into the nine stages of hell. Not again. You can go there on your own this time. I can't watch. I'm going to collect some things and . . . *I am leaving*. Do you understand?"

The words hung in the air as the reality of them seeped into Laura's consciousness. "Ryan, no. I'm just having a bad day. This is so *temporary*, such a small thing." She almost seemed confident as she spoke. Ryan had never actually walked out before, even though he had threatened to do so many times.

"*Life* is temporary, for Chrissake! When we were first going out, you were a force to be reckoned with—you had it all going for you! You were so smart in school, and we always knew you'd be good at whatever you decided to do. Your spirit and your love made my world turn. Without you in my life, it would have stopped and been empty. Now . . . just dark days. When you're drinking, the earth stops spinning and we're stuck on the dark side, until you smarten up and we can start living again. Ah, what's the point? You're not going to remember anything I say anyway." He thought he was done but added, "I don't know why you can't cope anymore. You have it all. And I can't think of how I can help you anymore. I'm out of ideas, out of love, and out of energy for you. You're not afraid to die—that's obvious—but you *are* afraid to live."

Ryan went upstairs and into their bedroom. He rummaged around for a large black sports duffle bag that had been folded up in the bedroom closet. It had the logo, VIC'S ATHLETICS - UNIVERSITY OF VICTORIA ROWING TEAM, on it. He threw it on the bed and opened his chest of drawers and started to fill the bag with clothes and his shaving kit. When the bag was full, he changed out of his street clothes and into a T-shirt and shorts. He tossed the dirty clothes into the hamper in the laundry room and went back downstairs.

Rosie stood stiff legged at the bottom of the stairs, wagging her tail in wonder at Ryan's body language. He took the duffle bag out to his SUV, returned to the house, and opened the main closet and picked out two jackets, his jogging/rowing gear, and shoes. He tossed them into the back seat and went back to the kitchen.

"Laura, I'm leaving," he said solemnly.

She looked up from the kitchen table with a glazed stare. "Okay," she said with no emotion.

Ryan sighed at her disassociated state and turned to leave. As she reached for the remains of her wine, Laura tipped the large glass over and it shattered when it hit the table. Ryan glared and shook his head at her sloppiness.

"Don't worry, I'll get it," Laura said with false calm.

"Oh brother. *I'll* get it. I'm always cleaning up after you." Ryan grabbed the garbage container from under the sink and with a paper towel carefully scraped the shards into the plastic pail. He replaced it under the sink and left the room.

"It's garbage day tomorrow," Laura called out a few seconds later.

"Oh my God, you just don't get it!" Ryan cried as he walked through to the garage. Nevertheless, he returned to the kitchen and grabbed the garbage. Without thinking, he took the cans and jars set out on the counter for recycling and put them in the bag also. He took the paper and an empty aluminum foil box and stuffed them in the white kitchen garbage bag. He went back out into the garage, crammed the bag into a larger green garbage bag, and tied the top.

Mounted on the wall of the garage was his single scull. This was a smaller, recreational version of a larger, more official rowing shell. Ryan hadn't been out on it for two summers. Leaving the garbage bag, he looked up at the sleek carbon fibre craft. He took off the coat and backpacks that had been hanging over it. He took a rag off his workbench and dusted the boat, then went over and pushed the button to open the garage door. Sunlight poured in, reminding him it was a beautiful day. He reached for the scull and with a grunt hoisted it above his head and walked it out to his SUV. With some effort he placed the side of the craft on the roof rack and pushed it into the centre of the vehicle. With two ratchet straps, the boat was secure and he returned to the garage to find the oars. He strapped them to the roof racks with special Velcro ties.

Ryan went back through the garage and into the house and announced to Laura, "I'm taking Rosie."

She looked up as if this had caught her attention as somewhat significant. "Why? She's fine here." She had poured a new round in a new glass, stemless this time.

"You keep Muss. I'm taking Rosie—she needs to get out. "

"Where are you going?"

"I'm not sure," he lied.

Ryan whistled a unique call that Rosie recognized as "Come here." As he was doing so, he reached for her leash on the hook intended for their keys by the garage door. He turned to the pantry and grabbed a large bag of dog food. "Come on, girl, let's go!" he said with a phony enthusiasm.

"Where are you going?" Laura sat as if chained to the kitchen table.

"I'll check in with you at some point," Ryan said. "Maybe in a few days." He exited with Rosie close behind. He tossed the dog food in the back of the SUV and shoved all his gear aside to make room for his travel companion.

"Up you go!" He patted the floor in the back of the vehicle. "Come on, girl. Up! Up!"

The dog just stood there, firm in her belief that her days of jumping that high were over.

"Oh brother. Come on, Rosie." She was too heavy to lift from the ground up. Ryan bent over and hoisted her front legs onto the back bumper. Rosie awkwardly moved into position, looking back at Ryan. He bent over and lifted her rump, then gave her a firm push.

He shut the hatchback, got in the driver's side, and started the car. He put it in gear with his eyes on the rear-view mirror, checking to see if Laura had gone to the garage. As he did so he realized he'd left the garage door open and hadn't taken the garbage to the curb. He put the vehicle in park and returned, reaching for the bag. In his haste he swung it roughly, forgetting its contents. As the bag quickly passed the side of his leg, a pointed shard of glass sliced him just below the knee, leaving a deep, jagged laceration.

"Goddammit!" he exclaimed in pain. It started to bleed profusely, "Jesus Christ." He couldn't believe he'd been so careless. He went back into the house and into the main-floor bathroom for a first aid kit.

Laura heard him return. "I thought you were leaving," she said, slurring her words. She was still stationed at the table.

"I am, I am. Just had a mishap." He tried to sound as calm as possible.

Laura got up from her chair, glassy eyed and foggy she went to the bathroom. Ryan was sitting on the closed toilet, his right leg extended as he fumbled with a Band-Aid box.

Laura went wide-eyed when she saw the gash and the blood dripping down his calf. "Holy shit, you really did a number on yourself." She perked up momentarily. "That's a mess. You're gonna need stitches, I'd say."

"I'll be fine. I just need to keep some pressure on it, and a couple of Band-Aids will work. That stupid broken glass got me—it was in the garbage bag I put out."

"Mmm," she murmured, then hesitated for a moment and went back to the kitchen.

Ryan put three Band-Aids over the cut, and one more across all three for good measure. He cleaned up the bathroom with some toilet paper and finally headed out. As he walked, he knew the gash was going to be problematic, as the skin could open up when the muscle was flexed. Hopefully, it would stop bleeding during the drive.

He returned to his vehicle and carefully manoeuvred himself into the driver's seat. Reaching to the visor, he pushed the button on the garage door remote. "Okay, Rosie girl, let's go!" He looked up at the rear-view mirror, hoping to see an enthusiastic face above the back seat, but the golden retriever remained out of sight.

When he was heading down the street, he let out a heavy sigh and pushed the hands-free button on the steering wheel. "Call Emily," he said.

"Calling Emily" was the reply, and the phone rang through the speakers.

"Hi, Dad." Emily seemed genuinely pleased to hear from him.

"Hi, Em, how are you?"

"I'm fine. Just heading back to the dorm. Had a busy day."

"That's good . . . Hey, I um, got some bad news."
"Uh-oh. That doesn't sound good. What's wrong?"

"Well . . . your mum. She's drinking again and—"

"Oh no, you can't be serious."

"Yes, I'm serious, and I'm really pissed off. After the last time, I thought we were out of the woods, with the detox and the therapy and the union and the school board writing her up. Things had really stabilized, but here we are back to the same old BS. The school sent her home. I think this is it—I think she's done at work." He started to speak more matter-of-factly. "So . . . I've left. I'm driving away. I've told her this is the last straw, and I have the dog and I'm heading . . . somewhere . . . away."

"Oh my God." Emily seemed stunned. "Do you mean that? You're splitting up? You've left her alone?"

Ryan paused briefly to calibrate his response. "I don't know what you call it, but yes, I'm leaving, and she is alone. I guess that's why I called. She'll need some help or supervision or some damn thing at some point soon."

"How is she right now? Is she coherent?"

"She was sitting at kitchen table, drinking and pretty nonchalant about the whole thing, really. Can you call her and check in?"

"Um . . . yeah, I can." Her voice seemed disconnected from her thoughts. "I'm not going to be able to get there tonight, because tomorrow I have a field trip booked with my practicum class. Jesus. What about Lazlo and Marta next door? Maybe they could look in on her?"

"Maybe, but it's not fair to them to—"

"You need to turn around and get back home! She needs help." Emily was adamant.

"I can't help her anymore, Em! I've helped her dozens of times. She needs some sort of reality check, and this is it."

"Where are you going?"

"I don't know."

Chapter 2

Ryan Hanson *did* know where he was going. He pushed a button on the steering wheel. "Call Walter mobile," he said. "Calling Walter mobile," the woman's voice replied.

The dial tone found its way to the stereo speakers. It rang four times and the recorded voice of a person who was obviously reading text said, "Hi, you have reached the confidential voice mail of Walter Rosenthal of Barrett, Burns & Pike. Please leave a message and I will get back to you as soon as I can. Thank you and have a great day." It beeped.

"Wally, its Ryan. Call me, buddy. Call my cell, please, as soon as you get this message. Thank you."

Walter and Ryan had met in university. They were quite close while in school and kept their friendship alive through business dealings and the occasional golf game. Walter was in the category of alumni from the Lower Mainland who had come to the University of Victoria (UVic) as a plan B. His first choice was to attend law school at the University of British Columbia in Vancouver where he grew up, but he didn't have the grades. UVic was his fall-back. Ryan, on the other hand, was born and raised on Vancouver Island and UVic was his dream. Ryan was a stellar computer science student, while Walter barely made it to the bar. Walter fell in love with Victoria when he lived there during school, and also fell in love when he met Claire in a criminality class. Claire was a local girl from Saanich, and they were married right out of school. She became a paralegal specializing in property transfers, and Walter started at the bottom as a rookie articled student at BB&P. Eventually, Walter moved up in the ranks and gained a solid reputation as a criminal lawyer. Maybe there would be an *R* in the company's abbreviation one day.

Ryan was pleased when the phone rang after only a few minutes. He saw the display on the screen on the dash and picked up. "Wally! Hey, thanks for calling back."

"No worries, buddy. What's up?"

"Well"—Ryan took a breath—"I'm sorry to say that Laura and I are on the outs. She's back to drinking again, and I'm out of . . . hope, ideas, whatever. I just can't do this anymore."

Dead silence for a couple of seconds, then Walter replied, "Oh man, I'm sorry, Ryan. Gee, you guys have invested so much time. Are you sure?"

"Right now I'm sure. I feel *very* sure. I'm spent and frustrated, and I really feel betrayed. She's decided to go back to the bottle, and I'm beyond the point of . . . sympathy or empathy, or whatever I'm trying to say."

Walter asked, "So how can I help? Do you need a place to stay, or do you want to meet, or . . . ?"

"I'm calling to let you know about us, but I'm also calling about the cabin. I know we said we'd kind of put it on hold for now, that you were free to look for other buyers, but I've really thought about it and would like to buy the cabin from you and Claire."

"Are you sure you've thought about this? I think you're stressed right now and need to give it some more time."

"Nope, nope. I made up my mind a few days ago. I was going to call you. I've wanted the cabin since you suggested it and said you were planning to go back to the Lower Mainland. I loved the place anytime we visited you guys there. And I loved it when we looked it over when we were thinking about buying. It was Laura who wasn't too keen. I just went along with her, hoping she'd come around. Now I don't care. I know it's a good fit, whatever happens. It's a good location when I need to go into work, the property is big enough to expand if we want . . . and I'd really like living on the lake."

"Hmm." Walter seemed surprised at these latest revelations. "I was just about to list it with a realtor. I was going to call her today."

"You don't need to do that, Wally—I'm in. I agree to your asking price—I know it's a good deal based on the market, since I've looked into it. I'm surprised you're even selling it. It's such a nice spot." There was hesitation on Walter's end. "Are you there?"

"Yes, yes, I'm here. Okay . . . well, this is bad news about you and Laura, but good news, I guess, about the cabin. Are you sure you can handle it? What about your work? Are you still doing the web design thing?"

"Yeah, yeah, I'm still doing website design. I can do that from anywhere. And I can handle the cabin. Financially, emotionally, I'll work it out."

"But I guess neither of you know what's in the future now," Walter said, cautioning Ryan.

"Wally, I've never been more sure of anything in my life. Let's get going on the paperwork."

"Okay, then. I'll get Claire working on the transaction. She has to get someone else to execute it, but she'll do all the rest of the work, so no charge for it. There's a little more red tape here since this is what we call a ninety-nine year lease. It's officially Native land."

"So is that a problem? Is it possible the lease transfer wouldn't be accepted, or they'd cancel the lease if they wanted you out?" Ryan asked.

"Not likely. They're actually expanding the number of lots on that side of the lake, and they'll be improving the road for better access. They may even reset the lease date to year one for you, so you have maximum time."

"So, they're good to deal with?"

"Um . . . yeah," Walter said hesitantly.

"Is there anything you aren't telling me? The lease is real, right? The cabin is sound?"

"Yeah, yeah, it's all on the up and up for sure. You've seen the structure. You've even looked underneath, right? The lake level is real stable. It's all good. I'll get Claire to send you the legal description and lease papers for the bank. You'll need to get home insurance—it's a little different based on the leasehold agreement, but we'll walk you through it."

"Okay, great," Ryan said. "So, you know what I'm going to ask you next?"

"Um . . . probably. You want to go there right now."

"Yup, you got it!"

"Uh, I guess so."

"You're hesitating, after all this time? You know my word is good." Ryan was offended.

"Hey, no, it's not that. But I do feel a little awkward, like I'm enabling your separation, that's all. I mean, we love Laura too. She probably needs your help right now."

"I'll be damned if I'm gonna feel guilty about leaving this time." Ryan said carefully, mostly to himself, "Let's face it—it's always been about her. I've bent over backwards for her and now *she's decided* this is what she wants. She knew the consequences very well! She knew how this movie would end."

"Okay, okay, okay . . . Jesus." Walter seemed prepared to support his friend at last. "I moved the hiding spot for the backup key. It's hanging on a nail under the deck. If you're looking at the lake, it's at the far-right corner—you have to really reach for it. Unhook the lattice on the side and it will bend back, then reach up to the top of the beam."

* * *

Walter was right. The gravel access road that ran along the back of the dozen or so existing cabins on the east side of the lake had recently been improved—widened and graded. A couple of pieces of heavy equipment, dirty yellow in colour, sat at the far end of the road. As Ryan turned down the densely treed track, he felt a rush of excitement. He had made a decision to start a new chapter in his life, and he suddenly felt free and alive. He instinctively knew he had done the right thing. Any underlying guilt he felt for suddenly leaving Laura he had suppressed. As he drove by the old sign that had marked the entrance to the original development, he thought it looked dated and dilapidated. The indian springs logo depicted a corny, cartoonish image of a Chief that would need to be changed to attract a more upscale clientele to the new development.

Walter and Claire's cabin—cabin seven—was in the best location of the entire row. About halfway down, it had the deepest lot, with a long private road that was perfectly discreet, narrow, and overgrown. The cabin was perched on a spit of land that jutted out into the lake. Trees mostly obscured the view of neighbours on either side. Ryan stopped at the entrance of the cabin road. A heavy chain with pink surveyor tape tied to it in spots as a visual reference blocked the way. Walter had once said that no trespassers had ever accessed the cabin from the road, and there had been no problem with vandalism or squatters in the neighbourhood. There was no other indication of the reason for the road—no sign, no family name—just a faded metal number seven no one noticed anymore, high on a tree. He got out of the car and unhooked the chain from the tree to the left and dropped it on the ground. He got back in the vehicle, drove over the chain, stopped again, and replaced it. Ryan meandered down the mossy track toward the lake, savouring the moment the lane would open up and he would see the cabin on the right and the lake view, beckoning like a page from a travel magazine. The early-evening light filtered through the canopy above. It gave the dense green such a saturated look that if it were a painting, you'd say it was overdone. Soon bright sunlight at the end of the lane called to him.

Ryan pulled up between a tool shed to the right, the cabin to the left, and shut off the vehicle. The view from his windshield was even better than he remembered. He couldn't believe his luck that Walter was selling the place and the price was so doable. He got out and opened the hatchback. Rosie was feeling the excitement also; she wagged her rear end in anticipation of exploring her new world.

"Let's go, girl! Come on!" He pulled her toward him by her collar. She was heavy, but lifting her from the car and putting her down was much easier than doing a deadlift from the ground. As he bent down, he felt the cut on his leg split open and he winced in pain. He looked down at the Band-Aids and saw new blood seep out.

"Damn it!" he said under his breath, not wanting to make the dog think he was angry at her, or let the pain undermine his elation at being there. He put his hand on his leg for a few seconds to apply pressure.

Rosie went around him and hobbled toward the water. She seemed genuinely happy to be there, in the warm evening sun, out of the car, and in a new environment. Instinctively, she waded into the lake and just stood there, appearing to smile as she panted. She looked back at her master. This made Ryan's heart glad. He laughed at the dog and decided to join her. He kicked off his runners and pulled off his half socks and waded in just above his ankles. The water was very cool, soothing, and refreshing. He looked out at the lake, over to the short dock to his right, then back at the cabin. This was going to work.

He rubbed his arms and let the dog remain where she was. Ryan made his way over to the elevated deck, pulled back the lattice, and groped around for the key. He found it with little trouble and unlocked the main door. As he unloaded the car, he let Rosie explore. She couldn't go far.

The cabin was basic in design. It was a standard wood frame, on pilings about four feet high to mitigate the effects of any high water. The deck, in need of some TLC, ran across the full width of the building, a wide stairway in the middle leading down to the ground. A single French door was centred in the front, and two large windows flanked it—one for the living room, the other for the kitchen. Inside, the ceiling rose; it had an unfinished feel but appeared vaulted. There was a pellet stove for heat, but electric baseboard heaters provided early-morning backup.

Ryan was anxious to get out on the water with the single scull. He unstrapped it from the roof racks, hoisted it onto his shoulder, and walked it over to the short floating dock. He swung it down and placed it on the silvery, weathered wood beside a single piling that stabilized the dock. He went back for the oars and placed them beside the boat. On the piling hung an old orange ring-shaped life preserver and rope that Walter had kept more for reasons of rustic charm than for practicality. Someone had painted indian springs along half the circle. Ryan looked out over the lake again and felt serene, while Rosie amused herself with a piece of driftwood along the water's edge.

* * *

Those first few days went by quickly. Ryan puttered around the cabin, cleaning and making plans, noting them on a white plastic memo board on the refrigerator. The weather was sunny and calm and he got out on the rower each day, in spite of the cut on his leg. He was motivated enough to jog each day and explore his surroundings, along the beach and down to the end of the road. He discovered a path opposite the main road that went deep into the Vancouver Island forest, winding around huge trees through a dark and damp world that saw little direct sunlight.

After several attempts to log into work from his computer, Ryan became frustrated with the quality of the internet connection, and the Wi-Fi range. On the Monday he opted to go into town and arrange for a higher quality internet service, a new router, and a Wi-Fi transmitter. He needed much more capacity if he was to work from home. He also stopped for groceries and dog food, then checked out the hardware store for a flashlight and some screws to secure the lattice that was flapping under the deck. In the hardware store, his phone rang.

"Hey, where are you?" It was Walter.

"I'm just in town running some errands. How are you? What's going on?"

"I'm good, real good for a Monday. Calling to let you know the paperwork is done. I'm sending it over by courier right away. I just wanted to make sure you were going to be there to sign for it."

"Um . . . okay. It will probably be forty-five minutes before I'll be back at the place."

"That works. I'm gonna say he'll be there around noon. I'll give him directions so he can find the place. Leave the chain down, please. Oh, and if you want, you could sign them right there and he can take them back with him. No rush, though. Keep them and look them over if you like, but it's exactly as we discussed—price, lease, everything the same."

"Hmm." Ryan was a little surprised at Walter's efficiency. "Okay, let me think about that."

"Are you enjoying the cabin?"

Ryan paused for only a second. "Totally. Love it. Really love it."

He finished up at the hardware store and headed straight back to the lake. As he dropped the chain and headed toward the bright light at the end of the canopied road, he thought about the courier and questioned himself about the impending reality of taking over the cabin. With or without Laura, did it make sense? If she came back into his life, she'd probably be pissed off about his buying the place. It wasn't her cup of tea. But what did *he* really want? He stopped the car, went to the hatchback, and let Rosie out. She jumped down and he grabbed some of the groceries. His mind was churning as he unlocked the door and propped it open with a bag. He put the rest of the bags on the table and looked out over the lake. It was a cloudy day, but there was still a gorgeous view. His rower called to him from the dock.

The courier arrived about twelve thirty. The rap on the door came as Ryan was fiddling with hooking up the new router. He let him in and asked him if he could hold on for just a couple of minutes. Ryan pulled open the plastic outer package, opened the thick envelope, and looked at the documents. Pink and yellow sticky arrows pointed to where he needed to sign. He sat down at the table and leafed through the papers.

The courier seemed very patient. "Nice place you got here," he said as he looked out the window.

"Yeah, thanks," Ryan replied absent-mindedly.

Everything seemed to be in order. Witness signatures were already conveniently in place; someone from Walter's office must have signed. Ryan paused briefly to look at the stack of papers. Such a lot of documents for a little cabin. The events of the recent past spun in his mind. Was he being too quick to jump into this? Was he being too selfish? Heck, he hadn't been selfish enough. He pictured Laura in her sober days; she would have been very annoyed with him for going through with it. But the price was right, and he could flip it if he had to. He signed and initialled the papers in multiple places, kept the copies marked for him, and stuck everything else back into the envelope and gave it to the courier.

"Can you please take these back to BB&P?"

"Yep, you bet. I was ready to do just that."

"Okay, thank you."

"Ciao," the courier said cheerfully as he jogged down the stairs and over to his van.

Ryan finished up with the Wi-Fi and tested his computer for connection. He got through the annoying set-up, wrote down the passwords, and was satisfied with the results. He had a functioning high-speed connection. His reward was to get himself out on the lake in the scull.

Whenever he started thinking about Laura, worrying about her condition, he forced himself out of it. Somehow, he felt he needed time and space. He wasn't anywhere near ready to reconsider a relationship that he felt had sucked the life out of him. Life was burgeoning anew in his spirit, and he focused on that.

Rosie was in her element also. She frolicked on the beach, in and out of the water for hours at a time. After a few nights, she jumped up on the bed to sleep with Ryan. She hadn't jumped up on the bed for years—not because she wasn't welcome, but because she just couldn't. Not being so sedentary was really agreeing with her. In the short time she'd been at the cabin, she had become slimmer and her coat healthier. Her eyes were clear and, like Ryan, she was getting back to her old self.

Chapter 3

As he was making coffee the next morning, Ryan looked out at the lake and was shocked to see two people standing in the water directly in front of the cabin. He stood bolt upright and stared out, perplexed, not sure what he was seeing. After backing away from the window, he turned off the lights in the cabin so he could look out without being seen. He crept to the side of the window and discreetly poked his head around. They were gone.

"Hmm." He puzzled over this. He resolved to head back to town that morning, pick up a few things he had forgotten, and check the hardware store for an appropriate sign he could post somewhere noticeable. That should do it.

At the hardware store in a display of various signs, he found a bright red-and-white no trespassing sign. When he got back to the cabin, he posted it on a tree using two long screws. He put it in a conspicuous place on the left side of the property where the sand turned into the underbrush. This must be where the people had entered, from down the beach. Now it would be clear to anyone that they weren't welcome.

The next morning, about the same time, Ryan was distressed to again see the same two people standing in front of his cabin.

"What the hell is this?" he said aloud. Rosie cocked her head, assuming he was talking to her.

Again he shut off the lights in the cabin, thinking he could look out without being seen. The two figures were just standing there, one near the water's edge, the other almost up to their waist. It appeared to be two women. They were chatting, calm and nonchalant. Ryan reached for his cell phone on the kitchen table and scrolled for Walter Rosenthal's number. He selected it and dialed.

When Walter answered, Ryan started talking without a hello. "Who are these people standing in the water in front of my cabin?" He tried to sound calm.

"What are you talking about?" Walter was clearly playing dumb.

"Wally, I think you know what I'm talking about," Ryan said more firmly as he continued to look out the front window. He paused to let Walter speak, but there was an awkward silence. "Walter, you *must* know what I'm talking about." He realized he sounded like a scolding parent. "I'm calling you at eight in the morning because there are two people on the property, standing in the water . . . Jesus, she just waved at me!" Ryan backed away from the window. "She must think I'm you!"

"Oh, she knows it's you," Walter admitted. He released a sigh. "I . . . I was sure this was over with. I had a chat with the band, and it was all good."

"I call bullshit on that, Wally. What the hell are they doing, anyway?"

"No, no, Ryan, really I did. I talked to them and said I'd sold the property to a friend and I wanted this to go well. Anyway, they won't come by that often. It's really not a problem."

Ryan was defiant. "Not a problem? I have strangers trespassing on my property, using *my* beach, and that's not a problem? This is not what I signed up for!"

"They mean no harm. I'm sure they'll only stay a short time. I can talk to them again if you like," Walter said, trying to settle Ryan down.

"I think I'll be the one doing the talking—or getting a different lawyer. You'd better do some explaining."

"Well, you know it's called Indian Springs for a reason." Walter's tone was dismissive. "They think the water is special, has healing properties or something. It's just Aboriginal lore, a legend, an old wives' tale. They just think the water will help . . . some things . . . or everything, I don't know. It's just a big placebo effect. Like holy water—they have baptisms and stuff."

"What's wrong with the water on their side? It's the same damn lake."

"They think it's better closer to the source," Wally explained. "If you look closely on a calm day, you'll see bubbles in the water about fifty - sixty feet out. Pretty sure that's where the spring fills the lake. They think the water is best right there. Just so happens our—I mean *your*—cabin is closest to the spring. They come around and make use of it."

"So this has been always going on and you said nothing about it?"

"Well, yeah. I guess it's always been happening. But coming over to the property and accessing the spring is pretty rare. Maybe someone's ill and they're trying to get closer to the source. For some reason they think morning is best . . . I don't know. They won't stay long—that water will be frickin' cold."

"If they want to get close to the source, they can damn well come over in a boat and not cross my property. I'm gonna go out there and tell them so. I'm sure they have boats over there."

"Ryan, I wouldn't do that if I were you. You need to get along with these people. They've never really been a problem, and in their minds, they own the place."

"I have a long-term lease! *I* own it. I'm reading that damn thing and getting some advice." Ryan did a double take and thought about what Walter had said earlier. "What do you mean, they know it's me?"

"They know it's not me because they know I sold the place. The deal is done, and they had to approve it. It's all in the paperwork. You signed it."

"So you *knew* they'd be trespassing on a regular basis!"

"No. Yes . . . well . . . they *have* done this before, but it's not frequent, and they just come and go."

Ryan hung up on Walter. "They just come and go," he said sarcastically to the dog. He peered out the window, only to see they were gone.

Ryan made plans to go back to the hardware store and get another sign he had seen while buying the first one. He remembered a private property sign he'd almost bought the first time. He would accompany the first sign with a second. That should get their attention. But before he could run errands, he had to log onto his computer, take care of some emails, do a short job on a client's website, and email his boss to ask for a few days' stress leave. All this took much longer than he anticipated.

He let Rosie out to roam. She seemed to naturally understand her boundaries and never went too far. She loved going in and out of the water, exploring the bush behind the cabin, and enjoying her new freedom.

It was after lunch before he set out to town. He stopped at the liquor store and bought some beer and wine. In light of Laura's issues, he had abstained from drinking at home for years. Now he had some space and thought he would have a couple of beers in the evening, maybe call Wally to come over. Maybe a face-to-face meeting would be more effective and defuse their recent conflict.

The next morning, things happened exactly as before. The two women arrived, oblivious to the signs, and one went in the water while the other stood at the water's edge. Frustrated, Ryan shook his head and resigned himself to the fact that he might have a long-term problem. He didn't want this; he wanted peace and privacy. The whole point of owning the cabin was to have an oasis to call his own. He fumed but opted not to confront them. His passive side held him back. Maybe tomorrow. Walter's voice echoed in his mind: *You need to get along with these people.* But at the same time, this was unacceptable and needed to be nipped in the bud. He sat at the kitchen table and watched them leave after about fifteen minutes.

He found himself at the hardware store yet again that day. This time he selected the beware of dog sign to complement his growing collection. He returned home, cracked open a beer, sat on the porch, and enjoyed the view. The afternoon was waning—it was close to suppertime—so he grabbed his screwdriver, two screws, and the new sign. He and Rosie made their way over to his sign tree. He started mounting the sign on top of the stack. No, it would look better at the bottom, so he moved it down.

"Hello." The female voice behind him was almost cheerful. Startled, Ryan turned, stumbling a bit in the sand. It was the two Native women.

"Uh . . . hello," Ryan replied.

"Are you having trouble with people on your property?" The pleasant-looking older woman, shorter than her companion, asked sincerely.

"Uh . . . yes." Ryan cocked an eyebrow, a little bewildered at the question.

"Hmm" was all she said, looking at the younger woman.

They continued to the water's edge. Rosie followed them, anxious to make friends. Ryan looked at his watch as if he didn't know the time of day. Shouldn't they have been there in the morning? Their timing was a surprise. He finished setting the second screw on the beware of dog sign and walked over to the women.

"Is this the dog?" the older one asked as she bent down and petted Rosie. Rosie wagged her tail, enjoying the attention.

"The dog?" Ryan was puzzled.

"The dog to *beware of.*"

"Oh yes. Yes, I guess it is."

"Pretty friendly dog."

"Um, yeah, I guess she is at that," Ryan admitted.

The older woman stood up and put out her hand. "I'm Owny. This is my daughter, Patsy."

"Oh, uh . . . hi. I'm Ryan." He shook her hand but was frustrated with himself for being too friendly. "Owny, you say?"

"Yes, Owny. My real name is Oneida, but everybody just calls me Owny." She had a bit of a Native accent. "Owny Wilson," she said, as if there were more Ownys to be aware of. "Pleased to meet you."

Patsy offered a small wave and said nothing. She waded into the water, leaving the two at the shore.

"You usually come in the morning," Ryan said, trying to reset the conversation.

"Yes, but we have an appointment tomorrow, so we came this evening."

"Hmm," Ryan muttered, mildly curious about the appointment.

"We have to go into Victoria tomorrow," Owny said. "Patsy has to have an assessment. She has cervical cancer and they're watching it closely. They may operate soon."

"Oh . . . I'm sorry to hear that." Ryan was sincere. "So this helps? Here at the lake?" He had a skepticism in his voice.

Owny took a beat, ignoring his tone. "Yes, I think so. We'll know more tomorrow. It's something we've always done. Some of our people don't think much of it, but some do. I do. I would come here with my parents. It's just part of our beliefs. Why not do everything I can to help Patsy? Traditional, non-traditional, anything."

Ryan's contempt rapidly drained out of his body. Suddenly, Rosie jumped up and ran down the beach a short distance. She grabbed a stick and brought it to Owny, thinking the group must be there to play with her. Owny tossed the stick toward Patsy in the water, and Rosie playfully waded in.

"I suppose it couldn't hurt," Ryan said.

They stood in silence briefly, and Patsy laughed at Rosie splashing around.

"How do you like the place?" Owny asked.

"Oh, I really love it. It's only been a few days, but I know this is for me."

"It's the best spot on the whole lake," she said. "Our village grew up on the other side of the lake only because it's closer to the salt water from there. It's just a couple of kilometers to Old Town, and it's a little more out of the wind."

"Old Town?"

"Oh, our village is split between the old part on the ocean and the newer part on the lake. We call them Old Town and New Town," Owny explained, then said suddenly, "Okay, Patsy, let's go!"

"That's it?" Ryan asked. He was now enjoying the chat.

"That's it!"

* * *

As Ryan expected, he had no visitors the next morning. He took the single scull out for a good workout up and down the length of the six-kilometer lake. When he returned to the dock, the sun emerged in earnest, and the heat of the day hit his back and amplified his body temperature from the workout. He went to the cabin and released Rosie, who had been cooped up during his excursion. He pulled off his shirt and kicked off his shoes and waded into the lake to cool off. It was cold, but he convinced himself to go completely in, and the dog eagerly followed.

Feeling refreshed and acclimatized to the water, Ryan swam out farther to explore the area where the bubbles were thickest. He could see them coming up from the bottom, and once he was in the middle of the effervescent plume, it was noticeably warmer. He called the dog closer and lingered there, imitating his four-legged friend in a stationary dog paddle. The bubbles seemed to improve the buoyancy, and he felt very much at peace, splashing Rosie and looking back at the appealing cabin.

Eventually, he swam back to shore and sat on the warm wood of the dock to dry off. He threw a ball for Rosie, who happily splashed in and out of the water, retrieving it for her master. Ryan's last conversation with Walter churned in the back of his mind. Since meeting Owny and Patsy, he thought perhaps he had overreacted. Still, he wasn't crazy about their feeling entitled to randomly access his property. Perhaps there was a way to work it out without too much conflict. He returned to the cabin, made Rosie stay on the deck to dry off, and decided to give Walter a call and let him know he'd met the locals.

"Hi, Ryan," Walter knew who was calling from the phone's display. He had a mild sense of anticipation in his voice, unsure of the purpose of Ryan's call.

"Hi, Walter, how's it going?"

"Okay for a Friday," he said, sounding a little surprised at the friendly tone.

"Hey, just wanted to call and say I've met the uh . . . visitors, and it went okay. You were right—they seem okay."

"Who was it?" Walter asked.

"Owny and, uh, what's her name? Patsy. They've come several times now. The last time was just last night."

"They came at night?" Walter sounded surprised.

"Well, no, I mean in the evening. Patsy had an appointment this morning in Victoria, so they didn't come by then."

"So what is the appointment for? Do you know?"

"Some sort of consultation with a specialist, I think. Patsy has cancer."

"Oh no, that's awful!"

"So you know them?"

"I don't really know Patsy. I know who she is—Owny's eldest daughter. I know Owny, of course. Everybody knows Owny."

"Why do you say that? She seems pretty low key."

"Owny is the Chief," Walter explained. "I guess you didn't know that. She's the head of the band."

"Really?" Ryan was genuinely surprised.

"Yeah, she's the Chief. She does come off as very down-to-earth—quiet, I guess. She's been the Chief for some years. She's very nice, but don't underestimate her—she's actually quite a force within the band. She's why they constructed the original cabin row, and why they're expanding it and other businesses on the reserve."

"Hmm. You sure wouldn't know it to meet her. She's pretty soft-spoken," Ryan said.

"Yeah, I know, but she's very progressive. She actually went to UVic. She has her degree in Aboriginal law, and other credits too, I think. We had a chat about it one day."

"So she's a lawyer?" Ryan said, even more surprised.

"No, no, it's a separate thing. But she really knows what she's doing in terms of their rights and how to navigate the system—that's for sure. It's good you've met them, Ryan. Get to know her. She's an important person in the whole region, actually. And too bad about Patsy. That's really the shits."

Rosie scratched at the door to get in, and Ryan, still on the phone, obliged her and opened the door. The golden retriever eagerly followed him around the room, still enthused from their foray into the lake. She started jumping, bouncing vertically as she vied for Ryan's attention.

"Wow, this dog is really loving the lake life! She's just bouncing around the place. Unreal! She couldn't do that a few days ago!"

The significance of the dog's behaviour started to sink into Ryan's consciousness. He sat down on a chair at the kitchen table and with his free hand peeled the bandage off of his right calf. There was no sign of the jagged scar that should have been there. Not a scab or any blemish at all.

"Say, Wally, how much time did you spend actually in the water here?"

"Not that much, really. We had the kayaks, did some fishing at the far end by the creek—over at the reeds on the other side—but not a lot of time swimming. We mostly just enjoyed the cabin and the lifestyle, I guess. Why?"

"Oh nothing . . . just wondering."

Chapter 4

Principal Phil Conner was feeling overwhelmed. The school year was rapidly coming to an end and there was still much to do. It was Tuesday, and Sports Day was under way after having been rescheduled from the week before. Phil was stressed by the visiting school board members, report cards, needy substitute teachers, and the daily demands of his job. The days would be long until the day after school was over.

An email had come in from Island Occupational Testing Lab, in a stack of dozens of emails he had to get to, but that wouldn't be today. He spent little time thinking about it; he was too distracted. The email would just set off a sequence of events that meant more work for him—more forms, more explaining, more heartache from the teachers' union. But his mind was made up about Laura, his justification for her suspension like an immovable object.

The next day started early, and somehow his transient optimism was back in place. He was buoyed knowing there were only eight school days until the end of the term. Sports Day, while a little disorganized, had been a success. The weather cooperated, and there were no incidents or injuries. He was resigned to grinding through the balance of the report cards, and in reality, the workload would be light from here on in; there was little instruction going on.

He made time to swing through a drive-through for a coffee, then got to his office and booted up his computer. Phil was determined to catch up on his neglected inbox. He looked down the stack and quickly deleted the junk mail and spam. He assessed the reduced volume of messages, sighed deeply, and clicked on the blood test company email with the subject line "Laura Hanson Results." He opened the attachment and saw a vaguely familiar form—he had seen this before. He scrolled down the page, seeking the single important fact. He found the cell, "Blood Alcohol Content."

0.00. Zero. He blinked and poked around the form with his mouse, thinking he must be missing something. He went back to the line; it was very clear. Blood alcohol content: zero. Zero? There must be some mistake.

He shook his head. No way this could be a zero. If it was, then the decision he had made had to change completely. Not only that, having already set the wheels in motion, he wondered if he could be personally liable or vulnerable in some way. At the very least, he had made a huge error in judgment. How could that be? It was so obvious at the time what was happening to Laura.

He decided to call the Island Occupational Testing Lab and clear this up. He got the phone number off the email signature and dialed. Requesting the manager, he referred to the number on the form and asked how the protocol worked.

"No chance of error, sir," the manager said. "This is what we do. Many of our tests determine people's health and welfare, their jobs, their future. We're very careful. Especially in this case. It would have been a random test, giving the person no chance to prepare or to falsify the results. They go into a private room with no paraphernalia—no purses, no bags, no additional clothing. A nurse supervises the whole process. The lab testing is carefully regulated. The specimen is tracked with a bar code and matched with the name, birthdate, and medical number. We stand by the results. Perhaps there's something else at issue here?"

Phil got off the phone and contemplated this. "Hmm, something else at issue." He drummed his fingers on his desk. Almost in a daze, he called out to the secretary working in the outer office. "Mary? Mary, you got a sec?"

Mary stopped what she was doing and came to his door.

"Last week when we sent Laura Hanson home . . . tell me what you were thinking." He preferred an open-ended question.

"What are you talking about?" She looked puzzled.

"I mean, what do you think was wrong with her?"

Mary shrugged slightly. "She was drunk, of course."

"Okay, thanks," Phil said, and Mary went back to her desk.

Phil knew he couldn't retest or question the results any further; that door was closed. He would have to contact Laura and work this out. However, he was perplexed as to exactly how to approach her and what to say, so he went on with his day. Procrastination wasn't his specialty, but he did need some time to think.

By the afternoon he had gotten over his denial of the accuracy of the test results. They were a fact, and now the mystery of her behaviour troubled him. He looked up her number in the school database and called her cell, as there was no land line indicated. His call went straight to voice mail.

"Hi, Laura, it's Phil Conner. Um, can you please call me back at this number as soon as you get this message? I'd like to talk to you. Thank you, and talk to you soon." He tried to sound friendly.

Phil pondered whether to let Mary in on the test results. He was thankful he'd enlisted her help that day with Laura, but he would let it go until Laura called back, and then decide.

The rest of the day's activities happened as usual. He shelved the thought of Laura's status for a while—he had left a message, after all.

The next day his internal dialogue about Laura started up again, and he resolved to call a second time. The call went straight to voice mail again, so he left a message virtually the same as the last, but this time stating the day and time. The day passed with no call back.

On Friday Phil went back into the school personnel database and looked for the next of kin number to call in case of an emergency. It referred to a Ryan Hanson with a different phone number. He called the number, and a confused woman answered, stating she knew no one named Hanson. The number was old, and the phone company must have reassigned it to someone else some years ago. While in the database, he jotted down Laura's home address. He looked up to see Mary at her desk and called her in. He got up and closed the door behind her as she sat down.

"So . . . I've been meaning to talk to you about Laura Hanson's lab test results. You remember I sent her for a blood test right after she left the school?" He suddenly looked out at the parking lot to see if her car was still there. Of course it was gone—he would have noticed it before. "The test results showed her blood alcohol content at *zero*."

Mary sat up in her chair and screwed up her face. "How can that be?" she asked. "There's no way. There must be some mistake."

"That's what I thought. I even called the lab. They're quite sure about the results. I-I'm starting to get worried about this. I tried calling Laura. I left two messages with no reply. I'll call again today, but if she doesn't call back, I'm going over to her house after school. I just wanted to let you know what was going on, to let someone know I'll be stopping by her place to check on her. Maybe she's gone away or something—I don't know. Maybe she's still upset and screening her calls. Maybe. But I feel I . . . someone should check on her."

"This is hard to believe." Mary shook her head. "Do you want me to go with you?"

"No thanks. She's likely out or just upset or something. I'll check it out."

Phil called again as he said he would, and again he left a voice mail stating the date and time. The day passed with no call back, so he decided to head over to her house before he went home.

* * *

From the address, Phil knew where Laura's neighbourhood was. He went directly to the street, noted house numbers, and followed them to the house at the end of a cul-de-sac. He parked behind Laura's car, exited his vehicle, and looked across the large fenced front yard to the older, well-kept bungalow. The house appeared dark and foreboding. The grass was getting long, and a local weekly paper was looking neglected on the welcome mat. He entered through the white picket gate. He picked up the paper and rang the doorbell.

A sound seemed to come from inside the house, but it was muffled and hard to discern. A cat appeared at the narrow full-length window beside the front door. It meowed in protest, or perhaps for help—he couldn't tell. He rang the doorbell again. No further sounds came from inside. Again he waited, then opened the screen door and knocked sharply on the wooden door with three narrow skewed windows at eye level. He refrained from looking in. Phil waited a few seconds and rapped again, this time calling, "Laura?" right after he knocked.

"She's home," a disembodied voice said from a distance.

Phil was surprised and looked up and down and then to the right. Behind the fence was short, tanned senior, the next-door neighbour. Phil focused on the older man.

"She's home, pretty sure," he said with a faint European accent. "Haven't seen her for a few days, but she must be in there. I think she might not be doing too well."

"How do you know?'

"We checked on her on . . . Monday or Tuesday. Not sure. After her daughter left—that must have been Sunday. So on Monday we checked. She's sick or . . . well, in a bad way, I think. We were worried and going to try to see her today."

"So is she sick or is she drinking?"

"Oh, she's drinking," the neighbour said firmly. He seemed to have some experience with Laura. "But it seems different this time. Worse. Ryan's gone. I think her daughter is busy or doesn't know what to do with her or something. She needs help."

The man's wife must have been standing on their front porch. The small poised woman, probably about seventy, came down the steps and stood beside her husband.

Phil let go a long "Phew!" and looked at his shoes. He wasn't sure he wanted to get involved, but he had passed the point of no return, not even realizing when that had happened.

"Okay, I guess we'll try to get her to come to the door." He knocked loudly and called Laura's name. The neighbours walked from their yard into the Hanson's to join him.

"Oh, I'm Phil Conner, the principal at the school Laura teaches at."

"Hi, Phil, I'm Lazlo, and this is my wife, Marta," Lazlo said in an understated tone. Marta just nodded.

"I was concerned about Laura too. I couldn't get her on the phone, so I wanted to check in," Phil said, for some reason feeling rather awkward.

He rapped on the door harder than ever. As if knowing what they wanted, the cat looked out the window but couldn't do anything for them except meow.

"Try the door," Lazlo said.

Little Marta stepped up and took the lead. She turned the knob. It was unlocked. She pushed the door open, and the cat emerged and made serpentine turns through their legs.

"Laura?" Marta called. "Laura, it's Marta!"

Nothing.

"Should we call 911?" Phil asked.

"We don't even know she's here for sure," Lazlo said, calming them. "Marta"—Lazlo gestured encouragingly to his wife—"you . . . you go look. Go see if she's here."

Marta's eyes widened. She shook her head in hesitation, as if to say, "This was not what I wanted to do today." She didn't look comfortable doing it at all. However, Phil felt her concern for the Hansons, and Laura specifically; he could sense they had some sort of bond. Marta looked sideways at her husband, sighed, and stepped into the dark house. Lazlo picked up the cat.

"Laura?" Marta called. "Laura?" She stepped through the foyer to the hall that opened up to the kitchen. It was in an uncharacteristic mess, with bags and bottles and dishes scattered carelessly. "Laura?" She looked back at her husband and Phil, both standing in the doorway.

Lazlo nodded at her and made a pushing motion with his hand.

Reluctantly, she crept forward and squinted into the gloom. "Laura?"

Phil and Lazlo watched Marta disappear around the corner, presumably into a bedroom. She was gone for a few seconds before they heard "Oh God."

"Are you okay?" Lazlo called out.

"She's here!" Marta yelled to her break-and-enter cohorts.

"Can we come in?" Lazlo asked cautiously.

Marta flicked on the guest bedroom light, and after a brief pause responded, "Yes! Come in."

Laura Hanson was incoherent. There was evidence of long-term drinking throughout the house, and this only confused Phil more. He knew they—he—needed to get Laura help right away. But he had never done anything like this before.

"So what's the best thing to do here?" he said to his partners. "Do we get her up and moving around? Do we try to get ahold of her family?"

Lazlo looked at Phil and then at Marta. "You know, we're not experts at this. She may be just sleeping it off, or maybe close to death—we don't know."

Marta continued to try to rouse Laura.

"I think it best that we call an ambulance and get her help right away." Lazlo was genuinely concerned. "What do you think?"

Phil hesitated for only a second. "I think you're right." He pulled his cell phone from his pocket and dialed 911.

The ambulance was there in short order. As per protocol, the fire department arrived almost simultaneously, so there was quite a scene at the end of the normally quiet cul-de-sac. When the two EMT personnel got a good look at Laura and the overall scene, they nodded to the fireman that they had this. The firemen turned off the flashing lights of the truck, which trundled out of the neighbourhood.

Phil and Lazlo and Marta stepped back and let the two EMT personnel do their work. The ambulance workers seemed very experienced. They worked efficiently and assessed Laura quickly. They started an IV and got her on a gurney as soon as they could negotiate the hallway through the house.

As they were about to close the ambulance doors, Phil asked, "So how is she?" He had no clue, as Laura was still unresponsive.

"Not good," the EMT said. "She's pretty far gone. You guys did the right thing."

"So you'll take her to the hospital?" Phil asked at the risk of asking the obvious. He wasn't sure if there were other options in Laura's case.

"Yes. Yes," the EMT said irritably as he slammed the back door on his partner. "She needs further assessment right away. She'll be there for a while." He walked around the vehicle to the driver's side. "Probably in the psych ward—that's where they put them."

"Where are you taking her?" Phil asked hastily.

"Royal Jube."

Chapter 5

Ryan woke up pondering the dog's health and how he felt himself, and wondering if there would be any morning visitors. Sure enough, Owny and Patsy showed up at about eight fifteen in their usual quiet fashion. Ryan was curious as to if this was a good sign or a bad sign for Patsy. He filled a travel mug with black coffee, and he and Rosie went out to the beach to say hi.

He walked up casually. "Good morning, ladies. How are you doing?"

Owny turned to him. "Good, Ryan. How are you?"

"I'm well, thanks. Can I ask how it went yesterday in Victoria?"

"Oh, just okay." Owny was noncommittal. "They say the tumour hasn't changed. We're hoping to start chemo and radiation soon to try and shrink it. They say it's quite big and irregular in shape and needs to be reduced before they consider surgery."

"I was hoping they'd say something encouraging. I know you're doing your best."

"We're trying. Patsy is on a strict diet and exercising to keep her fit for her fight. Doing all we can."

Owny stepped into the water with her flip-flops on, perhaps needing to feel the water herself as her daughter waded out. Ryan noticed some faded tattoos on the top of her feet but couldn't make them out.

"Why don't you get right out to the source?" Ryan asked. "I swam out yesterday—it's not too far. You can see the bubbles from here."

"Yes, I know. Patsy's not a good swimmer. Me neither—I'm scared of deep water. We never taught Patsy to swim like we should have."

Patsy stood waist deep in the water, shivering. Owny stepped back onto the sand, kicking cold water off of her feet like a cat that couldn't avoid stepping into a puddle.

"In that case, I've got an idea!"

Ryan felt proud of himself. He put his mug down and walked over to the tool shed. He dug around for a minute and came back with a life jacket. It was an old white canvas thing that had the big flotation pillow on the front and back.

Owny turned up her nose at it. "That looks like it came over on the *Titanic*." She twisted her face. "It stinks."

Ryan was a little embarrassed and banged it on the dock to shake the dust off. A cloud came off of it and floated down the beach. Patsy just looked back at Ryan without moving.

"I really think it's worth it to get right out there, Patsy." It was the first time he'd spoken directly to her.

"I'm not putting that thing on. It won't hold me anyway," Patsy said.

"I'm sure it will hold you. I'll clean it up." He shook it and hit it against the piling. "Try it on." He held it out toward her. She shook her head.

He had another idea. "How about the life jacket *and* the life ring?" He pointed to the orange life preserver hanging on the piling. "It has a rope. You put on the life jacket, get in the life ring, and we push you out to the bubbles!"

Owny and Patsy looked at each other as if to say, "Who is this guy?"

"When you're in the bubbles, it's warmer, and you can probably stay in longer. I think the bubbles themselves help too. They help you float."

Owny shook her head as if she was mulling this over. Finally relenting, she said, "Try it, Patsy. It's worth a try."

Patsy shrugged and waded out of the water. She cringed at the old life jacket but did as her mother bid. Ryan put it over her head, and Patsy tied the thick dangling ribbons, looping them as a crotch strap. Dripping with lake water, she walked down the dock. Ryan had the orange life ring off its hook and flat on the deck. She stepped into it and pulled it up to her waist. Patsy sat down on the very end of the dock.

"Okay, scootch in and see how it feels while you're close to the dock," Ryan suggested to get her confidence up. "We're right here."

Patsy slipped off the wood and into the water. She seemed to sense that the makeshift system would support her easily. Sure enough, she floated like a cork and looked confident.

"Are you okay?" Ryan asked.

Patsy nodded.

"Okay, I'm going to push you out. I have the rope, and I'll hold on all the time. And I can pull you back in at any time . . . Are you okay?" Ryan asked again to be reassuring.

"I'm okay," Patsy replied.

Ryan kneeled down, turned her toward her destination, and gave her shoulders a firm push. She looked like the Michelin Man bobbing out to sea.

"Paddle with your arms to get yourself going!" Ryan called encouragingly from the dock, making motions as if he himself was in the life preservers.

Patsy moved her arms and attempted to manoeuvre in her ungainly apparatus. In a couple of minutes, she was over the bubble plume.

She looked down in amazement. "It *is* warmer, Mum! A little warmer, anyway! The bubbles tickle!" It was as if she'd thought Ryan may have been exaggerating.

With Patsy out of earshot, Ryan asked quietly, "How is she doing . . . really?"

"Ah, I'm not sure," Owny said in despair. "She has less energy lately. She's keeping positive, but I'd really like her to start treatment soon. So we have a plan, a course of action, a mission, but I feel like we're in limbo." She looked at her daughter floating in the lake.

Suddenly, the scene seemed all too pathetic. Silence fell between Ryan and Owny for several minutes. Rosie waded back and forth in the water, as if thinking it might be a good idea to swim out to Patsy.

Owny bucked herself up and changed the subject. "So what do you do, Ryan?"

"I do website design. And maintain some of the sites I work on. They're mostly transportation, like car dealerships, trucking companies, that sort of thing. But I also have a coffee company, a sports retailer, and some municipal sites—small towns, tourism, and the like."

"That sounds like interesting work. You have your own company?"

"Not exactly. I work for a larger company, but I have a small stake in it, kind of like a junior partner. I have a boss, but we've

worked together for years, so he lets me do my own thing. I like it—
keeps me busy. It's great 'cause I can do a lot from home—anywhere,
really. I specialize in 'the story' of a company. I like to take my own
photos when they're local, to make the site really authentic and to
make it pop."

"So you went to school for that?"

"Uh, well, I took computer science at school. The website stuff
is mainly self-taught. I went to UVic."

"Oh yeah? Me too," Owny said. "You were on the rowing
team?" She gestured to his single scull upside down on the dock.

"Yes, I sure was!"

"Not me," Owny said flatly, then shouted to her daughter,
"How are you doing, Patsy?"

"I'm okay!"

"Maybe you could take a look at our website some time," Owny
suggested. "It hasn't been touched for a few years and it's really looking dated. I have lots of ideas for content, but our website person has
gotten busy with other things."

"Oh yeah? Who was that?"

"Me."

Ryan hesitated. He tried to maintain a poker face as he frantically searched his mind for a realistic excuse not to oblige. He failed.
"Um . . . . Okay. Sure, I could take a look if you like. I'm pretty busy
with my client base, but we do give free consults."

Owny gave Ryan the URL and said she would appreciate any
feedback. She let him know that her cell number was on the website
under the "Contact" tab.

When the time seemed right, Owny told Ryan to bring Patsy
in. He pulled her gently toward the dock, then down the dock to

the beach. Once the water was shallow enough, she waded in. She dropped the life ring and gave Ryan the wet life jacket back.

"Just take the jacket out of the shed if you come by and I'm not here," Ryan suggested.

"Okay. Thanks, Ryan." Owny seemed pleased. "Maybe tomorrow—we'll see."

Ryan and Rosie returned to the cabin, and he made himself some breakfast. Afterwards he booted up his computer, and with some trepidation he went to the local band's website. Owny was right: it looked like something from the beginning of the internet age with its poor graphics, terrible purple cursive fonts, green backgrounds, and low-quality content. What was the point of the website, anyway? What use was it to the band or anyone else? He'd have to put some thought into the message and meaning, but Ryan knew he could make huge improvements to the look and functionality of the site. However, he wasn't sure how far to take it. Walter's advice, *You need to get along with these people,* doggedly followed his mouse clicks.

The morning became grey and overcast. Clouds hung low over the lake and filtered the daylight to create muted tones in the water and trees. Since it was cool, he decided to go for a long jog and further explore the path through the trees across the road from the cabins. Website work could wait until later in the day. He was anxious to see how Rosie would do on the run. He wore shorts but dressed for rain with a light nylon jacket and a ball cap, and strapped on a water bottle. He ran down his cabin road with the golden retriever in tow, crossed the main road, and found the rough path.

As he entered the dense forest, the damp smell of vegetation was almost overpowering. He was reminded of how much he loved Vancouver Island as his eyes adjusted to the dark world, and he noticed the lower trunk of an enormous Douglas fir that must have been standing there for five hundred years. The path meandered through a grove of massive firs and cedars.

As he got deeper, he began to feel uneasy, vulnerable, remote. He shook the feeling off as simply unfamiliarity with the route. At the beginning of the run, Rosie was overjoyed to explore areas that were off the path. Now she settled in beside her master as the underbrush thickened and the high canopy darkened the way. The path seemed to fade out in places, making it was difficult to pick up the next section.

After about forty-five minutes, Ryan stopped and tried to get his bearings. Suddenly, he felt like a child, insignificant among the giant sentinels of the forest. He also felt as though he was being watched, but that was impossible. There would be no one within miles of this place on a day like today. His imagination was working overtime. Rosie looked up at him as if to say, "Now what?" He was a little spooked but still happy he was exploring the path. It started to rain, but because of the dense canopy, only some of the drops made it all the way to the ground. It felt good to run in the damp, green, earthy world.

The way back looked obscure, but he stroked the dog and gulped from the water bottle he had pulled out of his belt. He put some water in his palm, and Rosie lapped it up out of his hand. After putting the bottle back, he wiped his hand on his shorts, and said, "Let's go!" to the dog, and they started the jog back down the coniferous needle-strewn path. Twice he made a wrong decision about which way to go; the path closed in and disappeared. He worked his way back and got on the right track each time, but all along worried he had gone astray. After a bit, he sensed he was running toward the light, and as he passed another enormous tree, he hoped that moss was indeed growing on the north side. If it was, he was going in the right direction.

He got back to the trailhead almost two hours later. He was tired but relieved he'd made it back unscathed. Ryan was pleased that he had conquered the trail and allayed any fear of the giants' grove. He would be confident in his next attempt.

Rosie and Ryan traversed the main road and veered up his cabin access. He ran up the front stairs and into the cabin. After making Rosie lie on the mat at the front door, he stripped off and went straight to the shower to warm up. He emerged a little dizzy from fatigue and from lingering in the hot water too long. He pulled a towel off the rack and went into the main room.

Still woozy from the long shower and his exertion, he looked out the front window and saw a figure standing on the beach. It was a man facing the water and wearing a traditional Native blanket over his shoulders. The man dropped the blanket and walked awkwardly into the water. He was completely naked and staggered on a crude prosthetic leg. Once in deep enough, he took off the wooden leg and let it float beside him for a moment. He seemed to be rubbing his stump. Then he tucked it under his arm as if for flotation and swam out to the bubbles.

Ryan was aghast. He wiped his eyes with the towel and stared out at the water. "What the fuck is this?" Rosie stood up from her resting spot, cocking her head.

This time he would take care of this himself; he wouldn't phone a friend. He wasn't going to sit by and watch this transpire. Indigenous interlopers were one thing, but strangers intruding in the nude was quite another. He ran back into the bedroom, pulled open a drawer, and found some track pants and pulled them on. He grabbed the first T-shirt he saw, and he ran out of the bedroom barefoot while simultaneously pulling the shirt over his head. Rosie got out of the way as he went for the door.

He ran across the deck and down the stairs and onto the beach. The man was gone. The blanket was gone. Ryan ran frenetically in each direction at the water's edge, looking for the person with the prosthetic limb. At least that's what it had looked like. Had to be. He ran toward his sign tree and past the next cabin, and the one after that. Nothing. A woman was on the next cabin's deck, and she looked up from her book, clearly wondering who he was.

"Did you see someone go by just now?" Ryan asked frantically.

She just shook her head.

"No one at all?"

"Nope," she responded, still shaking her head, as if she were skeptical of Ryan because of his look and approach. She said nothing more.

"Okay. Sorry to bother you."

Ryan turned back, hiking up his pants as he walked. He returned to the cabin, knocked the sand off his feet, and booted up his computer.

He went to the band's website to get Owny's number so he could talk to her about this. Once he clicked on the "Contact" tab, he started punching the number into his phone. But before it rang he cancelled the call, thinking the conversation would be a little awkward. He wanted to address this but didn't want to come off as a busybody. He mulled this over for a few minutes, rubbing his still-damp hair.

He resolved to bring up the subject of the intruder the next time he saw her, probably when he gave her some ideas regarding the website. This gave him the determination to get something together for the site sooner than later. He returned to the home page. *It was hopeless*, he thought. He would recommend starting from scratch.

Chapter 6

True to his formula and his work ethic, Ryan wanted to develop his own take on the website's content. While there was still time in the afternoon, he changed clothes and drove to the other side of the lake to explore the village. He had never visited that part of the reserve and was hoping New Town and Old Town had some rustic charm he could develop into his concept. Perhaps there were some totem poles, or some sort of angle he could play up as a tourist attraction, and maybe Old Town had some historic significance.

When he rolled into New Town, he was disappointed to see nothing he could use as the subject of a single meaningful photograph. The settlement was very basic, just a grid of half a dozen gravel streets with houses in various states of repair. He came across the band office, which was modest and not particularly attractive. It had a tin sign on the front that read indian parking only. He assumed this was tongue-in-cheek, as the sign was probably intended for motorcycles. Someone had a sense of humour. Next door was a small fire hall that looked abandoned; he took a picture of it with his phone anyway. On the lake was a dilapidated set of floating docks with a few aluminum boats at the shore. At the north end of town was what looked to be a recreation centre, and at the end of the street was a small sawmill, also apparently deserted. A large shed had some logs stacked in it, and a couple of pieces of older log-moving equipment were parked by the main building. Ryan assumed there was an actual sawmill inside, but silence indicated production had stopped long ago. He took a few pictures in the hope there was some sort of potential here. Or perhaps something that wasn't jumping out at him now would translate into a good photograph.

After seeing all he could see in the village, Ryan easily found the road that led to Old Town. He was hoping for more potential at the end of the two-and-a-half-kilometer gravel track. As he emerged from the tree-lined road, the view looked promising, but it soon became apparent that Old Town was even smaller that New Town, and older and more rundown. However, at tidewater there was a dock system that looked fairly modern and had potential for further development. Several outbuildings stood off the waterfront area—including, perhaps, an old warehouse and net loft. Several gillnetters and nondescript boats were tied up to the three fingers of floats that lay at the bottom of a gangway that was currently at a steep pitch. Ryan let Rosie out of the back and walked down toward the boats. He took some pictures of the floating docks, went to the very end, turned around, and took a few pictures looking toward shore.

All in all, his short expedition revealed little potential. At least he had familiarized himself with the villages and understood what there was to work with. He knew he must be missing something, and that something would probably come from Owny when they met to discuss the website.

Ryan headed back to New Town, then around the lake to the familiar row of cabins. He stopped to snap a picture of the indian springs sign, then continued on to the dead end, where he expected to see something happening. He thought he would see evidence of the road being pushed farther down the lake, with perhaps some clearing of land and demarcation of lots. Ryan found only a bulldozer and a backhoe standing idle in the turnaround, waiting for someone to get in them and put them to work. He took a picture and returned to the cabin.

Sitting down at his computer, Ryan formulated a rough proposal for Owny. It wasn't much, and he would let her know he was struggling with an overall vision for the website and advise her that the existing site was okay (even though it wasn't). Maybe then he'd be off the hook. If she really pressed him, he would show her examples of other websites he'd created, but only the most basic ones. He really only wanted to address the trespassing on his property. Hopefully, she would understand. Something had to be done. How could they expect to attract other buyers to the area if intruders could come and go as they pleased?

Rather than call, Ryan sourced Owny's email address from the website and sent her a note that he was ready to discuss the site. After a few minutes, she responded from her phone with an invitation to come over to her house—right now was fine. Ryan was dismayed. He didn't want to discuss it right away since he hadn't completely formulated his non-pitch, and he really didn't want to go over to her house. He would much prefer his place, or the band office. Still, it would be good to get this over with. He noted the basic directions from her return email and replied that he was on his way. He folded up his laptop and put it in his backpack, gave Rosie some food and water, and drove over to Owny's place.

He found the little blue house right away: he had driven by it earlier, and the Wilson sign by the door was a dead giveaway. He knocked, and a shorter Indigenous man about his age answered the door.

"Hi, I'm Ryan. I'm here to see Owny."

"Hi, Ryan. Come on in." Coming up behind him was Owny herself.

"Hi, Ryan. This is my husband, Gerald."

"Hi, Gerald," Ryan was careful to be polite. "Nice to meet you."

The doorway brought him right into the living room. It was small but tidy. A young girl sat on the couch. "This is our daughter, Iris." Owny held out the palm of her hand toward the girl.

The teenager looked up quickly from the TV and gave a small wave.

"And we have another daughter, Aster—she's the youngest—but she's out with some friends. Patsy... we named Patsy after Patsy Cline you know. Our Patsy used to have a twin brother, Alan, but he's no longer with us. He was born with a hole in his heart, he only lived a few weeks."

Gerald shook his head as if to say, "You don't need to tell him everything."

"Come on into the kitchen." Owny waved Ryan into the next room.

Gerald returned to the easy chair in the living room and let Owny and Ryan have the kitchen. Ryan got the feeling that with Owny being the Chief, visitors were commonplace for the family. The kitchen was spotless, and Ryan was ashamed to be surprised at this. His preconceived stereotypes about Natives, and admittedly the rundown look of the reserve, made him expect the house would be a mess.

"Have a seat." Owny pulled out a chrome-legged chair from the table. "Let's see what you think."

"Well, I don't have much." Ryan didn't even pull out his laptop. He sat down and folded his hands on the green floral plastic tablecloth.

"Would you like some coffee?" Owny asked.

"Um . . . sure. Sure, sounds good." Ryan tried to relax.

The coffee was already prepared. Owny poured him a cup and one for herself. "Cream and sugar?"

"No, black is good, thanks." He wanted to get to the point and be on his way. "So, I've looked at your site." He shrugged a little. "Um, it's . . . it's—"

"It's awful," Owny admitted. "Nobody uses it, nobody goes there—it's bad. I've been thinking about it, and I want to scrap the whole thing. Start new."

Ryan couldn't help rolling his eyes.

"Show me some of your work!" Owny seemed eager to see what Ryan had to offer.

"Okay." Ryan reached down and pulled out his laptop. He opened it up and booted it up. "Do you have Wi-Fi?"

"Yes, the password is just *wilsonwifi.*"

"That's not very secure, Owny."

"It's never been a problem," she said dismissively.

Ryan navigated the set-up quickly and got to some of his established websites.

Owny was genuinely intrigued and commented with some acumen on the landing pages, banners, radio buttons, flow, and content. Ryan sensed her enthusiasm. He was proud of his vocation, his ideas, and his workmanship. He settled in and offered up most of his more elaborate websites. She liked his personal touch with the narratives and custom photography. Ryan was flattered by Owny's comments and felt she was truly impressed with of his body of work.

After revelling in his past accomplishments, Ryan knew he needed to address his lack of ideas for Owny's website, and his fruitless trip through the area trying to conjure up compelling images to post online.

"Earlier today I went through New Town and Old Town, just exploring and trying to get to know the area a little better. With thoughts of posting something, I took some photos of the dock area in Old Town, the band office here, the fire hall, and the, um . . . I guess it's a sawmill? I gotta tell you, Owny, there really isn't much I can work up into an interesting story or photo montage. Just wondering what you see as the enhancements or new theme for the site."

Owny scratched her head in contemplation. "I know to an outsider the town doesn't look like much. And I know we need to move to a better quality of life. Honestly, Ryan, that's what I see the website helping us do. I know just a website isn't the be-all and end-all, but a fresh new site that taps into the positive aspects of our culture, our land, our art, our businesses, our potential—that's what our people need. It can act as an impetus to inspire change. It can show us in the best light—not being untrue to ourselves or . . . false, but at our best. I see from what you've shown me, you can do that—you have the knack. It's what our young folks need, to show we're engaged and progressive. I want to put a positive face on our history, and our future. We all need a more functional site for our municipal affairs, for news and current events. It can be a real touchstone and a meeting place that can galvanize our people."

Ryan hung his head. This was a tall order given everything he saw and didn't see. He was surprised how well-spoken Owny could be, and how eloquent she was when she spoke of her vision. But he was stymied as to what possible subjects he could romanticize into a compelling story.

"So . . . tell me, Owny. I'm struggling on where to start. I've looked at the old website and a few pages I could perhaps carry over to a new site, but I'm really unsure about the overall new content. You mentioned many things, but I didn't see much of any of them. What about local art? Do you have local artists or artisans we could feature?"

"Well, we do, but honestly, they're limited. We've really let this slide. I know there's very good Native art on the coast, but locally we need to reach out to other bands to share best practices on re-energizing our art."

"Hmm." Ryan was disappointed. "You know, we're so close to Victoria, there must be some sort of tourist activity we could promote. I'm not sure what makes sense, but think about if you want that."

"I do very much if it's done right. It has to be respectful and not overly commercial, but yes, you're right—we could think of some sort of attraction. That's long term, but you're on the right track." She hesitated. "Except . . ."

"Except what?"

"Some people want to embrace change"—she spoke of her own tribe—"and some don't. We have both. Most want to move forward, but a few are determined to keep things more . . . status quo."

"Well, I'm sure when they see the overall benefits to everyone they'll understand." Ryan was being practical.

"Maybe . . ."

"Tell me about your businesses? You mentioned businesses, but I haven't seen much of that."

"Of course, we have the land development on the other side of the lake. I'd like to have a trailer or temporary building at the new site where we could have staff and promote the lots."

"How's that going?" Ryan asked, thinking of the stationary yellow iron at the end of the road.

"Slow," Owny said. "We have the sawmill, but there are some issues there. We lost a key customer when they went belly up. A forest fire the year before last really took a bite out of our woodlot. And we're getting some repairs done at the mill."

"How's that going?"

"Slow. I—*we*—have some other ideas of possible viable businesses for us. Perhaps we'll expand the docks at Old Town, maybe make it a stop for boats going up the West Coast. The location is quite good. Maybe open a gas bar to attract the fishermen and the recreational boaters, or a restaurant to promote authentic local food. Perhaps develop the bay with oysters or mussels, perhaps kelp. Maybe we'll start our own greenhouse and grow cannabis. Or build a small hydro dam on the creek. Maybe make a campsite farther down from the cabins. I've looked into it—it's possible."

"But these ideas are a long way out," Ryan said.

"Yes. But Ryan, they aren't just dreams. They're real. These and other possibly better ideas need to be pursued. Our land is at the end of the line. We don't have the benefit of a pipeline going through it, or minerals or oil, or construction projects on our reserve or nearby. Our people have had a rough go of it. We've lived on this island for centuries, and we've been relegated to this small piece of it—for better or for worse. We can't forget the past, and we sure as hell can't change it. What we *can* change is our future. We can't go on the way we have. We can't rely on Indian Affairs forever—it won't be there. We need to think of future generations of our people. We need to make the most of what we have. Maybe you can help in some way."

Ryan blinked and shifted in his chair. "We'll pay you," Owny said, as if sensing some hesitation. "I don't expect you to do it for nothing."

"Fair enough." Ryan was resigned to working on the website. "I like your ideas, but in terms of what we can actually promote right now, it's the cabin properties, and maybe the sawmill, right?"

"That's right," Owny admitted.

Ryan was emboldened by her hope for her people, but he still felt he'd been backed into a corner and needed to make a silk purse out of a sow's ear.

"Do you have a person in charge of the land development?" he asked.

"That's me."

"Is there someone in charge of the sawmill?"

"That's Ronny and Chester. If you intend on looking around there, you better let me talk to them first."

"There were quite a few logs in the shed by the mill. Are they waiting to go through the mill once it's working again?"

"No, I don't think so. The mill would be cutting mostly fir and pine for dimensional lumber for construction. The logs in the shed are Sitka spruce and cedar, I think. They've been set aside for maybe a separate run or hopefully some future demand—I'm not sure. Gerald would know, since he used to work at the mill before Ronny and Chester took over."

"Okay. Thanks." Ryan was tiring of the conversation. "There's one more thing I wanted to talk to you about, Owny."

"What's that?"

"It's about people on my property. I—"

"Me and Patsy?" she asked in surprise.

"No, no, no, not at all. I . . . you can come at any time, of course. You're welcome, always. I just don't want half the town traipsing through the property. I want to cooperate, I really do. I understand now the significance of the site. Really."

"So who else is coming by? Strangers? Kids? People from the village?"

Ryan hesitated briefly. "Who's the guy with the wooden leg?"

Owny stopped, suddenly frozen as she was sitting at the kitchen table. After a few seconds, she placed both of her hands on her face.

"Owny, I just don't want it to be Grand Central Station, you know. It's . . ." Ryan sensed he should stop talking.

Owny's chest started to heave slightly, like a precursor to an outburst. Ryan sat back in his chair, not knowing what to think. Then she crossed her forearms on the table and laid her forehead down on her wrists. Ryan was taken aback and let her be for a moment. Perhaps she was suddenly feeling unwell.

"Owny?"

She started to breathe rapidly. Ryan looked anxiously toward the living room, wondering if he should summon Gerald. Finally, she sat up and turned to look at Ryan. Her face had changed, her eyes showing her age now. She swallowed and asked in a phlegmy voice he could barely hear, "What did he do?"

"Well, he . . . I saw him standing at the beach where we go—you know, right in front of the place. He had an old blanket on. He dropped the blanket and walked buck naked into the water. Then he took off his leg, his wooden leg, and stuck it under his arm and swam out. You know, to the spot."

Just then Gerald came into the kitchen. He got a glass from a cupboard, filled it with water from the tap, and placed it on the table in front of Owny. He returned to the living room without saying a word. Owny didn't turn to her husband or acknowledge him in any way. She looked at Ryan again, then dropped her gaze down to the glass. She closed her eyes and rocked slightly sideways in her chair. Ryan thought she was going into a trance state.

And so she began the story.

Chapter 7

"His real name is Nigaani, which means "he leads" in the old language. After a time, this name would be forgotten, and he would forever be known as Stoneblanket. He is my great-grandfather's brother. He would eventually become the most powerful *halayt*, or shaman, of our people.

"One day Nigaani was with his young wife, Wenona. Wenona means "first-born daughter" in our language. They were foraging along the beach, not far from where Old Town is today. In the woods near Old Town, you can still see rough outlines of the original longhouses. It is a secret, sacred place, and no outsiders can go there.

"The tide was very low at that time of year, so Nigaani and Wenona were far out on the beach on some rocks. They were looking for abalone and sea urchins and limpets, sometimes diving into the water to get the bigger ones. They were so busy with what they were doing, they didn't notice that a canoe full of outsiders—raiders from the north—had come upon them. These were an oppressive, barbaric people. From time to time they would come down looking to capture slaves; this was their way. And even back then, they knew they had to bring in others to diversify their gene pool. They jumped out of their canoe and captured Nigaani and Wenona. They clubbed them on the head to subdue them, and they took them away back north in their canoe.

"Nigaani wasn't sure how long he had lain unconscious. He came to in an encampment, and Wenona was beside him. His captors saw him awaken, so they clubbed him again. Wenona was very close to death, and with this second clubbing, so was Nigaani. Then he had what we now think of as a near-death experience, except he was not alone—Wenona was there with him. Nigaani and Wenona went to the spirit world together. Nigaani was hurt, but Wenona was hurt worse. She wanted to stay—she had to stay—and she wanted Nigaani to stay with her. But he was strong and felt the pull back to the world of man. So he travelled back to the world of man alone. Again, he woke up in the encampment. This time Wenona wasn't by his side, and he felt very bad. Soon his enemies saw he was awake, and they clubbed him again, and again he travelled to the spirit world. He saw Wenona, and this time he also saw his ancestors. Wenona begged him to stay with her, but Nigaani wasn't ready to stay in the spirit world; he still had life in him and again felt the pull back to the world of man.

"This time when he awoke, they let him stay awake. He sat up and noticed they were dancing and celebrating. They were cooking something over a large fire. They cut pieces off of it and danced and ate. With one of these pieces, they taunted and teased Nigaani. They put it under his nose. They tried to push it into his mouth and rubbed it on his face. They ate the meat in front of him.

"Soon Nigaani looked down and saw that part of his leg was missing. A rope made of woven cedar bark strips soaked in oolichan grease and pitch was tied around his lower thigh. They were eating his own leg right in front of him, tormenting him with his own flesh! They took the leg off the fire—by now it was just his bones with a foot attached—and rubbed it under his nose to disrespect him. Nigaani passed out from the pain and the sight of his enemies eating part of him.

"Once again, he had a near-death experience. He travelled back to the spirit world, and this time stayed for quite a while. He saw Wenona, his ancestors, and his brother, who had died when they were teenagers. They knew he had been treated badly, and they told him to stay. Nigaani was tempted. It was good to see Wenona and not to be in pain. But he was a very strong man—and maybe the strongest-willed man of our people *ever*. He returned to the world of man once again. Maybe it was the thought of revenge that drew him back.

"While Nigaani was in the spirit world, the raiders returned in their canoe to our village. They brought Nigaani's lower leg with them. They came to our village and taunted our people, and they threw the leg onto the beach to shock them and instill fear. They said they had eaten Nigaani and Wenona, that the leg was the proof of it. In eating the flesh, they had taken on all of their strength, adding to their own. They said they would return and do the same to the rest of the people of our village. They wanted our people to live in fear, to intimidate us and disrupt our peaceful way of life. They thought they could return at will and dominate our tribe.

"Our people *were* peaceful. This was shocking and had never happened before. They knew it was Nigaani's lower leg because the foot was still attached, and he had a unique tattoo on the top of his foot that they could still see clearly. This type of tattoo is customary even today. The village went into weeks of mourning for Nigaani and Wenona. They built a mortuary pole in honour of them. The people tried to think of ways to defend themselves against the raiders, and they set up watchmen to keep vigil.

"The village shaman said the leg had powerful spirits around it. He felt the people needed to do everything possible to tap into its power, and that it could help defend them against the enemies to come. We believe that the soul doesn't live in the heart, or in the brain, but resides in the bones. In the marrow of our bones.

"Our people believed in a mythological creature called the Sisiutl. It is the god of warrior invincibility and one of the most powerful deities. It is represented in different ways, and details differ from nation to nation, but usually it is depicted as a man in the centre of a two-headed sea creature—a serpent, with horns of power. Sometimes it is also thought of as a war canoe with the serpent heads on each end and the man in the middle. The magical war canoe also has many meanings attached to it. This two-headed beast linked to a powerful man represents the *duality* that is the centrepiece to our forefathers' belief system. The Sisiutl's twin heads represent the gateway to two worlds, the spirit world, and the world of man.

"In the north where the raiders were from, the Sisiutl takes the form of a wand or sceptre and is usually made from the leg bone of a bear. The serpent's heads are carved on each end and a man's head is in the middle. Often it is adorned with mother-of-pearl and mica to make it more distinctive and powerful. This was what they called the Soulcatcher. It was a powerful idol that was the ticket to the spirit world. It was the key to prompting the soul to travel to that other world.

"Our shaman wanted to use Nigaani's shinbone, his tibia, to create a Soulcatcher. He said there could be nothing stronger to protect us, to overpower our enemies, and to guide any of our fallen to the spirit world. Fight fire with fire. Many people were against it, as this wasn't our form of the Sisiutl and the spirits would be angry. But he did it anyway. He took the shinbone from the mortuary pole and left the foot and other bones there. Over the next few weeks, he carefully carved the shinbone into a unique Soulcatcher. Because of the naturally flared ends of the tibia, the detailed monsters on each end were open mouthed and looked very fierce. He skilfully carved the middle section of the bone all over with mythic beings and as a spiral ribbon, revealing the inner channel where the marrow had been. Into this channel he inserted an intricately carved bone bead, representing the man. This little man was captured inside and could slide up and down the marrow tube, symbolically moving from the spirit world to the world of man and back again. If the shaman shook the Soulcatcher up and down, it made a clicking sound, almost like a rattle. This was a powerful sound; he could summon up spirits with the shake of the rattle. Once the new Soulcatcher was completed, the shaman held an elaborate ceremony to honour it, to evoke its power, and to honour the dead it so clearly represented.

"Not many days after the Soulcatcher ceremony, our watchmen saw a man coming toward them down the beach. He was moving slowly. He had crude crutches and part of one of his legs was missing, the stump end still tied with a rope. They ran out to him. It was Nigaani. They couldn't believe their eyes; he was supposed to be dead! Nigaani was in terrible shape. He was close to death yet again and incoherent. No one knew how far he had come, or where he had been. The watchmen carried Nigaani back to the village, and everyone was in disbelief that he was still alive. He was truly the strongest, most invincible warrior of our people. The shaman said this proved that the Soulcatcher he made had worked and had strong supernatural powers. The ceremony must have guided Nigaani home.

"The village banded together and nursed him back to health. It took many weeks, as he was very sick and his leg was badly infected and crawling with maggots. They moved him temporarily up to the lake, where we are now. There was no settlement here then. They brought him here and bathed him in the waters every day to keep his wound clean and to protect and isolate him. This is how the story of the healing power of the lake began. Eventually, Nigaani recovered. Because of his many near-death experiences—the many times he went back and forth from the spirit world and the world of man, he learned how to move between the two worlds. He could move when he was alive. Now he moves while he's dead.

"When Nigaani finally recovered, the entire village bestowed a special blanket on him. Blankets are especially important, practically and symbolically, in our beliefs. Woollen blankets, capes, and especially now our button blankets are important parts of our culture. Blankets are given to people who are held in extremely high esteem, to people who have had a life-altering experience, or to those with special accomplishments. Nigaani was all those things and more. His blanket had the symbol of the Soulcatcher on it, and the morning star. The morning star symbolizes the beginning of a new day, the rebirth of the spirit, and protection. He was never formally given the name "Stoneblanket," but it seemed preordained. He was Stoneblanket from that day forward, and I think everyone has forgotten his real name. Everyone except me.

"A couple of years passed, and the most likely successor to the old shaman was Stoneblanket. The shaman trained Stoneblanket in the spiritual ways. But from the very beginning of his studies, it was clear that Stoneblanket was already more powerful than the *halayt* who was teaching him. Through the terrible experience of his capture, Stoneblanket had become very strong, very brave, very wise, and most importantly, had learned how to travel to the spirit world and back again. No one had ever done that before. Stoneblanket could travel to the spirit world whenever he wanted; he created a special, secret mushroom ceremony that transported him.

"Eventually the old shaman died, and Stoneblanket guided him to the spirit world. When he returned, Stoneblanket was officially the *halayt* of our people. He remained so for over fifty years and had many adventures, helped many people from all over, settled many important issues, and safely guided those who passed to the spirit world.

"Unfortunately, Stoneblanket became more bitter over time— maybe from being hit on the head. Or maybe he was just impatient with those who didn't understand him. He never got over losing his wife and the damage the raiders inflicted on him when he was young. He was hurtful to some and absolutely ruthless to those who crossed him.

"Since he could move so effectively between the two worlds, when it came time for him to die, he easily made the transition. And after he died and went to the spirit world, he could also return to the world of man whenever he needed to.

"The Sisiutl is the myth, Stoneblanket is the personification of that myth, and the Soulcatcher is the catalyst."

* * *

Owny slumped in her chair, exhausted from recounting the story. Her face looked more aged under the old fluorescent kitchen light.

"So why does he 'need' to come now?" Ryan asked. He was skeptical of Owny's story, but still moved by it.

Owny shuddered and began to sob openly. "I'm scared he's come for Patsy!"

Gerald came into the kitchen and put his hand on Owny's shoulder. She turned slightly to acknowledge him, patting the back of his hand. She took a drink of the water, wiped her eyes, and composed herself, pulling at her top. Again she looked at Gerald. Then she stood up and left the room. Ryan thought she had gone into her bedroom; he heard some rustling from where she was. Gerald shook his head, saying nothing, looking for her to return.

Owny emerged, carrying an object about a foot and a half long in a worn black velvet drawstring bag. She went to the table and sat again. She laid the item down carefully, with reverence. She stroked the bag from the centre to the ends a few times, as if calming it, her right hand quivering slightly. Owny breathed in deeply and exhaled.

She worked her fingers into the drawstring and released the cord, then opened the bag gently and pulled it off from the bottom.

Ryan knew what was coming, but he was still surprised to actually see it and couldn't contain himself. "Whoa, whoa, whoa!" He pushed his chair back roughly and stood up, then backed away from the table. He didn't know what to do with his hands and wiped them on his jeans and continued to back away as if he thought she was going to make him touch the thing. Hearing the commotion, Iris appeared at the entrance to the kitchen, peering in from the other room. Patsy had also heard it; she came from her bedroom and looked over her sister's shoulder.

It had a dark brown patina and a grain to it. A thin ancient hand-woven rope was tied at the centre. The rope was tattered, about three feet long, and hung off it like a lanyard. The room had a musty odour now that the object was lying exposed on its bag. Wide-eyed, Ryan was impressed at how ornate it was. It was beautiful in its own way. The figures at each end were as Owny had described, but to see the actual workmanship was something to behold. It was narrow in the middle, and he couldn't see the little man. He didn't want to get too close.

Gerald was trying to be patient, but he was becoming agitated. "Do *not* shake that thing," he said emphatically, ostensibly to Owny, but also to anyone within earshot.

Owny started to talk to it in her Native language. It was as if she was speaking in tongues, as the language was slow and slurred and full of clicking sounds. She had her eyes closed, and she laid her hands on the bone as she spoke.

Gerald stood behind her with his hands on her shoulders, giving her support. He let her finish. "Let's put it away now," he said quietly.

Owny complied, slipping the black bag back over the bone. But Ryan had the feeling that she knew it would have to come out again. Soon.

Chapter 8

It had been two days since they had put Laura into the ambulance. Phil Conner was curious about her status, and the report from the lab still had him perplexed. He wasn't sure about detox sessions. How long did these things take? He wanted to give Laura the space she needed to get through her "valley of the shadow of death," and he certainly didn't picture himself holding a bucket and wearing rubber gloves and a plastic poncho for someone he didn't know all that well. He liked Laura from a professional standpoint, and had always thought she had a good sense of humour and a bright personality. This past school year she had been very engaged with her class and had volunteered for key extracurricular work, which always endeared a teacher to the supervisory staff. Her involvement made her recent decline that much more of a mystery. She seemed to have put her past troubles firmly behind her until the last few days of the school term.

He decided to give the hospital a call and inquire how she was doing. The nurse he spoke to stated she was doing "just okay," and that Laura was still some days away from being able to see visitors. This satisfied Phil, and he resolved to go and see her in a few days. He was happy to hear she was in the process and sticking to the program. To educate himself about what Laura was going through, he googled "alcohol detox stages." He learned the following:

Alcohol withdrawal occurs in three stages, with the exact time of onset of each stage varying from person to person:

- Stage 1: This usually starts eight hours after the last drink and is marked by symptoms such as anxiety, insomnia, nausea, and abdominal pain.

- Stage 2: One to three days after the last drink, Stage 2 begins. Confusion, along with high blood pressure, increased body temperature, and an atypical heart rate characterize this stage.

- Stage 3: The final stage is marked by fever, hallucinations, seizures, and agitation. This can begin two to four days after the last drink.

Symptoms typically decrease within five to seven days.

For sure Laura needed more time. Since she was a long-term alcoholic, and since she had been pretty far gone on this last bender, maybe going cold turkey would take a little longer this time.

Still busy with year-end tasks, Phil immersed himself in his job. He could afford the long hours; his personal life had been non-existent since his fifteen-year marriage had come to an abrupt end about a year ago when his wife left him suddenly. Later he discovered that a younger man had been waiting in the wings. She took the kids and managed to turn them against him. They had a seen his temper first hand, after all. At first he rolled with the punches, but recently he had become frustrated as he became more isolated. Work was his saviour, and as much as he wanted the school term to be over with, he had spent zero time planning or even thinking about what to do with himself for the summer. It was too late to sign up for teaching summer classes, and his heart wasn't in it anyway.

While researching the subject of alcohol withdrawal, he took it upon himself to google the symptoms Laura had displayed in the short time he'd seen her. He typed in "slurred speech," "lack of balance," and "look like you're drunk." The return information was vast and covered everything from stroke to brain tumour to side effects of drugs. He wasn't qualified to narrow this down, especially with what little information he had. He would get to the hospital as soon as it was practical and try to talk to Laura, maybe a health professional. He printed off the lab report with Laura's blood work and put it in his computer bag.

On day four of the detox he tried to call Laura's cell. No answer. He didn't leave a message. Day five he tried again with the same results. Day six came, and he had a lighter day with the school year almost over. He sneaked out for a few hours in the afternoon and made his way to the hospital. He checked at the main information desk for the location of the "psych ward." From there he found his way to the ward desk and asked about his employee.

The nurse seemed unsure of what to say. "She's . . . resting as comfortably as she can. She's having a rough go of it and isn't ready to see . . . Are you her husband?"

"No, no. I'm her . . . I'm Phil, the principal at the school she teaches at. I—*we*—were wondering how she was doing, so I thought I'd check in."

"She's still working through this and she's not ready to see anyone but close family, and even they sometimes have to be approved by the doctor. I—"

"Has any family been in to see her?"

"I haven't seen any, and I've been on day shift for a few days now. I'd say give us a call tomorrow to see how she's doing. I'll let her know you came by, Phil. Maybe she can take a call tomorrow. Maybe. Here, I'll give you the direct number to call this desk." She wrote it on a Post-it note and gave it to Phil.

"Okay, thanks. I'll check in tomorrow." Phil departed and returned to the school.

The next day he called the ward desk and managed to get the same nurse. She said there was some improvement and kept him on the line as she went to speak to Laura. Maybe she would come to the phone.

The nurse returned and said, "She said she won't come to the phone. She said she doesn't want to see you." She was much less friendly than before.

He should have been prepared for rejection, considering the circumstances of Laura's last day at school. Still, he was taken aback. She might not know he had precipitated her rescue, and she certainly wouldn't know about the lab results.

"Can you please ask her again, please? Tell her I have some information regarding her blood test that I'd like to share with her."

The nurse gave him dead air to demonstrate her disdain for his request to waste her time by going back to Laura's room.

"It will likely affect her insurance, and maybe WCB, BC Medical, all of it. It's important. I'm her employer."

She relented. "Okay, then. Hang on." She put him back on hold, for a longer wait than she had the first time. "She said she'd see you. Tomorrow, not today. I need to let the doctors know you're coming. Because she's still in detox, they may want to see you first."

"Oh, okay. Thanks, I'll come by tomorrow afternoon. What's the best time to come?"

"Visiting hours start at two," she informed him.

"Thanks. I'll be by then."

* * *

After lunch the next day, Principal Conner informed Mary he was going up to see Laura.

"She's still in the hospital?" Mary seemed surprised.

"Yeah, looks like this was rough for her. I'm not clear on what the whole process is, but I checked in a couple of times over the past few days. It seems to be going slowly, but it looks like she might finally be out of the woods. I'll let you know when I get back."

Phil made his way to the hospital. He thought briefly about bringing a small gift or flowers to cheer Laura up and break the ice. He soon dismissed it as inappropriate; just showing up would be enough. He went up to the ward desk and asked for Laura's room. Without hesitation, a different nurse told him it was 214 and pointed down the hall and to the left. He went to the room; the door was almost fully open. He sheepishly stuck his head in, knowing from the phone call she must be pissed off with him.

Laura was sitting up on a bed on the far side of the room by the window. She was reading something. The room seemed stark. There were no pictures on the walls, no cards or flowers on the nightstand. The only thing around her was a plastic cup on her overbed table with a bent straw in it. It was a four-room ward, but only one other bed looked lived in, and it was vacant.

"Hi . . . Laura?" Phil was surprised at how good she looked. He was expecting some sort of unkempt being. She appeared to have lost some weight, but she had colour in her face. She must have recently washed her hair and was surprisingly bright-eyed. "How are you doing?" he asked sincerely.

"I think I'm back in the land of the living, finally!" she said breezily.

"Nice to see you looking well! Are you able to get out soon?"

"No word on that at all. They're doing a bunch more tests for some reason. I . . . I . . ." Laura was at a loss for words. It was suddenly awkward for her to discuss her personal issues with him, her supervisor. Maybe she wished it was her husband checking on her, or her daughter. She sighed and looked at him standing there holding a piece of paper.

"More tests?" Phil said, trying to prompt her.

"Yes, more tests. I still feel unsteady on my feet. Can't seem to shake it. A few other symptoms seem to be . . . persisting, so yeah, more tests."

"I don't mean to be nosy, Laura. I . . . we . . . we're all thinking about you and concerned about you. Could there be any sort of permanent damage, any ongoing problems?

"Well, I'm not sure, really. Yeah, I probably have abused myself," she admitted, her eyes widening. "I'm really trying to put this behind me. I want this latest episode to be my last. I really thought it was all behind me." She shook her head, obviously disappointed in herself. "We had a good school year in general, right?"

Phil nodded as he pulled over a chair.

"I was accused of drinking and knew I was going to be fired. I was super stressed and upset, and . . . I guess thought if I was accused of it then I was screwed, so I might as well just drink. So I fell off the wagon. Not the right way to cope. It was not my finest hour. But Phil, I wasn't drinking that day! I don't know what the hell was wrong with me, *is* wrong with me, but I wasn't drinking at school that day. And for a long time before that." Laura was emphatic.

"I know."

"You know?" Laura sat up and her brow furrowed. "You know?"

"Well, that's one of the reasons I'm here." He looked down at lab report in his hand. "I was just . . . We all like you, Laura, but I can't have anyone intoxicated at the school. You know that. And I thought you were. It sure looked like it to me and Mary. Anyway, when I got the lab report back, I just couldn't believe it. I thought it was wrong. I called the lab and everything." He handed it to Laura and pointed to the box with the blood alcohol content beside it. "I believe you now. I guess I should have believed you from the start, but—"

"Phil, I've had a lot of time to think about this. I was upset for a long time because I felt you pushed me back into a terrible place. But I know now you were just doing what you thought was right. *I'm* responsible for how I react to situations—not anyone else. That's step ten . . . sort of, I think." She looked at the back cover of the book she was reading.

"When I got the results, I was really confused. I tried to call you a few times, then decided to go over to your place and check on you. Lazlo and his wife came over and we found you."

"Oh my God, you were there? Oh my God!" Laura put her hands to her mouth and closed her eyes in embarrassment. She was quiet for some time. She sighed deeply. "Wow. You're full of surprises." She shook her head in shame. Her cheeks bulged and she blew out air through pursed lips. She opened her eyes and blinked hard. "I thought it must have been just Marta and Lazlo. I need to thank them." Tears welled up in her eyes. "I guess I need to thank you too." She looked down at the orange bedspread, trying to blink the tears away.

"Marta and Lazlo are good people. And you don't need to thank me. I didn't do anything."

"You were concerned enough to check on me. That's more than other people have done."

Just then a doctor briskly walked in, whistling to himself. He was a tall South Asian man with thick black hair. "Hello, Laura, how are you doing today?" He had a slight accent.

"Much better. I've had some breakfast, a shower, and even a visitor! Things are looking up."

"That's good." He snuck a look at his clipboard. "And this is Mr. Hanson?"

"Oh, no, this is Phil Conner, the principal at the school where I work. Worked."

"Work," Phil said. He shook the doctor's hand.

"Oh, your principal, yes. Hi, I'm Doctor Patel." He turned to Laura but seemed to still be talking to Phil. "Laura has had a challenging week or so. I'm very glad to see her looking better today. We still have some . . . some things to determine so we can understand what's going on with her."

"Oh yes, Doctor," Phil said. "I came today to let Laura know the results of the blood test we had done the day of her . . . the day we sent her home. That day at the school, Laura looked . . . inebriated. She was slurring her words, staggering a bit, and was lethargic. It looked all the world to me like she'd been drinking, so I sent her home. Well, sent her for a blood test—then she went home. Here's the test." He handed it to Doctor Patel. "It shows her blood alcohol content at zero."

The doctor looked at the form and winced. "But Laura, you *had* been drinking. You were in a bad way when you arrived here."

"Yes, Doctor, I was drinking *after* I was sent home. I . . . relapsed, but it was after I got home. I was stressed. Stressed because nobody believed me, because I think there's something else wrong with me, because drinking is what happens when I really bottom out."

"Hmm," Doctor Patel said. "This is interesting, but Laura, you *are* an alcoholic."

"Yes, I am. Obviously. I'm not in denial about that. I've been here before. But I don't want to be here again. And I'd like to know what else is going on. Have I done some other damage? Whatever it is, I'd like to know."

"Okay, so tell me in more detail how you were feeling that day," Doctor Patel said. He looked at Phil, then back at Laura as if to ask, "Is it okay he's here for this?"

"It's okay," Laura said, sensing his concern. "Phil might have something to add. What he said about my condition that day was true, and I should have spoken up about it earlier. I was feeling funny for quite some time, and it would come and go. I thought it was . . . I don't know . . . blood sugar or fatigue or something. I was just trying to get through to the end of the school year and then rest and regroup. I thought maybe it would go away for good. At first it was hardly noticeable, and I'd feel a little dizzy, or off balance. Then it would go away. Then I was slurring my words, then having some kind of hot flashes."

"So how long have you felt this way, off and on?" the doctor asked.

"I was probably in denial about it for a while. It wasn't too big of a deal at first. But I'd say since about Easter maybe. A few months."

"Hmm," the doctor said as he processed this. "Okay, I'm going to schedule some tests. You're going to have to stay here for a few more days. I want to observe you, do some manual tests, and schedule you to see a specialist."

"What type of specialist?" Laura asked.

"A neurologist. We have a really good neurologist right here. I'll talk to him today. I want him to see you after we do an MRI, some blood work. Maybe a spinal tap."

Laura was concerned. "A spinal tap? I don't like the sound of that."

"Don't worry. It isn't too uncomfortable. We should probably test your spinal fluid. Okay?" Doctor Patel tried to sound reassuring. "So we have a plan. Let's get some data and get you in front of a specialist. Okay?"

"Okay." Laura seemed to feel better with a plan in place, even if she would be living in limbo for a while longer.

The doctor turned to Phil. "Thanks for coming in."

"No problem," Phil responded.

Doctor Patel turned to leave, then stopped and looked at the lab report. "What about THC?" He turned to Laura. "Cannabis. Do you use cannabis?"

"No." Laura shook her head, looking a little surprised at his question.

"Okay—just checking." Using the lab report to wave a friendly goodbye, he strode out.

Phil turned to Laura. "It's great to see you, to see you're on the mend. I'm gonna head back to school now and get some work done."

"Phil, thank you. Thank so much. I know now you were doing the right thing all along, and you've really come through for me."

"Not a problem. I try to look out for my teachers! Maybe I could stop by again soon? I'd like to see how you're doing."

"By all means. Um, I'll ask for my phone—I think I can have it now. They take it away from you for the first while. So I'll ask and charge it up and should be able to communicate with you. But feel free to come by anytime."

"Okay, thanks, and stay well! See you soon."

Phil exited the room, passing a nurse going in. He heard Laura ask for her phone and paused in the hall to hear the exchange.

"I'll check with the doctor, but not likely. You're still officially in detox and we really want to keep you focused on yourself. We need to keep outside influences to a minimum."

Chapter 9

Driving back around the lake in the dark, Ryan shook his head and muttered under his breath, lamenting what he had gotten himself into. He had really led himself astray throughout the whole thing: walking out on Laura, buying the cabin so impulsively, letting Walter process the sale so damn quickly, the stupid website, his beach visitors, and now the Soulcatcher performance. He felt as he was on a slippery slope with few options. He had created the sign tree on his property for a reason; he needed some boundaries, some space, some time alone to reflect. He just wasn't sure how to attain this now. Ryan decided to call his daughter, check in with her, and inquire about Laura. He didn't want to call Laura directly; he wasn't ready. He wasn't sure he would ever be ready.

Once back at the cabin, he took a quick look from the deck for any strangers on the beach; there was no sign of anyone. Rosie barked from the cabin, hearing her master on the stairs. She was anxious to get out. He unlocked the door and greeted the dog. She stood on her hind legs for some attention and then scampered down the steps and into the underbrush. Ryan went in, leaving the door open for her return. He turned on the stove to boil some water to make pasta. It was past his usual suppertime; he was hungry and needed to regroup. As the water heated, he called Emily. Instinctively, he sensed that as a daughter she would be in tune with her mother the most. He scrolled through his phone and tapped her mobile number.

"Hi, Dad."

"Hi, how are you?" Ryan asked.

"I'm okay. Have you heard from Mum?"

"Uh, no. That's why I am calling you. Have you talked to her recently?"

"No, I've called her cell, left messages, but nothing. It just goes straight to voice mail."

"Hmm. When did you last try?"

"That would be . . . yesterday. No, the day before."

"Could you please try again? I, uh, I don't feel like calling her myself right now. But I'm thinking she should be checked on." Ryan said, concerned.

"Okay, I can. I went over last weekend, just so you know. She definitely was drinking but seemed to be . . . I don't know . . . in control? I'm not a good judge of it, actually. She could carry on a conversation at least. I don't like being around her when she's drinking either—you know that. She's such a different person."

"Yeah, I know, I know. But right now I don't know if she's tapering off, gone all in, or what. I don't know what to think. Please try and call. As soon as you connect with her, call me back."

"Okay, I'll try now, but it may be tomorrow, or whenever, before I get a response," Emily explained. "So where are you? Where are you staying? You're not at the house."

"I'm at Walter Rosenthal's cabin. You know, your mum and I would visit them here sometimes. I have Rosie with me—though I guess you must know I have the dog if you saw your mum on the weekend." Ryan neglected to tell his daughter he'd actually bought the place. "Don't tell your mum where I am, okay? For now. Just keep trying to get ahold of her."

"No worries. As long as you're doing okay too. I'll keep trying and let you know. Love you."

"Love you too. Bye."

Ryan fed Rosie and had his pasta and a glass of red wine, then turned in right away. He knew he would have a fitful night. Visions of the Soulcatcher, worry about his wife and their relationship, concerns about his neglected work and the new expectations around Owny's website project, serious buyer's remorse, Emily. The endless loop played in his mind, until a few hours of sleep stopped the churn. He dreamed he was back in university, rowing. Things were simpler then.

The morning dawned misty and cool. The weather report promised a nice day once the fog burned off. The water was as smooth as glass, and the shore on the other side was obscured by low cloud. The lake called to Ryan when he looked out to inspect the beach. He expected visitors, but so far not a soul. Not a mother and daughter, not a one-legged Aboriginal going for a skinny dip, no one. All quiet on the Western Front. The serene morning reminded him of why he was there. If this was the new normal, all would be well.

Inspired by the promise of a beautiful summer's day, he dressed for a trip in the single scull. He tucked his phone in the pocket of his small blue foamy neck float and set it to music mode. He closed the door on Rosie; she was stuck in the cabin watching Ryan head to the dock. He prepped the boat, setting it in the water at the far end of the dock, locking in the long oars—pointed forward for the time being—and stepped carefully into the spindly craft. As he shifted to the familiar sitting position, he poked earbuds into place. He scrolled through his playlists for classical and selected his favourite for such an occasion, "Hornpipe" from Handel's *Water Music*, and touched Play. French horns and violas started taking turns with his auditory nerves. He shuddered from the damp coolness going through his back as he pushed away from the dock, but he knew it wouldn't last long.

He rowed in a shallow arc out to the centre of the lake, slowly at first, as he warmed up for a straight run to the south end. As he started to pull the oars in earnest, sunbeams shot through the low mist, right on cue. The filtered light became stronger, and it sparkled and danced on the surface as the fog dissipated. It was as if the vista of the lake was emerging just for him. His senses were as full as they had ever been, and he revelled in the moment.

It was obvious why New Town was here, why they had brought Stoneblanket here. It was obvious why anyone would want to protect this place, whether or not there was anything extra special about the water, or the source, or the bubbles. Just being at the lake, on the lake, or in the lake was an invigorating tonic.

Seeing he was closing in on the shoreline, Ryan coasted to a slow tempo, then cranked one oar to execute a tight 180-degree turn. He turned his head to ensure his direction was correct, and that no one else was on the lake, then put his back into a sprint down the waterway. He was determined to make it to the other end without stopping. In just over twenty minutes, he slowed as he approached the north shore. He turned, paused to rest for a moment, and then covered the same distance southbound.

Once back at the south end, he pulled out his earbuds and hunched forward, exhausted but satisfied with his workout. He paused briefly, then pulled on just his right oar, rotating the boat. He pointed the narrow craft roughly toward the centre of the cabin row in the distance and slowly propelled the boat back to his starting point. His body heat amplified the sun's radiance on his back, and vapour rose from his upper body from the perspiration.

After exiting the boat, he lay on the aging silvery wood of the dock, still breathing deeply. He held on to the boat with his right arm till he felt rested enough to wrestle with the scull. He told himself he needed to do this every day possible. It changed his spirit, his outlook, his physical fitness, all for the good.

Back at the cabin, he greeted his four-legged friend and jumped into the shower. He prepared the coffee maker and booted up his computer while he waited for the toaster. After a second cup of coffee, he addressed his Outlook inbox. For the next few hours, he responded to clients and updated several websites with new prices and rates furnished by the clients via email. By noon he had made the most critical changes and notified each person that he had updated the sites as requested.

Ryan keyed in the address for the local band's website and looked at the home page. Normally creative when it came to such things, he was drawing a blank. He knew he could refresh the site with an updated look—this might be enough to please Owny—but the content wasn't going to improve. He shook his head. The conversation about the website at the Wilson's last night was almost forgotten, overshadowed by Owny's soliloquy about Stoneblanket. Trying to recall it, he knew he only had two solid elements to promote: the new cabin development and the sawmill. As far as he was concerned, both were lost causes. For some reason no one was pushing the road farther down the lake or surveying the new cabin lots. The sawmill looked like an abandoned shell, with no activity at all. From his limited knowledge, Ryan knew that any working sawmill would have large stacks of logs awaiting the saw, and some lumber inventory ready for sale. Neither was there, except for some big logs stacked up in the shed.

He would need to ask Owny about the lack of activity when it came to the construction equipment. It must be expensive to rent it—or did they own it? Or did it belong to a contractor who was allowing it to lie idle for some reason? He couldn't remember if there were any company logos on the machines. He looked around the internet for other locations selling lakeside community lots in North America, which gave him some ideas, and his recent excursion on the lake inspired him. He knew he could work up a good subsite for real estate promotion once he knew more about the concept.

He was stymied regarding the sawmill and saw nothing positive. Maybe there was something they could do with the logs in the shed. On a lark he googled "spruce wood uses." There was a lot of information, and he soon realized there were several different species. He thought Owny had said Sitka spruce. He searched Wikipedia and lumber industry sites for information. One of the uses for high-quality Sitka spruce was making musical instruments.

"Hmm," he muttered. "I wonder . . ." He looked down at the dog, who was looking back at him. He recalled a forestry research centre at the university. Maybe they would have some information on the properties of wood for special applications. He went to the University of Victoria website and did a search. The Centre for Forest Biology came up; it had a large presence. At the bottom of the page he saw a link, "Tell Us Your Story."

"What the hell," Ryan said. He typed in a brief note stating he was assisting an Indigenous group and looking to get Sitka spruce analyzed for acoustic properties for commercial applications. He gave them his name and number. It was a shot in the dark, but he had nothing to lose.

Ryan stopped for a while and grabbed a sports drink out of the fridge, then went outside to appreciate the day. He sat in the old Adirondack- style deck chair. The sun had decided to hide behind some clouds, but it was still pleasantly warm that June afternoon. A light breeze tousled the leaves in the arbutus and alder trees between the cabins. After about twenty minutes, his cell phone rang, and he rushed inside to find it on the table beside the computer. An unknown number. He answered in a business voice, stating his name.

"Hi, Ryan, how are you?" The voice was friendly.

"I'm fine. Who's calling?"

"Hi, Ryan," the man said again. "I'm Mike Maguire with the University of Victoria Department of Biology."

"Holy smokes, that was quick! Thank you for calling back."

"No problem. The site sent me a copy of your note in an email, so I got it right away. Your timing was good—we're just starting our summer session, so we have staff and students, uh, engaged in studies currently."

"Interesting. So is there anyone there who knows anything about Sitka spruce?"

"Well, for sure someone here knows about it. But as far as its acoustical properties go, not so much. That's a very specialized thing."

"Hmm . . . too bad. I was hoping to explore the idea for an Indigenous group I'm working with. We're looking to diversify and come up with alternative uses for locally harvested wood products." Ryan was improvising.

"Well, actually, that's why I'm interested. We don't—I don't— know about how to test for acoustical properties, but I'd love to give that task to some students to do a research paper on. It would be right up our alley for a summer term project."

Ryan was thrilled with his luck. "That sounds really great, Mike. So what do you need? Where do we go from here?"

"I need to propose this to some students, but I really think it's something they'll jump at. The course is about alternative uses for local softwoods. We've been racking our brains for some new and interesting ideas. Like I said, your timing is good. We have a class tomorrow and I'll give you a call back, hopefully tomorrow, and let you know what we come up with."

"Awesome. Sounds good. Thanks, Mike. Oh, so just wondering . . . Will there be a cost to this?"

"At this point, I don't think so. The students may have some costs to cover, but I can't think of anything right now. Let's talk tomorrow."

"Okay, great. Thanks again for calling. I look forward to hearing back from you soon."

Ryan set the phone down and shouted, "Yeah! That's what I'm talkin' about!" He bent over the dog, scratching her under the neck. "This could work out good!" He looked at the half-finished sports drink on the table, closed the cap, and put it back in the fridge, instead opting to crack open a beer and celebrate his little idea.

His mind started to click in, and he thought back to a municipal website he'd developed from scratch about a year earlier. With new enthusiasm, he went to his files and found the original framework for the site. He quickly changed the wording on the home page, revised some tabs on the search banner to "Old Town," "New Town," "Upcoming Events," "Contact Information," "Real Estate Division," "Business Development," and "Specialty Spruce." He searched "West Coast Aboriginal art" and discovered some beautiful photos of carvings. Only as a placeholder, he downloaded a picture of a canoe painted to resemble the Sisiutl and placed it on the home page. He wanted to show the full potential of the site to Owny and whoever else would be interested.

The next morning, he arose early and started tweaking the website with ideas he had conjured up overnight. He downloaded a few pictures he took of the marina and used them as backgrounds for the Old Town section. He used a picture of the machinery at the end of the road under "Business Development," and the sawmill picture under "Specialty Spruce." In each subsite, he added some basic dialogue as placeholders.

He returned to the old website and was trying to understand why and how members would interact with it when he heard a shuffling noise outside. Rosie jumped to her feet and let out one loud bark, and she cocked her head and listened for more. Ryan stood up and shushed the golden retriever, trying to hear what direction the noise came from. He heard it again; it was coming from the south side of the cabin, by the shed. Ryan opened the door and peeked over the side of the deck. Patsy was peering in the shed doorway. Owny came out of the dark shed with the old life jacket.

"Good morning." Ryan smiled to his visitors.

"Good morning, Ryan. How are you?" Owny asked softly.

"Doing great, thank you."

"We decided to take you up on your offer and use the life jacket again. Patsy feels safer and can stay out longer." They walked together over to the beach.

"Absolutely," Ryan responded.

The two women organized themselves once they were on the dock. Patsy grimaced as the old life jacket went on over her head, but she quickly got into the mode, tying it and stepping into the circular life ring. She slipped into the water, and Owny held the rope. Patsy paddled out to the source.

Ryan saw an opportunity to chat with Owny. "I've been working on the website a bit!" he hollered. "Um, give me a sec." He held up his index finger, nodded, and furrowed his brow, as if she was in a hurry to leave. He went inside and grabbed his open laptop, unplugged the adaptor, and brought it out to show Owny his progress. He stood beside her, turning the computer slightly toward her as she manned the rope.

It had her attention immediately. "Oh, it looks good!" She was genuinely impressed. "What . . . where did this all come from?" she said as if she expected it to resemble to the old site, but it didn't at all.

"It's the framework of another project I did a while ago. Then I downloaded some stock photos and used some of the photos I took the other day." Ryan deftly used the laptop's mouse pad and clicked on the banner, showing his friend the content he had placed in each category.

She shook her head. "Wow, you are *fast!*"

"Ah, well, it's what I do. Most all of this is just placeholder stuff, just to show you the concept. I need to—*we need to*—really understand what you want out of this, what programs you want to administer from here, and what you want to show and promote to your band and the outside world."

She ran her index finger across the banner, taking in the titles. "We have a 'Real Estate Division'?"

"Well, kind of. I know I'm taking some liberties here, but I just want to show you the potential of the website, what it can do for you. If you want to promote the new cabin lots, you'll need a compelling website to get the word out. Honestly, anyone looking to buy would check it out on the website first. Everyone expects a professional pitch with information. Without it, it's a much harder sell. Here, look at this." For an example, Ryan quickly found one of the lake lot sites he'd explored the day before. But he was on the outside range of his Wi-Fi; annoyed, he turned the laptop to and fro. Owny got a glimpse of what Ryan was talking about before the computer froze.

"Oh yeah. I see what you mean." She nodded. "You're right."

"We could really do a good job of promoting this. Just thinking . . . How about a picture of the existing cabins from out in the water, looking this way?" Ryan nodded toward the water and back to the cabin. "That would be a great way to show the potential. Add a map of the lots, a Google map of the location of the site on the south part of the Island, and some contact info to "Real Estate Division," and Bob's your uncle."

"Gee, Ryan, you're really thinking." Ryan went back to the prototype home page and Owny looked at the subjects in the top banner again. "We have 'Business Development'?"

"That's for the other ideas you talked about. I haven't thought about it that much, but it could be a way to legitimize some of your ideas, shine a light on them, maybe attract investors, or just let your people know what the next priorities are. If you give these things a forum, some oxygen, they tend to become a reality, not just something you're talking about. I don't know . . . maybe a rough plan of the campsite, and call that the next project after the cabin development –indicate that it's the goal. Maybe something at the marina, that kind of thing."

"Hmm, well, okay. That's something." Owny appeared a little overwhelmed on her quiet morning outing with her daughter. "How you doing, Patsy?" she said.

"I'm getting cold. It seems colder this morning."

"Couple of more minutes." Owny turned again to the computer and pointed to the banner. "And what is 'Specialty Spruce'?" she said with both disbelief and curiosity.

"Well . . . I had an idea for all those logs in the shed at the sawmill. You said they were Sitka spruce, right?"

Owny nodded.

"I did some digging around for the best uses of Sitka spruce, and it's used for musical instruments and other things. I did a little more digging and approached the university for some help in assessing if the wood you have is good enough for instruments. I hope to hear today if some students will take the assessment on as a project. They're looking for projects on diversified uses for domestic timber."

"Ryan, I don't know what to say. You're a real dynamo!" Owny raised her eyebrows. "Okay, Patsy, time to come in!" She started to gently pull the rope, twisting Patsy a bit, then drawing her closer. Owny turned to Ryan as if she had been waiting for the right moment. "Did my story scare you the other day?"

"Um . . . a little. So to you Stoneblanket is real?"

"Well, you saw him, didn't you? You must have, that's why I felt I needed to tell you the story. You couldn't just make that up."

"No, for sure. I couldn't just make that up."

Chapter 10

Laura really wanted her phone. This was a double whammy—withdrawals from alcohol, and withdrawals from the phone and social media. The combination was becoming hard to bear. She recalled the lonely days of the virus isolation—but this was even worse. Something had to give. She asked Doctor Patel for her phone the next day as he was giving her a physical exam. He still declined.

"Maybe tomorrow," he said vaguely. "For the next few days, I really want you to focus on what we're doing here. This afternoon we'll do the lumbar puncture so we can test your spinal fluid, and tomorrow we hope to get you in for your MRI. After that, maybe as soon as tomorrow afternoon or the next day for the phone, okay? You're still in detox, right?"

"Okay," she said despondently. She felt like a schoolgirl who had lost privileges.

"Are you claustrophobic?"

"Why do you ask?"

"Have you ever had an MRI before?"

"No."

"Well, some people get a little uncomfortable in the machine. It's like you're in a tunnel, and it's a little, well, cramped in there. You'll be in it for at least several minutes, probably longer."

"I don't do well in confined spaces. I have to drive with the car window down half the time."

"Hmm. Okay, we'll give you something in the morning to calm your nerves."

"You better make it good."

Doctor Patel gave Laura a thorough exam, checking her eyes, her ears, and her neck glands, and he checked for lumps and moles. He took an exceptionally long time banging her knees and elbows with a little rubber hammer. Throughout this, he hemmed and hawed. He scheduled her to go down to the lab for blood work immediately after the exam. She was unsteady on her feet, so he asked for a wheelchair and a nurse to escort her. Laura had always been fiercely independent. She wasn't used to the detailed attention, the malaise, or the looming uncertainty.

Late in the afternoon she was brought into a small operating room for the lumbar puncture. She received freezing in her back, so the procedure was only mildly uncomfortable. It all happened quite quickly once she was in position. Almost immediately afterwards, she experienced a pounding headache and her left leg felt numb. She was taken back to her room, where she requested some painkillers. She didn't eat her supper and slept through to the morning.

In spite of the nagging anxiety about the MRI, her mood the next morning was optimistic. She was almost through the required exams and hoped there would be a light at the end of the MRI tunnel. Her back was a little sore, but her leg felt better and she'd had a good sleep. Laura waited in anticipation to be taken for the test. Just after lunch a nurse came in and advised her that due to emergencies and maintenance, they wouldn't be able to get her in that day but would put her at the front of the queue first thing early next morning. Laura half expected something to go wrong. She ordered a TV for her bed. Luckily, it came later in the afternoon.

A nurse came in early the next morning to rouse Laura. She handed her a little paper cup with a single white pill in it. The nurse called it Ativan and watched Laura carefully as she swallowed the dose. When the pill was down, she departed, stating she'd be back in about a half an hour and they would go for the MRI. Laura did little to prepare, just went to the bathroom and brushed her teeth.

Her escort arrived with a wheelchair and pushed her quickly down the hall to the elevator. The magnetic resonance imaging room was cool and dark. They flicked on the lights and booted up the machine; it seemed to have been asleep also. It hummed and ticked for several minutes. Laura looked at the big white beast and shuddered. The hole she would have to slide into looked very small. She hoped the Ativan would kick in soon.

The nurse left her there and a technician introduced herself and gave Laura a rundown of the procedure. Since she was having a detailed, full-body MRI, she would need at least forty-five minutes in the machine. Laura asked for another Ativan.

"I think you had one already," the technician retorted. "You'll be fine." She had a calming way about her. "Here, take this eye mask. Leave it on through the whole procedure—don't take it off. Think good thoughts . . . Imagine you're on a beach somewhere. We'll be done before you know it."

Luckily, the pill kicked in and Laura managed the tight quarters without a meltdown. Soon she was back out in the waiting room, where a couple of other patients were waiting. Laura didn't ask for assistance or wait for any advice; she pushed the wheels on the chair and got back to her room on her own steam.

Doctor Patel showed up later that morning. "Good morning, Laura. How did it go?"

"Fine. They finally got me in this morning. Do you have the results? What can you tell me?"

"Ah," the doctor said, as if he realized he hadn't completely apprised her of the steps involved. "I don't actually read the MRI. A trained radiologist will look at it, hopefully today. That report will go to me, and I'll ensure it gets to Doctor Wu as soon as I get it. He's the resident neurologist I spoke to you about. He and I will look at the images also." As if sensing her frustration, he added, "Listen, Laura, I know this has been a long haul for you. In the grand scheme of things, we've gotten a lot done over the past few days. Often it can take weeks or months to schedule these tests and get a diagnosis. Since you're here in the hospital, and since we're . . . well, we're all concerned about your symptoms, we're moving quickly. This is a mystery we need to solve. I hope and think we can come to a conclusion here today, or tomorrow, or soon . . . with Doctor Wu, and with good information. Be patient. We want what's best for you." Uncharacteristically, he reached out and held her hand. "I know you're a strong person. Be strong now. We'll have news soon. Prepare yourself. Probably you can have your phone . . . tomorrow. I'm going to give you some other meds today. Be sure to take them, okay?"

"Okay." Laura felt the sword of Damocles suspended above her head. She felt that it was hanging by a very thin thread and would fall at any second.

* * *

Laura was called down to Doctor Wu's office early the next afternoon, and Doctor Patel was with him. A nurse delivered her in a wheelchair.

"Hi, Laura. I'm Doctor Wu." The short Asian man had fine features, had no accent, and looked too young to be a doctor, let alone a specialist.

The nurse set the wheelchair directly in front of the desk in the small office and closed the door behind her as she left.

"Hi, Doctor." Laura mustered a smile and put out her hand.

"I see Doctor Patel has been taking good care of you!" Doctor Wu said cheerfully. "He's a good man—you're lucky to have him. He's been hounding me to look at your file. He's very thorough, very persistent."

"Yes, I suppose, but it's been quite an experience. I'm anxious—"

"Yes, Laura." He took a deep breath. "The tests you've taken so far have been helpful, but inconclusive." Laura felt frustrated. "I want to tell you what we're looking for. We're concerned you may have either ALS or MS. We're leaning toward MS, but we need to confirm it, if we can. Sometimes it's hard to tell, as they both can present in a very similar fashion." He spoke slowly and deliberately as Doctor Patel looked on.

Laura reeled: the initialisms didn't compute. "ALS . . . or . . . MS?" she said, trying to form a question.

"ALS is amyotrophic lateral sclerosis. You might have heard of Lou Gehrig's disease? It's that. MS is multiple sclerosis. They're both serious diseases, but ALS is much more serious. There's no cure for either, but ALS will progressively get worse and MS can come in several forms. The most common early-onset type is RRMS, that is, relapsing-remitting multiple sclerosis. It comes and goes. Since we can't see any sign of remission right now, and you haven't reported the symptoms going away in any meaningful way since this started, we're concerned you've skipped over to secondary progressive MS, or that you have ALS." He gave Laura a few seconds for his words to resonate. "I want you to take a couple of more tests. They're not hard, but we really need to confirm or eliminate ALS. The tests give us better insight as to how much damage, or what kind of damage, has been done to your nervous system. They accurately test your nerve conductivity, the speed at which your nerves react."

"So this is serious. It's hard to take it all in . . . I can't even think straight. If it is ALS, does that mean I'm going to die?"

"The prognosis for ALS is poor but improving all the time. Listen, let's cross that bridge when we get to it, okay? When we have all the facts, we can have a real discussion about what your future could be, okay?"

"Okay, I guess." An undercurrent of depression that had been unconscious become more defined and pushed its way to the surface.

Right after the meeting with the doctors, Laura had an electromyograph just a few doors down from the Doctor Wu's office. They put electrodes on her feet and hands, and on her head. She didn't really feel any effect from the current. In the same room they did a similar test, a nerve conduction velocity (NCV) test. She was back in her room in less than an hour.

* * *

Later in the afternoon, Laura was surprised to see Doctor Wu at her door. He scanned the space and saw that her roommate was present, in the bed opposite on the window side. He obviously wanted to talk to her in private. "How would you like to go for a ride?" he said in a friendly tone. "Let's head down to my office." Doctor Wu pulled the wheelchair to Laura's bedside.

"Wow, nothing but service!" she said, trying to make light of the real reason for his visit. She retied the sash on her housecoat, stepped into her slippers, and sat in the chair. They proceeded down the hall to the elevator, making small talk. When they got to Doctor Wu's office, he pushed some chairs out of the way from previous guests and set Laura's wheelchair immediately in front of his desk. For a second, he sat casually on the end of the desk, one foot on the floor, then thought better of it and sat in his chair behind the desk.

He quickly pushed some papers into a small stack and created an empty space in front of him.

"Okay, Laura." He placed both of his hands flat on his desk as if he was about to conduct a séance. He locked his eyes onto Laura's. "Thank you for your patience, and for taking those conductivity tests today—they really help with the diagnosis. To be clear with you, they're not definitive—it's hard to be one hundred percent sure—but I do have enough to make a judgment call I'm quite sure about. You'd think with all the technology at our disposal we could be very clear, but I hope you understand that symptoms can really overlap, especially when it comes to what's affecting you. We want to make sure we give you the right treatment for the right diagnosis." Just then a sharp rap on the office door interrupted the conversation.

"Come in!" Doctor Wu shouted.

Doctor Patel came in, swiftly opening and closing the door behind him. "Hi, hi," he said politely. Doctor Wu just glanced over to him, hardly acknowledging his colleague.

"Laura, as I was saying, I know it's been a long process for you. But we wanted to take advantage of your being here in the hospital, and we needed to be sure of the diagnosis, and we needed to . . . kind of coordinate this with your detox, and understand any symptomatology that might be clouded by your alcoholism." Laura looked down at her hands, hating the frank reference to her addiction.

"So, I have good news and bad news. The good news is we're quite sure it *isn't ALS*." He paused for a second. "However, the bad news is we're quite sure it's MS. Multiple sclerosis. If it was ALS, your nerve connectivity speed would likely be much slower. And the MRI confirms there's some damage to the myelin, the insulation around your nerves—in a few key places."

She knew they would come to a conclusion at some point, but actually hearing it was hard to bear. She bowed her head and let out a deep sob. It was a quiet, prolonged effort, and then she sucked in air like a baby that had scared itself. The two doctors looked at each other. Laura looked up at Doctor Wu, then turned to Doctor Patel, aware that her face was probably puffy and ashen. Tears were poised to flow down her cheeks. It wasn't just the news that had released what had been an undercurrent of emotion. It was her isolation, her long hospital stay without seeing those close to her.

Doctor Patel pulled a tissue from a box on the filing cabinet, passed it to her, and put his hand on her shoulder. "Laura, we're here to help," he said softly. "You can do this—we have a plan for you."

"I want my phone, and I want to get the hell out of here!" she demanded, shedding any politeness.

The doctors looked at each other again. Doctor Wu spoke up this time. "Laura, we still need you to stay with us a little while longer."

Laura shook her head with conviction.

"We're concerned." He tried to get her to acknowledge him. "We're concerned about two things unique to you. First, we need to get you into remission. We want to be positive about the diagnosis and get you on a path to . . . sustainable recovery. As far as we can tell, you haven't really gone into remission. We want to ensure you haven't skipped a step and gone straight to secondary progressive MS. We've never *seen* that, but we have to get you into remission to turn this around, and get you feeling better. We need to monitor that closely. The second concern is your alcoholism. We're very concerned you'd get home and start drinking again. We want you to be very stable when you leave here. MS manifests itself in many different ways, and we want to be sure how it's affecting you. There can be a depression component—not with all cases, but some. The combination of depression and personal issues could easily trigger your drinking. We'll work on giving you some tools to cope. It's very, very important that you do *not* mix alcohol with your meds."

"Cope. All I've been doing is coping. I just want to go home," Laura said, knowing she was about to be overruled.

Doctor Patel took a turn. "Laura, we aren't trying to be cruel. It's strict policy to keep a patient isolated during detox—away from most visitors and the phone and social media. I know it's been hard, but we have to continue that. Keeping outside influences away for a time and having a strict regimen is all part of the process."

"I need to call my family." Laura felt a little calmer and perhaps resigned to staying.

"Okay, for sure. I'll ask the nurse to get you your phone. But please think of your own well-being regarding who you choose to speak to."

"What are you talking about?" Laura was bewildered.

"Well, we don't know, everyone's different. We don't want you to be in contact with any individuals who could encourage you to drink, or who could cause your mood to deteriorate."

"You mean like 'drinking buddies'?" she asked disdainfully.

"Yes, like that. Please avoid that social pressure," Doctor Wu said.

"I don't have any drinking buddies." Laura was offended by all this talk about a problem she felt she could put firmly behind her.

"Let me give you a little background on your condition, Laura. Do you know much about MS?" Doctor Wu asked.

"No, I don't, and I won't be able to research it with no phone."

"Multiple sclerosis is actually an autoimmune disease, like arthritis or psoriasis. Unfortunately, the body turns on itself. With MS, the immune system attacks the myelin, the insulation around your nerves. Myelin is a fatty substance that coats and protects nerve fibres, like the insulation on a wire. It gets eaten away in various sites, which can affect most every bodily system. Numbness, weakness in the limbs, loss of vision, slurring of speech, fatigue, dizziness, bowel and bladder problems."

"Oh great—that's what I have to look forward to?"

"I'm just letting you know the common things that happen to patients. All these various symptoms make it so hard to diagnose. Everyone experiences MS differently, and most are in that remission-relapse cycle. We really want you to get into remission so we know we're on the right track with the regimen of meds." The doctor sighed. "Also, we mentioned depression. Dealing with the emotional side of MS can cause depression, but with you, we're concerned the disease *itself* is causing a depressed state, or even some cloudy thinking. It isn't very common, but if the brain myelin is compromised, it can change cognitive abilities. From the MRI, other tests, and our conversations, we think this might be an issue for you."

"Great. I'm fucked in the head too. You guys are full of good news." She paused. "But that might explain a few things. And there's no cure?"

"Unfortunately, no. MS is a mystery to us, even after all this time. But it's widely researched, so we hope for better controls or a cure at some point. It usually affects people between fifteen and sixty, affects women twice as much as men, and hits people of Northern European descent the most. There is something of a genetic component to the disease. We don't know why, but Canada has one of the highest rates of MS in the world. We've tried to link it to geography— lack of sunlight for prolonged periods in Canada causing vitamin D deficiency—but we can't make a definitive connection."

"Be patient for a little longer, please," Doctor Patel pleaded. "Work with us to get this in check, and we can set you up for the best quality of life possible and get you back home."

"Okay. I guess there's no other option. Can I have my phone . . . please?"

* * *

Once Laura was back in her room, a nurse soon entered her room with a plastic bag with her belongings in it. She opened the bag and rummaged through it quickly. There were only the clothes she arrived in. Of course, there was no phone or purse since she had been rushed away in an ambulance.

"Shit!" she exclaimed, throwing the bag across the bed. She was stymied again.

"Trouble?" A voice came from the door.

Laura looked up. The principal was standing in the open door with a cone-shaped bundle wrapped in green paper. "Oh, Phil! Phil! Am I glad to see you!"

"Well—that's nice!" Phil looked relieved to hear this. "I—we—thought you'd like some flowers to brighten up your room."

"Thank you so much! That's the nicest thing anyone's done for me in a very long time!" Laura's mood lifted instantly. "Can I borrow your phone?"

Chapter 11

Patsy put the wet life jacket back in the shed as Owny coiled the rope and replaced the life ring. Chief Owny thanked Ryan for the work on the website, and mother and daughter walked back down the cabin row beach. Ryan took his laptop into the cabin and decided to put the boat in the water for a quick jaunt up and down the lake. He didn't bother changing or getting his phone for music; he just tipped the boat into the water, stuck in the oars, and got in. Rosie obediently watched him from the shore. He felt wonderful being on the water, even though he constantly scanned the shoreline for unwelcome visitors.

While returning to the dock, he had an idea. His company had a drone they used for aerial shots of real estate and cityscapes. He had used it a couple of times previously. A flyby showing the existing cabins and the site of the prospective development could powerfully get the message across about how beautiful the lake was, and how exclusive the property really could be. Only a dozen or so lots would be developed in the new phase. Ryan was overdue to go in and have a sit-down with his boss and give him an update on his clients. He would broach the subject of using the drone. His boss might not be all that thrilled to accommodate Ryan on a project that so far was pro bono, but Ryan did have a good relationship with him. He thought he could sell him on it being a good cause, and that it would look good in their portfolio. He was determined to make the website a good as it could be.

Back to the cabin, he checked his emails. He discovered a message from Mike Maguire from the university. The Sitka spruce project was a go. He had two students that were interested in it. He needed some samples as soon as possible and had included some rough dimensions for a first analysis. Ryan responded to Mike right away and advised him he would get the samples to him as soon as possible. He then messaged his boss and asked if he was in town. Maybe he could kill two birds with one stone: visit the boss, and drop off the wood at the university. He picked up the phone and selected Owny from his contact list. She picked up right away.

"Hi, Owny, it's Ryan. How are you doing?"

"Good since we saw you last." She was mildly sarcastic since she and Patsy had just been at his cabin a few hours before.

"Hey, I have some good news. The university has a couple of students willing to do a research paper on the Sitka spruce acoustical properties project."

"Oh, that's really great, Ryan. That *is* good news."

"I need a couple of samples to take to the university. Is there something available at the sawmill? Or could someone cut me off some a couple of slabs. They wouldn't be very big."

"Hmm . . ." Owny seemed hesitant. "That might be, well . . . hmm. Let me make a call. The sawmill is kind of out of service right now. I think they're waiting for parts or something. There are two fellows who run it that I could contact. Um, maybe I can get Gerald over there to get your samples. He used to work there, until a couple of years ago."

Ryan was a little confused. It seemed like a simple request. "I can just go over there and look around for myself, although I'm not positive what I'll be looking at. It has to be the spruce, of course. And a—"

"No, no, no—don't go over there on your own, Ryan. We'll get you the wood. Let me make a couple of calls." Owny was insistent.

"Okay." Ryan was even more confused. Maybe it was a safety issue. "Let me know. I told them I'd get them something right away."

"Yup. Call you back. Bye." Owny hung up.

Ryan set the phone down and shook his head. His ideas were good, but there always seemed to be a wrinkle. Whatever that was.

* * *

Owny looked up at Gerald, who was sitting across the kitchen table from her. "Ryan has the university interested in doing a study on the spruce at the sawmill. He needs a couple of pieces to give them."

"What kind of study?" Gerald asked.

"He thinks Sitka spruce might be good for making musical instruments. He's researched it, or he knows something about it. Anyway, the school is interested in testing some samples and needs to get some pieces. Do you think you can get some for him?"

"You know how I feel about the sawmill. I swore I'd never set foot in that place again. I can't work with those two guys." Gerald was adamant.

"But this is a great opportunity. If I call Chester or Ronny, they'll just give me the run-around," Owny said. "*Please*, Gerald. For me. It's just a couple of pieces of wood."

Gerald looked her into the eyes from across the table and sighed. He said, "Okay, okay," but his true feelings were evident as he shook his head.

"Today?" Owny asked.

"Chester and Ronny think they own the place. If I go over there out of the blue and start looking around or cutting wood, they'll be all over me," Gerald said. "We didn't part on good terms. You know that."

"It's been a long time. And they *don't* own the place. They're supposed to run it, but they're never there. Okay, I'll call them and just frickin' tell them. We're going to collect a couple of samples for the university. That's it." Owny picked up her phone.

* * *

Chester Ghostkeeper and Ronald DeDeaux were legends in their own minds. They were also the bane of Owny's existence. The only thing that kept them in civil communication with Owny and in some sort of distant orbit around her was that Chester was her brother's son (Owny's maiden name was Ghostkeeper, after all), and Ronny was his lifelong friend.

Over the years, the two had bestowed upon themselves the function of unofficial opposition party leaders within the nation. Whenever Owny or the band council put forward a progressive idea, Ronny and Chester would take the contrary position. They had neither formal status nor much credibility with the general population, but they still managed to create doubt and sow discourse on virtually every initiative. If Owny said black, they would say white, even if it was obviously black, and black was a good idea.

Chester and Ronny also had the unabashed temerity to consider themselves elder stewards of the reserve's natural resources—the land and waters. In fact, they were self-serving—walking contradictions to the conservation they espoused.

Their behaviour was tolerated for several reasons. First, tolerance and abstaining from overt conflict was the Native way. Second, they were classic bullies who could creatively intimidate the meek. And third, social undercurrents within the clan suggested that maybe Owny did need a counterpoint to her enthusiasm. According to Chester and Ronny, Owny's ideas were all too risky and had little benefit to the group. She was a dreamer who needed to be reined in, and she would "sell them down the river just to make a buck."

Both Chester and Ronny were legendary drinkers, and they had proven it over and over again. So much so that no one even bothered pronouncing Ronny's last name anymore—that was too much work. He was simply "Ronny Two Livers" in recognition of his years of service to the bottle, and to distinguish him from any other local Ronny. Chester and Ronny were two peas in a bad pod, and everyone knew it. Everyone except Ryan Hanson.

* * *

Owny called her nephew, Chester, but he didn't acknowledge her call. She hung up and considered calling Ronny but thought the better of it, as he was even more contrary than Chester. She called Chester back and left a voice mail for him, explaining that Gerald would be stopping by the sawmill to gather a couple of pieces of spruce. Sounded simple enough.

"Okay, Gerald," Owny said softly yet firmly, "I left a message for Chester. He knows we'll be out to the sawmill. All we're doing is getting a couple of pieces of wood! We have every right to be there and do this. The band runs the sawmill. Chester and Ronny just work there—they don't run it."

"Run it into the ground," Gerald said, seemingly to himself. "Okay. No big deal." He spoke as if he was talking himself into it. "I'll go over and get the wood."

"Thank you. Uh, I'll come with you. We're making too big a deal about this. I'll call Ryan. You'll probably need a hand, and he knows the sizes the students are looking for."

Owny stopped by the band office and picked up spare keys to the main door of the sawmill. She and Gerald met Ryan there. They were all pleased to see some traction for an idea of what to do with some unused logs. The group looked around the mill and found no usable pieces of spruce. They went back out to the large shed to look at the logs.

"We're sure this is Sitka spruce?" Ryan tried to ask without being offensive.

"Oh yes, for sure," Gerald said. "We're not starting up the mill to cut these pieces for you. It's a big deal to start the whole thing up, so that's out. I'll get a chainsaw and cut something close to the right size for you. Then maybe we can take it over to the small planer and push it through to clean it up. Should work."

Gerald went back into the mill and soon came out with a large chainsaw. He selected a log that was sticking out of the stack, one of smaller diameter so he could effectively run the chainsaw into the end grain to create a slab. He tugged on the pull cord of the chainsaw several times, flicking and squeezing things. It fluttered but wouldn't start. He set it on a log, checked the gas level, checked the oil, and shrugged. After placing it on the log, he gave it a strong tug, and it sprang to life with a roar and a sputter and a cloud of exhaust. Gerald revved the machine madly as if he was afraid it was going to stall. He positioned himself at the end of the log, and with surprising skill put the saw into the end of it, then pushed the hungry chain into the wood. He cut into the log about two feet, pulled out the saw, and made a parallel cut. Then he drew the saw out again and cut off the end of the log, creating a slab. The pieces fell to the ground and he silenced the chainsaw.

"That's slick!" Ryan said while their ears were still ringing. Gerald had cut a nice slab from the heartwood.

"Okay, let's take it over the planer and clean it up," Gerald said. He picked up the wood and they went into the sawmill. He moved some metal rollers away from the receiving end of the planer, set the wood on the flat surface, and raised the cutter to accept the slab. He started it up and pushed the wood through with a stick that sat beside the machine. It spat out bits of wood as it smoothed the surface. He put the wood through several times, each time lowering the cutter a little. Within a few minutes he had a nice plank, smooth on both sides.

"So now we should cut this in half?" he asked Ryan.

"Yes, that's what they're looking for—two samples, about a foot square."

Gerald nodded and took the wood over to an ancient band saw that sat close to the wall. He set the wood on the metal saw table and then hesitated. Gerald went over to a work bench and found a measuring tape and a pencil. He measured the wood, found the exact middle of the slab, and started up the saw. It too was loud, and Owny and Ryan stuck their fingers in their ears as they stood watching Gerald expertly guide the wood through the diving blade.

Suddenly, a hand tapped Gerald sharply on the shoulder three or four times. Gerald turned, probably thinking it was Ryan or Owny interrupting him for some reason, but it was Chester, and Ronny who stood behind him. He carefully stopped pushing the wood into the blade and shut off the machine.

"What's going on?" Chester asked loudly. He and Ronny stood there in indignant surprise, as if they had discovered intruders in their own home. Chester was of average height and verging on heavy-set. He had thick black hair combed into something reminiscent of a pompadour. Ronny Two Livers, standing back from the group, was slightly shorter and had two long braids that went down the front of his jean jacket. He was swarthier than Chester, quite thin, and with a pockmarked face.

"I left you a message on your phone," Owny said. "Did you get it?"

Chester just bobbed his head ambiguously, as if to say "Maybe, maybe not."

"The university is looking for some samples of wood to do a study on this species. It's about diversification of wood products."

"Are they going to pay for it?" Chester was argumentative as usual.

"We aren't going to charge the school for two small pieces of wood for something that may ultimately help us!" Owny pushed back.

"Who's this?" Ronny said, nodding and looking directly at Ryan. "Are you from the university?"

"No, he's not," Owny replied. "This is Ryan. He's helping us with some stuff on the website. He got the university interested in the wood . . . and he bought Walter's cabin."

Chester and Ronny looked at each other; they couldn't hide their surprise.

"I thought we got rid of Walter," Ronny said, looking defiantly at Ryan. "So this is the *new* Walter? Your days are numbered here, my friend."

Owny shifted in her stance, looking at Ryan sheepishly as her secret troubles became evident to the newcomer. Ryan bristled at Ronny's comment but said nothing, looking back at Owny.

"You leave Ryan alone. He's the rightful owner of the cabin, and—"

"*We* are the rightful owners of the cabins," Chester said.

"Ryan is the rightful owner of the cabin," Owny said emphatically. "And he's been very helpful already, with some great work on a new website for us and other ideas."

"We don't need no help from a white man," Ronny said with venom in his voice, looking at Chester for his reaction. "The wood stays here."

"Like hell it does!" Owny said. "Start that saw, Gerald. Finish that cut and let's go!"

Gerald looked at Ryan, then at Ronny and Chester, then back at Owny. He started the saw, finished the cut, and then shut it off.

"Let's go," Owny said.

The three of them left the sawmill unmolested. Ronny and Chester just watched as they exited from the main door, leaving it ajar as they left.

"Sorry about that, Ryan," Owny said as they approached their vehicles. "That's why I didn't want you coming here by yourself."

Ryan finally found his voice. "Jesus, you mean to say they harassed Walter to the point that he wanted out? Were you aware of that?" He was getting flushed.

"No, not exactly," Owny answered.

"What is that supposed to mean?"

"It means I wasn't aware of them hassling Walter—not until now. But knowing them, it doesn't surprise me, and I guess I had my suspicions. Walter never complained to me about anything."

"Things are starting to make a lot more sense now . . . unfortunately," Ryan said. He looked at Owny and Gerald. "Walter was real quick to make the sale. Come to think of it now, it seems awfully quiet around the cabins, in spite of the good weather. Hmm."

"Those two have been feeding the wrong dog for too long," Owny said, looking at Gerald.

"What's that?" Ryan asked, puzzled.

"Oh, nothing," Owny replied. "It's just a saying. Why don't you come over to the house for a bit? We can have a coffee and chat."

Ryan didn't answer right away. Then he shook his head but said, "Okay."

Chapter 12

Owny reached into the cupboard for a large container of coffee. She took off the lid and began scooping the contents into the coffee maker with a plastic spoon that resided in the can. Gerald and Ryan sat down at the kitchen table.

"When does the university need the wood?" she asked as she counted the scoops.

"I'm going into the city tomorrow. I'll drop off the wood and hopefully meet the students and the prof. I also need to stop into work. I haven't caught up with my boss in a while. Um, I can't guarantee it, but I'm going to ask for permission to use a drone we use for aerial video shots. I thought that video would be a great way to showcase the new cabin development. Something simple, like a shot moving down the beach from the existing cabins to the new lots, or maybe a wide shot from out over the lake. Hopefully, we'll have a sunny evening with low wind. The light would be best then, I think."

"Gee, Ryan, you think you can get it?" Owny was impressed. "That would really give a professional look to the website."

"Yeah, it would. Anything we've done with the drone has looked real good. You can edit it pretty quickly and uploaded without too much trouble," Ryan responded. "Have you given any thought to having someone manage the real estate sales pitch for the properties? I don't know . . . maybe a trailer with information, lot maps, pricing, that kind of thing. Or maybe you want to contract it to a real estate company to handle?"

"We've thought of it for sure. Over the summer we'll have some students returning from school. I thought it would be good experience for them, but maybe you have something there, getting the professionals involved. The only problem is, we'd be paying for commissions, but it could be what we need to get more exposure. But it might make sense to keep it within band . . ."

"So why is the construction equipment at the end of the road just sitting there, Owny? Is there a contractor ready to go? Has it been surveyed and all that?" Ryan asked.

"Hmm." Owny measured her words carefully and said, "We have some . . . challenges getting things done sometimes. We need to address a few issues before we can really get going."

"I don't get it. It must have been a go if the equipment is on site, no? But maybe it isn't. Why have it there if it isn't approved or you don't have permits and everything?"

"It's approved—and the permits are in place," Owny said.

"So what's the hold up?" Ryan asked.

"Oh, politics," Owny said quietly.

"Politics like the politics with the two at the sawmill?"

"You could say that," Owny admitted.

"What did you mean when you said something about their dog?" Ryan asked.

"About their dog? I don't know . . . Oh, I said they've been feeding the wrong dog. It's just a saying we have. Part of a story with a moral. An old school story."

"I still don't get it."

"Well, you know we have our own traditions, our own stories and lessons," Owny went on. "It's about the two things inside of us, the duality. Maybe it's a little like the angel on one shoulder and the devil the other. Except the story of the two dogs actually makes more sense." Owny hesitated as though she didn't want to elaborate, then continued. "Inside you there are two dogs. A good dog and an evil dog—or a bad dog. If you feed the bad dog, it will get stronger and dominate and control you, and fight off the good dog—maybe even kill it altogether. If you only feed the good dog, the bad dog will starve and have no power. The good dog is the dog of family, love, culture, art, the environment. The bad dog is the drinking dog, the sex dog, the incest dog, the gang dog, the lazy dog. Ronny Two Livers and Chester Ghostkeeper have been feeding the bad dog for a very long time. I think their good dog ran away."

"How about you guys?" Ryan asked sincerely.

Gerald spoke for himself and his wife. "We try our best, like most people. It's not perfect, but we have for many years tried to feed only the good dog. Our family is our world. Our kids are our life. They're good kids. And the band is an extension of that—for Owny especially. She's stepped up and done her best to bring positive change as Chief. It hasn't been easy sometimes. Not everyone wants change, or if they do, they just want it given to them."

"So there are those in the band who are letting the bad dog live?" Ryan asked.

"Oh, of course. In any group of people there'll be some feeding the wrong dog, maybe both dogs at the same time. Maybe we all do from time to time," Owny answered. "But we're proud of our village and our nation, Ryan. Our people—most of our people—have a solid moral compass, and things have really improved over the last ten years or so with better communication, better role models in the community, and better employment opportunities. More respect."

"So you try not to feed the wrong dog in your family, but you feed the wrong dog in the community." Ryan was pushing her buttons.

"What do you mean by that?" Owny didn't understand.

"Ronny and Chester. I think you enable them," Ryan said flatly. "I'm worried about those two."

Gerald looked at Owny as if to say *I told you so,* and raised his eyebrows at the fact that Ryan was perceptive enough to pick up on it so quickly, and blunt enough to just blurt it out. "If they've run Walter off, what have they done to the rest of the cabin owners? The sawmill isn't running, and construction is stalled."

"Ryan, we know we have issues with them and a few others. It's never come to a head quite like this before. I'll be addressing it soon. I need to think about it and ask some more questions. I will. But right now, I'm busy getting ready for a conference. There's a big meeting in Nanaimo tomorrow, and for the rest of the week. I'm doing a presentation on water quality, and we'll be reviewing nominations for Grand Chief of the island. I'm thinking of running."

Ryan could see that Owny was feeling the pressure. She was often low key and seemed slow to react to situations, but ultimately, she was a political animal. Owny instinctively knew the pace of change that would be tolerated. She placed three cups of coffee on the table.

"Well, if there's any trouble from Chester and Ronny, I'm going to the police," Ryan said. "I don't want the hassle, but I've got too much invested in the cabin and this new stage of my life to live in fear of those two jokers." He sipped from the cup. "I'll have visitors and eventually people staying over, I'm sure, and I don't want any issues."

"You have family that will come by?" Owny seemed interested in his past but was careful not to pry. "You have kids?"

"Yes, a daughter. She's grown up and basically on her own. She's in university. My wife, well . . . that's why I got the cabin from Walter. We've recently split. She has some issues and I finally had enough. I really love the cabin and the lake. It's ideal, really, except for this. This recent turn of events, I mean."

"Hmm," Owny said. "Do you think you'll ever get back together? She'd like the cabin too?"

"I don't know if we'll get back together. Right now, I can't see it. And she won't be happy about the cabin. I don't care. She's messed up."

A pregnant pause followed, and Gerald drummed his fingers on the green plastic tablecloth.

Owny changed the subject. "So we have a busy day tomorrow! You're off to the university, I'm off to Nanaimo, and Gerald has to take Patsy for her first chemo treatment at the Royal Jubilee Hospital."

Ryan rushed through his coffee despite its heat. "I'm heading out. Good luck tomorrow."

"You too," Owny and Gerald said in unison.

* * *

Ryan hoped to get out on the lake first thing in the morning, but the dawn was clammy. Overnight rain had changed to a light drizzle, so he decided to skip the rowing workout. He fed Rosie and poured some cereal into a bowl. The familiar sound of the shed door being opened and the low murmurs of voices exchanging short sentences prompted Ryan to step out onto the deck. It was Gerald and Patsy this time, here for some local therapy before the first day of chemo at the cancer centre.

"Good morning," Ryan said calmly.

"Hi, Ryan. Good morning," Gerald replied. Even Patsy mustered up a "Morning."

"I came to see how this is done!" Gerald made light of the fact he was filling in for his wife for the day. "Kind of chilly this morning."

"Yeah, not the best," Ryan said. "You're getting the full treatment today, aren't you, Patsy?"

"Yep," she said quietly.

"How do you feel about getting your first chemo session?" Ryan said, trying to engage with the shy girl.

Gerald caught Ryan's eye and subtly shook his head so only Ryan could see. Ryan felt bad; he had unwittingly hit a nerve.

Patsy said, "Well, I think it's just fear of the unknown that's bothering me." She looked at her father as if they were starting up a previous conversation. "I just don't want to feel sick. I'm sick of feeling sick."

Ryan looked at Gerald but spoke to Patsy. "You know, they've come a long way in that department, I understand." He gauged Gerald's reaction and turned to the girl. "There's anti-nausea medication they give you at the same time, I think. That whole feeling sick thing has really improved. I bet it won't be that bad."

"Hmm. Well, that's good." She looked up and then over at Gerald. "And I don't want my hair to fall out. That's another thing."

"It'll grow back," Gerald said gently.

Patsy looked into her father's eyes as if finally relenting to an inevitable force. "I guess it's good we're finally doing something other than freezing my butt off in this lake." She attempted a smile.

Gerald gave her a hug. She pulled on the life jacket and walked onto the dock, her father not far behind. Ryan and Rosie tagged along. Patsy stepped into the life ring and handed her father the end of the rope. She moved with familiar steps, kicked off her flip-flops, and sat down at the end of the floats, dangling her feet into the water. She recoiled at the cold water and turned to Gerald and winced in pain. "It's really cold, Dad."

"Just go in for a few minutes. It'll do you good," Gerald said, trying to encourage his daughter. "Your mum says you gotta do this."

"Aieeee!" She flapped her hands like it may ward off the cold, and slipped into the water. Patsy gasped several times and looked uncomfortable. She pushed away from the dock, paddling backwards as she stroked with her arms to get to her destination. Gerald gave her some slack as she moved away.

"Works good," Gerald observed, then whispered to Ryan beside him, "Looks frickin' cold!"

Rosie waded in from the beach and stood in water up to her belly in support of Patsy. The dog whined, barely noticeable to the others as she watched the young woman. Her eyes flitted between Patsy and the two men on the dock. Patsy's lower jaw started to tremble involuntarily.

"So Owny is gone for the rest of the week?" Ryan asked.

"Yup. Till Friday. It's a big day for her. Um, tomorrow is, I guess. She's gone with Cecil and his wife. Cecil is the Assistant Chief. Don't think you've met him?"

Ryan shook his head.

"They left early. They have to pick up someone in Duncan, then go on to the AGM."

The two stood in silence for a few minutes watching Patsy as the drizzle turned to mist and the day grew clearer.

Gerald's cell phone rang. He fumbled to get it out of his jacket pocket. "Hello?" He didn't say another word for several seconds as he shook his head. Ryan thought he could hear Owny but wasn't positive. Gerald looked intently at him as he listened closely. "Just a minute," Gerald said. He called to Patsy. "It's Mum—they've been in an accident!" He spoke into the phone again. "Just a minute. I'm going to put you on speakerphone."

Patsy paddled in as fast as she could.

The shift to speakerphone caught Owny in mid-sentence. "—and it's pissing down rain here," she said in an animated tone.

"Is everyone okay?" Gerald raised his voice.

"Yes, we're okay. The car is . . . I don't know if it's totalled, but it isn't drivable. Some looky-loos stopped in the middle of the road. I don't know what they were looking at." Someone spoke in the background. "Oh, they hit a deer. Or the people in front of them hit a deer, and Cecil piled into them. Then someone piled into us. Visibility is the shits! Rainy and foggy. We weren't going all that fast. Is it raining there? Where are you?"

"It's stopped here," Gerald replied, looking to the cloudy sky. "We're at Ryan's. Patsy is just getting out of the water."

Ryan went over to Patsy and helped to pull her onto the dock.

"I gotta go. I'll call you right back," Owny said, distracted from the conversation.

Patsy pulled off her life preservers. They walked off the dock with the dripping jacket.

"Um, come into the cabin where it's warm." Ryan sensed Patsy's cold and the stress of the situation. They had just gotten into the warmth of the living room when Gerald's phone rang again.

"What's going on?" Gerald asked as he switched to speakerphone.

"Cops just showed up. We pushed the cars off to the side. Cecil's talking to them. Here comes a tow truck."

"So what are you going to do? Where are you, exactly?" Gerald hollered.

"Just a sec . . ." Owny was talking to someone. "Maybe we can get a lift into Duncan with someone behind us. Nope, they just took off."

"What about the tow truck?" Gerald asked. Can you get a ride back with them?"

"I don't think so. He has a helper, so we won't all fit. Can you come to get us? We're just on top of the Malahat."

"I have to get Patsy to her chemo! We're due there in an hour." Gerald looked at Ryan.

"You're still at Ryan's?" Owny asked.

"Yes, we're in the cabin with him. I've got you on speaker."

"Ah . . ." Owny was thinking out loud. "I know it's not the best, but Ryan . . . are you there?"

"Yes, I'm here!"

"Ryan, could you get Patsy to her treatment? I'm sorry to ask you, but you're going into the city as it is. I don't think it will be too far out of the way for you. Maybe you could drop her off and then pick her up when you're done? She could wait. Patsy, are you okay with that? Are you there?"

Patsy bobbed her head ambiguously. "Yes, it's okay," she said.

"Ryan, is it okay with you?" Owny asked.

"Yes, it's okay. I'll get her there. Where is it again?"

"Royal Jube," Gerald said, abbreviating the name of the Royal Jubilee Hospital.

"Yep, it's fine. It's not too far out of the way."

"Okay, I'll be there as soon as I can," Gerald told his wife.

"I'll get off the phone and give you a better location from the map app," Owny replied. "I'll call you back or text you."

"Okay, bye."

Ryan said to Gerald, "Just let me get organized. Meet you and Patsy back at your place? She can get ready, and I'll be there shortly."

"Thanks, Ryan. I'll probably be gone before you get there." Gerald was as intense as Ryan had ever seen him.

Ryan pulled up to the Wilson's home. He put the vehicle in park and watched the front door for Patsy. Sure enough, the pretty young woman had been watching for him; she came out in street clothes, carrying a cloth shopping bag brimming with a sweater and magazines. She hopped in the passenger side and stretched to put the bag in the back seat.

Ryan did a U-turn and headed out of the village toward the main highway, first turning west, then joining the Island Highway going south. Patsy was painfully quiet as usual.

Ryan broke the silence. "So do you know where we're going? Where we check into? There must be a specific department."

"My dad said to just check in at the main reception and they'd give me directions."

"Fair enough. And your appointment is when? Ten?"

"Yup, ten."

"And how long will it take?"

"Not sure—three or four hours maybe. Maybe longer for the first time?"

"Okay, that should work out good. And I'm sure you'll do fine." Ryan was trying to be encouraging since she was going solo for her first chemo treatment.

They drove on in silence. The windshield wipers kicked in intermittently as the rain began; it was threatening to start up again in earnest.

They pulled up to the main entrance to the hospital with about fifteen minutes to spare. Patsy grabbed her bag and opened the door.

"So I'll meet you right back here when I get back, okay? There are some benches over there." Ryan pointed to some white wire mesh benches. "Or you can watch from inside. Timing should work out about right."

"Okay, see you back here," Patsy said. She exited the vehicle and bravely marched into the hospital.

Ryan pulled through the drop-off zone and set out for the short drive to the university. He called Mike Maguire at the school and left him a voice mail that he was en route and would be there in a few minutes. The rain abated, and as he drove north the sky seemed less grey.

Ryan found the correct building. It was good to meet Mike personally and chat about confirming if the two Sitka spruce samples had good acoustic properties. Mike informed him that the two students had already done some research into what makes a specific species better for musical instrument applications than others. He said they would analyze the samples in several ways: cellular level, weight-to-density ratio, conduction of physical and tonal vibration, correct curing process, and anything else they could come up with. It sounded like an excellent start to Ryan, and Mike's enthusiasm would ensure a timely result.

Ryan thanked Mike and advised he would check back in a few days. He headed back to his vehicle and drove south to his company's offices close to the centre of town on Government Street. Ryan loved the feel of downtown Victoria. It was busy and bustling, but without the intensity of a big city like Vancouver. He went directly into his boss's office and they had a long chat. They had known each other for years, so Ryan was comfortable revealing his recent personal issues. He assured him that his work wasn't suffering and went over his accounts and discussed in detail updates, billings, and creative concepts for each one.

He admitted he was doing some "volunteer" work for the Indigenous band where his new home was located. He pitched the idea as an experimental beta site that would ultimately open a new market for their company as they demonstrated that they could understand and service Indigenous internet needs. Ryan explained that dozens of Indigenous clans had websites in need of a professional facelift; it was an untapped market. The results of this first site would lead to other groups wanting the professional look and functionality he could offer. The word-of-mouth validation would be invaluable. He sold his idea.

Then he asked for use of the drone for the aerial real estate shots, and his boss was fine with it. They invited his boss's partner for lunch and headed down the street for a light meal. After lunch, Ryan went into the storage room and picked up the big black plastic case that housed the drone and its controls. He put it in the back of his vehicle and returned to the hospital to pick up Patsy.

Chapter 13

Laura was exasperated as she looked at Phil's cell phone. He had punched in his password and got to the keypad screen for her, but she was drawing a blank on the next step. She couldn't remember her daughter's phone number. All her commonly called numbers were programmed into her phone, so she didn't need to remember them. She could think of the first few digits, but the rest escaped her.

"Damn it," she said, stalled.

"What's wrong?" Phil asked.

Laura shook her head rapidly in frustration. "I can't remember the number! Darn it. They're programmed into my phone."

"Ah, I know," Phil said consolingly. "We don't memorize anything anymore. I'm the same way. I can hardly remember my own cell phone number, let alone anyone else's." He paused in thought. "How much longer do you think you're in here for?"

"Not sure. A few more days, I'd say. They have to get my meds on track, and I have to get a little more mobile."

"I can maybe go get your phone for you. I don't mind." Phil looked at his watch. "I should be able to just go over and come back. Um . . . keys. Do you have your house keys? Would your neighbours have them?"

"Jesus, I don't know. I left the house in . . . Well, I don't even remember leaving the house, as you know. Anyway, I know it would be asking a lot, but I really could use that phone. There's a window on the right side of the house. It's usually open a crack for fresh air—you could get in that way. It's up from the ground a ways, but you could ask Lazlo for a stepladder. We've had to get in that way before."

"Yeah, I can do that. For sure." Phil looked at his watch again, then took his phone back from Laura. He looked happy he could be a saviour in some small way. "I'll be back as soon as I can. Do you know where the phone will be? You'll need a charger too."

"It's likely on the island in the kitchen. The charger should be plugged in there too. If not, try the bedside table. Thanks, Phil. Thank you so much. And thanks for the flowers—they're beautiful. Made my day!"

Phil smiled and simply said, "I'll be back!"

He had been gone for just a few minutes when a nurse came in and told Laura, "You're on the move. We're moving you to another room."

"I'm being moved? Why?"

"We need the bed. You'll be out of the psych ward and closer to the autoimmune specialists."

"But I . . . Someone—a friend—is coming back to bring me something. Can we wait a half hour or so?"

"'Fraid not. We have to make room right away. Can you just give them a call and let them know?"

Laura sputtered, "'Fraid not!"

The nurse opened the drawers beside the bed and gestured with a circular motion for Laura to speed up. Laura only had a few things, and she put them into a reusable shopping bag, carefully picked up her flowers, and sat down in the wheelchair. The nurse pushed her through the door at warp speed.

Laura's new room was in a completely different wing of the hospital, and on the third floor. Once she arrived and stood up, the nurse pointed to her bed and exited with the wheelchair immediately. She placed the bag in her bedside stand and put the flowers on the windowsill. As she did this, she noticed that the sun was starting to drive the clouds away, and she suddenly felt invigorated by the brightening day. She looked over at a walker that stood beside her new bed. She looked out the window again, and back at the walker. Laura decided to go down to the main entrance and wait for Phil to arrive; she could head him off at the pass. Thinking about walking down unaided, she reconsidered because of her recent lack of exercise and the distance involved. Instead, she would take the walker for a spin.

She started off, moving slowly down to the elevator, then down to the main floor and into the main atrium. It felt good to get moving on her own steam. She made her way out the automatic doors and saw a small group of people near a white wire bench enjoying the sun. She sat down beside a pretty, young Indigenous girl. She was wearing a beautifully knitted Cowichan sweater and looking at her phone.

"Lovely day," Laura said to her bench mate.

"Yup" was the only response, made without eye contact.

Laura wasn't offended; she simply gazed out at the busy traffic coming off the main road and into the hospital. Phil should be back soon if all went well. Watching the endless stream of cars flowing up the smaller road, turning this way and that, she was surprised to see what looked like Ryan's SUV pulling into the main entrance and stopping immediately in front of the benches. Could it be? It *was* Ryan!

"Ryan?" Laura said aloud, but not loud enough for him to hear.

The girl beside her stopped gawking at her phone and spun her head to look at Laura. Ryan put his four-way flashers on and got out of the vehicle. He stopped as he closed the door and looked over the roof at Laura and the girl. He gulped and walked around his vehicle and up to them. They both stood up.

"Ryan, you found out I was here! You came to see me!" Laura was ebullient.

"I . . . I didn't know you were here, Laura."

"But . . . you were checking . . . looking. Checking for me at the hospital?"

Just then Phil walked up to them, crossing the street from the paid parking. "Oh Phil. Hi, Phil—you're back." Phil appeared to be carefully hiding his emotions as he watched Laura talking to Ryan.

"Who's this?" Ryan asked.

"Oh, this is Phil Conner. You've met him before, Ryan. He's the principal at my school."

The two men barely nodded to each other—no handshake.

"So how did you find out I was here?" Laura asked Ryan.

"I told you, I didn't know you were here. I'm here to pick up Patsy." Ryan gestured to the person standing to Laura's left.

Laura turned to Patsy, then to Phil, and back to Ryan. She couldn't process the information right away. "You're here to pick up this Indian girl?" she said in disbelief. "You didn't come to see me?"

"*I didn't know you were here,*" Ryan repeated emphatically. "I don't think anyone knows you're here. Does Em know?"

"No, I haven't been able to contact her. I've been in the . . . ward, unable to communicate." Laura suddenly felt awkward about entering into a private conversation in front of a stranger, and with Phil present.

"So don't be upset if I didn't know you were here," Ryan said bluntly.

Phil couldn't help but say something. "Hey, hey, Ryan. Laura's been through a lot here. She hasn't been able to reach out—"

"What the hell does this have to do with you, anyway? What are you doing here? Aren't you the one who put her here in the first place?" Ryan's blood was starting to boil.

Laura stepped in. "Ryan, Phil has been incredibly supportive and helpful to me! Without him, I'd be in much worse off!"

Ryan's brow furrowed and he lowered his chin and glowered at the taller man.

"So why are you picking up this person?" Laura asked.

Ryan began to speak and then hesitated as if trying to find the right words. "She's a friend. I'm doing a favour, that's all."

"A friend? A favour? What?"

"Hey, I don't have to explain myself to you. I'm here, I came to pick her up, and now we're leaving. C'mon Patsy, let's go." Ryan nodded to the vehicle a few meters away, its lights flashing.

"Ryan, we need to talk." Laura wanted to tell him about her new diagnosis.

"We've been talking for twenty-five years. I'm done talking. There's nothing to talk about." He reverted to an obstinate, defensive mode Laura had seen many times before.

Phil spoke up. "Ryan, Laura needs to talk to you about why she's still in the hospital and—"

"Listen, baldy, this is absolutely none of your business—not Laura, not what you think who needs to say what to whom, nothing. Stay out of it!" Ryan put his hands on his hips in a display of righteous indignation.

Phil stopped making eye contact with Laura's rude husband. He shook his head. Then he looked again at Ryan. "You're really a piece of work, man. She just wants a few words with you!"

"This isn't the time or place. It's none of your business, understand? This is between me and her. I'll talk to her when I get around to it."

"When you get around to it? What goes around comes around, buddy."

"I ain't your buddy."

Ryan picked up Patsy's bag, reminding Laura of how he used to pick up a diaper bag for her years earlier. He took Patsy's arm and walked her to the passenger door as if he was escorting a new mother from the hospital. Patsy said nothing, but looked back as she got in the car, as if she was reviewing the scene to make sure it had really happened. Laura and Phil looked on in disbelief. Ryan jumped in the driver's side; the car lurched as he slammed it into drive. Laura and Phil didn't look at each other until Ryan's vehicle was well on its way.

Phil spoke first. "Well, that went well," he said sarcastically. "I'm still confused, I guess. Did he, or did he not, know you were here?"

"Not, I guess." Laura hid her wounded spirit. "And how does he know the Indian girl?"

* * *

Ryan and Patsy drove for several minutes in silence until Ryan felt a little more composed. If Patsy was uncomfortable with the whole situation, she didn't show it.

"Sorry you had to see that," he said sincerely. "I know I probably came off as an ass back there, but there's a lot of history, a lot of build-up. My wife, Laura, we broke up. I mean, I left . . . went to the cabin, you know. Because she was drinking. I'd finally had enough after years and years of on-again-off-again drinking. Done, just done. This isn't the first time—we've been through it many times. She'll get out, but she'll be back in there soon enough. I have to get off the merry-go-round. I know I was rough, but I can't get invested it that sympathy cycle anymore. It's too hard to bear. I guess it's just a way of keeping my guard up. I'm not really that much of a prick. Really."

Patsy looked over at him. "You don't have to explain anything to me."

"Well, I do, I think. You were there. I was a hard-ass to Laura, and I thought I recognized that guy. What was his name again?"

"Phil, I think."

"Yeah, Phil. I've met him before. Never liked the guy. Something about him." Ryan then tried to change the subject. "Did you talk to Laura?" he said, as if Patsy must have ESP and had known who she was sitting beside.

"No, not really. I don't know her, Ryan. I didn't know it was your wife."

"Course not." Ryan reset his demeanour, calming himself. "That Phil guy, I'm going to check him out." He then realized he had said this out loud and noticed Patsy looking sideways at him. She had one eyebrow cocked as if to say, "Jealous much?" He scrambled to change the subject. "How did the chemo go? You made out okay on your own?"

"Yeah, it went okay. They were a little surprised I showed up for my first chemo treatment by myself. People usually have someone with them. Some people were there on their own, but they were older, and it wasn't their first time."

"Was it busy? Did you have to wait?"

"Yeah, it was busy, and I had to wait just a few minutes. I'm shocked at how many people need chemo. There's an afternoon session too, I guess. Lots of people. Some not looking so good. There's some pretty sad sights when you walk through that cancer ward." Patsy turned away from Ryan and wiped her cheeks.

Ryan sensed he wasn't equipped for this conversation. It had never dawned on him how she would react to navigating by herself for the first time through a cancer ward. Poor kid. Nevertheless, he forged on. "How do you feel? You aren't feeling sick, are you?"

"No, I feel a little queasy, but not too bad. You were right— they give you a whole bag of some anti-nausea drug in the IV before they give you the chemo stuff." She looked at Ryan and tried to smile. "I got two big bags of something, and then a small bag that had red stuff in it. Everyone calls it 'the red shit.' Not sure, but I think it's harsh."

Ryan tried to channel the times he'd had heart-to-hearts talks with Emily. "You'll do fine. You're young, you've got a good support network. You'll get through this with flying colours. When's your next treatment?"

"Three weeks. It's every three weeks for me."

They rode in silence for a few minutes before Ryan said, "Have you heard from your mum?"

"Yup. Dad got there, and they made it to Nanaimo. Haven't heard how bad the car is yet. They're okay, though. I need to check on the girls as soon as I get back." It was sinking into Ryan how tight the Wilson family was. Though awfully quiet, this was a good, strong kid. A stoic quality was emerging in her. She got that from her parents.

Just under an hour later, they arrived back at the Wilson's home. Ryan dropped Patsy off and headed down the road that made the familiar arc around the south end of the lake, back to the secluded row of cabins. As he neared the old indian springs sign, he could see people on the road. There was new graffiti on the sign; he couldn't tell what the spray paint said, but it blotted out the word "Indian." As he pulled to a stop, he saw that Chester Ghostkeeper, Ronny Two Livers, and two others were standing behind a black-and-yellow wooden barricade set across the gravel road. Ronny put up his hand like a flag person. He had some papers in his other hand.

"Now what?" Ryan said as Ronny approached the driver's side.

"New Walter!" Ronny was not unfriendly.

"My name is Ryan."

"Okay, Ryan New Walter. We have something for you."

"What's this?" Ryan reached for the piece of paper Ronny was passing to him.

"This is an information statement to inform you of the rights of the Indigenous people who own this land," he said, trying for an official tone.

"I own my property. I have my own piece of paper that says just that." Ryan tried to maintain a level speaking voice. "You can't keep me from it."

He started to read the text. It was printed on plain paper with no letterhead and was crudely presented. He read the first few lines, which stated that this was tribal land and the clan held historic claim to it. The property had been ceded to them officially in 1903. It stated they held sovereign claim to all properties within the boundaries of the reserve.

"We thought you needed a history lesson," said Ronny.

"I know about the history of your tribe, Ronny. You and Chester have been feeding the wrong dog."

Ronny looked surprised to hear the reference; he dropped his hands to his side and shook his head in defiance. Ryan crumpled up the paper and threw it on the passenger seat.

"You've been listening to Owny's stupid stories, haven't you? Don't give me that two-dog crap—you know nothing of our people!"

"Maybe not, but I know my rights. You bastards aren't going run me off like you did Walter!"

With that, he slammed the vehicle into reverse to move away from Ronny, then put it in drive and spun the wheels in the gravel. He went forward, turning sharply to the far left of the road, into the ditch and around the barrier. As he scooted away, he looked in the rear-view mirror at the group in the middle of the road. He couldn't refrain from sticking his left arm out the window to provide the middle finger salute. His regret about his circumstances grew, but from it his recalcitrance grew, and at a greater rate. He knew he would be in for more conflict, but somehow, he also knew his stubbornness would carry him through.

As he pulled up to his usual spot between the cabin and the shed, Rosie emerged from the bushes near the beach. She looked forlorn and nervous. First she sat, then lay down, then sat again, up and down several times as though she didn't know what to do. In his haste to leave, Ryan had let Rosie out for a pee, then left the property. She had been out the whole time. Ryan cursed himself as he went to the back of the vehicle and removed the big black plastic case that held the drone.

He walked up to the golden retriever, who was back down on her belly, her right front paw across her nose and her eyes darting back and forth as if she knew she was in trouble.

"Hi, Rosie. Hi, girl," Ryan said as he set the case down and fell to one knee to give her a thorough two-handed neck scratch.

An overpowering musky smell assailed his olfactory nerves and he stood up in dismay.

"What have you gotten into?" he asked.

Rosie whimpered in despair; it was clear she was having a difficult time coping.

"Oh man. Wow." Ryan tried to block his nose with his forearm. He looked out over the lake. "This has been a heck of a day. What are we going to do with you? You're a mess." Thinking a dip in the lake might dissipate the odour, Ryan grabbed a piece of driftwood from Rosie's current selection and tossed it into the water. "Go get it, girl! Go on!"

The dog hesitated, then jumped in after it. She grabbed the stick and returned it to her master. There wasn't much improvement. Ryan realized she must have been in the lake earlier herself, for she had been damp when he approached. Now she just smelled like a wet dog and strong musk.

As he tossed the stick in again, he noticed a woman on the beach a few cabins down. He had seen her before. He waved to her, and she returned the wave and disappeared, climbing the stairs to her deck. Curious and smelly, Ryan walked over to her cabin as Rosie followed, wet and with a stick in her mouth.

"Hello, um . . . Hi there," Ryan said to her. She was wearing a broad-brimmed sun hat and a tank top with capri pants. Her auburn hair hung loose at her shoulders, and she was tall and had a long face beneath large sunglasses.

"Hello," she said suspiciously, looking over her glasses as clouds scudded overhead to darken the sky.

"Hi, I'm Ryan," he said awkwardly. "I'm just a couple of cabins over. Have we met?"

"I don't think so," she replied, not volunteering her name.

"Do you happen to have any tomato juice?"

"Tomato juice? You're looking for tomato juice?"

"Yes, my dog has been sprayed by a skunk. She reeks." He turned to the dog to keep her back. "Sit. Stay. Rosie, stay." The dog sat and dropped the stick.

"There aren't any skunks on Vancouver Island," the woman informed Ryan.

"Oh really? Hmm . . . I guess I knew that, now that you mention it. Well, anyway, she's gotten into something god-awful."

The woman descended the stairs and took a closer look at the dog, and at Ryan. She got a whiff of the problem. "Whew! Yes, she's gotten into something for sure. Not sure what, though. Maybe a possum? I think they stink."

"Possums stink? I didn't know that. They play dead, I know. They play possum."

"They play dead, but I think they can smell dead too."

"They can smell dead too? I didn't know that. They must be very convincing!" Ryan tried to be chatty.

"Sorry, no tomato juice." She cocked her head and turned her palms skyward in the universal gesture meaning "I have nothing for you."

"Okay, then. Thanks anyway." Ryan backed away, turned, and spoke to the dog. "Let's go! Get your stick!"

They walked back to their cabin. Ryan went to the shed, as he thought he remembered a large washtub in the rafters. Sure enough, there was an old galvanized tub. He struggled to get it down but finally managed to fit it sideways between the beams. He took it to the front of the cabin and half filled it with water from the hose. Entering the cabin, he brought the drone box with him for safekeeping. He filled a large pot with hot water from the kitchen sink and brought it to the tub, along with some liquid hand soap. He squirted a small amount of soap in the tub and poured in the hot water.

"Rosie, come on. You get in! Come on!" The dog wasn't going to volunteer, so Ryan went over and picked her up and placed her in the tub. He held his breath and began to pour water over her with the pot and scrub her. Focused on his task, he didn't hear footsteps in the sand coming up behind him.

"Clamato!"

Ryan nearly jumped out of his skin. He was always on edge, always wondering when unwanted visitors would arrive. "You scared me!" He stood up, wet and soapy.

"Sorry. Didn't mean to." It was his neighbour. She was holding a large plastic jug. "Clamato juice!" She waved it in front of him as if it was a prize. "I thought it would do in a pinch. It's mostly tomato juice, I think!" Ryan looked at it and caught on to what she was saying, still a little rattled.

"Yes, of course! Good thinking. Thank you!" Ryan took the container and unscrewed the cap. He went down on his knees and poured water over the dog, then poured the Clamato juice sparingly over her back. He worked it in with his fingers.

The woman watched for a moment, then took off her hat and glasses. On the other side of the tub, she kneeled down and pitched in.

"Thank you again," Ryan said. "I think this is going to work."

She finally introduced herself. "I'm Meaghan."

"I'm Ryan. This is Rosie."

"Hi, Rosie." She turned the dog's head to face her as she spoke. Then she turned to Ryan. "Hi, Ryan."

Chapter 14

Ryan went in to get more hot water while Meaghan worked on Rosie. The dog was sensing the bath was doing what it should, so she settled in and patiently panted as she was scrubbed. Ryan returned with the pot and poured more water over the dog to begin rinsing. He was curious about his neighbour, and happy to have finally met someone in the cabin row.

"Have you had the cabin long?" Ryan wanted his words to be general enough to not seem nosy but still elicit some information.

"Oh, it's not mine. I'm just, um, renting. I've been here since the beginning of May."

"How do you like it? "

"Oh, I love it. It's so peaceful. I really love it."

"Me too. I've only been here a few weeks, but I know it's for me. It *is* peaceful. Usually, anyway, but I've had some . . . issues."

"Issues? Like what?"

"Well, like today there was a roadblock on the road out by the sign. The Natives are restless. I think some of them don't want us here."

"There was a roadblock? Like a protest?" Meaghan seemed oblivious.

"Something like that. More like harassment."

"Did they threaten you?"

"No, not exactly. Not physically. It's more of an intimidation campaign."

"I didn't see it. That's not good." Meaghan seemed concerned.

"Well, somehow we need to resolve it, that's for sure. These Natives are hard to figure out. I think I have the information they gave me in the car. I'll show you in a bit." As a local, Meaghan should be informed, he thought.

Ryan commented on Rosie. "Hey, this is working good! I can still smell it, but it's way better." He poured the rest of the warm water over her back and carefully over her head and face, then squeegeed it out with his hands. "I'm going to get her out and take the hose to her, then let her shake it off." He picked her up out of the tub, getting wet dog all over his pants and shirt. He placed her on a patch of grass close to the stairs. "Stay! Stay, Rosie. Stay." Ryan pulled the hose over, adjusted the nozzle to a medium spray, and rinsed off the dog. She whimpered at the cold but stood firm.

"She really loves the cabin. She's improved so much since we've been here. She used to be really crippled—now you can hardly tell."

"She's bound to be more active out here at the lake," Meaghan said.

They paused and looked at each other, wet and soapy. Meaghan's front was saturated. Ryan thought, *If this was a wet T-shirt contest, she'd be winning.*

"She sure is." Ryan shut off the hose.

"Okay, go!" He gestured to Rosie to move on, but she stood there and shook thoroughly, starting from her nose and ending with her tail, twice. Ryan and Meaghan backed off, shielding themselves with their hands. They laughed and complained at the same time. Rosie dove into the grass and rolled around on it. She then romped off, shaking her butt and back legs mightily, delighted with being clean. Ryan dumped the reddened water from the tub into the grass, hosed down the tub, and tipped it on its side to drain against the deck post.

"Let me grab a couple of towels. Come on in if you like." Ryan dropped the hose and went up the stairs to the deck. He entered the cabin and picked up the mat from the front door and put it out on the deck. "Rosie, come!" The dog bounded up the stairs and looked at him. He flopped the mat down. "Lie down! Stay. Stay." Rosie lay down on the mat, panting. "Come in, come in," he said to Meaghan.

Ryan went to the back and found two towels and gave her the cleanest one. They towelled off over their clothes as best they could.

"I tell you, I've had a heck of a day. I'm going to pour a glass of wine. Can I get you one too?"

"Uh, sure. That sounds good."

"White or red?"

"Red is good."

"Red it is." Ryan went to the fridge and took out a bottle.

"You keep red in the fridge?"

"Yeah, I prefer it these days. In summer, I mean. The fridge is probably too cold for it, but it's better than too warm at room temperature." He took two stemless glasses down and poured the wine into them. He handed one to Meaghan. "Cheers!"

"Cheers," Meaghan responded. They clinked glasses. "You're right. It's good. More refreshing."

"Yup. If the wine isn't so great, the coolness makes it a little more palatable. So you saved the day! Thank you. I'll replace your Clamato juice as soon as I can get to the store."

"No need to really, that's okay."

"Oh God, no, I insist. I'll get you some."

"Well, okay. I do need my daily Caesar!"

"Absolutely. Spicy or regular?"

"Regular is good."

"Okay, done. Hey, I'm going to grab that information I was telling you about." Ryan put down his glass and ran out to the car.

* * *

Before he was down the stairs, Meaghan had opened Ryan's wallet, which he had left on the kitchen table. A small stack of twenty-dollar bills were inside. Meaghan helped herself to two of them. She stuffed them into her pants pocket, carefully returned the wallet to its original location, tweaked its position to make it look as though she hadn't moved it, picked up her glass, and moved to the window. She looked out innocently over the lake.

* * *

Ryan returned and tried to smooth the crumpled paper. He quickly finished reading it and handed it to Meaghan. She read it over and put it on the table.

"This sounds serious," she said. "Why do they want to reclaim this area, and develop new cabins at the same time? It doesn't make sense."

"No, not much. There's some conflict around here. I think most of them *do* want development, but a few people are resisting, and cabin owners are caught in the middle. It needs to be resolved, but in the meantime, I'm not going to let them push me around. I bought this place fair and square. They need to understand that, and back off." Meaghan looked a little surprised at his militant tone. "I'm going to show this to the Chief. I know her." He tapped his finger on the table near the paper.

"That might be a good idea." Meaghan sipped her wine, then downed the rest of the glass in one gulp. "Well, gotta go!"

"So soon? That went down quick."

"Yeah, I'm gonna go. Thanks for the drink."

"Okay, then. Thanks again."

Ryan opened the door for his neighbour, and she half ran across the deck. He watched her as she passed the sign tree and headed toward her cabin.

* * *

True to his word, Ryan picked up a large jug of Clamato juice the next day. While in town, he stopped at the liquor store and bought a small bottle of Grey Goose to complement the juice, making it a gift for his new friend. Maybe Meaghan would make him a Caesar.

As he arrived back at the cabin, the sun was forcing the morning clouds apart. The brightening day, and the passing of a little time, diminished the troubles of the day before. The wind was low and the light was good, so Ryan took the big black box that held the drone and put it out on the sundeck. He undid the heavy plastic latches that secured the lid and took out the drone and the remote-control console. He looked at the buttons and levers and fiddled with the joysticks to reacquaint himself with the machine.

After getting his laptop, he placed it on the wide handrail and booted it up. Ryan connected the remote control to the laptop to enable video from the four-prop flying machine. Then he powered the thing up and practised short vertical take-offs and landings. Once he was confident he could control the craft, he took it up to about a hundred feet and flew it out to the centre of the lake. He pushed record and soon had a panoramic shot of the cabin row from high up over the water. He flew the drone over the first cabin and down the shoreline, past his own cabin and on down the line. The drone backed away and got a great context shot of the site of the new cabins, then a low shot back along the beach. Then he took it back out to the middle of the lake where he began. He brought the buzzing flyer back toward his cabin and hovered over the bubbles.

Rosie spotted the drone returning and ran out to the end of the dock. Ryan brought it toward the dog. She barked and jumped up, her front feet near the machine. He made the drone dance back and forth, and Rosie followed it playfully. Ryan laughed at his pet going crazy, and he got it all on video. He landed the drone on the grass where he had bathed Rosie.

He disconnected it, took the laptop to his kitchen table, and reviewed the short video. He copied the main portion of the flight to a new file and added a title to the first frames of the panorama shot: "Indian Springs Recreational Cabin Development." He posted it to the new website, exited, then went back into the site to ensure it was working. It looked great. The perspective from the air and light quality were perfect. He would text Owny and ask her to take a look when she had a chance.

Happy with his work, Ryan brought the drone inside and headed out onto the lake in his single scull. Conditions were still calm, and it felt great to get out and experience the lake he was promoting. When he returned to his dock, he could see the top of Meaghan's hat. She was sitting on her deck, probably reading. He got the boat out of the water and pondered when and how he would give her the jug of juice and the vodka.

He got back into the cabin and looked at the drone. The mesh pouch on its belly could unlatch remotely. "Hmm." He took the drone outside, returned for his laptop, and set up the machine for flight again. Then he went back for the little bottle of Grey Goose and slipped it into the mesh belly pouch. It barely fit and most of it stuck out. He rummaged around for a Post-it note, wrote "Come over for the Clam," and stuck it on the bottle. He tried to take off. The drone could barely lift the bottle, but it did eventually make it to altitude. He flew it the short distance to Meaghan's cabin and let it hover out along the shoreline for a few moments, as he didn't want to scare her.

Meaghan stood up and looked directly at the drone. As it approached her deck, she looked concerned and quickly went into her cabin, then looked out the window at the intruder. Ryan landed the drone on the old wooden picnic table on her sundeck. He dropped its cargo and gently backed off. The bottle landed on its side, then rolled off the table, bounced off the bench seat, and landed on the deck, where it clunked but didn't break. He pulled the drone back and it hovered over the beach again. Meaghan stepped out onto the deck and picked the bottle up, plucking off the Post-in note. Looking back at the awaiting drone, she waved the bottle at it and turned to go back inside. Ryan returned the flyer to his property and landed it carefully on the deck.

* * *

The Caesars were good. For the first round, Ryan had managed to scrape up a couple of celery sticks that weren't too limp and some Tabasco, and he spiced the rims with what he had on hand. Meaghan deemed hers wasn't nearly strong enough, so she took it upon herself to mix the second round, sans the frills. After that, the little bottle of Grey Goose was almost gone.

Ryan remained curious about her past, her age, and how she came to be living in the cabin she was in and how long she planned to stay. Meaghan didn't talk about herself much. That worried Ryan, but he liked her—she was a free spirit. Carefree and winsome were qualities very opposite to Ryan's personality, and that was exciting. He decided that her past wasn't that important right now. After all, he wasn't prepared to tell her much about his own situation. Still, there were things that bothered him about her. Once in a while when she was talking, a hint of ungraciousness betrayed her. There was something very rough about Meaghan that she couldn't completely hide.

"What do you do for a living, Ryan? Are you retired?" Meaghan asked.

"No, no, not retired. I'm a website designer."

"So you're kind of freelance, then? On your own?"

"Nope, I work for a company. I've worked for them for about fifteen years."

"Wow, that's quite a while. You wouldn't think of going out on your own?"

"Oh, I've thought about it. I could at any time, really. But I like my boss. It's a small company, but we have a good reputation and solid clients. We have history, you know. He's good about including me in . . . the business, I mean. How about you? What do you do?" Ryan felt it was okay to ask since she'd asked him.

"Um, I'm between jobs right now. The owners of the cabin have given me a great deal, so I can stay here for cheap."

"So, any prospects? What are you looking for?"

"I'm not looking right now. I'm just"—she bobbed her head—"taking some time right now, decompressing a bit, getting some space."

"Me too, kinda. This is a good place for that. Are the owners of your cabin planning to spend some time here this summer? It's been a pretty nice so far, weather-wise. I'm sure they'd want to enjoy it."

"Oh, they have several places. Not sure if they'll come this summer at all." She remained vague.

"Hmm," Ryan thought he would ask Owny about the owners—maybe *all* the owners if things didn't improve with Ronny and Chester.

"Hey, I'm going to make some spaghetti. Would you like to stay for some? It's my specialty." As he asked, he felt old and predatory even though he wasn't sure about their age difference. Still, Ryan was hopeful she wouldn't reject him.

Meaghan wasn't surprised at the offer but remained coy. "Well, I don't know. I really should be getting back."

"You've got other plans?"

"Mmm, not exactly pressing."

"Then stay. We'll have a glass of wine. I have a nicer bottle of red this time."

"Okay. Sounds good."

Ryan's pasta was very basic, but it was hot and fresh, and parmesan cheese made it better. They toasted the day. They chatted about Rosie, the lake, the drone, and the landing of the Grey Goose. Meaghan did admit she was from Vancouver, and Ryan let it slip he was on the outs with his wife. The wine had lubricated the conversation.

After dinner Meaghan said she needed to go home for a bit, and that she would return with more vodka. Ryan was skeptical she would come back, thinking it was a ruse to get away. He accepted she was probably gone for the night—maybe for good. He gave Rosie a treat and kept busy by picking up the dishes and running water in the sink.

When he heard the door open as Meaghan let herself in without knocking, Ryan was relieved and encouraged. He was very careful to be casual about her return, not showing any surprise that she'd come back. He continued with the dishes as she plunked a large bottle of vodka on the table.

"Would you like one?" she asked.

"Um, no thank you. I've got a glass of wine going," Ryan said sincerely.

She went to the cupboard, then the fridge for juice and ice. He finished rinsing the dishes and left them to dry on the plastic rack beside the sink. He picked up his wineglass and sat down beside Meaghan. Again, they toasted and he said, "Cheers!"

"Cheers," Meaghan responded. "Here's to good neighbours!" They each took a sip.

Over on the counter, Ryan's phone lit up with a message. He got up to check it. It was from Emily: *Need to talk to you about Mum, please call.* Ryan had expected some sort of fallout from the conflict at the hospital; this must be it. He set the phone down, shutting off the message screen. He grimaced.

"Trouble?" Meaghan asked.

"Nope—no big deal."

Ryan sat down beside Meaghan again. Though they had only known each other a short time, Ryan felt that the barriers of awkwardness had dissolved. He was pleased to have a woman in his cabin, and the conversation became very natural. The kiss he offered was an obvious step Meaghan accepted; after all, she had returned to Ryan's place with reinforcements. They moved to the bedroom, and she produced a condom at just the right moment.

* * *

When Meaghan keeled over as Ryan came out of the bathroom, he could only watch in disbelief. They had reconvened to the living room; Ryan had left her on the couch only briefly. She slumped forward, drool hanging from her mouth, then folded over, arms on her lap, her head dropping forward slowly to rest on her knees. She listed to the left, then awkwardly fell sideways onto her left side on the couch cushions, feet on the floor, her gangly legs askew.

"Meaghan? Meaghan!" Ryan rushed over to her and kneeled down, pushing the coffee table out of the way. "Meaghan!" He gently patted her right cheek. "Hey! Talk to me!" She was unresponsive. Panic rushed over him as her face went ashen, her breathing shallow, then stopping altogether. "Jesus Christ!"

He snapped into action but was nervously uncertain what to do. He kicked the coffee table farther back, grabbed Meaghan by the shoulders, and pulled her off the couch and onto her back on the floor. He put his ear to her chest. Nothing. "Shit!" He pulled open her blouse, popping buttons as he did. Her chest braless, he tried to recall the CPR training he had had years before. He pushed on her chest three times, then held her nose and breathed into her mouth. Rosie came over, curious, and licked Ryan's ear. He didn't respond to the dog. "Come on!" Ryan repeated the chest compressions.

Rosie turned away from the two on the floor and barked toward the front door. A *step, clump, step, clump* sound was coming from the front stairs. Ryan barely noticed. He was mostly aware of Meaghan's lips turning blue, and her mouth lifeless as he held her nose and breathed into her again. He looked at his phone for a half second but dismissed calling 911. *No time. No time.* He pushed on her chest again, frantic in frustration. "Meaghan! Don't do this!" He looked toward the front of the cabin, desperate for a miracle. He pushed his arms underneath her back. Adrenalin helped him lift her effortlessly off the floor. He rushed to the door, fumbling for the doorknob. "Stay with me! Stay with me!" He pulled the door back and stepped out onto the deck.

The night was dark and still, but as he took a step, he felt as if he had entered a wind tunnel. He couldn't move forward as a strange force pushed him back, keeping him from stepping forward, though he shifted in the wind. Rosie barked at his feet, but the sound of her protests was remote and muted. Deafening wind rushed past his ears. Looking forward, he saw what looked like northern lights streaming in a brilliant display, brightening as he tried to push forward. Rosie seemed to float up behind him, dog paddling. Ryan held Meaghan as tight as he could to his chest and put his head down. He bellowed like an Olympic weightlifter on his final attempt. He staggered and weaved as Rosie barked and whined. Another rush of adrenalin enabled him to make a mighty push forward; he managed a step, then a second, then a third.

By the time he reached the stairs, the strange, coloured storm had dwindled into the night. He stumbled and slipped down the stairs and across the beach. Without hesitation, he waded into the water up to his waist. He lowered Meaghan, keeping his hands under her for support, letting her float on her back. Rosie started barking again at something on the beach.

"Meaghan! Come on! Talk to me!" She was cold and lifeless, pale even in the darkness. He let her sink slightly below the surface so the water covered her face. Rosie barked. He lifted her up again. "Meaghan," he said more calmly now, despair replacing panic. He immersed her again. Nothing. He raised her up. "Meaghan, please." Nothing. He dropped her down, letting her float a little on her own. Rosie wouldn't shut up.

Ryan wasn't sure if you could baptize the dead. Can you purify a soul if it has already been taken? Can a wandering soul travel back from the spirit world? Can you get back into your body as though you were putting on yesterday's pants?

Ryan felt the frigid water now. He had been oblivious to the temperature until his heart went dark; only then did the cold invade him. Meaghan seemed peaceful in the dim light. He studied her face as she floated just below the surface. A shiver went up his back. Then her eyes opened suddenly as if she'd been awakened from a tormented sleep. Disoriented, she turned her head and opened her mouth. She breathed in, said something, then burst into a panic as she realized she was under water. She flailed and kicked, and Ryan put his arms under her back and attempted to get her upright. Rosie stopped barking at last. Meaghan found the bottom with her feet, coughing violently and hacking up water. She coughed hard several more times. Eventually, her faculties returned, and she was able to get her bearings. She looked at the cabin, then back at Ryan.

"What the fuck are you doing?" she yelled, coughing through it. "You tryin' ta fuckin' kill me?" She staggered like a drunk in the sand, the soft bottom and the waves affecting her balance. "You tryin' ta drown me, you fucker!" Meaghan wiped her mouth roughly and splayed her fingers across her eyes. She twisted her body as she pulled her feet into a first step toward the shore, then another, her hands dripping and skimming the water's surface. Obviously feeling threatened, she tried to pick up her pace and pulled her blouse shut. She looked down at the sopping wet shirt, bewildered as to why she couldn't button it up.

"I was trying to help you! You passed out—you were out of it. I was just trying to revive you. I tried CPR, I tried to—"

"Like hell you did." She spat into the water. "You can't do this to people. You got yourself a mess of trouble. This is bullshit. You're a sick bastard!" She made it to the shoreline and walked solemnly toward her cabin.

"Meaghan, you passed out! You stopped breathing!" Ryan yelled from the water.

She glanced backwards as she crossed the property line at the sign tree to see if he was following her. He wasn't.

Chapter 15

When the RCMP came, Ryan was upset that they didn't turn off their lights after they parked. He recognized the marked Ford SUV; it was the local reserve constable. He was Indigenous and well known in the village; his name tag read corky smoke. He must have called for backup, as a second car pulled past the Ford and parked directly in front of the cabin, its flashing lights illuminating the entire lake. The second constable was white and must have come in from town; they didn't seem to know each other.

Ryan opened the door and walked out onto the deck. "Would you mind shutting your lights off?" He tried to sound calm.

They ignored the request and stopped at the bottom of the stairs.

"Are you Ryan Hanson?" the local cop asked.

"Yes."

"Do you know why we're here?"

"I have an idea."

"Can we come in and talk about it?"

Ryan backed up from the top of the stairs, pushing a nosy Rosie back. "Yup. Come in."

The two police officers climbed the stairs and entered the cabin. They both looked around the premises in that suspicious way. Both had one hand on their belts.

"So what happened here tonight?" Corky Smoke asked firmly.

"Meaghan is still upset?"

"Upset? Yes, I guess you could say that."

"Have you seen her?"

"No, we came here first. She said you tried to kill her."

Ryan hung his head and slumped into a kitchen chair. "I didn't try to kill her. I tried to save her. I *did* save her. She stopped breathing, and I performed CPR. I did everything I could, I—"

"Did you call 911?" the white cop asked, knowing the answer.

"No, no, I didn't call. I thought about it, but she wasn't responsive. She wasn't breathing, her heart stopped, she was turning blue. I knew there was no time to call or to wait for help to come. I just did what I could to get her breathing."

"Were you guys doing drugs?" Corky asked.

"We were drinking. I mean, we had some drinks with dinner. We weren't intoxicated. At least I wasn't. I went to the bathroom. When I came out, she had passed out. I'm thinking maybe she did some drugs? Not here, but she was in a bad way, like she'd OD'd or something."

"Then what did you do?" the town cop asked.

"I . . . well, the CPR wasn't working. I tried several times, but no go. I panicked, I suppose. The only thing I could think of to do was to get her into the lake. I was hoping the water would revive her."

The two constables looked at each other. "So you threw her in the lake? This was your idea of saving her?" This from the white sidekick.

"I didn't throw her into the lake! I carried her out and waded in. I held her on her back. It took a bit, but eventually she came to."

"So you thought the lake would help." This wasn't a question; Corky seemed to be trying to connect some dots. "Then what?"

"Well, it did. It did help. Then, well, she freaked out. She woke up in the water, and I guess that was a shock to the system. She yelled and screamed and buggered off. I tried to explain to her, but she was mad."

"Did you two have sex?" the white constable asked.

"Yes, we did—earlier."

"Did you pay her for it?" he asked bluntly.

Ryan was taken aback. He shook his head in disbelief. "What the fuck are you talking about? We're friends, I guess. We've only known each other a short time, but we . . . it was consensual. We had like a date, dinner, whatever." Ryan gestured at the dishes in the sink and on the counter.

"Did you hit her?" the white cop said. "Did you abuse her after she passed out?"

"Oh, for fuck's sakes. Listen, we had an evening together and she must have had too much to drink, or something more I wasn't aware of. She passed out, like *dead*. Unresponsive. Not breathing. Get it? I revived her. I swear. That's it."

The two policemen looked at each other again, and Corky nodded for the two of them to go outside. Ryan watched them talk in low tones on the deck. Corky was the more animated of the two; he pointed to the lake, and they talked for some time.

Just the white cop came back into the cabin. "He's going over to speak with the accuser. I'll stay here with you till he gets back." He pulled up a kitchen chair across from Ryan.

They sat there in uncomfortable silence. Ryan got up and busied himself with straightening up the living space. After about ten minutes Corky came back to the cabin and entered without knocking. Ryan and his constable companion looked at him inquisitively.

"Meaghan Smith is known to us," Corky spoke in a calm, measured tone. "I believe *she believes* she was threatened. But we had a chat and she's calmed down. She says she had taken some drugs. Prescription pills, she says. I said I believe Mr. Hanson wasn't trying to hurt her. I suggested she was under the influence of those pills and might have had too many. They might have clouded her understanding of the situation. She was scared, but I think she's reconsidering her charges. I want you two to stay away from each other. I'll file a report and check back here tomorrow." Corky seemed very level-headed. "Does that sound reasonable to you?"

"Yes, yes, that's fine. I won't bother her."

The next morning, Ryan felt lonely for the first time since coming to the cabin. Before now, he had been preoccupied with all things lake related, work related, dog related, and website related. Now all that seemed less important. He was alone, rejected, misunderstood, ashamed, and uncertain of any of his relationships. He didn't know if he needed to make amends or just move on, in any direction.

He heard a rustle outside and he went out to the deck. His heart brightened for a moment as he hoped it was Patsy and Owny or Gerald, but it was just the wind flicking a stem from a bush that had recently grown long enough to touch the wall of the shed. Time to do some yard work around the place. He didn't have a lawn mower or trimmer; he needed to take care of that. If the Wilsons came by, maybe that would mean the whole lake wasn't aware of the events of the previous night. If they didn't come by ever again, that would be a blow.

Ryan lay down on the couch and replayed the previous night in his mind yet again. His recollection of that night would prove quite durable. The fun with the drone, the dinner, the lovemaking. Then the fiasco with Meaghan passing out and his not being able to get across the deck. *Oh yeah, nearly forgot about that. What was that?* Some kind of gravitational field, a weird colour storm that got brighter as he forced his way against it, then through it. Was he recalling that correctly? Did it really happen? Was that Stoneblanket trying to do his thing? Rosie's relentless barking seemed to indicate as much. *Maybe you should baptize the dead,* he thought. *Better late than never.* He wondered when Corky would come by. He thought Corky understood him. Didn't like the white guy. Sleep came as his mind wandered through the maze of his thoughts.

Footfalls on the dock and muffled voices awoke him from his fitful slumber. Rosie was looking through the glass in the front door, her tail wagging and tongue lolling. Ryan got up and looked out; this time there really were visitors. Gerald was on the dock holding the rope for Patsy, who was out in the water. Ryan was about to step out when he saw Owny walking onto the property from the left, maybe from Meaghan's. She gestured to Gerald that she was going to go up the cabin stairs. He just nodded. Owny was about to knock when she saw Ryan through the glass.

Ryan attempted a pathetic smile and opened the door. "Hi, Owny."

"Good morning, Ryan."

"Come in, come in. Can I get you a coffee?"

"No, I've had my quota this morning. Thanks anyway."

"How is Patsy?"

Owny turned and looked at the sight that had become normal, but that from this vantage point seemed preposterous. "She's coping, but I'm worried. She's losing weight, has no energy."

"Sorry to hear, but she'll come around. She's got a whole team working for her."

"Hmm." Owny was clearly worried about her grown daughter. An awkward silence followed. "So you've had some trouble, Ryan."

"You could say that. I didn't mean for it to be trouble. You know the story already?"

"I talked to Corky." Owny got right to the point. "Meaghan's a con artist, Ryan. I knew there was someone staying there in cabin four, and that it wasn't the owners. I didn't think too much about it at first. Owners have friends stay, or even rent the cabins out sometimes. But this time it seemed odd. I spoke to her once as we went by, and she was very evasive. Anyway, I just came from there." Owny pulled out a chair at the table and quietly sat down. She unzipped her pea-green nylon jacket and looked at Ryan earnestly. "We had a little chat. She's bad news, Ryan. You should stay away from her. I'm pretty sure she's just squatting there and the owners don't know. Pretty sure. I'm going to contact them. She must know them somehow—enough to know where they are and that they won't be at the cabin for a while."

"She's batshit crazy."

"Could be . . . You've been feeding the wrong dog, Ryan. You're better than this. Or am I wrong about you too? I'm worried now that we shouldn't have let you alone with Patsy."

This offended Ryan, and he felt as if he was being scolded by his mother. But under the circumstances he could understand Owny's concern for her daughter.

"I wouldn't do anything to hurt anyone. I didn't mean to hurt Meaghan, if I ever did. I just tried to revive her. She was drunk, stoned—or both, I guess."

"And you too?"

"I had a few drinks, that's all. I tried to save her. I *did* save her!"

"Maybe you did. Maybe you did, Ryan. We take a very dim view of domestic violence around here. It's something we clamp down on immediately. That's why Corky came right away, and that's why he called for backup. When she called in, she was frantic."

"This wasn't domestic violence. How come you know everything all the time?"

"It's my job. I'm the Chief. I care about what goes on around here. She's still upset, but I think she's sobered up and realizes she may be mistaken about what happened. She doesn't know about the lake's powers, Ryan. That's why you took her into the water, right? It would be a strange thing to wake up under water."

"For sure. I couldn't get through to her when she came to. But at least she came to."

"So you think it worked? Getting her into the lake made the difference?"

"Damn straight. She'd stopped breathing for quite a while. Stoneblanket came for her."

"Oh my God! Are you sure?" Owny fidgeted in her chair.

"Pretty sure. I didn't see him, not in a bodily form at least, but Rosie must've. He made it hard for me to get her to the lake. I had to push through some sort of weird . . . force. It was like being in some sort of windy, freaky colour storm. Crazy shitshow, that's what it was, right here on the deck. I was carrying Meaghan and finally was able to push through it. It took all the strength I had just to get to the stairs. Then it went away, and I got her out in the water. It took some time for her to wake up. But she did, thank God."

"Hmm." Owny looked around the room and twisted her lips. She tapped her index finger on her bottom lip, then got up and went to the window and looked out at the dock. Patsy was getting out of the water, and her doting father put a towel over her back and replaced the life ring. Patsy shivered and adjusted the towel. She was pale. Soon her hair would be falling out. A tear streamed down Owny's cheek, her face close to the glass. She subtly wiped it away, as if hoping Ryan didn't see her emotion.

"Stoneblanket," she said intensely under her breath, as if he was a problem she needed to solve.

Chapter 16

Ryan was still lamenting the episode with Meaghan. He knew she must have had some demons, but he constantly returned to those few fun moments: giving Rosie a bath, having dinner, making love. Especially making love, that baser human instinct. Her runners and bra were still at his cabin. He wasn't sure whether to keep them, toss them, or get them back to her. He put them in a reusable shopping bag and made up his mind to return them to her—maybe just discreetly hang them on her doorknob. That might at least show he was thinking of her and meant no harm.

He picked up the bag and exited the cabin, ensuring Rosie stayed inside so he could sneak over. As he got to the sign tree, he stopped and stood beside it, poking his head around it to look past the adjacent cabins to see if the coast was clear. As he did, he heard a door close. Craning his neck, he saw Ronny Two Livers walk swiftly from Meaghan's front door and across the deck, then bound down the stairs. He was stuffing something in his pocket as he half walked, half ran down the side of the cabin.

Ryan was shocked to see that Ronny had some sort of relationship with Meaghan. That was very disappointing, no matter what that relationship was. This was something he had to think about, so he waited a few seconds, then returned to his cabin, retaining the bag with Meaghan's things in it.

That low level of loneliness he'd managed to tamp down had just ratcheted up a notch. Meaghan and Ronny? What the hell?

This was a wrinkle that meant things really were over with her. He booted up his computer, poured a coffee, and inspected his phone. He reviewed his text messages and realized he needed to call Emily.

"Finally!" Emily said as she answered her phone. "I was starting to get worried about you."

"Oh, I've been busy with some stuff for work. How are you?"

"I'm fine. So you talked to Mum?"

"Well, sort of, not exactly. I saw her, but we didn't say much."

"So you don't know?"

"Don't know what?"

"About her diagnosis?"

"What, they've just confirmed she's an alcoholic?" he said sarcastically.

"Dad, no. You're so out of it. You need to return some phone calls."

"I'm calling you right now. What is it?"

"So Mum has MS . . . multiple sclerosis. That's why she's been in the hospital so long."

Ryan paused. He was confused. He wasn't positive what MS was, so he wasn't sure how to react. "What is that, exactly? Is it bad? Is she okay?"

"It's a disease—a major disease. She has, like, nerve damage and stuff. It affects her balance and speech, and her whole life, I guess. They discovered it when she was in the hospital."

"I thought she was just in rehab. Maybe she needed a longer stay this time."

"Well, she was in rehab, of course. But then she needed to stay on to get the MS thing taken care of. She's still in. I'm going to see her today. Do you want to come with me?"

"No, no, I don't think so. She's still in the hospital? Wow, that's a long haul."

"Why not come with me?"

"I'm not ready. I'm not ready to see her."

"She's your wife, Dad. Besides, you already saw her, right?"

"That was just by chance. I didn't set out to see her."

"I don't understand." Now Emily was confused.

"I happened to be at the hospital and just ran into her. Listen, I'm still pissed off with her. I may *never* want to see her again, to be honest with you. She's messed this up and I'm moving on." Ryan knew he was being overly dramatic and seeking empathy from his daughter.

"Dad, it hasn't been that long. She needs all of us now. This is new information. This is a big deal."

"Emily, I know it's a big deal. You're right." Ryan sighed. "Let me think about this. It's a big deal all around, Em. I know I need to talk to her at some point, but on our own terms. Nobody else around. Just us. Tell you what? Call me after you've seen her and give me an update. Maybe don't tell her you're doing that, but call me when you can. I'm concerned about her too. Okay?"

"Okay. You're being stubborn. You should come." Emily gave it one last try.

"I will not. Just call me later. Bye."

"Bye."

* * *

Ryan went to his laptop and googled "MS." He had an idea what it was, but his search enlightened him. He was ambivalent when reading the prognosis. Emily was right—not necessarily about going to see Laura, but about him being stubborn. Born stubborn.

Still in research mode, he googled the name "Phil Conner" and came up with seven million hits. Not discouraged, he checked out LinkedIn, guessing Conner was a University of Victoria alumnus. He discovered a Phillip Conner, but there was little information. Ryan narrowed his search to "Principal Phillip Conner" and got some school and provincial school board websites. On a hunch he plugged in "Phillip Conner News" and scrolled through a long list of unrelated sites. On page four he was about to give up when he came across "SOMNIA: Spotlight on Military News and International Affairs." In the second line under "Archives" was the tagline: "Infantry makes an example of Corporal Phillip Conner." It dated to over twenty years ago. On a deeper dive he found the information very revealing, but he had to ensure this was indeed the correct Phil Conner. There were millions of them, after all. An hour flew by as he read through the military archive database.

Feeling drained, he rubbed his eyes and looked up at the big black plastic drone box, packed up and ready to go back to his office downtown. He realized that in all the kerfuffle, he had forgotten to tell Owny to look at the website for the aerial footage of the lake and cabin row. Ryan shot her a quick email and included a link to it so she could just click on the line and get to the new views.

As he did, a window popped up informing him he had a message from Mark Maguire. He went to the email and read that Mark's two keeners had already done a preliminary analysis of the spruce samples and the findings were very promising. To round out their mini thesis, the two were looking to come out to see some stands of the timber. Ryan was pleased to see positive feedback and such quick progress. He was also pleased for the distraction of doing something productive in the midst of his own malaise. He forwarded the email from the university to Owny. He would give her some time to get to the emails, then follow up with a phone call. Get back in her good graces. In the meantime, he acknowledged Mark's email with a note to say thanks, and that he would get back to him as soon as possible to organize something with him and the students.

Ryan killed some time by letting Rosie out, and flicked on the TV news. Soon he gave Owny a call.

She was pleased with the video. "It looks really great, Ryan. Really great. I don't think I've seen the lake in that way before. You really captured the cabin setting. Super job. I'll show it to the council next meeting."

"So you'll be moving ahead with the road construction, then?" Ryan said.

"Yes." She sounded positive, but Ryan detected a waver in her voice. "Yes. We need to tie up some loose ends, but we want to move forward as soon as possible."

"That sounds good. Did you see the email from the university?"

"Yes!" Owny appeared happy to change the subject. "Yes, that's great news. I'm so surprised they're interested. You really pulled that out of your hat."

"Can we give these students some time, get them out into the forest somewhere?"

"I don't see why not. I haven't . . . Just a sec. Gerald?" Ryan heard Owny talking to him away from the phone. Then she put the phone on speaker. "Take a look at this email from Ryan, from the university." She waited a few seconds for him to read the text. "Can you think of a suitable place to take them? I'm not sure."

"Yes, I know a spot. Just north of Old Town. There's a spruce grove. Nice area."

"Can you drive there? The road doesn't go that far in, does it?"

"Yeah, we can only get so far, but we could walk the rest of the way. Shouldn't be too much." Gerald thought a bit. "Or we could take a boat. Probably a better view from the water, and it's only a short way. Maybe talk to Tom White. We could take just a skiff. Or maybe even his gillnetter."

"Okay. That sounds good. We'll call Tom and get back to you, Ryan."

"You don't mind being a guide, Gerald?" Ryan said.

"No, don't mind at all. I'll get back to you. So when do you want to do this?"

"Dunno. Maybe tomorrow or the next day?" Ryan needed to confirm a date.

"Okay. Talk to you soon."

Ryan emailed Mark back and asked about when they could make the trip with the students. "The sooner the better" was the response. The students would share their preliminary findings when they arrived. Ryan tentatively suggested tomorrow afternoon. He texted Owny with the news. Soon his phone rang.

"We've got a great idea." Owny sounded cheerful. "Gerald thought of it. We take the canoe up to the point with the students."

"Canoe? There will be a few people, Owny. Not sure how that's going to work—"

"It's a big canoe, our big dugout canoe. It's down at the Old Town dock all the time. We should get it out anyway. We'll get a few paddlers and give the students a good tour. It's an honour for them, really. The weather looks good. Tom will have it ready at the dock. We paddle up, they look around, then we come back. Should be fun."

"Okay, sure. I didn't see a big canoe down there," Ryan said.

"It's in its own shed. It's a beauty. Wait till you see it. It's beautifully carved and painted on the side with the Sisiutl."

"That should be interesting. So are we okay for tomorrow?" Ryan asked.

"Yes, let's all meet at the band office and see what they have so far. Then we can go to Old Town and take the canoe to the spruce grove."

Ryan said goodbye to Owny and Gerald. He responded to Mark, inviting him and the others for the next day, and he added the coordinates for the band office.

Ryan went out to his dock and put the single scull in the water. He needed to clear his head and put the day's happenings into some sort of context. Rowing down the lake would settle his thoughts and put his mind into a place where he could process the news about Laura, and Meaghan, and think about what the next day might bring. He put on some tunes and hit the water.

* * *

The students arrived on time at the band office. Ryan was early and brought the drone, just in case the canoe trip proved to be interesting for the website, or the students. Owny, Gerald, Cecil and his wife, as well as Patsy and her two sisters, Iris and Aster, were there. Owny seemed genuinely excited to meet the students, see their research, and show off the canoe and some positive aspects of the reserve.

The students were Jason and James. Jason was of Asian descent, while James was Caucasian. Everyone went into the band office boardroom and sat around the table. Jason and James were bright faced, smart, and confident, and very much in their element as they spoke about what they had found. Jason started up his laptop and asked to connect to the flat screen TV on the wall.

"First, we'd like to thank you for the opportunity to take a closer look at different uses for domestic wood products. We're looking for all types of applications for local lumber, and this specific product use hadn't occurred to us, so thanks for bringing it to our attention." Jason sounded like a businessman.

James took over. "So we've done a few things recently. We've researched the desirable qualities of wood, and Sitka spruce specifically, for instrument manufacturing, and the acoustic properties of wood that lend themselves to stringed instrument applications. We analyzed the samples at a microscopic level and researched what luthiers look for in selecting wood, especially for the top section of an instrument. We'll share that briefly with you. Also, we're looking forward to seeing actual standing timber so we can understand the habitat of the species. When we're there, we'll take GPS coordinates, photographs, soil samples, branch samples, and a core sample from a couple of trees that will include bark and deeper ring layers."

Jason jumped in. "Thank you for your invite today! Seeing this first-hand really adds to our research experience."

"Yes, thanks for having us," James added.

"We welcome you on behalf of our whole clan. We're happy you have come to our village," Owny responded formally. "We're also anxious to see what new things we can do in a sustainable way with the resources on our land."

Jason and James explained what they had found out about properties instrument makers look for in wood. For hundreds of years, Sitka spruce has been the most desirable wood for manufacturing the top soundboard of most stringed instruments: violins, violas, cellos, bass fiddles, guitars, mandolins, and the like. The prime product has a specific cellular structure—very even grain—and stabilized with a patient curing process. They showed photos of microscopic views of the spruce samples, commenting on the incredibly uniform tubular cells. They give a crisp, clean resonance, and an even vibration across the structure. The sustain of the vibration is excellent. The structure improves strength, makes the wood easier to carve, and is more rigid—less likely to crack over time. The wood grain— the yearly rings of wood—was very uniform, speaking to the consistent seasonality of the species' environment.

"You guys are saying this is good quality Sitka spruce?" Ryan knew he was stating the obvious but he wanted to get involved in the discussion.

"So far, from what we've found, we believe this may very well be the best Sitka spruce in the world," James said.

Everyone around the table just looked at each other.

"Sitka spruce is grown all around the world. It's been transplanted all over the northern hemisphere for decades. It's harvested and replanted consistently in dozens of countries. However, the northern coast of North America is where it originated. There's a reason for that. We want to dig deeper into this. The quality is so good, we feel the trees here have adapted over time to become a pristine species. It may have developed properties to fend off parasites, especially insects—we found no signs of infestation whatsoever. And it may moderate its nitrogen intake, giving it the structural uniformity we see. Also, water availability is key. Geographically, this is ground zero for the most excellent old-growth stands of Sitka spruce. Kind of like the Goldilocks zone of habitats—not too hot, not too cold. Just right."

Ryan couldn't contain himself. "Goldilocks zone. I love that! Can I use that on the website?"

"Sure, knock yourself out," James responded. "It's a common term."

"Can I use the university's name as the source for the research to be mentioned on the website?"

"That I'm not so sure about. You better check with the prof, but I doubt it. We aren't a commercial venture."

"Okay, will do. Can I say, 'As researched by a prominent university'?"

Jason and James looked at each other and shrugged as if to say, "We have no idea."

"Ryan, as usual you're getting ahead of things," Owny said, then turned to the others. "The idea to explore the quality of our spruce and get the university involved was Ryan's idea. He's been very helpful with our website and other initiatives. Thank you, Ryan." Owny was sincere about recognizing him publicly. She took control of the meeting. "Let's get more information, get our student friends out to the old growth, and take it from there." Owny paused. "We have a surprise for you! We're taking you down to Old Town, the original part of our village, at tidewater. From there, we'll make a short trip in an authentic dugout canoe to the spruce grove. It's a beautiful day for a ride in the canoe!"

Jason and James looked at each other again and smiled and nodded.

The group travelled to Old Town in a caravan of vehicles. As they came down the hill to the marina, they could see the elaborately painted large canoe sitting out at the far end of the floats, ready for them with paddles and life jackets. A man was standing with it, tying a rope. He stood up and gave a friendly wave as they approached. Everyone made their way down to the gangway and the floating dock. Ryan didn't ask—he just brought Rosie along—and grabbed the box with the drone. The group congregated beside the canoe and were introduced to the man, who was Tom White, the caretaker. He would be at the back of the canoe. Onlookers remarked on the drone as Ryan unpacked it. He commented that the trip was such a good photo-op he couldn't resist, and the video could be particularly useful. Ryan took some stills of the canoe with his phone, then fired up the drone and let it idle on the dock.

Everyone piled into the canoe under Tom's direction. He passed out long exquisitely painted paddles to anyone who wanted to help propel the dugout. He offered Patsy a place of honour at the bow and gave her a hand drum and a bent stick so she could give some rhythm to the ride. Tom mentioned Patsy's past rides, and that she seemed to enjoy the experience more than most.

Ryan struggled with both the remote for the drone and a paddle. He settled down, took a spot in the canoe, and launched the flyer. He had it hover about a hundred feet out and fifty feet up, then set it to follow the base remote on autopilot. It would automatically follow the canoe and capture a smooth picture. Rosie was excited but stayed at Ryan's feet.

With a push off the dock by the inside paddlers, they set off. Tom called to Patsy to get drumming, and she started to hit the skin. Soon she had found the rhythm and the group leaned into their task.

"This is awesome!" Jason shouted at the top of his lungs.

"We didn't expect to be doing *this* today!" James added.

A slight mist drifted off the point they were heading to. As they took the short route to the spruce grove, the mist thinned and evaporated, like a veil lifted from a thing of beauty.

Keeping the canoe at speed proved to be a workout, but this only added to the experience. Soon Gerald pointed his paddle at the trees he was thinking of, and Tom responded by giving some rudder to the boat, turning toward the shore. They hit the sand firmly, and Gerald, Cecil, and several others jumped out of the heavy craft and pulled it up the beach as far as they could. The rest got out of the canoe, each awkwardly stretching down the side of it to touch the sand. Once on the beach, Jason and James opened their arms in awe as they looked up at the pristine stand of trees, perfectly positioned as if planted by the hand of God. Ryan remained in the canoe and picked up the remote for the drone. Rosie was anxious to participate; she jumped up to be with her friend Patsy. Gerald helped Rosie and Patsy get out of the dugout.

Ryan switched the machine off auto and took it straight up for a bird's-eye view of the setting. The drone slowly approached the canopy, inspecting the treetops and an eagle's nest, currently uninhabited. It circled inland a bit, and then he brought the drone down, close to the trunk of one of the largest trees he could pick out. Once close to the ground, it circled the students, then landed on the beach. Ryan shut down the drone and caught up to the students, who were enthusiastically gathering their data.

"These trees like it here, that's for sure," James said. "There's a perfect balance of yearly light, moisture, nutrients, and pest control. They're tall and straight and uniform in appearance. They seem to like southern exposure, and a slope, which probably gives them better exposure to light—like a spectator has a better view from tiered seating."

Jason dug deep below the moss layer with a hand spade and retrieved a small amount of soil at the roots of a couple of trees. James took some core samples through bark with a large hollow corkscrew-like auger.

Gerald, Tom, and Cecil had made a small fire on the beach out of driftwood. Owny opened a basket she had brought along and spread a cloth over a large log that lay perpendicular to the water. She picked up a few small rocks and placed them on the edges to keep it in place. She pulled out a Tupperware container and pulled off the top to reveal a generous heap of smoked salmon, cut into individual pieces. In another container she displayed elk jerky. She put the basket on the log and told everyone to dig in. There was also pop keeping cool in the basket.

Jason and James returned to the beach and were overwhelmed by the display of hospitality. Jason sounded a little choked up as he commented on the food Owny had put out. He walked down to the water and washed off some dark soil and, returning, wiped his hands on his jacket. He selected a piece of smoked salmon and took a bite.

"This is wonderful. Thank you," Jason said. "I think I'm starting to understand why things grow so well here! This salmon is really good. Just right. Just right."

"Thank you, Jason," Owny said. "Good smoked salmon is an art. Not too wet, not too dry, just the right cure. My people *have* had a little practice."

"I'd say so. About ten thousand years!" Jason said.

"Yup. And maybe more, you know. It's possible the last ice age didn't take in the islands on the West Coast of BC."

"Hmm." Jason's gaze drifted to the side. "That would make for a very long stretch of time, culturally speaking."

"Yes, it could very well be." Owny was happy he was beginning to understand the timeline of her people.

"That's a lot of smoked salmon!" Jason said.

Gerald and Tom came over to Jason and James. "Have you got all you need?" Gerald asked.

"Yes, we've got our samples and GPS data, thank you," Jason said.

Gerald spoke to the group. "Okay, finish up everyone. Then let's pack up and head back!"

The stay was brief, but it was meant to be. Perhaps there would be another time to get together with the students. Tom and Cecil broke up the fire, and Owny repacked her basket with a lighter load. The group headed down to the boat and clambered in. They took a more leisurely pace back to their destination; they were moving with the tide this time.

Chapter 17

Laura found herself sitting in front of her doctors once again. She was anxious to find out about her progress. She was feeling more positive about herself, despite running into Ryan and the girl. Doctor Patel and Doctor Wu were again double teaming her in Doctor Patel's office.

"Now Laura, how are you feeling?" Doctor Wu said.

"Better. Improved. Just a few days ago, I really relied on the walker, and I felt dizzy from time to time. I don't need the walker at all now, really, and I feel pretty clear-headed. My appetite is coming back."

"Okay. That's great. Really good to hear." Doctor Patel seemed encouraged. "Just to recap, we've confirmed you have multiple sclerosis. Specifically, it's relapsing-remitting multiple sclerosis—RRMS. There will likely be a cycle to your disease. You'll relapse sometimes and your symptoms will get worse. Then, with treatment, they'll usually lessen and you'll go into remission. We want to ensure you're in remission most of the time so that your quality of life is as close to normal as we can get it. We're not so sure where you are on the RRMS spectrum. It's possible you've had this for quite some time, and you may be closer to secondary progressive MS that may not go into remission, or the remission sessions may be brief." Doctor Patel adjusted himself in his chair and looked at Doctor Wu.

Doctor Wu took over the conversation. "But Laura, we're really encouraged by your progress, and your feedback today tells us we're on the right track. We have you on a blend of drugs, kind of a cocktail we need to tweak to the right recipe for you. One drug you're taking suppresses your immune system. This is to stop your body from turning on itself—to stop it from thinking that the coating of your nerves is a foreign substance it needs to attack. We also have you on a steroid to reduce inflammation, an antidepressant, and a pain reliever. All of these drugs have side effects. We want to get you on the correct dose to both counter your symptoms and lessen the side effects.

"You need your immune system to fight off other infections, so we can only suppress it so much. The long-term side effects of steroid use can be harsh, and we'd like to wean you off the antidepressants. The painkillers may be with you for a while, but how many of them you take on a day-to-day basis will likely be your call. Over the next couple of days, we'll back off on the immunotherapy prescription just a little. We'll determine the amount of inflammation with another MRI, then reduce or even eliminate the steroid if we can. The antidepressant we'll cut in half, and then eliminate in a few weeks. We'll replace it with a healthy lifestyle. Right?" The doctor tried to sound upbeat.

Doctor Patel said, "You're doing well—exactly what we want to see. In addition to fine tuning your meds and getting you another MRI, we'll get you in to physio for a few sessions. Then we think you can go home. You have some support at home?"

"Um, yes." Laura maintained a poker face. "I have my daughter . . . It will be fine. I'd love to get out of here!"

"Okay, great." Doctor Patel stood up. "We're close now, Laura. Let's get this thing in full remission and you can get on with your life. Get out and walk as much as you can. Don't overdo it, but get back into a normal routine. I'll get the physiotherapist to give you an exercise plan, and we'll get the dietician to stop by and give you some meal ideas. Keep up the positive attitude. It's important! Your mental state can really affect this disease."

Laura said goodbye and thanked the two doctors who were key to her recovery. She walked slowly back to her room, looking at her phone, and texted Emily with the latest news. A few more days. Leaving couldn't come soon enough. As she walked, she made a commitment to herself to work hard to ensure the best outcome. When she got back to her room, she sat up on her bed for a brief rest, then texted Principal Phil. He responded immediately with a happy face emoji and said he would come by in the afternoon. He suggested going for a walk outside. After a few minutes Laura got up and folded up the walker beside her bed and leaned it against the wall; she promised herself she wouldn't be needing it anymore.

By the time Phil arrived shortly after two o'clock, Laura had already met with the physiotherapist and the dietician. She had physio appointments scheduled for the next two days, and he gave her exercises to help with her strength and balance when she got home. She met the advice from the dietician was less enthusiasm. The suggested meals sounded like more hospital food. All Laura wanted was a steak or turkey with all the trimmings.

"Are you up for a walk outside?" Phil asked.

Laura was happy to see a friendly face and do something normal for a change.

"It's nice out," he continued. "I think there's a corner store that sells ice cream just a couple of blocks up Fort Street."

"Sounds great. Just give me a couple of minutes to change." It had been ages since Laura had put on her street clothes. They weren't clean, but it still felt good to put on clothing that didn't tie in the back; it confirmed she was well into recovery.

As they made their way through the hospital maze, Laura worked hard to have a spring in her step. She forced herself to walk just a little quicker than she was comfortable with.

Phil noticed her pace as they left the hospital from the main doors, past the famous white benches. "Holy cow! You're really motoring! You must have a new lease on life!"

"I do, Phil. I really do. I'm not crazy about my MS diagnosis, of course. But I've been looking into it, and I know thousands of people live with it. I'm determined to get back to normal and be myself again."

"And get back to work?" Phil asked, smiling.

"I . . . I sure would. That would kind of be up to you, though."

"I s'pose, but more accurately, it's up to you. I've talked to Betty on the school board, and to the union. They want a report of some kind. Maybe like something Workers' Compensation would get. Then I'm sure you'd be clear to resume your position in the fall."

"Wow, that's great. Thank you. I don't know how I'll feel then, but it really gives me something to work toward."

"Hey, Laura . . . I wanted to say I'm sorry. I've thought about it a lot, and I feel terrible about that last day at school. I didn't believe you. I should have handled it differently. Better, I mean. Obviously, what I did set off a sequence of events that has changed your life."

"You know, that's true. I guess I never really thought of it like that. But it seems I had to go through that to get where I am now. I've thought a lot about it too, Phil. You did what you had to do—I know that. I'm sure it looked for all the world like I fell off the wagon that day. It was your follow-up on the blood test and checking in on me that got me the help I needed. If it wasn't for that—for *you*—I might very well be dead. I know from this last kick at the cat in rehab that I'm responsible for my own actions. I can choose how I react to things. I made the wrong choice that day after the blood test. It was a super stressful, effed-up day, but still. I took that fork in the road, not you. I went to the dark side because I was feeling sorry for myself. No more dark side for me. I can't afford it, and I'm not going to let it happen again."

"That's the spirit! I've learned something too. You can't judge a book by its cover. And don't jump to conclusions. Listen a little more, and reach out sooner."

Phil's comment seemed heartfelt, but the irony of it didn't escape Laura. If Ryan had done those things, they would still have a relationship.

Sure enough, as Phil predicted, there was the corner store, and it advertised twelve flavours of hard ice cream. They went in and made their selections, then back out to the sidewalk to sit on a rickety picnic table just outside the store.

"So, what about you?" Laura felt confident enough to be forward with her friend. "What's your story? You seem to have a lot of time on your hands these days. Time enough for a charity case like me, at least."

Phil was hesitant. "You're not a charity case . . . It's summer! That's when we teachers have time on our hands." He smiled awkwardly at Laura, then transitioned to his own story. "I grew up here in Victoria. Went to Oak Bay High School, thought I was a jock. I was in the military for a while, then went to university to be a teacher. Like you." He stopped and smiled awkwardly again. "I think you met my wife, Mara. Once, maybe?"

"A couple of times. At the Christmas party a couple of years ago for sure. Before that too."

"We're not together anymore." Once the words were out of his mouth, Phil clammed up, as if speaking of it was harder than he thought it would be.

"Thought so," Laura said, sensing his mood shift. "That was the talk in the staff room, anyway. These things happen. I can vouch for that!" She raised her ice cream cone as if it was a drink. "You don't have to talk about it if you don't want to."

"Yeah, it's a touchy subject." Phil looked out into the street at the busy traffic and at the passers-by on the sidewalk. He paused, took a bite of his waffle-cone, and looked down at the concrete. "I miss seeing my kids every day most of all . . ." He looked directly at Laura. "You know, it occurs to me I've never really told a soul about the whole thing. I've told some friends about bits and pieces of the how and why, but not the whole context. Maybe I haven't told it all to myself. Relationships come apart for a reason. We just need to learn from them."

Laura took in his story with the patience of a therapist. She sensed he might be glossing over some details, but that was to be expected. Her own story was no fairy tale, so she couldn't be judgmental or the least bit surprised at anything Phil said. Besides, Phil had been a real stand-up guy. That meant something. He'd been there for her when no one else was. She had been forced into isolation—first by rehab and then by the secondary diagnosis—but Phil was genuinely concerned with his staff member's well-being. His motivation appeared altruistic from the time he got the lab results to when Laura got stuffed into the ambulance. She realized she was perhaps filling a large vacuum in his life by spending time with Phil, but she was okay with that as she felt herself being gently sucked in. Besides, she had acquired a pretty big void of her own, and nature abhors a vacuum.

Phil explained that his relationship with his wife had probably been a marriage of convenience all along. When they met they were both well into their thirties, and both felt beyond the dating scene. Mara's biological clock was ticking very loudly, and Phil's success rate with previous relationships was mediocre. They had always had their differences. Mara had a strong personality with a classic case of ego ideal control issues – she was a control freak. But the fall-back explanation of their incongruous relationship was "opposites attract." Phil eventually rebelled and took it out on the kids. While the girls looked alike, the oldest was more like him personality-wise, the youngest more like Mara. Both were young enough and malleable enough to acquiesce to their mother every time. Just as they did when they left Phil alone for good.

"I'm sorry." Laura stared intently at Phil as he stopped speaking. She was worried he was on the verge of breaking down. If he was, he suppressed it well. She reached across the weathered table and put her hand on Phil's. He didn't move a muscle. After a moment he nodded in recognition. He was done with the story, for the time being at least.

"Let's go." Laura nodded toward the hospital. "Thanks for the ice cream!" she said, trying to lighten the mood.

They squirmed out of the little picnic table and started walking. Each tossed their napkins into a garbage can on the sidewalk.

"I am so looking forward to getting home and out of that damn hospital."

"I bet you are. Two more sleeps, maybe?"

"Yep, two more, I hope. Not completely sure, but I'm going to do my best to make that work." Laura was dedicated to her cause.

They made their way back to the hospital, and Phil said goodbye at the front door. It was an awkward parting this time. Was it an occasion for a hug? He looked a little preoccupied; perhaps he was concerned about the after-effects of his story on her psyche. Phil gave a slight wave and started to walk away. Laura mustered a "Bye" and a wave back.

Before she entered the doors, he turned back and shouted, "See you tomorrow?"

Laura turned and smiled. "I'd like that!" She entered the hospital with renewed hope for the next day.

* * *

The next two days dragged by. Laura was in full communication with Emily, who came to visit her each day. She was concerned for her mother's well-being and felt the need to be available for her in light of her father's conspicuous absence. Emily offered to take Laura home when she was eventually sprung from the hospital and was a little confused when her mother told her she would be okay, and that Phil would take her home. He was available and Emily wouldn't need to miss any summer classes.

Through casual conversation with Laura, Phil had learned when Emily usually visited. He tried to make sure his visits didn't coincide with hers, but they did overlap a couple of times.

Emily called her dad and kept him apprised of her mother's progress.

"I did a little digging around about this Phil guy your mother is seeing."

"I'm not sure she's 'seeing' him, Dad. He's her principal. I guess he's been helping her out a bit. I think she's needed it."

"Have you met him?"

"Just briefly. I was leaving Mum's room the other day, and he was just coming in. He seems nice enough. Anyway, what do you mean, 'digging around'? Trolling the internet for information on people isn't appropriate, you know. Or whatever it is you've been doing. You've backed away from her—you made that clear. She's a big girl and can do whatever she wants."

"I know, I know. So yeah, I've been a little nosy. But I wouldn't mention this if I didn't think it was important. He's got a few red flags in his past. It was a long time ago, and maybe it's all water under the bridge, but it's something she should at least be aware of. I don't want her to get hurt. If the information comes from me, she'll just throw it back in my face. If it comes from you, she might be more apt to listen. Anyway, you be the judge. I'm going to send you a couple of links to some websites, and you can take a look. If you think I'm overreacting or sticking my nose where it doesn't belong, I know you'll say so. Okay?"

Emily was disappointed she had to deal with her parents as if they were high schoolers. "Yeah, I guess."

Within a few minutes, she received an email embedded with links to SOMNIA and the Canadian Military Psychiatric Crime Database and Disciplinary Actions.

An hour later Emily texted her dad. *Are you sure this is the same guy?*

Ryan replied, *Yup very sure.*

* * *

The day before Laura's release, Emily visited her mother once again. They went down to the cafeteria to have a coffee.

"So is your dad back at the house?" Laura asked, wanting to be sure what to expect. She and Ryan had been married for twenty-five years and together for almost three decades, so it was surreal to think of him not being there. Her mind's eye saw him there, in spite of the lack of communication and the incident in front of the hospital.

"No, Mum. No. I told you, he's living on his own. He's not at the house." Emily was matter of fact.

"So where is he? With that Indian girl?"

"He's at Walter's cabin. You know, at the lake. And no, I'm pretty sure he's not with 'that Indian girl.'"

"He always liked that stupid cabin," Laura said. "I can't imagine why."

"He's always wanted to be on the water. You know that. Pretty sure he bought it off Walter, Mum."

"What? He bought the thing? He's not just staying there?"

"Pretty sure it's official."

"He told you that? That he bought it?"

"Yes. He said he moved on it pretty quickly, but that he has no regrets."

"Jesus Christ. What the hell was he thinking? We can't afford that."

Emily paused as if considering her next words. "I don't think he's thinking in terms of 'we' right now, Mum."

"What the hell?" Laura was disillusioned at the news. Emily had obviously been holding back this information for a time her mother was feeling better and able to cope with it. Laura sensed this and turned away from her daughter. She stared at the people holding trays, waiting to pay a cafeteria worker in a light yellow uniform behind a plexi-glass barrier.

"Hmph. I guess he's really pissed off." But even as Laura spoke, her thoughts flickered back to Phil and what would happen in her near future.

"I don't think he's pissed off, exactly. At least not anymore. I guess he *was*. You know Dad—he can be a little hot-headed. He's been busy with work and stuff. He's rowing on the lake. That's why he likes the cabin. And I think Walter gave him a deal."

"I'm going to call Walter and see if my name is on that cabin."

"I'm pretty sure he did it on his own, Mum. I didn't ask, but I'm sure he swung it on his own." Emily switched gears. "So you've really gotten to know your friend Phil?"

Laura's brow furrowed at the question. "I've known him for years. He's the principal at my school. What do you mean?"

"Oh, just curious if you're maybe getting . . . Well, are you dating, that kind of thing?"

"I think 'that kind of thing' is likely, yes. He's how I got into this mess, but he's helped me get out of it."

"And he's talked about his past with you?"

"I'm not sure what the heck you're getting at. But yes, if you must know, he's been very open about his past. He's separated from his wife if that's what you're worried about. He's been very candid about it all."

"Okay, okay, that's great. Just a little concerned, that's all. You've had a lot to deal with over the past few weeks. A lot." Emily seemed to be beating around the bush.

Laura's eyes widened. "I am not on the rebound."

* * *

Laura had been in the hospital almost a whole month. On the day she was scheduled to be released, Phil arrived a little early. He looked unsure of himself, as if he wasn't clear how their relationship would progress once Laura re-established herself at home. She sensed he felt honoured in some small way to be the person who would take her home. He had been the one to remove her from the school, and to help extricate her from the house. It was somehow fitting and rewarding that he should be the person to bring her home again. The contrast between her condition when she left her home, and her condition now was remarkable.

Lazlo and Marta had clearly received a heads-up from Phil that Laura's return was imminent. When she and Phil pulled up to the house, they saw a small dollar store welcome home banner tacked across the front door and flapping in the wind. Lazlo, widely known in the neighbourhood as an ardent gardener, had placed two beautiful lavender plants in stout terracotta pots on each side of the doorway to give the stoop colour. They created a welcoming, lived-in look to the quiet home. The lawn had been cut and trimmed.

If Laura had any trepidation about returning to an empty house, it evaporated as she walked up the sidewalk and got a closer look at the banner and the plants. She glanced next door to see if Lazlo and Marta were on their front porch swing but couldn't spot her friends. She carefully unpinned the banner from the door jamb and entered the house she had spent over twenty years in with Ryan and their daughter. Her concerns over the state of decay she must have left it in were quickly dispelled as she entered the kitchen; it was utterly clean and cheery, with cut flowers in a vase on the table and a few groceries on the counter.

Laura teared up. "Did you do all this?" she asked Phil.

"No . . . well, a little. It was Marta and Lazlo. Mostly Marta, I think. She really went to town cleaning up. When I came back for your cell phone, I kind of gave them access . . . just to watch the place, I thought. I hope that was okay."

Almost in a daze, Laura went into her bedroom and then into the other main-floor rooms. All were clean and fresh. The windows were open a crack, sunlight was pouring in, and the whole place shone like a new dime. Laura returned to the kitchen and placed her hands together over her nose and mouth. She closed her eyes. A wave of shame flooded her as she tried to remember the house as she'd left it, as she'd lived in it at the end. The shame soon dissipated as she told herself it was over, in the past. For good. Lovely Marta.

Laura trembled, and tears came to her eyes. She tried to contain herself, but sobbed openly. Phil couldn't help embracing her, holding her naturally as she let her emotions out. The kitchen took on a new aura as he comforted Laura. The room spun around them as the breeze pushed the curtains in a gentle dance.

"Hello?" A familiar voice came with a light tap on the front door, which they had left partially open, signalled the neighbours' arrival.

"Hello, hello!" Laura backed away from Phil and quickly wiped her eyes. "Come in, come in!" She approached the entranceway and saw Marta with Lazlo, who carried Laura's cat. She was happy and surprised to see them. Marta suddenly looked so much older than she had before. Thinking of all the work she must have done to get the house back to normal deepened Laura's gratitude.

Laura reached out to Marta and held her by both hands. "Thank you. Thank you both." She looked over at Lazlo. "I can't tell you how much this means to me. I know I haven't been much of a neighbour lately! I shudder to think of what this house must have been like. Thank you."

"We all chipped in," Marta said modestly. "It's so nice to have you back! You look great. Really great. We didn't know what to expect." She glanced over at Lazlo and stopped talking as if she felt she had said too much.

Phil picked up the conversation. "I told Marta and Lazlo about your diagnosis. I hope that's okay. They were very concerned about you." He turned to Marta. "Laura has made real progress with her MS—it seems to be in remission. I think she's feeling as good as she looks!" He put his arm over her shoulder and gave her a squeeze.

"You come here, you!" Laura reached out and pulled the cat away from Lazlo. Muss purred loudly and rubbed his head under Laura's chin.

Laura looked back at Phil and smiled. "I do feel great. And it feels great to be home. In my own home, with friends." She turned to Lazlo and Marta and gestured to the kitchen table. "Sit, please, sit! I'll make some coffee." She placed the cat on the floor.

As Laura busied herself with the coffee maker, the other three sat at the table and made small talk.

"This reminds me of old times!" Lazlo said.

He was being positive, but it wasn't lost on Laura that things were different now. There was a different man in her life. That was surreal. And back then she wasn't fresh out of rehab or struggling with a new diagnosis of a major illness. Laura looked over at Phil as if to confirm her thoughts. He was quite different from Ryan. Phil was tall and bald with a stubbly beard, quiet and thoughtful, perhaps a little secretive. Ryan was shorter, had salt and pepper hair, and was clean-shaven, and more impulsive and intense. Phil's casual strength suited Laura, especially under these new conditions.

The coffee came and they chatted about the weather, the garden next door, lavender, and the rest of the summer. Phil spoke openly about Laura's possible return to work.

After barely finishing her coffee, Marta said to Lazlo, "Let's go, Grampa!"

"So soon? We just sat down!"

"Yes, so soon. Let's leave these two alone."

Chapter 18

Ryan was inspired by the canoe trip to the Sitka spruce grove and invigorated by the enthusiasm of Jason and James. When he and Rosie finally got back to the cabin, he immediately opened up his computer and started to research fine instrument manufacturers. At first he couldn't really find any names, so he went to music store sites that specialized in stringed instruments and got brand names from there. He then googled the company names and created a database of manufacturers; they were primarily in Europe, though some were in North America. He had compiled quite a list by the time he'd tapped all his energy. He went to bed, intending to close the loop on the Sitka spruce concept in the morning.

After he'd had a restless sleep, his morning routine unfolded as usual. He fed Rosie, had a light breakfast, and went out onto the water in the single scull. This always settled his mind. Upon his return, he indeed felt he had a clearer path and knew the next steps to take for the website.

He went into the background design software for the website and went to the "Specialty Spruce" tab. He wrote a rather flamboyant piece on the attributes of Sitka spruce, adding everything he'd noted about the students' presentation, including the Goldilocks zone comment. He included a map of Western Canada and highlighted a magnified inset of Vancouver Island. After very little tweaking, he included his photos of the canoe trip. He then downloaded the drone video. He edited out some of the paddling and focused on the final pass over the trees. The drone's view of the forest canopy carried a powerful message that brought home a sense of wonder at the habitat that was the source of the product.

He was happy with the results but felt there was something missing. Despite the information, the video, and the photo montage, it was hard to make a slab of wood exciting. Ryan was blanking on ideas, so as a computer geek, he did what he often did—just randomly googled words, looking for inspiration. He googled "board," "North Coast," "Native," "wood," "spruce." He scrolled through many pages of information that was useless to him. Eventually, he came across an art form he had never seen before. He was surprised to see a North Coast artist depicting a totem, but it was painted flat on a rectangular board. The art was beautiful, with traditional colours of red and black. Below it was a caption that read "Powerboard." Powerboard. That was a concept he could work with. He captured the photo and saved it.

Ryan finished up the website design for the time being. It needed more work, but it was at least presentable. He emailed Owny to take a look at what he had done and included a link directly to "Specialty Spruce." He also included the photo of the powerboard and asked if she knew much about this art form, or the artist.

About an hour later his phone rang. It was Owny. "You've been a busy little beaver," she said with some restraint.

"What do you think about the Specialty Spruce pitch?"

"I think you have quite a gift. Not that I think any of it is BS, because it isn't, but you can certainly take an idea and make it, well . . . larger than life? It's just a piece of wood, after all."

Ryan was slightly offended. "Not just any piece of wood! It's the best damn spruce on the planet. Anyway, you need to elaborate on the story. You don't sell the steak—you sell the sizzle. Speaking of sizzle, what about the powerboard idea? Are they sacred or anything?"

"I don't think they're sacred, exactly. Powerboards are a real thing. They're kind of a two-dimensional totem pole. Flat, painted. Sometimes carved in relief. What are you thinking?"

"I was just trying to think of a brand, or a way to promote the wood from a Native angle. I think it would appeal to people to have wood from an ancient forest—from an ancient people. We could call the brand Powerboard, and maybe package it with a printed paper cover over the wood for when it's delivered, or maybe have a burned-in logo on the wood."

"Those are really good ideas. I think you have too much time on your hands. Are you getting your own work done? And are you in touch with your daughter?"

"Yes and yes. Maybe if this starts to turn a profit, I'll send you a bill one day."

"Let's not get too carried away," Owny was half joking. "The site looks really good, Ryan."

"I think it needs a little more work, but I'm going to reach out to some companies I've researched and see if we get any interest. Don't hold your breath, though. I'm sure these companies have existing suppliers they might have dealt with for years. But let's run it up the flagpole and see who salutes."

"Sounds good. Thanks again, Ryan."

* * *

Ryan opened his email the next morning and was thrilled to see a response from a small company in Romania. They specialized in bass violins, and they needed a source of large-dimension Sitka spruce of the highest quality. They wanted to experiment with a deeper back bowl to create a more parabolic sound reflection, and if the wood really was of excellent quality, they would attempt a full front piece and full back piece with no glue joints. They loved the Goldilocks story, and the Native source. They provided dimensions; these were the biggest stringed instruments made.

Ryan was confident in the quality, but not so much when it came to the sizes they needed. He forwarded the email to Owny and said he would give her a call in a bit. Instead, his phone rang; it was Gerald and Owny.

"So do you think you can supply the sizes this company needs?" Ryan asked.

"Yes and no, Ryan," Gerald replied. "I'm pretty sure we have the wood, and some of it is big enough for sure. They're really nice pieces. The problem is cutting the logs. We don't have a saw blade big enough, so I doubt the mill can handle the dimension. That's one of the reasons the logs are still sitting there—they're too big for the mill."

"Why didn't you say that before?" Ryan was perturbed.

"I had no idea what sizes would be needed, what you would turn up. Who knew that this would be the first inquiry?" Gerald replied.

"You're right, you're right. I was surprised at the ask also. But this could be a good opportunity. They're obviously interested, have a unique need."

"Oh yeah, you bet." Gerald sounded more upbeat. "Tell you what . . . I know a fellow at the big mill up in Chemainus. He's a very experienced sawmill guy, so maybe he has a blade we can rent or borrow. He could tell me if our mill can handle the blade, if we can push that big a log through it."

"You would do that?" Ryan asked.

"Of course, of course. This is great! I gotta tell you, though, Chester and Ronny are going to be a problem. They'll either try to control anything to do with the mill, or they'll try to block it altogether. They're very protective of the place, and as you know they don't want anyone sticking their nose in there. That's why I don't go there anymore. I used to work there, with them. There was just too much drama and too much bullshit—Owny could tell you. I needed to get out. So we aren't on the best of terms. I can picture them saying the mill can't handle the blade or the log, or whatever."

"But this could be the start of something really great. I know there's still a lot to get done, but it could be nice little business— for them."

Gerald was blunt. "Something tells me they don't want your business ideas. Anyway…" Ryan could tell he was turning away from the phone. "I guess that's really Owny's problem."

"Hmm. Probably true." Ryan didn't envy Owny's responsibilities.

"I'll get ahold of my guy in Chemainus and get back to you," Gerald said.

Owny piped up in the background, "I'll call Chester."

* * *

Gerald wanted to reacquaint himself with the main saw at the mill. He thought he could recall the basics, but he wanted to be very sure before he contacted the fellow in Chemainus. He would confirm the specs of the main saw, the motor that drove it, and the bolt pattern mount, and he would measure the diameter of the largest of the circular blades on hand. He went to the band office and got the spare keys to the mill. Though it was close enough to walk there, he drove over.

Once inside, he turned on the main lights and went into the workshop to get a measuring tape, a flashlight, and a pencil, and he found a piece of cardboard to write on. He wrote down the name-plate data from the big green saw table and crawled under the thing to get to the information on the motor. He crawled back out and slapped the sawdust off his clothes. Next, Gerald made his way to the far side of the mill, near the band saw where they'd cut the original spruce samples. There was a seldom-used room nearby where they used to sharpen the main circular blades before they started sending them away to be done. Now it was just used for storage. He would be sure to find the big round spare blades there.

The door was locked. Gerald rattled the doorknob and looked up at the old orange steel door as if it was thwarting him. He tried again and pushed the door. It didn't budge. He pulled out the keys and tried all three, but none fit. He stood back and looked at the door.

"What the hell?" There was nothing of value that he could imagine, nothing worth locking up. He rubbed his stubbled chin. Knowing Ronny and Chester, he thought for a second. He reached up to the door frame and ran his fingers along the dusty edge. He touched something metal, and a key fell and clanked as it hit the concrete floor. He unlocked the door with it and flicked on the light.

Upon entering the main door, he thought he had smelled something sweet, but sometimes sawdust smells that way. Once inside the storeroom, though, he noticed that the smell was much stronger. Gerald squinted, not understanding at first what he was seeing. There were plastic barrels, stainless steel tanks, copper coils, and bags of what he at first thought were cement stacked up.

"What the hell?" He shook his head, bewildered. He approached a plastic drum and lifted the lid. The unmistakable smell of alcohol assailed his senses. "What the hell!" He stood back and looked around the room. "Unbelievable." Gerald pulled out his cell phone and called his wife. She picked up right away.

"You better get over here," he said.

"Over where? Where are you?"

"At the sawmill. Unbelievable."

"What? What is it?"

"You're not going to believe this. They've got a still here. A still! They're making booze, here in the sawmill. In the storeroom."

"Are you sure it's a still?"

"Well, I've never actually seen one before, but I can tell you for sure, it's a still."

"I'll be right over." Owny had mentioned she'd heard rumours of Chester and Ronny having access to some "real good porch climber." Now it made sense.

Gerald realized he hadn't checked the size of the blade mounted on the saw motor itself. He exited the room, closing the door behind him. He found a chair and carefully stepped onto it, then climbed over a guardrail and onto the large saw table. He made small steps on the steel plate, as if he was walking on ice to the dormant blade. He pulled the measuring tape out several feet and attempted to slip it down to the shaft of the motor; he would just measure the radius of the blade.

As he fiddled with placing the measuring tape, he heard a clunk from the far wall, then the unmistakable sizzle of the saw motor being energized. The blade started to rotate! Gerald pulled his hands back instantly and lurched backward on the slippery surface, falling on his butt and pushing himself back from the blade with his heels. He dropped the measuring tape, and it hit the deck and spun in a circle as it retracted sharply. The saw spun and roared, then shriek like a monster that was rudely awakened. His heart pounded and his hands shook as he reached for the guardrail and climbed over, then searched for the chair with his toe. He found it and lowered himself. The saw stopped screaming.

"What are you doing here, old man?" It was Ronny Two Livers. "You could get yourself killed, you know!"

Gerald was breathing so rapidly, he couldn't speak. His chest heaved and he gasped for air. He raised his hand, about to say something, but couldn't get it out. He was still hyperventilating.

"What are you doing up there, old man?" Ronny asked. Chester was now beside Ronny.

"Measure the blade," was all Gerald could say.

"Measure the blade? What for?" Chester asked brusquely.

"Cut the spruce." Gerald was still breathless.

"Cut the spruce? For what?"

"Maybe a buyer, for the spruce."

"Another one of Owny' stupid ideas! This is a dangerous place, Gerald. You know that. And you know, you didn't follow the proper lockout procedure on the saw, did you?" Chester was harsh.

Ronny pulled Gerald up by his lapels and got into his face. "You're lucky we were so careful when we were testing the saw. Next time you won't be so lucky. People are hurt in sawmills all the time, especially trespassers that don't follow the rules!"

They pushed Gerald toward the door, and he stumbled and fell to the floor.

Just then, Owny came in the main door, down by the end of the saw table. "What's going on here?" She was aghast.

Chester and Ronny looked up as if they had been caught beating up a schoolmate by a teacher.

Owny rushed over and helped Gerald get up. "Are you okay, Gerald?" Her voice was full of concern.

Gerald was still speechless but he nodded, reassuring his wife. "Yeah, I'm okay," he finally said. His pride was bruised more than his body. He reflexively wiped the front of his jacket. He nodded and pointed at the storage room door.

Owny didn't say word but glowered at Ronny and her nephew. The two didn't react as she walked over to the door; they must have assumed it was safely locked. To their surprise, the door offered itself up to the Chief without complaint, and she entered the room. Within seconds she was out and walking toward them, pointing back at the dirty orange open door.

"What the fuck is this? What the fuck is going on here?" Owny screamed, incensed at the duo for abusing Gerald, and for using the premises for illegal purposes. Gerald wondered if she was also angry with herself for letting them allow the sawmill fall into decline.

"You guys are done here! Get out! Get out now!"

"You can't tell us what to do," Ronny said, bluffing. "You need council approval to do anything."

"You wanna bet? You're fired. You're both fired. You get the fuck out of here, and don't come back!"

"You just want the still for yourself! That's our stock—we made it!" Ronny tried to match Owny's furious tone.

Owny looked stunned, as if she couldn't believe what she was hearing. Without saying anything more, she pulled a large fire axe off the wall and went into the storeroom. With all of her might, she swung the axe and wreaked havoc on the still. The contents of the drums spilled onto the floor and ran out the door. She splashed through the liquor and out the door and dropped the axe on the floor.

"That's what I think of your stupid porch climber! Get the fuck out of here!"

"We'll take this to council! To . . . to labour relations!" Ronny threatened. "You won't get away with this!"

"I don't give a shit what you do!" Owny stood beside her husband, holding his arm. She pointed to the main exit. "Out! You're just lucky I don't call Corky Smoke about this! Out!"

Chapter 19

I
t had been a few days since Owny had brought Patsy to the lake. When they arrived, unannounced of course, Ryan went out on to the deck to say hi. He was shocked by Patsy's appearance. His heart sank as she walked across the sand, holding hands with her mother. There was no confidence in her stride, and she was getting thinner by the day.

Rosie rushed down the stairs to greet them, wagging and seeking a welcoming hand. She went to Owny, then to Patsy. Rosie stopped in her tracks and tried to smell Patsy's crotch.

"Rosie, get over here!" Ryan called. "Smarten up!"

The dog turned, tail wagging again. She returned only to the foot of the stairs, looking up at her master. Ryan descended the steps and went to the shed to get the life jacket. Owny and Patsy walked out onto the dock. In silence, Ryan and Owny prepared the girl for her float. Patsy descended into the lake, holding her breath as she adapted to the cold. Owny held the rope as Patsy paddled out to the bubbles.

"How is she doing?" Ryan asked quietly.

"Not good. The chemo sessions have really hit her hard. Too hard. They're talking about changing the chemo cocktail to something else, some other combination. I'm not really sure how it works. Something about the 'red shit'?" Owny was despondent but wanted to talk. "Remember I told you Patsy was a twin? She had a twin

204

brother, but he died after only about two weeks. He had a hole in his heart. They say it was caused by my gestational diabetes. As she gets worse, I think of that time more. I don't want to lose her too! Alan— we called him Alan. Patsy and Alan." Her expression became vacant; briefly, she had gone back in time.

Ryan didn't know want to say about the family's tragedy. And he didn't want to mention the change in Patsy since he saw her last. He was at a loss for words. He could only nod and look out at the girl in the life preservers.

Owny sensed his mood and changed the subject. "Had some trouble at the sawmill."

"Trouble? Was there a breakdown? Did Gerald get in touch with his friend in Chemainus?"

"No, not that. Had a big blow-up with Chester and Ronny." Owny paused as if choosing her words carefully. "Gerald went over there to check out the saw situation but had a run-in with those two. They really scared him and roughed him up a bit."

"Oh no! Is he okay?"

"Not really. They started the saw to scare the shit out of him."

"What?"

"Yup. Before that, he'd called me. Gerald discovered a still in the storeroom. Big one. They were making booze. That's why they don't want anybody around. They were selling it and making money. And sampling their own wares, I'm sure."

"Oh my God—I didn't see that coming." Ryan was shocked. "Is Gerald okay? What exactly happened?"

"Well, I was furious with them. They never did get along with Gerald. They were rough with him, and that was unacceptable. When I saw the still, I lost it. I took an axe to it. Kicked them out of the sawmill. Fired them. They're bad news. Told them they were lucky I didn't call the cops."

"So why didn't you call the cops?"

"Uh, I dunno. Nobody was killed or anything. I thought firing them and getting rid of the still was punishment enough."

"Unbelievable. That's unreal, Owny. What's going to happen? What do you think they might do? Are you worried?"

"A little. But I should've done something a long time ago. I shouldn't have taken their word about what was wrong at the sawmill. I should have checked things out more. It's hard 'cause Chester is my nephew, but that's no excuse. I've let this go too long. His dad—my brother—will probably be pissed off at me, but I don't care. They can't intimidate others, and they for sure can't be making booze."

"So they're out of the sawmill? Completely?"

"Oh yeah, they're out."

"Is it capable of running?"

"Oh, I think so. It was all bullshit. I think it's fine—might need some maintenance, I suppose. Gerald will take care of it."

"Does Gerald still feel up to working on the spruce?"

"Yes, absolutely. He's more set on it than ever. He's really determined not to let those two get to him. He likes your idea and wants it to succeed."

"Is he working on getting a larger saw from Chemainus?"

"Well, he tried to call the guy he knew from the mill there. Willy, I think. Couldn't get ahold of him but finally tracked him down through the head office in Vancouver. We've hit a bit of a snag. The mill in Chemainus is closed down. We didn't know. They can't help with a saw blade. Our mill probably couldn't handle it anyway."

"Well, that sucks. We're screwed, then, on the dimensions we've been asked for?"

"Maybe not. The fellow Gerald called said he'd come down and help him figure something out. That will be great. I don't want Gerald alone at the mill, for a few reasons. They think they can get to the right size by first squaring off a log with a chainsaw, then feeding it into the saw. The blade we have should do it—they hope. Maybe they can flip the square log and cut it carefully all the way through. That's the plan anyway. Hope so."

"What's the timeline for this? Maybe I should get in touch with the customer if this is going to take a while."

"Oh no—Gerald has Willy coming over today. I hope they can figure something out."

Patsy broke into the conversation, ignoring what Ryan and Patsy were saying. "I'm cold, Mum. It's really cold."

"Just give it a couple of more minutes, Patsy. It's been a while since you've been here, so we need to catch up!" Owny tried to sound encouraging.

Patsy shivered. Rosie whimpered at her from the dock.

* * *

With Chester Ghostkeeper and Ronny Two Livers out of the picture—or at least the conflict exposed and the lines drawn—Owny felt emboldened. She knew there would be repercussions; that was inevitable. She hadn't handled the incident at the sawmill as professionally as she could have, but she didn't care—at least she'd handled it. She naturally and authentically exercised her authority, and brought to bear her sense of protectiveness and moral outrage. She told those two where to go, and how to get there. She could justify all of her actions to the band council, and besides, Chester and Ronny's reputation preceded them. Just in case there was any dispute, she and Gerald returned to the sawmill later to take pictures of the still with her phone. She also took pictures of the main disconnect switch for the saw, still in the on position, as well as the operator's console.

As she processed the fiasco, she felt encouraged that ultimately it was a blessing in disguise. She had always tried to keep peace within the band ever since she was installed as Chief. She'd even tried to defend Chester at times, thinking blood was thicker than water. Often she looked the other way when Chester and Ronny were up to no good, yet they continued to make her life miserable, and oppose her at every opportunity. That was over; she was cutting them loose. They were the bad dogs in her tribe, the worst dogs, and she was going to stop feeding them. She would now pursue the plans she had laid, come what may.

* * *

When Willy Dubois, a tall weathered white man, arrived at the sawmill, Gerald told him the story from the beginning, starting with Ryan's idea, then the website, the University of Victoria's research, and the Romanian company's request. Gerald glossed over the falling-out with Chester and Ronny, just saying the sawmill staff was elsewhere and unable to help. Willy was impressed. He was willing to help, at least for the day. He was close to retirement and hadn't worked for several months. He was happy to get his hands dirty and try to get to the dimensions Gerald needed.

The two men worked well together. They set a prime log in position for trimming, bucked it into a shorter length to make it more manageable, and squared it off with a large chainsaw. Once done, Gerald called Ryan to confirm the dimensions needed. Then they took it to the saw and carefully guided it through the blade.

By mid-afternoon Gerald called Ryan back and proudly told him the wood was sitting on a pallet on the loading dock, ready for wrapping. Willy Dubois had been a big help. They had even cut several extra slabs.

Chapter 20

As Marta and Lazlo departed, Phil and Laura prepared themselves for an awkward silence. Standing in the little foyer, Phil wasn't sure what to do next. It had been a long time since he had been in a situation like this. He improvised as best he could.

"Are you okay?" he asked, mostly to create conversation.

"I'm fine. I'm great, really." Laura gave Phil a hug. "Thank you. Thank you for everything."

Phil wanted to kiss her but refrained. He wanted to go out and buy a bottle of wine and bring it back to celebrate, but that obviously wasn't a great idea. He wanted to drag her into the bedroom, but that was just his caveman instinct kicking in. "Maybe I should go."

"Um . . ." She pretended to be mulling it over. "Nope. No, I don't think so." She took him by the hand and pulled him back to the kitchen. "Now where were we before we were interrupted?"

Phil had to think about it. They stood looking at each other. "Let me see . . . We were about here?" He embraced Laura. She clearly welcomed his careful kiss.

Coming from outside were the strains of "Three Blind Mice" from an approaching ice cream truck. It was slowly turning into the cul-de-sac. "Shall we dance?" Phil asked. Laura smiled as they started to waltz across the kitchen floor. They continued for a few minutes even after the tinny music faded away.

"Now I really should go," Phil informed his dance partner. "You need to get settled, get comfortable now that you're back in your own home." He didn't want to screw this up. He needed to balance their relationship with the right amount of both space and support. She had been married for twenty-five years, after all. His feelings were starting to overwhelm him. Did it really make sense to get involved with a person with serious health issues, an alcoholic, and a co-worker to boot? But she was charming. They had shared some challenging times lately, and relationships are born from understanding each other's grace under fire. And she hadn't balked when he'd told her his own story that day over ice cream.

Conscious that Laura might sense he was churning something over in his mind, he gently pulled away. "I'm gonna go. I'll give you a call tomorrow."

"Okay, if you insist."

Maybe that was for the best. He was sure she could use some time to call her daughter and do some things around the house. Reacquaint herself with the cat. She needed to feel she was on solid ground emotionally.

* * *

The next day Phil called quite early and suggested they do some touristy things down in the Inner Harbour in Victoria—walk the seawall, do lunch, maybe see the museum. Laura was less than enthusiastic, what with the many summer tourists, and she had seen the harbour a million times. Still, she relented. It was a nice day, and it had probably been a year or so since she had been down to the beautiful promenade. She needed to keep busy and to keep moving; Phil must have sensed this.

The touristy trip proved to be a tonic. Phil had a knack for making the mundane seem special, and he had an easygoing demeanour that made little decisions and conversation effortless. Phil and Laura had a superficial, very businesslike relationship at school. What was happening now wasn't like that at all; it was warm and held potential for something more. Consciously or unconsciously, they were becoming a couple. This was a date. Laura glowed at the attention and was optimistic about the next steps.

Phil splurged on lunch at the famous Empress Hotel, and then they wandered outside the Parliament buildings. At the seawall Phil insisted Laura sit for one of the artists. After the twenty-minute sitting, the pencil portrait was done, and it turned out to be a particularly good likeness. "That's for me!" Phil said as he paid the artist. He carefully rolled the sketch up, snapping an elastic band in place.

They extended their walk to look at a tall ship that was moored farther up the mouth of the harbour. The afternoon passed quickly, and they chatted about what to do next. A red double-decker bus with a huge Union Jack painted on the side roared past them.

"All this Englishness has got me thinking of tea!" Laura exclaimed. "How about we head back to my place and have a spot? It's about that time."

Phil shrugged. "Sure, why not?" They made their way back to his car and sped northward to Laura's house.

The tea was good, and sitting on the back porch was better. When Laura gently pulled Phil into the bedroom, it was better yet.

* * *

The two new lovers discovered they had a lot in common. They were both teachers, after all; they shared a love of learning and teaching. That magnanimous motivation can diminish over time, especially at their ages, but the spark still existed for each of them. They both had children, though Phil's were younger and estranged. He could work on that, though, and having Laura seemed to give him the backing he needed to reach out to them with more maturity and patience. They both had attended the University of Victoria and graduated only a few years apart. They had worked together for several years, and over that time their mutual respect had grown.

The new school year was looming on the horizon. Phil wanted Laura to come back to her post full time. He knew that immersing herself fully in work would do her good, keep her busy. She'd had an excellent previous year, notwithstanding the last few days of school. He thought they should be discreet about their relationship, for the foreseeable future at least, and that suited Laura also.

They both knew that rumours would be swirling about the circumstances of her departure. Phil was known for being a very pragmatic leader, and his instincts about group dynamics were exceptionally good. He would find the right person to put out the story of Laura's multiple sclerosis diagnosis. That would explain the difficult days of the last term, and why Laura should be allowed back without question. Then he would let nature takes its course. The story would permeate the staff quickly, and by the first day of school there would be very few questions about why Laura was back. She would probably even be elevated to martyr status.

Chapter 21

R yan went directly to the sawmill to see the spruce slabs. He brought the address for the Romanian company, and a makeshift logo he'd thrown together with internet art and printed on standard-sized paper. It wasn't very authentic to the tribe and needed some work, but it was the right idea: a classic black-and-red North Coast rendition of a bear with a frog in its mouth. Above it was the words "Powerboard" and "Authentic North Coast Sitka Spruce," and on the bottom in small print were the band office address and website URL.

Gerald and Willy were still there. They were doing some clean up around the main saw and attempting some sorely needed main-tenance. Ryan met them on the loading dock. He was introduced to Willy and thanked him profusely for his help. Gerald chimed in and thanked Willy again.

While he was unsure precisely what the customer was looking for, Ryan was impressed at the finished product; he marvelled at the clean dimensions. Each piece was straight grained and free of any knots. They stapled the labels to the slabs, then wrapped each slab in shrink wrap. The slabs were sturdy enough to make the trip without crating. Ryan gave FedEx a call, and Gerald said he would watch for the driver, who would come the next day. Ryan had arranged for the Romanian company to cover the freight, while the band had offered the first two pieces of wood as free samples. It seemed like a fair exchange to facilitate a new relationship. He gave Gerald the destination address and shipping account number to back up his online booking with the freight company. Ryan said his goodbyes and headed back around the lake to the cabin row.

The next morning, Ryan and Rosie set out for a run on the old-growth path on the route they had developed since they arrived in the area. When they got down to the main cabin access, Ryan was surprised to see activity on the road. A survey team was pounding stakes with pink ribbons into the weeds back from the edge of the road, and a service truck was at the dead end attending to the big yellow iron that had been sitting there for weeks. As he crossed the road, the bulldozer coughed and sputtered and belched out black smoke. It started with a roar. People yelled at each other over the noise. From the far entrance, another extended pickup truck appeared with tree fallers and large chainsaws in the back.

Ryan and Rosie entered the woods as they usually did and started to run past the giant trees. Somehow the trees rejuvenated him; being close to these enormous living things buoyed his spirit. Ryan always felt small when he made his way into the ancient forest; however, this time he didn't feel quite so small. He knew where he was going, and he felt as if he was starting to belong, as the trees had seen him before. And he felt as though he was starting to make a difference. Owny specifically, as well as the band, was getting their priorities in order; her handling of the incident at the sawmill and now the renewed construction on the cabin row extension were a testament to that. She was also getting the respect she deserved.

The run in the damp, dark world was refreshing. Rosie revelled in the trip, as she had also become more familiar with the route. The golden retriever was much braver and had become stronger over the last few weeks. Her heavy gut, stiff legs, and lethargy were long gone. She ventured farther and farther off the rough trail. Ryan had to whistle and call when she was out of sight for long. She always came bounding back, with her tongue lolling out and her tail wagging, looking pleased, as if she had gotten away with something.

The run had evolved into about a one-hour return trip that circled back to the starting point at the main road. It was always a solitary journey; they never saw a soul on the deep green route, yet the odd sense of being watched persisted. When Ryan and Rosie emerged into the open, another big truck was passing. It was dragging a large trailer, apparently an office-lunchroom combination. It was followed by a pickup with two plastic Porta Potties in it—a green one and a pink one. Ryan and the dog stopped and looked down at the dead end to briefly watch the activity, then crossed the dirt road and headed back up to his cabin, number seven, coming through the mossy access to the best spot on the lake.

When he got to the front of the cabin, rather that heading straight to the shower, he did what had become a new part of his regimen. He stripped down to just his running shorts, waded into the lake, and side-stroked out to the bubble plume. He encouraged Rosie to join him. As the dog paddled above the source, she circled him. Ryan chatted to her and playfully splashed her face. She yipped and huffed as she inadvertently breathed in a little water. After a few minutes they returned to the deck. If it was warm enough, Ryan would simply drip-dry outside and refrain from having a shower till later in the day. Rosie always just shook off the excess, starting with a slow wiggle of the nose that amplified to a full-body shake. Since following this routine, Ryan felt serene and fit. His fifty-something bones had never felt better, and his mind was clear and energy levels excellent. He had also added the dip in the lake to his routine when he returned from a row in the single scull on the lake.

He reflected upon his own attitude and how it had evolved since the first weeks at the cabin. He was in a much better place. Of course, the cabin itself hadn't changed, and he needed to return to the family home for more clothes and supplies, but he felt positive about living at the lake and saw it as a long-term solution. The situation wasn't perfect, and there were challenges to sort out, but it was a special place that he needed to protect.

He awoke the next day with a nagging thought, one he hadn't been conscious of: he needed to talk to Laura. He felt no compunction to return to a relationship, but he did want to check on her to see how she was making out after her struggles. And to put the incident at the hospital behind them. Though this was overdue, he would also be responding to his daughter's request to make sure he checked in with her mother in some meaningful way. As far as he knew, Emily still hadn't informed Laura of their concerns about Phil, and he wanted to leave that up to her.

He thought a two-stage approach would be best; he would text Laura first, asking if she was free for a call. He picked up his phone and, after some mulling and false starts, composed a terse text that fit the bill; he sent it off into the ether.

A couple of hours passed before her response made its way to the text string. Perhaps she'd needed time to think about her return message, or perhaps she was busy. Laura conceded to a call later in the afternoon. Ryan responded quickly, saying he would call around four. In the interim he opened his laptop and did some real work for neglected clients.

* * *

"Thought I should check in, see how you're doing." Ryan sounded a little sheepish; probably he was considering how much time had elapsed.

"So soon?" Laura was sarcastic. "I thought you forgot about me."

"I didn't forget about you," he said matter-of-factly, as if he were a scolded boy.

Incredulous, she went straight to the point. "So you bought Walter's cabin?"

"Yes, yes, I bought Walter's cabin," he admitted.

"I hope it's just your name on the loan."

"Yes, yes, it's just me. I wouldn't do that to you."

"Hmph. I'm not so sure. You've been such an ass."

"Wow, this is gonna go well. I really just wanted to reach out to see if you were okay."

"Oh, bullshit—you always have some other motive. You just want to see if I'm drinking again. I wasn't drinking that day at the school, you know. Did you know that? I wasn't drinking." Laura was indignant.

"Well, you were sure drinking at the house. You were drinking—that's all that matters."

"You never took the time to give a shit. You just jumped to a conclusion—"

"Listen, I don't want to argue about this." Ryan tried to be the calm one, a bit of a stretch for him. "I really just wanted to . . . whatever . . . acknowledge your condition."

"What the hell does that mean? My 'condition' is my business, not yours."

"Okay, fine. I'm wrong, as usual."

"Are you still seeing your little girlfriend?" Laura poked him again.

"She is *not* my girlfriend. She's a friend's daughter. That's it. She's just a kid. A real sick kid." Ryan was frustrated at having to explain his actions. He tried to turn the tables. "What about your principal friend. Are you still seeing him?"

"That's none of your effing business either! You can go to hell." A slight pause followed.

Ryan was the first to speak. "So do you feel better, now that you've told me off?"

"A little, actually."

"You've gotten it out of your system?"

"Hardly. What you did will never get out of my system."

"What I did? What did I do? I did what I warned you a dozen times that I'd do. I said I'd be gone if you fell off the wagon again. So I was. You're the one who screwed up."

"You left when I needed you most. That's what you did. It's unforgivable."

"What's unforgivable is your dysfunctional personality! Every time the chips are down, you hit the bottle."

"Fuck you!" Laura hit the red button on the screen and tossed her phone onto the kitchen table. The urge to drink swelled up like a demon inside her. She absolutely *craved* a drink after that exchange. Damn Ryan. That fuckin' Ryan. She went over to the kitchen cupboard where she kept her stash; it had been cleaned out. She slammed the cupboard door and cursed herself for even thinking about it. She instantly regressed again and went to the garage, where she sometimes had backup. No luck. Her friends had been thorough.

She returned to the kitchen and heard her phone's ring tone. She looked at the screen. It was Ryan calling back. It went to voice mail before she could decide whether she wanted to take it or not. The screen faded; he didn't leave a message. She thought for a few seconds, staring at the phone. He must actually be feeling bad. It was possible. And maybe it would be best if she talked through this sudden urge to fall back. Or maybe she should reach out to a coun-sellor at the hospital? She hit the call-back button.

"What?" she simply said.

"What do you mean, *what*?" Ryan was trying to figure this out. "Don't do anything stupid. Listen, I'm sorry to upset you, okay? That wasn't my intention. Please, I know you—just take a beat. I'm genu-inely concerned about my ex-wife."

"Ex-wife? That has a nice ring to it. You're such a prick."

"Okay, I'm sorry—that came out wrong."

"I think it came out right, because that's the way it is. That's it, over. Finis. Nearly thirty years down the drain."

"They *aren't* down the drain."

"Well, where are they, then? They're down the friggin' drain. Fuck all to show for it." Laura was starting to wallow in self-pity, her usual MO.

"Listen, stop it," Ryan said. "You've got a lot to look forward to. I know your diagnosis was probably a shocker, but at least you know what your problem is now. It's something you can work with."

"How the hell do you know? You haven't a clue. 'Work with.' Bah!" The conversation stalled.

"At some point I need to come over and get a few things," Ryan finally said.

"Like what? You've got everything you're entitled to. The clothes on your back."

"Come on—I do need a few things. Some more clothes, winter stuff, my fishing gear, my passport, just some basics."

"Okay, I guess. When?"

"Not sure. Tomorrow or the next day. I'm busy with some work I need to get through." It sounded as if he was stretching the truth. "I'll let you know."

"Whatever . . . Bye."

* * *

Ryan put down the phone and looked at the blank screen. Although the conversation had been stressful, he did feel better about making contact and setting up a return to the house to get some supplies. He went to a drawer and pulled out a notepad and jotted down the items he needed. Best to have a list; he would add to it over the next day or so. He also wanted to check in with Emily about when she should chat with her mother about Phil's checkered past. He called her and she was embarrassed she hadn't done it yet.

"This is a little awkward, Dad. But it's important, I know. I'll get it done today. Today or tomorrow."

* * *

Emily called her mother on the pretext of asking her if she could do some shopping for her. After that she carefully broached the subject of Phil's sketchy past.

"Mum, you know I want you to be happy—whatever that looks like now."

"Sure. I want you to be happy too."

"Whether it's with Phil, or Dad, whoever. Or whatever. Just so you know, I guess I wish you and Dad *could* get back together, but if that can't happen, I'm still behind you one hundred percent on whatever partner or path you choose."

"Okay, Em. Thank you—that's great."

"And I want you to be safe. Happy and safe."
"Okay. What's this about?"

"So Mum, I have some information. I basically stumbled across it. It's old and maybe totally irrelevant now. However, it's something I want you to be aware of, okay?"

"Okay, okay. Just tell me. What's this about?"

"It's about Phil, Mum. Just some information that was in the news a long time ago, when he was in the military. Stuff I think you should know about. Maybe you already do? It may be nothing. You've gotten to know him, and he's been forthcoming, right?"

"Absolutely. He's told me a lot. Some gaps maybe." Laura had a nagging concern about why Phil never was in contact with his daughters, and he rarely if ever referred to them.

"Okay, so it's probably best if I just email you a couple of articles, links to websites, and you read them and make up your own mind. Does that work?"

"Sure, whatever. Send me over what you're so concerned about. I'll take a look."

* * *

Laura was concerned enough about what she read that she confronted Phil the next day. She said he needed to give her more information on his time in the military.

"So why are asking me this? How did you find out about this?" Phil stared intently at her.

Laura scrambled to react. "Um . . . I was just looking to friend you on social media. We haven't done that. I checked you out on Facebook, business sites, and teacher sites. Then I went a little deeper and googled your name. Some old articles came up—details about your military service."

"Phil Conner is a very common name, you know. I bet there are hundreds of Phil Conners and Phillip Conners, or Conner—people with the same and similar spellings—on those sites."

"For sure. That's why I'm asking. You said you were in the military for a while, didn't you? You said that."

Phil sighed, clearly regretting the comment. He fidgeted and scratched the back of his head intensely in frustration. "Yes, I said that. I was in the army. I was very young. I entered when I was basically right out of high school."

"What I read was that you had a dishonourable discharge. Is that right?"

"No, that's not right." He wiped his hands roughly over his mouth, pinching his bottom lip.

"Then the story is about some other Phil Conner? Or is it false somehow?"

"What story? What's this story you're talking about?"

Laura circled back to her first question. She felt like a lawyer, but wanted the facts. "Did you or did you not get a dishonourable discharge?"

"No. That's not what they call it. That's an American term."

"What do they call it, then?"

"Just 'dismissed.'"

"That's it? Like you quit or were fired? That's not how I read it."

"Read what? Okay, for Chrissakes, it's called 'dismissed for misconduct.'" He raised his hands briefly in an *I give up* posture.

"Dismissed for misconduct? And then you were court martialled."

"Absolutely not. No way. I was never court martialled. That was dropped. I just got the dismissal. It was like a plea deal. I'm sure you're going to google that. For God's sake, I was just a kid. There was a bunch of us. It was called 'dismissed with disgrace for misconduct.' There. Are you happy? That's it." Phil looked down at the floor and shook his head.

"Wow. Yeah, that sounds way better than 'dishonourable discharge,'" Laura said sarcastically. "They said some female soldiers were hurt. Is that true?"

"For God's sake, I was just a kid. Had been in the military two or three years. Back then—not so much now—we had initiation parties. It was quite common. Nobody really got hurt. It was just a bit of fun, a way to *improve* morale. I was initiated when I first joined up. We did it to new recruits, and it's been going on since the beginning of time. Seriously. I just had the misfortune of being in a group that was singled out. Bad luck, really. I was never charged. *We* were never charged."

"You mean it was like a hazing ritual?"

"Yes, exactly— a hazing ritual. Like in college or on a sports team. A bit of fun with the newbies. Horseplay. A tickle party. That's all. The military wanted to clamp down on it, so they made an example of us."

"But there were girls involved."

"So what? There *are* female new recruits, you know. It was a joke we played on all new recruits. Everybody got the treatment."

"So what was 'the treatment'?"

"It's actually something that's supposed to be a secret tradition within the regiment. Really. You don't ask the Masons or the Shriners or the frickin' Kinsmen about their indoctrination customs, do you? They have them, you know! It's very much a part of their tradition. To this day, anybody who's gone through it doesn't talk about it."

"The article says that this particular time was more hurtful and went too far—it was sadistic, even. A hazing ritual for male recruits might be inappropriate for a woman to go through."

"Ugh. Laura, come on. Please—this is ancient history. I was a kid. Yeah, I suppose hazing could get a little weird. But we didn't make it up. We might have embellished it a little. It's been passed on for generations. The brass tolerated it, encouraged it by letting it go on. Eventually, it was deemed politically incorrect—or whatever you call it—and they cracked down. They happened to choose our regiment to pull the pin on it. It was the fault of timing, pressure from the media, and a few recruits."

"But you were a ringleader then. They must have warned you to stop it *before* they clamped down. You disobeyed the order, did the hazing anyway. Which was even harder on the girls. They wouldn't dismiss everyone—only a couple of you."

"Listen!" Phil raised his voice. "I was never charged with anything!" He slapped his hand down flat on the table. Laura was getting under his skin. "All the assault allegations were dropped. No charges whatsoever, to me or anyone else. Just the dismissal. And damn it, when I got out of the military, I worked hard to put it behind me. I got a job, and I put myself through university and got my degree. Started a career. A st-stupid st-stint in the army a thousand years ago does *not* define me. We are d-done with this conversation!"

Laura stopped pushing the subject. Phil was getting agitated, and his body language was getting erratic; he was scratching the back of his arms and kicking the chair leg. She had never heard him stutter before. Maybe he really *was* a victim of circumstance but bringing up this part of his past certainly aggravated him. But the fact that he had encouraged, organized, and participated in a demeaning humiliation ceremony was cause for concern. And did he say tickle party?

Chapter 22

R yan emailed Owny and congratulated her on mobilizing the construction crew on the cabin road. He offered to expand the website to include new pictures of this activity. He sent it off and relaxed with a cup of herbal tea.

After about an hour his phone went off. "Hi, Ryan." Owny sounded relaxed.

"Hi, Owny. You got my email?"

"Yes, thank you. Please, if you don't mind, add to the site whatever pictures you think best. I'd really like to show the development in full swing. I also wanted to tell you we've gone into a partnership with Island Realtors. They're going to promote the properties, like on MLS or whatever they do. They'll give us the expertise we need to make transactions—you know, look professional. And they'll hire two of our people to man a trailer we'll put out there to handle on-site visits. They'll train them and get them up to speed. Island will create some marketing collateral . . . They'd like to know if they can use some of your pictures."

"Yes, no problem. If they want, I can email them directly, so they don't have to grab them off the site. Better resolution. I'll get out there and take some more images that show the work."

"Great. Thank you. I'll email you a vCard for the contact at Island Realtors. I'll give them a call and let them know we've had a chat. Thanks again, Ryan. You've been a real big help to me. We need to talk about how to pay you for your services."

* * *

The next morning, Ryan set out to take some photos of the construction. He left Rosie in the cabin, as he didn't want her running around with the large moving equipment in the vicinity. As he approached the end of the road, he saw it was a hive of activity. The office trailer was set up and the Porta Potties were placed next to it. Trees were down a couple of hundred meters beyond the road's end, and a skidder was dragging the logs out to a landing that the bulldozer had created. Ryan could see clearly how the road was being carved out of the dense forest. Survey stakes were placed at regular intervals beyond the last cabin. These new lots appeared wider than those of the first phase. That made sense: they had the space, and a larger footprint would command higher prices.

Ryan came to the realization that this project involved greater effort than he'd first imagined. Just creating a road in this environment was a monumental task. He found some high ground on the edge of the cleared land and took some photos with his phone. It looked like a bomb had gone off. As he walked back up the road, he took pictures of the overall site. It was certainly a going concern. Turning up his cabin road access, he emailed the pictures to himself so he could work with them on his computer.

Once back at the cabin, he cropped and enhanced the raw images. He organized them in a file and posted a few to the band website. He received the contact information for Island Realtors and decided to give them a call. As he had to go into town the next day anyway, he offered to meet them in person and have a chat. They cheerfully accepted.

Ryan was up early the next morning and set out to town with Rosie before any construction workers arrived. Once he hit the main highway, he was reminded of why he hated the commute into Victoria at peak times. The traffic was dense, so he pulled off and hit a Starbucks for some strong coffee to make the trip a little more pleasurable. Once into town he stopped at work for a meeting about upcoming software upgrades, and then on to Island Realtors. He met with the owner, Martin Pembrooke, who was excited about the proposition. Ryan showed him the recent photos, and he was shocked to see such progress early on. Ryan got the feeling Martin had initially been skeptical that much was happening with the project. This progress was a positive sign for the real estate firm and having Ryan as their resident information source was a good turn of events.

Ryan emailed key photos and the drone footage to Martin while in their office. He finished up with Island Realtors and headed back home.

As he rounded the turn near the old indian springs sign, Ryan was aghast to see a glut of vehicles and people blocking the road. "What now?" Rosie thought he was talking to her and sat up and peered over the back seat, first at Ryan, then out the windshield at the commotion.

There were construction pickup trucks, service trucks, a large gas tanker, cars, and SUVs. He pulled over to the side at the end of the string of vehicles and got out. He made his way to the front of the traffic jam, looking for a clue to the cause of the disruption. At the front were two wooden traffic barricades and several people standing defiantly behind them. One person was in front of the line; he was directing traffic, keeping people and vehicles in the right lane. Ryan counted six men blocking access, all with bandanas over their faces. He was sure he could pick out Ronny Two Livers and Chester Wilson. Ronny's braids were a dead giveaway. Two of the disguised men held rifles, and two others held dark makeshift flags that Ryan didn't recognize. Ronny was yelling about putting a stop to the exploitation of "their land."

Ryan scanned the situation and shook his head in frustration. One of the militants standing back a bit from the rest seemed less engaged and had a slight build. They wore a snapback ball cap pulled down low, sunglasses, a black bandana, an oversized checkered red jacket, and dirty jeans. He paused, thinking he also knew this person—the way they stood, the way they held their arms.

"Oh my God," Ryan said under his breath. He'd put his finger on it—it was Meaghan. Had to be. Somehow the tense situation had just became even more complicated.

Ryan pushed his way to the very front and yelled over Ronny, "Hey, assholes! I live here. I have every right to access my own property!"

Ronny stopped yelling and looked at Ryan defiantly. "This is our land. You're not welcome here. Nobody's gettin' through here today!"

Ryan scanned the group members one by one, and his gaze stopped on Meaghan. He pulled out his cell phone and snapped a photo of the group behind the barriers. He tapped the screen and sent it directly to Owny with no text. Then he took a few more photos, focusing on the firearms. He dialed Owny to follow up.

"I know, I know!" Owny didn't say hello but simply blew up. "I know, I know! I'm on my way. I'm coming with Corky! I'm just waiting for him." She hung up without a goodbye.

Ryan decided to retreat from the front line to avoid any further escalation with Ronny or anyone else. This was not an information picket line he could walk through or drive around; this was something more serious. The dormant pang of "What did I get myself into?" reared its ugly head again. He went back to his SUV and rolled down the windows to give Rosie some air, then reclined the driver's seat a little and waited for the cavalry to arrive.

Chapter 23

Within a few minutes Ryan saw Constable Corky Smoke's white police SUV appear in his rear-view mirror. He was approaching rapidly with lights ablaze and dust billowing up from behind. As the vehicle slowed down and passed where Ryan had pulled over, he saw Owny in the passenger seat. She was looking intently at the cluster of people and vehicles. Corky made the siren chirp, signifying to onlookers he was moving around them and onto the left side of the road, which had access all the way up to the barricade. He pulled in as close as he could to the masked group, perhaps trying to get in their face. Stopping slightly askew, he turned to the centre of the road. Leaving his lights on, Corky exited the vehicle briskly, putting on his hat, securing his side arm, and inserting a baton into his belt. Owny emerged looking grim as she assessed the situation. They joined each other at the barricade and stopped and said nothing to the insurgents behind the symbolic line. The opponents stared each other down briefly.

Ryan made his way back up the parade of vehicles. He stood back and to the side of the group. Sensing the impending drama, he started filming the scene with his phone. Ryan knew it would come to this. This is what they wanted.

He thought Ronny Two Livers must have practised his speech. "We are warriors!" he proclaimed, as if to everyone, but he was really yelling at Owny and Corky. The group behind him cheered, raising their rifles and pumping the flags up and down. Owny didn't respond, and Ronny continued. "We are warriors defending our land!" Again, the dark group cheered, while the onlookers were mute and motionless. "We're here to stop the desecration of our ancestral land! We stand united for eternity to defend the rights of our people!"

Owny was fuming and finally found her voice. "What you're doing is illegal!"

Corky put his hands on his belt and sidled a step closer to the Chief. Owny continued. "This project was voted on and approved by the band council! It is sanctioned and permitted by the federal and provincial governments! This is the will of our people! You had your chance to—"

"This is not the will of our people!" Ronny shouted. "Our people want to preserve our way of life, not prostitute our future!"

"Do you have a permit for a demonstration?" Corky entered the debate, knowing the answer to the question.

"We don't need no stinking permit on our own land! This is our nation. This is our home! We don't need permission to do things in our own nation!"

Corky put his hand to his radio microphone perched near his left shoulder. Backup would be a good idea.

"This is sacred land! This is a sacred lake! This is our land! These are our waters! Our ancestors have lived here in harmony with nature for thousands of years!" More cheers came from behind.

"You could have participated in the public hearing! Many people did, and their concerns were all addressed." Owny was becoming flushed. "You troublemakers are in the minority! You're bad actors, acting outside of the law! You need to stop this right now!"

"We're only just beginning, you stupid woman!"

"You're feeding the wrong dog, you people. This is the dark side of the world you live in. Don't use violence and fear. It's misguided—"

Just then a piece of machinery roared to life behind the insurgent group. It surprised all the onlookers, including Owny and Corky. It clanked into gear and lurched forward. As it did, the group of six picked up the wooden barricades and pushed back the crowd. Corky got in front of Owny and tried to push back, but he was outnumbered; none of the onlookers were willing to step in. The insurgents advanced aggressively in one fluid motion, and two dozen people backed away quickly, many turning and running. The left barricade turned in sharply; as they moved forward, they worked it around the police SUV and pushed past it, as far as they could until they got to the first construction truck at the front of the line of vehicles. As he was pushed back, Corky was cursing, fumbling for his baton and his microphone at the same time. The six established a new line about thirty feet beyond the first, entrapping the police cruiser.

The big yellow machine that roared behind them was a skidder, with a blade like a bulldozer. It slammed hard into the police vehicle and attempted to lift it, but could only hoist the driver's side about three feet. It tried to tip the vehicle sideways, attempting to get underneath it, and when it couldn't lift the thing any farther, it stopped. One armed insurgent remained at the new line, and the rest ran to the RCMP cruiser and positioned themselves on either side of the skidder blade. They heaved hard and tipped the vehicle all the way so that it wobbled onto the passenger side, disabled like discarded toy at Christmas. The lights remained on, cockeyed and impotent. The police vehicle was now blocking half the road. The skidder backed up and moved beside it to completely block the right lane. The driver of the skidder, a seventh insurgent, shut it down and jumped out, joining the rest of his group.

"Shit!" Corky yelled, mostly to himself. He looked inconsolable. Bystanders surrounded him but stood back, giving him space. Shaking his head, he had his hands on his knees. He had lost his hat in the shoving match. An insurgent tossed the lost cap over the barricade toward the disgruntled cop. Constable Smoke didn't look to see where it came from; he just stooped down and picked it up. "Goddammit! Shit!" The disguised squad had clearly outsmarted him, setting Corky up all the way. They had positioned the construction vehicles and individuals, giving a clear path to the barricade for the cop car. They had the drop on the policeman, seemingly as usual. Reluctantly, Corky clicked his microphone button and called for backup, talking in code numbers. The bewildered crowd knew he would be in trouble from his superiors for this.

About twenty minutes later two police cruisers rushed in with lights on and sirens blaring. Five minutes later two more showed up. At first, they engaged Corky openly, then retreated to their vehicles. Corky sat in the back seat like criminal. In the meantime, the demonstrators produced a few lawn chairs and looked satisfied and relaxed, yet defiant, by their impermeable roadblock. Several construction vehicles backed out and left, their drivers knowing the conflict wasn't going to be resolved anytime soon. Others remained to see what would happen next.

Ryan returned to his vehicle, needing to regroup. He turned and looked at Rosie. At least she was with him. If he hadn't brought her, she would be stuck alone on the other side of the roadblock. He drummed his fingers on the steering wheel. His options were limited. Call Laura and ask for a room? Call Walter? Ask Owny? Get a hotel room? His daughter had no room for him, as she was in a shared dorm. How long was this going to go on? He opted to call Walter; after all, he had got him into this mess. No answer. He left a voice mail asking him to call him back as soon as possible.

It made some sort of sense to call Laura—the house was still half his, after all, and Rosie needed accommodation. He dialed his estranged wife. It rang so long he thought it would go to voice mail.

She finally answered. "Hello, Ryan," she said flatly.

"Hi. Um . . . I have a bit of a situation here. I can't get into the cabin because there's a demonstration, a roadblock. I can't get in. I have Rosie with me, and I was hoping I could stay at the house. I could take one of the spare rooms."

"Just a minute." The phone made a crackling sound and then went silent; he was on mute. After about thirty seconds, she returned. "This is not a good time."

Ryan blew through his lips in frustration. "I wouldn't ask if it wasn't a real problem. I'm in a jam. Rosie needs . . . I mean, I probably can't get a hotel room with the dog, and Walter isn't answering. I can't get into my place!"

"Sucks to be you." Laura sounded empowered. Sassy. She never would have reacted like that before.

"Oh, come on! I still have some sort of claim on the house. I have some rights here."

"Don't think so. Possession is nine-tenths of the law. You gave up your rights when you walked out the door." Ryan heard someone in the background who seemed to be coaching her. "You got yourself into this—you need to get yourself out. You can't come running home to Mama every time you skin your knee. Bye." She hung up.

"Goddamn it!" Ryan threw his phone onto the passenger seat. "Now what?" Rosie cocked her head and raised her eyebrow.

Ryan looked up and saw Owny walking alone, away from the centre of the conflict. She was talking on her cell phone and moving her free hand vigorously. She didn't seem to notice him or his vehicle. He rolled down the window the rest of the way and called to her. "You look like you lost your ride!"

Owny looked up, recognized him, and shrugged as if to say, "You think?"

"Hop in. I'll take you over."

She held up her index finger to say, "Just a sec." Owny spoke into the phone for a few more seconds, poked it to hang up, and then said, "I have to talk to the cops. I'll just be a couple of minutes. But yes, if you don't mind, give me ride to New Town. We need to have an emergency council meeting."

"You bet. I'll turn around and wait for you."

After a few minutes, Owny pulled the door handle on the passenger side. It was locked by mistake. Ryan fumbled with the button in his armrest and Owny got in. "What a shemozzle." She sounded amazingly calm. If Oneida Wilson had considered Ryan's being temporarily homeless, she didn't acknowledge it.

Ryan put the car in gear and headed over to New Town. Where was he going to go after he dropped her off? What about the dog? After a few minutes, he asked, "Has this happened before?"

"Well, yeah, it has. Not like this, though—not with the guns and the cop car turned over. Not like this."

"What are the cops going to do? Will this be over today, do you think?"

"The cops want us to settle this ourselves. I think we can, but it won't happen today. Maybe not tomorrow. I know those guys. I know who they are—mostly, anyway. There might be a couple of out-of-towners. They seem very sure of themselves right now, but give it some time and they'll change their tune."

"What makes you so sure?"

"I'm not that sure, actually—I'm just being a little optimistic, I guess. They're being very militant, but honestly, I think they have a short attention span."

"Well, that sounds a little better than what I was thinking. Right now I'm kind of stuck. I can't get to my cabin, and I don't have many options."

"Hmm . . . I guess you're right." Owny gazed out the window at the passing trees. A few moments passed. "So, it's not a great idea, but it's an idea. There's an old wooden rowboat at the dock. It's sort of community property. It's old and heavy, but it will get you across the lake if you want to go at it that way. You could park safely in New Town, row across to your cabin."

Ryan perked up at the idea. He was a good rower, after all, and he could bring the dog. "What do you think the guys at the road-block will be doing? Will they go door to door checking out the cabins? Will it be safe? Will they see me crossing the lake?"

"You know, Ryan, I'm not sure. Like I said, it isn't a great idea. Just an idea. Those guys are badass and they look intimidating, but if history is any guide, their bark is worse than their bite."

"They have guns. That's a big deal. You said they've never used guns before. They're serious this time."

"Maybe I shouldn't have mentioned the idea."

"If it were you, would you feel safe at the cabin?"

"Um . . . yes, I think I would. But I'm not you. You're seven cabins in. They'll be preoccupied with watching the roadblock."

"I think one of them is Meaghan."

"What?" Owny seemed surprised.

"I think one of the roadblock guys is actually Meaghan. Pretty sure."

"Meaghan from cabin . . . cabin four, is it?"

"Yup. They're in cahoots somehow. Not sure of the connection. I saw Ronny leave there the other day. Maybe drugs. Maybe other stuff."

Owny started to connect the dots. "So they might be using that cabin as a base. That will give them some staying power. They've probably stocked up. I thought they'd get tired of being outside pretty quickly. I guess they're more organized than I thought. I dunno, Ryan. Maybe staying at your cabin isn't such a great idea."

"Let's take a look at the boat. Let me think about this."

"I'm gonna have to tell the cops about the cabin. And Meaghan, I mean. You sure it's her?"

"Ninety-nine percent. Took me a minute to put my finger on it, but she backed away when I went to the barricade. It's her."

"You went to the barricade?"

"Well, yeah, when I first arrived, to see what was going on. I sent you the pictures."

"Oh yes, of course. Did you say anything to them?"

"You know me. I called them a bunch of assholes, I think."

* * *

Ryan opted for the rowboat. It was as Owny had described it: old, wooden, and heavy. He had to bail it out before the twenty-minute crossing. Rosie tried to avoid the water in the bottom of the boat by standing in the bow, and seemed to be gauging the distance to her home.

All was quiet when Ryan arrived. He tied the boat securely to his dock, quietly made his way to the cabin, and crashed on the couch, fatigued from the day.

The next morning Ryan called Owny to let her know he had crossed without incident, and that there had been no trouble at his cabin overnight. She was glad to hear from him, but she was preoccupied with something. Patsy. She wasn't doing well at all. Could Ryan take her in the rowboat to the bubbles? Maybe that evening?

Chapter 24

Ryan looked up from watching Patsy shiver in the dark water to see a familiar figure standing in the trees between the properties. He did a double take and looked again. His eyes widened. It was standing quietly in the impending gloom. His heart sank and a tremor went through him. Could he trust his eyes in this dim light? Yes, it was him. Damn it. The psychopomp himself. Stoneblanket. The harbinger of death, staring at them. Who was he here for? Patsy? Himself?

"Out of the water!" he said sharply to Patsy.

"What? Mum said I needed to stay—"

"Out of the water right now!" he yanked sharply on the yellow rope and pulled her toward him hand over hand. Keeping the figure in his peripheral vision, he rushed Patsy out of the water, pulling off the life ring roughly and tossing it onto the dock. "Get in the boat!"

Patsy was bewildered. "Did you see some guys from the road-block? Are they coming here?"

"Something like that. In the boat." The dog started to bark. "Rosie! Come! Get in the boat!" Ryan said sharply to the dog. Standing on the dock near the shore, she was hesitant to obey. "Come!" he yelled. Rosie complied grudgingly.

Patsy sat down at the stern of the rowboat, shivering. Ryan hastily untied the ungainly craft and jumped in. He pushed it away from the dock and fumbled with getting the oars in the water. Once in position, he pulled on them with several mighty heaves and felt his back crack as if he was under the knee of a sadistic chiropractor. This created some momentum and the heavy boat pulled away from the shore.

All the while, Ryan closely monitored the figure, staring over Patsy's shoulder as he rowed. Stoneblanket turned and lurched down the shoreline. He passed cabins six and five. He stopped at Meaghan's cabin, cabin four, looked back at the escaping boat, then turned his attention to the cabin; he raised his arms.

Rosie took notice and steadied herself on her four paws, feeling the movement of the boat. She glowered at the beach and began a deliberate, steady bark. Like cold smoke, a mist came up on the lake. The rowboat slowed on the still water as Ryan stopped rowing. It pivoted, drifting parallel to the beach.

Patsy was mystified. "What's going on?" She looked to where Ryan was gazing intently. "What . . .?" Patsy's eyes widened. "Is that Stoneblanket?"

"Yes," Ryan said quietly. He put his finger to his lips to shush her.

They all stared across the water at the one-legged spectre. In the silence they could hear Stoneblanket. Now ignoring his audience, he was chanting. Ryan sensed they were spectators of some sort of ritual. An aura emanated from his body. He must have just come out of the water. *He does like to take a dip every now and then,* Ryan thought. Stoneblanket's chant increased in intensity. At first, it looked as if he was staggering around. Then Ryan realized it was a dance of sorts. His wooden leg hampered his movements, causing him to lurch from side to side in the soft sand. He twisted his shoulders and stretched his neck. After a few moments, Stoneblanket turned and made his way to the base of the stairs to cabin four. He pulled his way up the stairs and across the deck, and the aura entered the house without the door being opened.

The northern lights started up in the cabin. It was the shitshow Ryan had seen when he pushed to get Meaghan into the lake. Intense beams of energy emanated from every orifice of the building. It was as if a weather system was developing from the inside, bringing a swirl of wind and pressure. The siding shuddered, the screen door banged, the windows rattled, and the light was too bright to look at directly. It broke through the mist like a million-watt light bulb flailing at the end of a wire. Ryan, Patsy, and Rosie stared silently, Ryan shielding his eyes with his hand. They sat in the old boat gazing at the spectacle as if it was a fireworks show for their eyes only. Evidently, Stoneblanket hadn't come for Patsy. Or him.

The light show stopped suddenly, leaving a strange silence that echoed in their ears. Spots danced before their eyes. A cold darkness made Ryan's entire body shiver. The mist seeped into his clothes and into his pores; he felt damp to the bone. An intense sense of melancholy blackened his heart. Rosie seemed to feel it too; she shook, rocking the boat, and turned to look at her master. If Ryan was cold, Patsy was much colder. She shuddered and rubbed the backs of her arms.

"Okay, let's get you home!" Ryan took off his jacket and put it over Patsy's shoulders. He pulled as hard as he could on the oars to create some momentum.

"What was that all about?" Patsy was clearly shaken at what they had just witnessed.

"Damned if I know. Let's get you home."

* * *

Ryan walked Patsy to her house. Only Aster was home to greet them. Returning to the dock, Ryan somehow knew he could safely return to his cabin—St. Peter wasn't calling for him. He and

Rosie climbed in, and he got to work rowing back across the lake. He beached the craft rather than tying it to the dock. After tugging the heavy thing a few more feet up the beach to ensure a wave wouldn't set it adrift, he and Rosie went up the stairs and he unlocked the door. He switched on the lights and looked around the room, trying to process the last hour. He turned to Rosie as if to say, "That really just happened, right?" Now what? What had happened over at cabin four? He could guess.

Ryan grabbed his flashlight from under the sink; he flicked it on to test it. "You stay here," he said to the dog. He exited the cabin, ensuring the door was securely latched. The flashlight lit the way past the sign tree to the foot of Meaghan's cabin. He waved the light over the sand, trying to spot the unique impressions of the one-legged visitor, but he could see no sign of a footprint with a stick print beside it. Stopping the search, he looked up at the door. He felt that deep melancholy again; it made it hard to climb the stairs. He shone the flashlight in the kitchen window and could see nothing remarkable. He shifted to the living room window and moved the light through the room. He stopped on a body that was slumped on the couch. It was an insurgent. The man's hat and coat and bandana were off, and it looked like Chester. He wasn't moving. Ryan scanned the coffee table; it was covered in Mason jars and glasses and drug paraphernalia. He moved to change his vantage point and shot the light into the main bedroom. He could see some legs on the bed, clad in skinny jeans, again not moving. His flashlight trained on Chester, he banged on the window. No movement. He tried again, checking the bedroom, then went back to Chester. Nothing. He went to the front door and tried the knob. It was locked.

"Oh man," he exclaimed, knowing that what came next would be a shitshow of its own. He stepped back and placed the flashlight on the picnic table, shining it straight up. He dialed his phone and talked to Owny. He caught her just as she was leaving the band office.

"You sure they're dead? They could just be passed out, Ryan," she said, unconvinced things were that bad. "I mean, if you can't get into the cabin, how can you be totally sure?"

"Oh, I'm pretty sure. Very sure. I can't get in to check their pulses. But they just had a visit from Stoneblanket. You should have seen the light show. Wow!"

Owny grew serious. "You saw him? You're sure?"

"Sure I'm sure. We were starting to row back across the lake, Patsy and I, and we saw him. The cabin lit up like a frickin' Christmas tree. They're dead. Dead and gone."

"Patsy saw it too? She was there? Is she okay?" Owny intensified.

"She's fine. I got her home. I think she was pretty surprised at the whole thing, but she's safe."

"I need to get home. What do you want me to do? Do you want me to call Corky, or—"

"No, no, don't get involved just yet. I guess I need to do this. I'll call them and tell them what I've found. I guess I just call 911?"

"Whatever you do, they'll come in like storm troopers. They'll have to."

"Yeah, I guess you're right."

Chapter 25

"You handled that well!" Phil said. He wanted to moderate his relationship with Laura, to get on an even keel again. He had gathered the gist of her conversation with Ryan, even though it wasn't on speakerphone. The thought of Ryan returning to the house, even for a single night, didn't compute with him at all. The story sounded like an excuse.

"What did he say about a roadblock?" Phil asked.

"He said there was a protest or something at the lake where he's staying . . . I mean living." She shook her head. "Whatever. Some sort of blockade or picket line. Said he couldn't get to the cabin."

"Hmm. Sounds odd. He didn't mean the road was closed for construction? Or it was washed out or something?"

"No. He said a roadblock. Surely if it was closed for construction, it would still be open to local traffic. Especially in the evenings. And the weather's been good."

Phil went into the living room and searched for the remote control. He turned on the TV and sought out local news stations. "Nothing on the TV about it," he said after a cursory check of a few channels. He returned to the kitchen, where Laura was sipping some tea.

Phil felt uncomfortable. They had gone through a rocky patch, so he wanted clarity right away. "I know we're pretty new in this relationship, but you wouldn't consider having him back here under any circumstances, would you? After all, he left you high and dry."

"No, no, course not." She didn't sound terribly convincing. "But in theory he still has half the house, I s'pose. He did sound a little desperate. He does have the dog."

Phil pulled out his phone and searched local news sites for any mention of a protest or picket line.

Laura was thoughtful. "I do miss Rosie. She's such a card." She smiled. "I think I miss her more than Ryan!" As soon as she said it, she looked sheepish, knowing she had put her foot firmly in her mouth.

Phil couldn't believe his ears. "So you *do* miss him!" He was hurt.

"No, no! That came out all wrong! I was just thinking about the dog. I miss the *dog*. I miss Rosie. She was such a part of the . . . We had her for almost ten years, I think—I can't remember exactly. A long time. I think the cat misses her too. That's all."

"Didn't sound like that to me."

"Listen, Phil, please. Don't worry. It *is* hard to move on without a thought after almost thirty years with someone. You have to admit it's true. But you've helped me. You've been great. I told you that, and I mean it. He's not coming back here. That's it—that's what I told him. You heard me. I meant it."

Phil liked what he heard, but skepticism lurked in his heart. He continued to search for the roadblock story on his phone, but without success. "Where did you say the cabin is?"

"I didn't, I don't think. It's at Indian Springs. You know—it used to be called Charlene Lake, but they changed it some years ago. The real name is some convoluted Native word. Can't remember. I'd know it if I saw it, though."

"Whereabouts on the lake is it?"

"There's only one set of cabins on the lake, other than the Native village. It's across the lake from the village, as I recall. I've only been there a couple of times. It never really appealed to me. It was Walter Rosenthal's place. Wally sold it to him. He's our lawyer. *Was* our lawyer. He went to school with Ryan. Maybe he's Ryan's lawyer! I never thought of that. I should be looking into that, I guess."

Phil jumped on the concept. "Yes, you need to be thinking about a lawyer. The sooner, the better. You need to know what your rights are and get the ground rules straight for the separation phase—like what you do about the house, anything you own together, RRSPs, the whole nine yards. You'd have some sort of claim on his pension, I think." Phil had some experience with separation law based on personal experience.

"I think the reverse is more likely. He doesn't have much of a pension, so he could have a claim on mine, my teacher's pension. That's a wrinkle. Maybe he wouldn't pursue it."

"Don't count on it."

"I think we're getting a little ahead of ourselves."

"Not really!" Phil put his coaching hat on. "You need to plan for this. I know it's hard to think in these terms, but it's the reality now. The sooner you think of it as a business negotiation, the better. Try to keep the emotion out of it. Let the lawyer do the communicating." Phil knew he might be coming on too strong, but he couldn't help himself.

"I'm a teacher, not a businessperson. I'm not great at that stuff. That's why I became a teacher, not a banker." Laura seemed ambivalent.

Phil sensed the tension the conversation had created and scrambled to bring it down. "Hey, let's go out for dinner. Forget about this stuff. Wherever you want. What do you think?"

Chapter 26

As soon as the police heard reports of deaths on the other side of the roadblock, they stopped patiently waiting for an internal settlement. A dozen members of the force donned riot gear, complete with helmets, gas masks, and large Plexiglas shields. One policeman got on the bullhorn and announced that they were coming in. Of course, the insurgents thought they were bluffing and stood their ground—at least until the cops formed a solid line and a tear gas canister bounced sharply off the yellow skidder.

They marched forward, stomping their feet in unison, and hitting the fronts of their shields with their batons in a show of solidarity and intimidation. Snipers trained loaded assault rifles on the protesters who had guns. The masked squad members looked at each other, not knowing what to do next. One insurgent tried to call someone on his cell phone, and another bolted for the bush. Three cops dropped their shields and chased the escaping protester. Ronny started yelling rhetoric, making political statements to the very last.

One reporter was on hand and videoed the whole scene. A policewoman did the same. The protesters were likely to wind up in court, and a picture is worth a thousand words.

Police manhandled the remaining protesters, pushing them to the ground, knees on their backs, then handcuffing them. They pulled off their bandanas and hustled them into police cars. A tow truck appeared after a few minutes and went to work righting the tipped cruiser. The police wanted that thing upright and off the property as soon as possible. It was a black eye to the force.

As soon as the insurgents were down, two plainclothes officers picked their way through the melee and walked up the road, looking for cabin four.

Ryan had walked down to the entrance of his access road and turned down the main road toward the roadblock. To remain discreet, he lurked close to the bushes on the side of the road. He wanted to monitor the action from a safe distance but know when the police had pushed through. Tear gas wafted down the channel the road created in the dense trees. He heard Ronny babbling. A commotion erupted in the trees across the road and down a bit. Soon two figures emerged from the confusion. They were both shining flashlights, which picked up the mist and smoke. They were looking at each cabin road entrance, searching for a number. Ryan approached them near the entrance to cabin four.

"Hello!" he called out to them, holding his hand up to wave.

They stopped in surprise.

"I'm Ryan Hanson. I called 911!"

Their flashlight beams seemed to relax a bit, and one called, "Come forward!" They pointed their beams directly at him.

"They're up here—cabin four." Ryan pointed; the dark and rusty number, slowly being devoured by moss, was hardly noticeable on the trunk of a tree. He considered asking them for ID but decided not to; only a police officer would be able to walk through the ongoing chaos down the road.

"Okay, lead on," the other one said, pointing his flashlight up the lane. They took the brief walk in silence. Their flashlights lit the back of the cabin, and then they could smell the beach and hear the water.

As they mounted the stairs, one of the detectives spoke. "So how did you find them? Why did you come over here?"

"Just heard a commotion. I live in cabin seven, down the beach from here." He pointed into the blackness. I had second thoughts about coming over, with the protest and all, and didn't do it right away."

"What kind of commotion?"

"Well . . . it was . . . "

Ryan's hesitation instinctively raised doubts. "Well, what was it?" the cop said.

"Sounded like an argument or something." Ryan didn't even consider telling the truth; it would be harder to believe than a thin story. "I heard some loud voices. When it died down, I thought about it for a few minutes, then checked it out. I just looked through here." He directed the cops to illuminate the living room window with their flashlights. Chester was in the same position. They were surprised. "Also, through the doorway there . . . I think there's someone on the bed." They moved the light, and sure enough the denim-clad legs were still there.

One of the officers immediately banged on the window. "Hey! Hey!" he yelled, but Chester didn't move.

The other officer tried the door. It was locked. They glanced at each other, and one gave a brief nod. The detective who had tried the doorknob stood back and gave the lock a solid kick. The door hardly budged. He gave it another, and another. Success came on the fourth attempt. He rushed in and went straight to Chester, touching his throat for a pulse. Nothing.

"You stay outside!" he yelled at Ryan. He went into the bedroom and turned on the light, then came out in a few seconds. "They're dead, all right."

"Is it a girl in there?" Ryan asked.

The detective didn't respond. He looked around the living room briefly, talked into his cell phone, then came back out onto the deck. He spoke to the second officer. "Get back down to the end of the lane to direct the forensics team once they can get through. I'll stay here with our friend."

The cop bounded down the stairs and around the cabin and down the lane.

"Turn around," the remaining detective said to Ryan. "Put your hands behind your back."

"What are you talking about?" Ryan was perplexed.

"Just do as I say." The detective produced some handcuffs and flicked them open, but Ryan didn't respond. "Just turn around!" he shouted.

"This is bullshit!"

"Better yet, come over here. Get over here!" He dragged Ryan by the arm to the picnic table on the deck. "Sit down. Sit down! Straddle the leg." The cop put the handcuffs on one wrist, then got down on one knee and pulled Ryan's other arm under the table. He placed the other handcuff on the other wrist. Ryan was bent down and handcuffed around a picnic table leg.

"I've done nothing wrong! I just found them and called you guys!"

"Just keep quiet. I'll get back to you in a minute."

"Jesus Christ," Ryan exclaimed, needing to lay his head on the cool table to take the strain off his back. He composed himself and lifted his head so he could watch the detective through the wide window.

Once back inside, the cop turned on the lights in every room. He looked closely at the disarray on the coffee table, then pulled some latex gloves out of his jacket pocket and snapped them on. He took out his phone and took about twenty photos from every angle. Then he carefully searched for Chester's wallet; he found it in his back pocket, opened it, and gave it a quick scan. Then he went into the bedroom for a few seconds and emerged again. He found Meaghan's purse in the bathroom. He opened it, looking for her ID. He placed Chester's and Meaghan's driver's licences on the kitchen table and took individual photos of them. His phone rang and he answered it, mumbling to the caller. They spoke briefly, and he looked out at Ryan as he talked. After completing the call, he crouched down in front of Chester and scrutinized his dead face. He rose and sighed. He turned to look out the open door, the door frame dangling askew from some determined nails.

The detective returned to the deck and looked at his captive. "You know these people." It was a statement, not a question.

"Yeah, I know them. I know who they are."

"There was an incident with the girl some time ago. She accused you of trying to kill her."

Ryan raised his head and shook it. "You fuckin' guys. I never tried to kill her. I tried to save her. I *did* save her!"

"I think you came over here to finish the job. You saw them here and you were jealous, so you killed them."

"Oh, come on! That's nuts! They were doing drugs or something! That's obvious! The door was locked."

"You could have been with them and locked the door behind you. You had a thing for her, didn't you? Statistics show that the person who claims they've discovered the victims is often the perpetrator."

"Oh God." Ryan paused, incredulous. He sensed he was on a slippery slope and sought to clarify his position. "Okay, so I knew them. It's a small place—everyone knows everyone else. I heard noises, I came over, I saw them here, I called for help. That's it!"

Flashing lights illuminated the trees at the side of the cabin. A black van and an ambulance nosed around to the front of the deck. The quiet cabin became engulfed in a flurry of activity as two EMTs pulled gurneys up the stairs and other police arrived and started a more formal processing of the scene. The cop left Ryan awkwardly confined the entire time. Eventually, the other detective returned and sat down at the picnic table across from him.

Ryan, his cheek back on the table, didn't lift his head. "Either arrest me or let me go. Either way, get these damn cuffs off me. You know what's happened here. It's pretty damn obvious. I had nothing to do with it. Let me go."

The cop sat in silence as if weighing the options. He got up and moved to the side of the table, kneeled down, reached under the table leg, and undid the handcuffs. Ryan sat up, then stood up, rubbing his neck and the small of his back. The cop called over a tech and they proceeded to take his fingerprints.

The cop was in his face. "You stay in town. Do not leave the province. Do not leave the island. Do you hear me?"

Ryan rolled his eyes and shook his head. He wanted to say something in retaliation but bit his tongue. "Yes, I hear you," he said, sensing his impending freedom. "I'm right there in cabin seven. That's where I live."

Chapter 27

The next morning, Ryan received a text from Laura. *Are you all right?*

He was surprised to see the question from his ex. *Yes, I'm okay. What's up?*

The roadblock, the deaths, they're on TV. Cops stormed the place. It made the national news.

Yeah, I know. I saw the news. I kind of caused them to come in.

Why does that not surprise me?

After a pause in texting, Ryan's phone rang. It was Laura. Guarded at first, they had their first normal conversation since before Ryan had moved out. The news of the day had validated Ryan's story, and Laura seemed genuinely concerned about his plight. He wasn't just meddling or being manipulative or needy. Plus, the events were dramatic and close to home. Ryan recounted what had happened at the roadblock, as well as what he'd told the police about discovering the bodies at the nearby cabin, his confinement to the picnic table, and his release. Laura noted that he always seemed to get in the middle of things quickly, push people's buttons, or simply get caught up in seemingly random events.

As they spoke, Ryan was secretly nostalgic for the casualness of their conversation. His loneliness and uncertainty about his recent choices were banished as they chatted. Laura seemed like her old self, making fun of him a little but somehow still showing she cared. She was curious about whether Ryan had a partner or not, but he didn't volunteer any details. Toward the end of the exchange, Laura seemed preoccupied and only gave one-word answers. There was also some noise in the background. After that, they soon finished the call.

* * *

Laura turned to Phil a few minutes after she got off the phone. "I think we should go for a drive and check out that incident at the lake."

"Check what out?"

"The trouble at the lake."

"Well, I think that's over, isn't it? That's what the news said. The cops broke it up and the troublemakers were arrested, taken away. Besides, they say two people were killed there. It's not something we should be nosing around in. We should leave this alone."

"Two people died, they said. They weren't *killed*." Laura knew more than she let on.

"What's the difference? They're dead. They're dead before their time, right? That's killed."

"I s'pose. Still, it's big news, and not very far from here. I used to teach some kids from around there."

"There will be nothing to see," Phil said emphatically.

"Well, maybe I'll just go on my own, then."

Phil couldn't help having an outburst. "You're not going on your own! That's not going to happen!" Clearly, he didn't want her anywhere near Ryan's cabin.

She turned into a statue. Phil's last few words had frozen her in space and time. After a few moments, she shifted and looked sideways at him. Slowly and carefully she walked out of the kitchen to get some breathing room, then went to the upstairs bathroom.

* * *

Once Laura was out of the room, Phil grabbed her phone before it locked down. He swiped the screen frantically to keep it awake, then tapped on her messages icon. He saw that the last exchange was initiated by Laura and read the text. He scrolled back, then viewed the call log to confirm it was Ryan she had been talking to when he came in. He looked down the list and noted how often Ryan's name came up under the "Recents" list. They were on familiar terms again. What to do? He carefully placed the phone back in its original spot.

Phil certainly didn't want Laura going to the lake on her own. That could be a disaster for him. But he may have just ensured she would do just that. He knew his last words to Laura were probably a little jarring to her. This reminded him of how he was with his ex-wife, Mara, near the end. That didn't work out well. He needed to walk this back. He needed Laura more than she needed him. Going there on her own was a non-starter, but how could he stop that delicately? Should he relent and take her for a drive to see that there was nothing to see? Maybe a bit of recon *would* make sense. At least he could control the situation and get the lay of the land. He waited for Laura to come back down.

"Okay, let's go," he said when she reappeared.

"What? Go where?" Laura was taken aback.

"Let's go to the lake."

"You just said we weren't going!"

"So I was wrong. See? I can admit when I'm wrong. I'm sorry. I just think it could be a waste of time. But no worries—let's go for a drive. We need to get out anyway. What do you think? Let's go."

Laura shook her head, baffled by the quick turnaround. "I can't figure you out sometimes."

Phil ignored this and tried to sound cheerful. "I need to get gas. Let's stop for a coffee to take with us."

"Okay . . . ?" Laura said this as if it was a question.

The couple drove in relative silence and made the pit stops. Laura gave Phil some basic directions to Indian Springs.

As they turned off the main road and down toward the cabin row, they saw the old sign now defaced with spray paint. Laura said, "This is where I pictured the roadblock. Right around here." Sure enough, there were deep tire impressions from large vehicles that had churned up the soft gravel roadbed. The bushes at the edge of the track had taken something of a beating also. They slowly moved over the bumpy portion and proceeded down the road.

"Wow, they've been doing some work here," Laura said as she saw the construction equipment in the distance. From the corner of her eye, she noticed a movement to her left. "Hey! Hey! It's Rosie! I'm sure of it!"

The golden retriever appeared out of the bush just down the road. On closer inspection they could see that she'd emerged from an overgrown access road with a hard-to-see number seven on a large tree.

"Rosie!" she called out as if the dog could hear her through the closed window. "Rosie!" She fumbled with the button to drop the passenger window, then fumbled to unlock her door. "Stop the car!" Laura jumped out and called to the dog.

Rosie was crossing the road and stopped in her tracks. She looked for a few seconds at Laura and then realized who it was. She changed course and bounded to the mistress she hadn't seen in months. As she did, Ryan emerged from the same point, wearing his jogging gear, and looked around to see where his dog had gotten to.

Phil punched the steering wheel as the scene unfolded. *This is probably what Laura wanted to happen all along,* he thought. He was a sucker. How could he compete with an animal act and nearly three decades years of history?

Rosie jumped up on Laura in complete bliss, as if to say, "Is it really you?"

"Oh my God, you look fantastic!" Laura's tone was effervescent. She scratched the dog hard under the neck and let her stand up against her on her hind legs. "The last time I saw you I thought I was going to have to put you down!"

Ryan looked surprised to see who Rosie was cavorting with. He approached Laura and their dog.

"And I thought the same about you!" Laura exclaimed, and Ryan shook his head at the bad joke. "She looks five years younger." Rosie was svelte, her coat shimmered, and her eyes were bright.

Phil thought he heard Laura add to Ryan, "I think maybe you do too."

The light must have been reflecting off the windshield, so Ryan squinted to see who was driving the vehicle Laura had just gotten out of. Phil didn't offer a word or a wave.

"So what are you doing here?" Ryan asked.

"We just were out for a drive and thought we'd check out where all the action was. I haven't been by here for a long time."

"Laura, let's go!" Phil called from the window.

"Hold your horses, numb-nuts!" Ryan responded, as if to say, "Laura can decide when she wants to leave."

"Gotta go." Laura gave Ryan a little smirk and a raised eyebrow.

Chapter 28

C hester's body was finally returned to the village after three weeks. No one seemed to know whatever had happened to Meaghan's body. If Ronny knew, he never mentioned it. It was assumed they found her family, and that was that.

Chester's funeral was an awkward affair, with the whole village turning out. Ronny's Rebels (what was left of them) attended; they were all out on bail and stayed together in their clique. They pretended to be defiant with their matching bandanas around their necks, intent on not showing how demoralized they really were. The rest of the tribe tolerated the group within the close quarters of the rec centre, where the ceremony took place. All attendees respected the tradition of a peaceful celebration of life, but the dysfunctional split in the clan was painfully obvious.

Ryan was no expert on drug use, but he knew the toxicology reports would indicate high levels of drugs, bad booze, or both. Sure enough, they did. Fatal dosages of fentanyl, along with potentially toxic levels of alcohol were in their systems. The search of the premises showed the source of the drugs, and the booze. Chester's and Meaghan's fingerprints were on everything, and Ryan's prints weren't found anywhere inside the cabin. He got this news from Owny; the cops never acknowledged him after the fateful night he discovered Meaghan's and Chester's bodies.

Ryan assumed Ronny Two Livers blamed him for Chester and Meaghan's death. The newcomer to cabin row had tried to "kill" her once before, after all. In Ronny's view, Ryan must have been involved since Chester and Meaghan were experienced drug users and wouldn't have died without some help.

Ryan knew it was just a matter of time before Ronny would exact his wrath on him. He was watchful when travelling or walking in the area, and swimming or boating on the lake. He thought of how Ronny might rationalize his recent behaviour. Ryan had created havoc for Ronny since he became the New Walter. It was Ryan's crazy idea that got him and Chester kicked out of the sawmill. He lost the still, lost his friends, and lost his pride. His band of rebels was greatly diminished; the out-of-towners involved in the roadblock had to stay away because of a peace bond, and Chester and Meaghan were dead. The sawmill's new mandate didn't include him, and the cabin row construction was under way. Ronny was losing his grip on being able to carry out another insurrection attempt. All these were good reasons to give "both" of his livers a good workout.

* * *

Things settled down after the funeral, which Ryan of course didn't attend. He'd had no feedback from the university students on their detailed findings. He knew the Romanian company had received their shipment, but they hadn't communicated their opinion of the wood. Ryan was up to date in his website work. Gerald and Willy had gotten the sawmill in shipshape condition and were awaiting new orders. Construction had resumed in earnest, extending the road and developing the new cabin lots. The real estate company had set up shop in a construction trailer where the new road began and hired two students from New Town.

Ryan hadn't been in touch with Owny for many days, but he knew she must be tied up with her ailing daughter. Owny hadn't been herself. He feared Patsy wasn't faring well. The last time they came for a dip, she looked terrible. Based on her condition, Ryan assumed they hadn't been back because Patsy was too weak to make it. The chemo was ravaging her, and she was going downhill fast. Ryan couldn't help but think that Stoneblanket was watching, waiting. He couldn't help himself from constantly keeping a lookout for the psychopomp.

* * *

Despite her enthusiasm for returning to work, and Phil's attempts to set her up for acceptance among her peers, Laura quickly went into relapse. In a matter of a few weeks, she was unable to negotiate the stairs at school and her energy was depleting rapidly. Her immune system appeared to be shutting down, which was a serious concern; if confronted with a virulent virus, it could be curtains.

She had checked in with her doctors in late August, and things had looked fine. In less than a month, she was in front of Doctor Patel again. He did a cursory examination and insisted she stop teaching full time. He got her back on a regimen of strong medications to mitigate the relapse; he had seen this process play out before in many other patients.

Laura had been trying valiantly to keep her decline a secret from Phil and the rest of the staff, but she was on a slippery slope, and it was starting to rain. She was devastated when she left Doctor Patel, as relapse was exactly what they didn't want to happen. Maybe she'd overdone it; she had bitten off more than she could chew at the school. Maybe she was being triggered by the stress subtly developing between her Phil, who was now staying full time at her place. The honeymoon phase was over, and an odd form of passive-aggressive control was starting to become apparent in her new partner. She knew she had to tell Phil about her deterioration as soon as she got home.

"So I went to see the doctor today. About my MS, I mean."

"And?"

"And . . . he said I need to stop teaching." Laura's words hung in the air. "I've relapsed and it's . . . well, it's serious. I have to stop schoolwork and get back into remission. I can't do both—Dr. Patel says so."

Phil looked perturbed but said nothing at first. "It's only been a few weeks—the school year's just starting. I got you reinstated with the school board . . ." He stopped talking, perhaps realizing he was dwelling on his own self-interest. "Um . . . how are you feeling? What's going on?"

"Well, it feels like it did when I was down and out at the end of the last term. Worse, I think. Except this time I know what it is, and I have support." She tried to smile.

Phil tried to smile too. "You bet. You bet you do. Let's get you well again! Don't worry about school. I'll get a sub in until we can find a more permanent solution. You'd be okay to share your plans and give the sub some mentoring at first?"

"Oh yes, of course. I'm sorry." Laura started to cry.

"Hey, hey, you have nothing to be sorry about. This isn't your fault. It's just rotten luck, that's all. It can happen to anybody."

"I feel like I'm letting you down. I don't mean to."

"We gave it a shot. I'm probably as much to blame as anyone. Maybe I forced you into it. I just wanted you to get back to normal, be busy. You're a good teacher! It's your calling. And you were in remission for a good while, right?"

"Right. I was. And I will be again. Need to work it out. I did it once, I'll do it again, and this time I'll figure out what set me back."

"Atta girl. That's the spirit."

Phil was smart enough to say all the right things, but his words came out trite and flat. She felt unsure of the relationship's success. Laura couldn't help but miss her old life.

Chapter 29

Ryan hadn't been out rowing his single scull for many days, and he was due for a tour of the lake. Summer was waning, and the lake was calling him to take advantage of it before the autumn rains dampened his spirits and chilled the island. He opted to go out without his music, without distraction. Just him, at one with the boat. He wanted the peace and quiet, the lapping of the water on the narrow hull, the soft creak of the oarlocks, the sun on his back, his breath wafting over the water.

Rosie was left inside, watching him from the cabin window. He put the craft in the water, arranged the oars once he'd settled into position, and pushed away from the dock. Pulling hard, he watched the shoreline become distant, and he turned in the centre of the waterway to sprint down the length of lake. Once at the north end, he made a wide turn and proceeded the way he came. He leaned into his workout for the second, longer leg. Toward the end, as he stopped rowing and coasted, he noticed a familiar boat in the distance, fishing near some reeds. He thought it was an acquaintance from New Town, Lawrence Manywounds, along with a child. He gave them a wave, which they returned. He resumed a slower pace, started a long wide turn to the east, then drifted to a stop toward the south end. He rested and took in the view.

As he leaned forward to stretch his back to counter the strain of rowing, an odd zing went past his head. He sat up, curious at the sound and the strange sensation in the air, like a dragonfly on steroids. A second zing passed by, and he noticed its Doppler effect: a high pitch approaching, a lower pitch after it passed. The next zing hit the side of the rower, crackling into the fibreglass and out the other side. It skipped across the water's surface for several meters. Immediately, a fourth zing hit the hull again, this time only striking one side, followed by the sound of rattling in the front of the boat.

Ryan had never been shot at before. The realization that this was indeed what was happening sank in only after the fourth volley. His heart leaped and he panicked, bending over as far as he could and frantically clutching his knees. Another zing close to his shoulder. He couldn't get low enough in the boat. Another zing hit the side of the craft, then it must have ricocheted into his calf.

He cried out. The pain shocked him, and he knew he needed to reduce his profile. He rolled out of the rower into the water, opposite to the side where he'd been hit, and tried to keep his head below the top of the scull. He held on to the craft and moved to the stern. Maybe they would think he'd been hit. Shouldn't there be a loud bang to warn you? Maybe they would go away. He realized his hanging on to the boat was probably affecting how it looked in the water, so he reduced contact and began to tread water. His calf was burning, blood filled the water around him, but he could still move his legs. He took off his cap and let it float out behind the stern. The shooting had stopped. Surely they wouldn't hang around the shore for long after discharging a gun in broad daylight?

He couldn't control his mind. He felt utterly helpless, a sitting duck. Wounded and without a plan, he was getting colder by the second, and his extremities were stiffening. Was he going into shock? If you can ask yourself that, are you really going into shock? Should he remain with the boat and try to push it to shore? Should he swim underwater as far as he could and leave the boat? Could he get far enough away to surface unnoticed? Not likely. Then he would really be exposed. He told himself to calm down. *Calm down.* He tried to take a look at his leg but couldn't really see it. It stung in the water, but he still had mobility. *Calm down. Think this through.* His chin shivered involuntarily.

Ryan heard a voice from the distance. "Are you okay?"

He turned to see a small skiff approaching with two occupants. It was the fishers he'd seen earlier.

"Are you okay?" Lawrence Manywounds asked again as he got closer. The craft made little noise, as only a small electric motor propelled it.

"My God, I'm glad to see you! No, I'm not okay. Be careful! Someone's been shooting at me!" Ryan sputtered.

"What?" Lawrence looked shocked. "Are you sure?"

"Yes! I've been hit. My boat's been hit."

"Holy shit!" Lawrence couldn't help himself. "Get down!" He pushed the young boy he was with into the bottom of the boat and clumsily ducked down himself. He let his boat glide close to Ryan and bravely grabbed him by the back of his shirt, then pulled him hurriedly into his boat. The three of them hunkered down in the bottom of the skiff.

"You're sure?" Lawrence asked, doubtful.

"Yes!" Ryan squirmed to get a look at his leg. Sure enough, a gash gaped across the middle of his calf.

"What the hell?" Lawrence couldn't believe his eyes. "How long have you been in the water?"

"Maybe twenty minutes."

"When was the last shot?"

"There were four or five shots in a row. Then I ducked into the water. Nothing since then. Maybe they thought they got me." Ryan wiped water off his face.

Lawrence poked his head up and looked at the shore. There was no sign of anything. "This is crazy," he said, as if to himself. "We need to call the cops." He pulled out his cell phone, scrolled with his thumb, and tapped the screen. Ryan assumed he was calling Corky Smoke directly, rather than 911. For sure it was Corky who answered. Lawrence told him the story quickly and asked Ryan to confirm his name for the constable. When Lawrence said, "Ryan Hanson," there was a pregnant pause. Lawrence put him on speakerphone.

Corky said, "Lawrence, I need you to mark your spot—with your phone, I mean. Are you still there, at the exact location of the shots?"

"Yes, we're right here. I want to get out of here—I have my grandson with me."

"Just go to "Maps." Tap your location on the map. Then you'll get a prompt, and you can send it to me. Real simple. Then get Ryan to the medicentre."

"I'm not going to the hospital," Ryan responded.

"You need to get this checked out!" Lawrence insisted. "You probably need some stitches, some medical attention!"

"I'm fine. If you could get me back to my cabin, I'd really appreciate it."

Corky heard Ryan's request. Perhaps skeptical of Lawrence's story, he didn't push the medicentre idea. "Ryan, I'll meet you at your place," Corky said.

"That's fine," Ryan said with some trepidation.

Lawrence fiddled with the maps on his phone for a few seconds, then leaned over and grabbed the single scull and pulled it to the rear of his own skiff. He instructed his grandson to fasten a rope onto a cleat bolted to the rower's bow so they could tow the narrow craft behind them. The small electric motor made little headway at first, but soon they were moving along toward the cabin row. In fifteen minutes they were at Ryan's dock. Corky was waiting there to greet them. He was less than sympathetic.

"Did you get the text with the location?" Lawrence asked the Indigenous constable.

"Yes, it worked. Thank you. Let's see your leg." He motioned to Ryan as he got out of the skiff. After taking a brief look, he said, "Hmm. Could be a gunshot wound, I guess."

"Could be? It is, for Chrissakes!" Ryan stood on the dock and favoured his wounded leg. "Look at the boat."

The single scull was half submerged. Lawrence untied it, pulled it around his boat, and pushed it toward the beach. Corky went down the dock and onto the sand to pull the now heavy scull hard up the beach. Water pissed out of the small holes in its side.

"Huh." Corky lifted his cap and scratched his head. He appeared convinced that this wasn't a fabrication on Ryan's part. "Real small holes. Must be a twenty-two."

"Would a twenty-two kill you?" Ryan was somewhat ignorant of firearms.

"Oh yeah, it will kill you, all right. Not the gun of choice for shooting accurately over any great distance, though." Corky's gaze turned to the end of the lake where the incident had taken place.

Ryan limped down the dock and looked at the bullet holes for himself.

Corky raised his chin and spoke to Lawrence Manywounds. "So, Lawrence, you were out fishing and just noticed this boat. Is that right?"

"That's right. We were fishing near the reeds on the other side, southwest end. I looked up and saw the boat with nobody in it. We'd seen Ryan rowing it earlier, so it was odd that suddenly there was nobody in it. We went over to check it out. We saw him in the water. He seemed to be hiding behind the boat."

"Did you hear any shots?"

"Nope, don't think so. Did you?" he asked his grandson. The boy just shook his head. "Nope," Lawrence said, confirming his grandson's answer, as if he needed to.

"Okay, thank you," Corky said. "You guys can go. I got the coordinates you sent."

"Okay, then," Lawrence replied. He looked at Ryan. "Good luck."

Ryan almost forgot to acknowledge the two who had saved him. "Thank you. Thank you. I'd still be out there if it wasn't for you. Thanks."

Lawrence nodded and backed his boat away from the dock and quietly putted off. He steered his skiff in an arc toward the far shore, creating a greater distance between his boat and the spot where the shots must have originated.

When Lawrence was out of earshot, Corky said, "You know, in all the time I've been working on this reserve, I've never been called to any of these cabins. Since you've been here, it's been a regular occurrence! Trouble seems to follow you around, Ryan. Man . . . the Meaghan thing, the night of the roadblock, Meaghan and Chester. Now this. This is serious. This is attempted murder! I need to get some detectives in here. *Again.* Jesus." Corky insisted that Ryan go to the medicentre, but Ryan wouldn't have any of it.

"It's not all that bad, now that I've had a better look at it. I can take care of it here. Just take a picture of the cut," Ryan said. "That's proof enough. It's a wound from a passing bullet for sure. I'll just bandage it up, and it'll be fine. A little time in the lake and it'll be gone."

Corky did take a couple of pictures of Ryan's leg, then some of the side of the fibreglass rower. "You know, I don't think you're safe here, Ryan. You should think about finding somewhere else to go. Somebody's out to get you, and it's likely they'll be back. Maybe they think they got you, but it won't be long till they know you're still alive." Corky seemed to want to get rid of Ryan and his baggage.

"I've got nowhere else to go," Ryan said flatly. Rosie emitted a couple of barks from the cabin window. "I gotta get my dog." He limped across the sand and up the stairs. Rosie jumped up and greeted her master. She ran down the stairs and into the bush to relieve herself.

Corky followed Ryan into the cabin. "You better let me take a closer look at that thing."

"I'm fine. I'll take care of it."

"No, really. Do you have a first aid kit? Get it and I'll wrap the wound for you."

Ryan suddenly felt very fatigued, so he accepted Corky's offer. He got the first aid kit from under the sink, sat down, and put one leg on a kitchen chair to give the constable access to his calf.

Corky cleaned the wound and found some butterfly bandages. Ryan winced at the pain of the disinfectant. "So who'd want to hurt you, Ryan?" Corky finally asked.

Ryan was silent.

"You might as well talk to me about this. It'll be me or the detectives, as soon as they get here."

Ryan relented. "Hmm . . . well, maybe Ronny. Ronny Two Livers. Or one of his guys, possibly. I'm thinking they aren't too happy with me helping Owny with some stuff. I never did anything to them directly, but I'm sure I've cramped their style at the saw-mill. Then there was the roadblock thing. I had nothing to do with Meaghan and Chester's deaths, but he probably thinks I did. Wants to blame somebody. Wants revenge. Just guessing."

"Anyone else?"

"Can't think of anyone. Could be some random asshole? Just an idiot taking potshots?"

"For sure. It's possible. But that's never happened around here before."

"There's always a first time."

"We'll get to the bottom of it." Corky sounded confident.

* * *

The same two detectives who had conducted the investigation at Meaghan's cabin and held Ryan that night arrived a few hours later. They hadn't introduced themselves then, but Ryan learned later that one was called Detective Felder. They didn't bother to introduce themselves now, or to offer to show their ID. Corky had long departed. Their attitude toward Ryan hadn't changed; they were skeptical, dismissive, and abrupt. They interviewed Ryan and talked among themselves. They looked at the pictures Corky had sent them of Ryan's wounded leg and looked at the bandages.

The two policemen walked out onto the dock, pointed around the lake, and talked on their phones. They looked over the rowing shell for quite a spell. They took out a ruler and placed it beside the bullet holes and took more pictures. They lifted the boat and shook it till they came up with a slug, captive in the front footwell. Without saying goodbye, they got into their unmarked car and drove off. Ryan shook his head at their rudeness, sure they didn't believe him at all.

A few hours later, he was surprised to see the two curt detectives knocking on his door. They looked dishevelled, as if they'd been out for a long walk. Despite his disdain for the pair, Ryan offered them some iced tea. They took it readily.

"So what's up?" Ryan knew they had to be back for a reason.

"Well, we think we found the place where the shooter fired from." The detective named Felder spoke with a little less derision than before. He produced two small baggies from his pocket: one with a tiny spent brass .22 shell casing, and one with a smeared piece of lead—a bullet. "Whoever did this was either really smart or really stupid. We're not quite sure . . . I'm leaning toward stupid, or just inexperienced."

Ryan was perplexed. "What in the world does that mean?"

"Well, see this shell? It's kind of unique. There's a tiny logo on it. They aren't very common. It's actually from a fairly low-grain bullet—not all that powerful. It has low muzzle velocity. It's not what you'd use to shoot someone way out on a lake. Never mind that the gun was only a twenty-two. But like I said, it's uncommon." Felder scratched his head, then held up the other baggie. "This bullet is subsonic. It's so slow, it doesn't break the sound barrier. It only travels about seven hundred miles an hour, so it doesn't make a very loud bang. It's quiet. Someone shooting from a heavily wooded area, like he was, might not be detected from any distance. That's why you didn't hear it coming. Same with the folks who found you. They were on the lake at the same time and never heard it either, correct?"

Ryan nodded.

"It would make a sound for sure, but it's much quieter than a normal gunshot." The detective handed the baggies over to his partner. "So . . . like I said, he was either real smart or real dumb. Smart to pick a bullet that was comparatively quiet so he could get away with it. Or dumb because it's hard to be accurate with a twenty-two over a great distance, and this low muzzle velocity bullet makes it even less accurate."

"Well, he hit me. And he hit the boat several times. So he had to have had some sort of experience. Could it have been a handgun?"

"Maybe, but not likely. This bullet *could* go in a handgun, but handguns are pretty rare here and would be way less accurate at that distance. It was a rifle. Anyway, this is the only shell we could find. We looked thoroughly. We were lucky to find it. Whoever did the shooting must have stopped to clean up before leaving. We really caught a break. This bullet from the boat helps too. No other clues, no good footprints, no tire tracks, nothing."

"You caught a break? How so?"

"Not many places sell this type of ammo. It's oddball. A little legwork might lead us to who bought it—if it's recent."

The two cops looked at each other and exited the cabin without another word. They sat in their vehicle for several minutes, then turned around in front of the cabin and departed.

Chapter 30

From Ryan's growing experience with the police, he knew it could be quite some time before he heard back from them. If and when they did contact him, it would be out of the blue. Ryan remained worried about the attempt on his life. Instinctively, he knew the shots were meant for him; it wasn't a random act. Corky, or maybe even the detectives from the city, would be talking to Ronny Two Livers. That could either defuse or exacerbate the situation. Who knew which? He only knew he had to be on his guard, but he didn't want the incident to define his day-to-day life either.

Over the next few days, he nursed the bullet wound across the back of his leg. On day two he waded into the lake. The next day he swam out to the bubbles with Rosie. By day three it was feeling good and he'd lost his limp, and the scab was lifting a bit at the edges. He kept it clean. By day six he was ready to get walking, even jogging a bit. He missed physical activity, be it rowing or running. Since his precious single scull was sitting perforated on the beach right where they'd left it, rowing was out of the question. He was spooked about going out on the lake anyway.

Feeling as though he was getting back to normal, he stepped out onto his deck with a cup of morning coffee and contemplated his next steps. The boat needed some fibreglass repairs, but he wasn't sure he had the skill set to do a good job of it. He hadn't heard from Owny or any of her family since before the shooting incident. He thought Corky might keep her apprised of what had happened but wasn't sure how far police confidentiality extended within the reserve. He missed their visits and decided he would text her later and check in.

As he surveyed his surroundings, something caught his eye up in a tree adjacent to his sign tree, something he hadn't noticed before. He did a double take. It looked like a camera. It couldn't have been there all that long, but how long? He stopped staring at the device, pretended to look down the beach, and tried to use his peripheral vision to confirm what it was. That wasn't working, so he casually went back inside and found his binoculars. He grabbed a bag of trash from under the sink and pretended to take it out to the garbage can, concealing the binoculars. He lifted the lid and walked away to where he thought he would be out of view. At a sharp angle he trained the glasses on the tree.

"Son of a bitch," he said. "Son of a bitch. How long has that been there?" His mind raced. Who had put it there? The cops? Whoever was out to get him? The absent owners of the cabin next to him? Had it always been there and he'd just never noticed? No, it had to be fairly new. He would have noticed it when the foliage was thinner, when he was out on the deck dozens of times looking around. He'd spotted it now, though, hadn't he? He felt violated. His instinct was to take a hammer to the thing. Sonsabitches. He could probably reach it with one of the long oars. Smack it to smithereens. He went back into the cabin to consider his options.

Against his outrage and general contrariness, he decided on a more subtle approach. He took an ancient stepladder that resided in the shed and harvested a healthy, dense limb from a cedar tree down the access road. He approached the camera from behind, and using the stepladder to get partway up, he climbed the rest of the way and tied the limb securely in front of the camera's aperture. It would look as if a natural obstruction had gotten in the way, and he would have his privacy back. When he was up there, he saw an antenna on the camera and a wire leading to a large battery attached with a Velcro strap to the limb above. As he replaced the stepladder and returned to the cabin, he couldn't help thinking about what Detective Felder had said about the shooter: either really smart or really stupid. The cranky cop thought the latter, but Ryan was starting to worry it was the former.

He was fed up with his convalescence. Surprisingly, he had been utterly patient with himself since being shot, but he was overdue to get back to normal. Things had been very quiet on the social front. He had heard nothing regarding the spruce shipment, and nothing from Owny or her family. His work was up to date, and he missed his daughter. He even missed Meaghan, or at least some sort of company on the cabin row. He missed Laura. He decided to reach out to everyone he could. He called Emily; it went to voice mail, so he left a message. He texted Owny to check in, but there was no reply. He got himself worked up about the camera again, so he called Corky. Corky denied any knowledge of a camera installed by the police, and according to him, he would know. He said it had always been there and that Ryan was just being paranoid.

"Just because you're paranoid, it doesn't mean they're not out to get you," Ryan replied. "Has anyone talked to Ronny?"

"Yes, I did, and Detective Felder has also. He absolutely denies any aggression toward you or anyone."

"What about the whole roadblock thing? That was an act of aggression, if you ask me."

"Maybe so, but it seems legit. Anyway, they got a search warrant and seized his guns and his ammo. And he was pretty pissed off about it, being on "his land" and all. They're in the process of testing it now. They should be able to link that shell to a rifle."

"What's the holdup? It's been almost a week."

"This ain't the movies, Ryan—these things take time. Should know soon. Soon as we do, I'll let you know."

Ryan was frustrated but somehow refreshed that he'd at least talked to someone, and they were actually following through. He checked his computer, replied to a few work-related emails, and went through his phone. He returned to the texts he had exchanged with Laura and reread them all.

Ryan plucked up the courage to send a new text Laura. He simply sent out a *How's it going?*, and waited.

After an hour or so she replied, *Just so-so. How about you?*

Same as you. Had some challenges here lately.

Several minutes went by. *Why does that not surprise me?* She was being cheeky again, this seemed more like her old self. Happy to be chatting, Ryan asked, *Think we could get together for coffee sometime soon?*

Another extended pause. *Sure, that could be a plan. I'm working again, so not sure how to fit it in. Having my challenges too.* Another long pause. *I'll get back to you.* The three grey dots, the typing indicator, pulsated and faded, with no return.

Ryan couldn't help himself. *Miss you.*

The exchange was hardly a promise of a renewed relationship, but Ryan was happy he'd had the guts to text his estranged wife and that she hadn't rejected him outright. He took it as a positive sign and decided to let himself be happy.

* * *

The next morning, he decided to sleep in a bit, then went for a brief wade in the lake. Refreshed, he put on his jogging gear and decided to test his leg with running and walking intervals. Picking up on what the clothing change meant, Rosie was ebullient; Ryan didn't have to say a thing, for she knew what was coming next. She jumped vertically several times until they got under way. Walking at first, they set out down the access road, across the main road, and into the path in the tall trees. In spite of the creepiness he'd felt the first few times he explored the trail, Ryan felt safe there now. It was remote and he never saw another soul. He was encouraged that he had the energy to go all the way on his standard route. Not far off his slowest pace, he turned to make the return trip. Tiring and his calf beginning to tighten up, he walked and jogged off and on.

This time when he heard it, Ryan knew it for what it was. That airy zing, the quick Doppler effect he would never forget. It sped by his head, just inches away. Panicked, he ducked behind a giant Douglas fir just as the second shot chipped bark off it. His heart pounded, forcing deep breaths. He looked around for his dog without exposing himself to the gunfire. He whistled. He heard Rosie bounding toward him through the thick underbrush. She emerged, far to his left, bouncing up and down over the thick dewy ferns and black huckleberry bushes as she tried to locate Ryan.

A noticeable pop. A yelp. Then silence. No movement from the low bushes near him where she'd dropped. His heart blackened. She could only be a few feet away, hidden in the thick brush. It was two or three feet high; maybe he could pull her toward him. He didn't have long to think about this. As he crouched down to try to see his dog, a man came into view, circling his tree, keeping a safe distance. He was holding a rifle at waist height. A shovel with a bright yellow handle held awkwardly under one arm. Ryan recognized the shovel. It was his.

"One down, one to go!" the man said with phony glee. He leaned the shovel against a tree and got a firm grip on the rifle.

It took a second to sink in who it was. Phil Conner. Ryan was stunned. He rose to his feet and stared at his assailant in the shadows. He didn't know what he was expecting, but it wasn't this. He struggled to wrap his mind around what was happening. "What are you doing?"

"What does it look like I'm doing?"

"Killing a harmless pet," Ryan said, as if oblivious to his own peril.

"Her time was up. Everybody has to go sometime. I thought your time was up on the lake, but I guess you got lucky. So here we are." Phil sighed like a bad actor.

"Why are you doing this? I haven't done anything to you!"

"Throw me your phone."

"Fuck that."

"Throw me your fucking phone."

"Why are you so bent out of shape? I'm not interested in Laura anymore," Ryan lied.

"I'm correcting the course of a ship. Setting the world straight," Phil explained. "You're a selfish bastard and you'll just drive Laura into the ground again. I know you've been whispering in her ear. You're the googlemeister, aren't you? Laura and Emily didn't find those things about me on their own." Phil stumbled and regained his footing on the uneven ground. "You treated her like shit and left her to die. That's the way it's always been with you, isn't it? Now it's your turn. She's been the victim of your bullshit for years. That's not going to happen again, and you need to be accountable for your behaviour. What goes around comes around!"

"They're gonna know it's you, numb-nuts. You're not gonna get away with it!"

"That's where you're wrong. You're such an abrasive little prick. You've made so many enemies, they won't know where to start. And I'll get your stupid phone eventually. I'll get it unlocked, and then you're going on a nice long trip. You're way overdue. You and the dog."

"Listen, Phil. Come on. I told you—I'm not interested in Laura."

"Yeah, you've got that young Native girl. Pretty thing. Way too young for an old fart like you, though. You couldn't keep up."

"She's not a girlfriend, she's just a kid for Chrissakes. And I've left Laura alone. We've gone our separate ways—for good!"

"You haven't let her alone. You can't bullshit a bullshitter." Phil paused for some reason, then went on. "There's an old saying that you can't compete with animals or children."

"Rosie's the animal, but who's the child?"

"You, of course. You act like a fuckin' child."

"So you're just eliminating the competition? You're bent. And shooting a helpless dog!"

"It got your attention, didn't it?" Phil smiled and reached for the shovel. He hoisted it like an Olympic torch. "Here, start digging."

"Fuck you." Ryan was raging as he saw his options dwindle.

"Your dog is dead and she needs a decent burial, Ryan!"

Rosie lay in the underbrush near Ryan's feet. He could see her now and noticed her eyebrows flicker. This gave Ryan a glimmer of hope. His spiking emotions moderated immediately. He looked down at the dog again. This time her eyelid struggled to open a little. It exposed only the white of her eye, but she was still alive. Ryan considered his limited options. Having a big shovel in his hand might not be a bad idea. "Give me that fucking thing."

"Now you're thinking." Standing well back and keeping the rifle pointed at Ryan, Phil tossed the spade over the knee-high bushes.

Looking for an opening—some way to distract Phil or lure him closer—Ryan started digging like a madman. He flung mud and dirt frantically. His desperate idea was to make quick, exaggerated movements, so maybe—just maybe—Phil wouldn't react to a sudden change of direction with the shovel.

"What are you doing? You're not even digging! You're just being an idiot! You gotta dig a big hole—that's a big dog!"

"Yeah, right." Ryan was becoming breathless. "A *big* hole."

Phil looked wary of Ryan's antics and kept his distance. Ryan slowed his pace, as his distraction efforts weren't working; he now dug in a measured way. Soon he stopped.

"That should do it." Ryan pointed to the shallow hole.

Phil didn't move. He wouldn't be able to see it very well from where he stood; the underbrush was thick in the clearing. "I doubt it. Keep going."

"It's deep enough." Ryan strategically put the shovel down and attempted to lift Rosie. All this just to bring Phil a few steps closer. He pretended it was too difficult to deadlift her from the ground. He gently pulled her back legs.

As Phil saw Ryan commit to moving the dog, he moved a few steps closer, trying to look over the brush but from a safe distance. Ryan grabbed the shovel, stepped sideways over the dog, and made a mad swing with the shovel, extending it as far as possible. He got nowhere near Phil, but he did manage to tap the very tip of the rifle, moving it a few inches. The firearm discharged, the bullet buzzing by Ryan's ear. Ryan didn't know a lot about guns, but he knew enough to see that the rifle was bolt action. Phil would need to reset the bolt to take another shot.

This was his chance. As Phil fumbled with the bolt, Ryan swung the shovel at the rifle again, this time harder and in the opposite direction. In spite of this, Phil managed to reset the bolt, but now Ryan was preparing for swing number three. With a sickening clank, he caught Phil flush on the side of the head. The rifle sent a bullet into the ground. Phil rocked and swayed, still holding the rifle, but he didn't go down. Ryan changed his grip on the long yellow handle, held the digger like a spear at shoulder height, and drove its point into Phil's face. It stabbed him deeply into the bridge of his nose. Blood spurted out. The rifle fell from Phil's hands as he crumpled backwards, his knees buckling awkwardly beneath him. Ryan grabbed the gun and tossed it as far as he could.

Ryan knew two things: he needed to do everything he could to save Rosie, and he needed to call the cops. He dropped the improvised weapon and turned back to his pet. He struggled to lift her. He managed to get upright with his arms under her belly, her legs dangling. Feeling the movement, she whimpered, giving him a sign she was still alive. Carrying the heavy dog was awkward, but Ryan knew the trail well and walked out of the dense forest as briskly as he could. He knew from experience he wouldn't have any cell phone service until he got to the road. Within ten minutes of his exhausting half-run, the trail opened up, the brightness of the cabin row road beckoning him onward.

At the edge of the road, he set Rosie down and pulled out his cell phone. "Corky?"

"What is it, Ryan?"

Winded and distressed, Ryan couldn't sound calm. "Corky, I've been attacked again. This time we had it out. He tried to shoot me, and he shot my dog! I hit him with a shovel. I'm pretty sure I killed him."

"Where are you?"

"Uh . . . there's a path that goes into the woods opposite the road into my place. Right across the main road from the turn into my cabin. Across the way." He gasped for air. "He's in there about—"

Ryan couldn't complete his sentence because the shovel rang like a bell as it struck the back of his skull. He fell face first into the gravel. Phil pulled the yellow shovel back, bringing it up and vertical. He kicked Ryan onto his back.

Maybe it was Ryan's stubbornness, or maybe it was the adrenalin. Maybe it was his fitness, or his utter animosity toward Phil Conner. Whatever it was, Ryan shook off the smack to the head. He came to just as Phil was poised to drive the shovel into his face, perhaps even all the way to the back of his skull. He raised both hands and slowed the blade's descent. Phil put all of his dripping, bloody effort into pushing it home. Ryan directed the blade to the side and pushed his body back away from it; it cut his hands as it slid through them into the gravel. Then Ryan curled his body around the shovel so his adversary couldn't easily pull it back. His knees up, he pushed Phil off and gained control of the shovel. He scrambled to his feet, and used the butt end of the handle to shatter Phil's sternum. The blood-soaked attacker's lungs collapsed; he fell backwards into the long grass that lined the side of the road.

Ryan ignored the blood running down his back, the cuts on his hands, and the intense pounding in his brain. He mustered all his strength to hoist Rosie into his arms. He stood up, woozy and trying to focus. He staggered across the road, barely able to hear the siren of Corky's SUV in the distance. Ignoring everything else, he continued up the access road to his cabin, utterly focused on completing his mission to get Rosie into the lake.

Ryan staggered into the water and put the dog down on the dock at about waist height so he could assess her. Rosie had been shot in the head. It seemed to have pierced her right eye, and there was no exit wound to be seen. He was concerned the bullet had become lodged in her brain; if so, she would be a goner for sure. He tried to examine the hole in her eyelid and eye to confirm some sort of trajectory, but it was impossible to determine this with the bloody eye rolling back into her head.

He simply picked her up again and waded in as deep as possible. He dunked her head, not submerging it for too long; he had made that mistake before. He bobbed her head several times more, but to no avail. He waded with the dog back to the dock and pulled the orange life ring with the rope from its perch. It fell onto the dock, and he dunked it under Rosie in the water, taking the weight off his back and legs. With her lying on the life ring as if she was on a plate, he could more effectively maintain control of her head. He waded back out as far as he could toward the bubbles. He managed to twist her to get her head and eyes below the surface and keep her mouth and nose out. He attempted mouth-to-mouth resuscitation, but it seemed ineffective. He bobbed, he blew. He bobbed, he blew. Minutes passed. Rosie's good eye opened slightly, then closed. He bobbed her head yet again. The good eye opened completely. Then she fidgeted and twisted on the ring, sensing her precarious position.

"Whoa, whoa, Rosie! It's okay. It's okay."

The dog genuinely understood the words. She calmed herself and lifted her head to look around, craning her neck since she was only using one eye. He floated her back to the sand. Miraculously, she found her legs and stood groggily on the beach. Not having the capacity to shake her head, she gave her behind a brief shake. She stood panting and dripping on the soft sand.

"Good girl, Rosie! Good girl!"

She wagged her tail slightly, as she had pleased her master. The golden retriever stood blinking, then lifted a paw to touch her wounded eye.

"No! No, Rosie." Ryan intervened and pushed her paw down. He decided to lift her again, to get her to the deck and get her warm. Then he'd get her to a vet. He told her to stay and went in search of two big bath towels from the cabin. He coaxed her to lie down on one and dried her with the other. She tried to touch her bad eye again, and again Ryan gently admonished her.

Ryan sensed a vehicle coming up from behind the cabin. Corky's cruiser pulled up, and as he stopped, he shut off his lights.

The panicked phone call, the mangled white man on the side of the road, the dog's condition, and Ryan's own neglected state told a story, but Corky needed to confirm it. "So you know this guy?" he said.

Ryan nodded and continued to dry Rosie.

"Who is he?"

"He's my wife's—my ex-wife's—boyfriend."

"Hmm. You must've had some conflict with him in the past?"

"Yeah, I s'pose. But not huge. Just minor stuff. Nothing to try to kill somebody over, that's for sure."

"Were you maybe getting back together with your wife?"

Ryan shrugged noncommittally. "I need to get this dog to a vet. She's been shot in the head."

"You're not going anywhere." Then Corky took a closer look at the back of Ryan's head. "Okay, maybe you are." He squeezed the microphone on his chest and called the ambulance to come up the road to cabin number seven. Two casualties.

* * *

The EMTs got Ryan to the hospital and were kind enough to take Rosie to a vet right after that. He needed five staples to close a deep gash on the back of his head. They gave him some painkillers and told him to keep still for a couple of hours. He would be observed and tested for concussion. As he lay there in the emergency ward, he heard the kerfuffle from two bays down.

They were working on Phil—it had to be. He heard a man react to the patient's facial injury, and the sounds of two other voices and machines being moved. It must have been a doctor who said he was going into cardiac arrest, and apparently they'd started CPR. But it was impossible with the state of his sternum. Soon the frantic voices stopped. Felder and his partner showed up at the foot of Ryan's bed just as he heard Phil's medical team call for a gurney to take his body to the morgue.

"You've had another busy day." Felder was deadpan.

"I had to protect myself. He tried to kill me. Twice. He shot my dog."

Felder nodded. "We know. We were just heading over to question him when we got the call from Corky Smoke. He was on video buying ammunition a few weeks ago. We finally narrowed it down."

Ryan slumped down, deeply relieved they believed his story. It was the truth, of course, but sometimes the truth can get turned on its head. Everything had become a surreal blur.

"We'll need you to come in and make a statement, but you get home and get some rest. We'll call you in a few days.

"Do you know where my dog is?"

"Nope. No idea."

"Could you do me one favour?"

"What is it?"

"Could you call my wife and tell her about Phil? Tell her everything that happened? Please?" Ryan struggled to keep himself from becoming emotional. "The fight in the woods, Rosie, my . . . *our* dog?

And what happened here?" Ryan nodded to the bay where Phil had expired.

Felder looked over and his partner and paused. He nodded. "You bet. We can do that."

Chapter 31

Ryan's phone lit up a couple of days later as he was changing the dressing on Rosie's eye. It rang a few times and then stopped. It was across the room, and he didn't want to leave the dog unattended and without the plastic cone around her neck; she would scratch her face for sure. He completed applying the ointment on the patch, set it on the dog's stitches, and reattached the awkward plastic cone. She seemed to hate the cone more than the pain in her eye socket. Ryan tried to reassure the golden retriever. "Won't be long now, girl. Couple of more days and we'll get you in the water again. It's just about healed."

He picked up his phone and saw Laura's phone number at the top of the "Recents" list. No message. He knew they needed to talk, whatever form that would take. He wanted to. With the evidence of her call, his heart felt a little lighter, despite there being no message. *She* had called him. *She* had reached out. Pocket dial? Maybe, but not likely. She just didn't want to leave a message. He could understand that. This was a heavy time. Heavy for him, doubly so for her.

That morning was the first morning he didn't wake up with a pounding headache. His memories of the altercation with Phil played over and over in his mind. He had been scared. Scared for his life. Not to mention for Rosie. His nerves got the better of him whenever he dwelled on how close he was to being killed. On the boat. In the woods, and finally at the road. The brutal finish. He'd been sure Rosie was a goner; what a dog. Laura didn't need to know all the details. He wanted to respond to her while she was still available and hopefully still in a talking mood. He touched her number on the screen of his phone.

"Hi, Ryan." She sounded calm and clear.

"Laura, hi. I see you called. Sorry I couldn't pick up—I was tending to Rosie. She has the stupid cone thing—you know."

"How is she doing?"

"Great, really. She just hates the cone. She lost her eye. Not sure if you knew. Her left eye. She has some scarring where they stitched up her eyelid—it'll be permanently closed. Some stitches internally there, too. Other than that, she's coping really well. Yesterday she kind of got her appetite back, and we went for a bit of a walk."

"I'd like to see her."

"Absolutely. No problem. She'd love to see you."

"So how about you? How are you doing?"

"Yeah, um . . . I have some stitches too." He tried to sound matter of fact. "Five in the back of my head. Staples, actually. Today is a good day—I'm much improved. Not much of a headache to speak of, so I haven't taken any Tylenol. I have a few other cuts on my hands and stuff."

"Ryan, I'm so sorry!" Emotion crept into her voice. "I don't know what to say . . ."

"Hey, hey, it's not your fault. You didn't have any idea, I'm sure. Did you?" Ryan knew the answer.

"No, no. God no. When the cops came, I was completely shocked." Laura sniffled into the phone. "It floored me. I still can't believe it. I'm just sick about it. I'm sorry I didn't see this coming at all, I never would have wished for this."

"I know, I know. It came right out of left field. How are you doing? How's your health and so on . . . ?" Ryan wasn't sure how to take a dignified approach to asking Laura about her MS.

"I'm not great. I was in some sort of relapse before this whole thing erupted. Now it's full blown, I'm sorry to say. I have to go to the doctor tomorrow for a consult."

"So would you like to see Rosie? Do you want to meet us somewhere?"

"I could come over. Should be doable, I think. I'll come over this afternoon."

* * *

Ryan made an effort to clean up around the place. He'd had other priorities for several days, what with the two of them convalescing. The cabin was in a state of upheaval and neglect. It felt good to prepare for Laura's visit. Maybe his subconscious had been scheming for this to happen all along. Too bad it had taken a tragedy to bring it about.

Several hours later Ryan noticed Laura pull up as he sat in his chair at the kitchen table. The familiar sight of her little grey car pleased him. He stepped out onto the deck, Rosie following and unaware of the arrival of a visitor. When she saw the car, her tail began to wag. As soon as Laura emerged from the vehicle, Rosie couldn't help herself; she barked and made her way down the stairs as briskly as she could, wobbling a little as she navigated with a single eye and the floppy cone. She walked around the front of the car to meet Laura and rose on her hind legs to get as close as possible to her mistress. Laura cooed over the injured dog for several minutes. When Rosie got down, Laura looked up at Ryan.

"I went to the wrong cabin at first! I couldn't remember if it was six or seven. Went to six and had to back all the way out. C'mon Rosie!" Laura sounded upbeat, but her movements betrayed her. She was tentative when she walked and attempted to keep away from the dog so Rosie wouldn't jostle her. She held her arms out slightly as if there was an earthquake and she needed outriggers to help her keep her balance. She took the stairs slowly.

Ryan tried to contain his concern, but what he saw worried him. "Should you be driving?"

Laura stopped at the top of the stairs and looked as if she was trying not to take offence. She glanced at Ryan. "Well, that's a good question. Driving was okay. Just okay. Have to make sure the meds are all working just right—kind of balance myself out before I head out."

Ryan shook his head. He stepped up to give Laura a hug; it seemed natural and long overdue. She reciprocated and patted him on the back as they embraced. She fought back tears. Rosie sat and watched, panting she tried to scratch her neck with her back leg.

Ryan said as they separated, "It's really been only a couple of months or so, but so much has happened!"

Laura ignored the statement, as if she didn't want to jump into past events immediately. "Turn around—let me look at you." She turned him around and looked at the back of his head.

Ryan had seen it in the mirror and knew it was partially shaved, and five shiny staples formed a diagonal line from two o'clock to seven o'clock. It gave him a perfectly ghoulish aura. The gash was deep and crusty. It looked as though someone had accessed his brain through the back of his skull.

"My God." Laura shook her head and looked down at Rosie. "What the hell did he do to you?"

"Maybe he beat some sense into me," Ryan said jokingly. "He tried to kill me. You know that, don't you? The police gave you some background, I hope?"

"They did, but it was brief. I know he shot the dog and you had to fight him off. I can't believe he snapped like that."

"Evidently, you're quite a prize. Worth fighting for."

"What does that mean?"

"Well, he wanted me out of the picture. I had to fight for my life. But yes, you *are* worth fighting for. I see that now." Ryan looked down at the floor and summoned some strength. "I'm sorry I bailed on you . . . so sorry. I was trying so hard not to give a damn, and I convinced myself it was the right thing to do."

"And I shouldn't have started drinking after being sent home. Big mistake. It set me back weeks and months when I should have acknowledged there was something wrong."

"We're only human." Ryan looked down at the dog. "Except you, Rosie! You're better than that!" He said to Laura, "Come in, come in. I'll make you some tea." It felt good to communicate with her again. Good to clear the air.

Ryan wasn't sure if they could reset their relationship after all that had happened. Could they get back together? Would they just be friends? The next few days would tell. Over the course of the afternoon, they discussed Ryan's harrowing experience in the woods and on the lake, but it was difficult to address. He described parts of the ordeal incompletely, and Laura didn't want to elaborate too much on her relationship with Ryan's assailant. She changed the subject and they discussed Emily, commiserating over her latest challenges at university. She was having difficulty in a few courses. Maybe they could tag team her with some help.

Eventually, Ryan described coming to the cabin and his exchanges with Walter. He pointed out his sign tree and described meeting Owny and Patsy. He carefully explained his relationship with the area's First Nations group and mentioned that it was their land he was occupying. He told Laura how it was his idea to get Patsy into the two life preservers. They had a little laugh about the process and how preposterous it looked. That opened up the conversation about the healing waters, but Ryan carefully omitted the story of Meaghan and Stoneblanket from his narrative.

"So they really believe that strongly in the lake? That the water can actually help cure what ails you?" Laura had never heard of the local waters being medicinal.

"They do. Well, most do. I think some of their people take it with a grain of salt."

"How about you? What do you think?"

"I think there's some merit to it."

Laura was surprised. "Really? You do?"

"Yup, I do. What first got me thinking there was something to it was Rosie. She's had the setback with her eye, of course, but you saw her a while ago. You were surprised at how great she looked, weren't you? She's a new dog. I swear it's the lake that's helping her. Somehow . . . Me too. Remember the day I left and I cut my leg on the garage? Maybe you don't. It was deep. Once I got out here to the lake and spent a little time in the water, it healed up real quick. Couple of days. Look, not even a scar." Ryan rolled up his pant leg. "And I used to feel a little arthritic after a jog or rowing hard on the lake—especially the next day. Now I go for a dip after a workout, and I swear it takes the joint pain away. I feel twenty years younger."

"I think you've been drinking the local Kool-Aid."

"I guess I am. You know, I have a filter bottle, and now I'm drinking water straight from the lake. I feel like a million bucks. I think you should go for a dip. It could really help you."

"Wow. You're really sold on this."

"I am. Even if it's a placebo effect, what the hell—*something's* working. But it isn't just my imagination. When Rosie was shot in the head, I got her into the lake, and she came to. I'm not saying the lake completely saved her, but it was a factor. Enough to ensure she survived, with more care. I'm sure of it."

"And did it save your little girl friend? What's her name?"

Ryan took a beat, ignoring the compunction to clarify his relationship with Patsy yet again. "Not sure on that one. She's Patsy. She has a tough prognosis. I know her mum, Owny, thinks it will make a difference. That's why they come here."

"Why can't they just jump in the lake over at the village?"

"Cause over here is the main spring that feeds the lake. See?" Ryan pointed at the water. "See the white foamy area just out there? Those are bubbles coming up from the bottom. That's where the spring fills the lake. It feels a little warmer right there, and you float a bit better there too." Ryan paused for dramatic effect. "Look at me." He wanted her to focus. "It could help you too—I really think it would be beneficial. Get out there and try it. It won't hurt you— that's for sure."

"I'm not so sure about that. That water will be real cold now."

Ryan didn't want to belabour the point. He knew she would be skeptical. "Anyway, just think about it. Food for thought."

"You seem sold. Okay, maybe I will." Laura paused and looked around at the cabin. "I should get going. I need to get some stuff done, and then tomorrow I have my doctor's appointment."

Ryan refrained from offering to go with her, though he considered the idea briefly. "Okay, sounds good. It was really great to see you. We enjoyed seeing you."

"Me too."

"Say, uh . . . maybe you could come by after your doctor's visit tomorrow? Still lots to talk about."

Laura thought about it for a second. "Sure. Um, sure. That could work. Let's see . . . around three-thirty?"

"Great. We look forward to it." Somehow including the dog with the 'we' seemed to underscore the family unit. They gave each other a polite hug. No kiss. Then Laura gingerly moved out the door, across the deck, down the stairs and into her car.

Not long after she departed, Ryan felt sad and happy at the same time. At their parting hug, her scent had triggered the conflicting emotions. He didn't immediately understand the source of his feelings. He was encouraged now that he was on speaking terms with his estranged wife but was sad to see her condition, and he had nagging guilt that harkened back to the day he walked out. If he had just stayed and got her through her relapse, the terrible events that followed wouldn't have happened. He called to Rosie to go for a walk. He needed to think about his actions and his own impetuousness. He was getting too old for the luxury of behaving that way.

* * *

The next day Laura texted that she was finished at the doctor's and on her way over. Ryan had been fairly sure she'd still want to come over, but with all that had happened he was prepared for anything. It was gratifying to see she was on her way. He wanted to make the most of this opportunity to renew their relationship. Laura arrived just as she had the day before, except directly at cabin seven.

As she climbed the stairs, she looked a little more mobile and less tentative. Laura was dressed a little more formally than she was the day before and carried a large purse.

"Hi there! You look great. You must be feeling better?"

"Hi. I do feel better. A little anyway. The doctor was very understanding, very helpful. I have to go and get some blood work done and pick up a new prescription. How about you? How's the head?"

"Well, that's a big question! The back of my head feels fine. Inside my head is in a better state too, I think. So I'm better on both counts. It was nice to talk yesterday."

Just then Rosie came out of the bushes to investigate. She was obviously happy to see Laura and wagged her butt, and her cone wobbled as she did so.

"You're just in time for the unveiling!" Ryan sounded cheerful.

"What are we unveiling?"

"Oh, we're just going to see if Rosie is ready to live without that darn cone. Thought I'd get her into the water for a swim."

Laura took a close look at the dog. "Oh, it does look better. Even since yesterday. As long as it isn't too itchy, I think she might be okay."

"Let's give it a try. Come, Rosie, come!" Ryan kneeled down and undid the collar of the cone and gently rubbed her permanently closed eyelid. She didn't seem bothered by it. "Let's get you into the lake!"

"So she'll go in on her own?"

"Oh yeah, for sure. She loves it. But you know, I think I'll go in with her, just for a quick dip. I want to get her out to the bubbles."

"Hmm. Well, I must be crazy, but can I join you? I brought a bathing suit just in case."

"Really? That's a great idea! Oh, that's great."

Laura changed in the bathroom and Ryan got ready in the bedroom. He ensured Rosie stayed with him so she didn't paw her head. She seemed to sense some activity was about to occur. Laura and Ryan emerged from changing and stood on the deck.

"Just to warn you, it's pretty cold," Ryan said. "But you just need to just suck it up and get out to the bubbles. It's warmer and you can last for a bit out there. Then it's cold again, of course, for the scoot back."

"Oh, I dread the thought of it, but let's go!" Laura replied.

The three of them made their way down the stairs. Laura and Ryan placed their towels on the dock and stepped into the frigid water. Laura cringed and let out a "Jesus Christ!"

"You just have to get right in and get to the source as quickly as possible!"

Ryan made a quick dive and Rosie swam enthusiastically beside him. After a second's hesitation, Laura followed suit. They regrouped at the bubbles.

"You're right—it's warmer. A little warmer, at least!"

"Told you . . . Come here, Rosie!" Ryan paddled with the dog and splashed water on her eyelid. The dog was surprisingly obliging; she seemed to understand why he was doing it. Laura gave Rosie a few splashes too. Ryan let the back of his head soak for a few moments. They laughed and enjoyed themselves as the water united them as a family again. Maybe it could heal relationships too.

They lasted only a few minutes, then made their way back to the beach. The air seemed warmer as Ryan and Laura towelled off, a good distance from Rosie as she shook from nose to tail. The dog revelled in the moment, as if sensing her family was complete again.

Ryan and Laura went back into the cabin to warm up, get into dry clothes, and have a coffee.

"I couldn't sleep last night," Ryan admitted.

"How come? Was your head bothering you?"

"No, not too bad. Just thinking about . . . how you're doing. How we got here. Where we go from here."

Laura blinked at Ryan and got right to the point. "Do you still love me?"

"Oh God, of course. I think I've learned something in the past months. I screwed up. I left the love of my life when she needed me the most. I see that now. I need to make amends somehow. I was an ass. I'm sorry."

"Thank you, I think. I know I screwed up too. It's hard to live with an alcoholic, even when they aren't drinking. You have to change the way you live for them—I know that. And I knew better than anyone that it was my third strike. Trouble is, the umpire called me out on a bad pitch and I couldn't cope with the call. Fell off the wagon." She looked Ryan straight in the eye. "That's not going to happen again."

"Did you still have feelings for Phil?"

"Yes . . . No. I did, though. He was there for me, at least at first. That stopped suddenly when I found out what he'd done. But even before that, I had some doubts about him because of some things that had cropped up about his past. I can't believe he thought the terrible things he did would somehow be acceptable to me."

"He started feeding the wrong dog."

"What?"

"Oh nothing. Just a saying." Ryan reached for her hand. "Can we start again? Can we be a family again? I miss you. I miss what we had. I want to be a better husband, to show you that I can."

Laura grew thoughtful and didn't answer right away. "Yes." She nodded firmly. "But this has to be the real thing. We both need to be in this for each other. This can't just be the path of least resistance. We need to have real love."

"After all we've been through, we will. Come stay here at the cabin for a while. Let me take care of you. Let's get you in the lake regularly. How do you feel now?"

"About the same. I still think the lake thing is a little far-fetched."

"I know it must seem that way. Anyway, whatever outside things influence us or happen to us, we know we'll have each other's back. Okay?"

"Okay."

Chapter 32

Owny found herself in Patsy's room, standing beside her daughter's bed with a glass of water in her hand. Tears welled up in her eyes as she looked at the bald, emaciated girl lying before her. "The wasting disease"—that's what their people called it in prehistoric times. She set the water down and crawled into the old brown metal-framed single bed beside her daughter. She cuddled behind her, just as she had when Patsy was three years old and she had the croup. Owny had always comforted her when she was sick. She got better from the croup because Owny nursed her back to health. Nursed all of her girls. Patsy would have forgotten all about the croup, forgotten about herself as a child, and now couldn't acknowledge her mother as she lay down beside her.

This wasn't the croup. All the love and attention Owny could give her wasn't helping. The chemo wasn't helping. The doctors weren't helping. Owny was deeply troubled that she couldn't nurse her daughter out of this. Death in slow motion. It was gradually spiralling out of her control.

She carefully raised her head and looked at the bedroom door. Soon Stoneblanket would come. *Must do something. Anything.* Patsy was too weak to get any farther than the bathroom, and soon that would be too much. Tears streamed sideways off Owny's face and onto the pillow. She struggled to keep her intense grief from Patsy. She tried to rest with her daughter, her hand on her shoulder, sensing her shallow breathing. A type of sleep came.

After about an hour, Owny awoke and gently moved off the bed so as not to disturb Patsy. She slipped out, closing the bedroom door behind her. She knew Gerald would be in the living room watching TV. She perched on the edge of the couch beside his easy chair, preparing herself for what she was about to say.

"Gerald" was all she said.

That was his cue. Gerald calmly raised the remote and turned the TV volume almost all the way down.

"I don't know what to do anymore." Owny pulled a tissue from the box on the coffee table and started to sob quietly into it. A rare display of tears from the Chief.

Gerald wasn't upset she had interrupted his program. He got up out of his chair and sat beside her on the sofa. He put his arm around her, pulling her toward him. She cried openly in his arms. He tried to rock her slightly, as if she were a child. He let her continue for several minutes, let her get it out.

"We must be missing something?" he said, trying to sound a little encouraging.

"I don't know what," she said, sobbing. "The doctors are preparing us for the worst. I can tell by the way they've been talking during the last two visits."

"What about traditional medicine? Can we try that again?" Gerald asked.

"Maybe, but that hasn't worked either. I got some advice from Halayt Jona Mason from Alert Bay. He's the oldest, most experienced shaman I know. Patsy hasn't responded to his suggestions at all."

"Back to the lake?" Gerald said.

"She's in no shape to do that. She can barely get out of bed."

"How about we carry her, at least to the dock here in New Town?"

"If we go to the lake, we need to get to the source. It really is best there. Not diluted. But she's not strong enough to get all geared up and over there."

"So we carry her."

"I . . . just can't see it. I don't think she'd want it. It seems so . . . undignified or something. She won't go for it. I dunno, it might be a shock to her system—she's pretty frail."

"A wheelchair? Maybe we could wheel her down to the water and in?"

"Maybe."

"There's a wheelchair at the medicentre. We'll wheel her down to the water, or even drive her over to the other side—even better—and wheel her in."

"You know it hurts her to sit for any length of time. She can't sit at all."

"Hmm." Gerald was running out of ideas.

"What about a stretcher? Maybe put it in the back of a pickup and get her down to the water, or over to the other side."

"Maybe. Seems pretty desperate," Gerald said.

"I think we're desperate," Owny quietly replied.

"I don't think she'd go for it. I'm worried she's resigned herself to . . . what will come." Gerald's voice tapered off into a whisper.

"Me too." Owny joined him in whispering, her chin slightly quivering. "But we need to do something to turn this around. Damn it. Kick-start something, wake her up, get her in the water and then back to—"

"The land of the living? How about we get a stretcher onto a boat at the dock, get her over to the other side that way."

"Maybe. Maybe we could have a bit of a ceremony for her, get her thinking about some traditional stuff. It could motivate her. She'd still need to get into the water somehow when we got over there. That could be tricky."

"We'll figure that out. If she was right there, she'd be into it—I hope."

The next morning Patsy seemed a little more lucid, so Owny pitched the idea to her. The stretcher, the boat ride across the lake, a traditional procession, some smudging—cedar and sweetgrass. She would have none of it.

* * *

Owny waited until Gerald went to the sawmill. She knew her husband wouldn't approve and would try to stop her. She padded over to Iris and Aster's bedroom and looked in, just to confirm they weren't there. Owny closed the door, then checked on her eldest daughter. As expected, the gaunt, hairless girl was lying motionless on her bed. Without a sound, Owny discreetly closed the bedroom door. She returned to her bedroom, to the closet, and pulled out the long black bag that held the Soulcatcher.

She took it to the kitchen and laid it on the table. After a few seconds, preparing herself with a deep breath, she untied the end and slipped the covering off the leg bone. The musty smell filled her senses, and she couldn't help but indulge herself for a few moments and take a close look at the ornate carving. She wished she had asked more questions about its power, its use. The images spoke to her. The concept of the Soulcatcher was speaking to her now, almost making an appeal. Perhaps it was her motivation. Perhaps it was her conviction. Perhaps it was her maturity . . . at last. She wasn't afraid anymore. Oneida Wilson needed to understand the object's power. She had shed the uncertainty, the lack of clarity. Death would be hers if need be. She poked her finger into the spiral opening in the bone. She wanted to see the little man. She wanted to make sure he was loose, free to move back and forth if she needed to shake the Soulcatcher. The features of his little face were hard to make out, as the carving was worn from his travels back and forth. She set the piece down on the old black velvet bag.

Owny felt strange, dizzy. She needed to sit down. She pulled a kitchen chair back from the table, all the way to the wall. She sat down and looked at the thing from a distance. The silence of the house was overpowering. Clouds moved away from the afternoon sun, allowing beams of light to stream into the kitchen from the small window above the sink. The light pierced the miasma that had filled the room. There was some power there, for sure. The Chief needed to understand how the power worked, to sort things out. Understand how to bring things together for the best outcome.

Owny headed back into her bedroom and undressed. She went to the bottom drawer of her bureau and found the white cotton underthings used only for ceremonies. These consisted of a button-front chemise with little lace frills around a wide neck, and white cotton bloomers that fell below the knee and had little frills at the hem. In her closet in the shelf above the hanging clothes was a box that held her handmade moccasins, beaded and embellished with real porcupine quills and dyed hollow prawn legs. She looked at them briefly, running her hand over the decoration. She sat on the bed and put them on, lightly rubbing the tattoos she had on the top of each foot. After returning to the closet, she unzipped a black plastic garment bag. She pulled her ceremonial cape off the hanger inside the bag. Again she paused and examined the craftsmanship that went into garment. Her mother's craftsmanship. She laid the cape out on her bed.

If she'd had trepidation about taking out the Soulcatcher, she now had equal trepidation about getting the Sisiutl mask from the attic. Soon she would wear it in the ceremony. She had never put it on before. She'd never had the need, the authority, or the strength until now. In her moccasins and bloomers, Owny Wilson pulled the attic ladder down with a cord that dangled in the hall. There was a squeak as she pulled the trap door away and unfolded the steep, wobbly steps.

* * *

Somehow, the sound of the unfolding ladder resonated with Patsy. The squeaking permeated the air in the stuffy bedroom. Her eyes opened. The sounds stimulated a dimmed sense of childish curiosity. She knew something significant was afoot. Was it her sisters? Don't think so. Her dad? Maybe. Or maybe it was something more. Somehow some energy came to her. She sat up, put her feet to the floor, and tiptoed to her closed door. She opened it a crack and saw her mother, in bloomers and a chemise, gingerly balancing on the ladder, trying to be quiet. The old wooden treads strained and snapped in protest. She waited and watched, her mother's secret audience.

* * *

Owny climbed to the top and into the attic. She pulled the short chain on the hanging bulb that awaited visitors to the storage space. Light burst into the darkness. She knew exactly where it was. It had weighed on her mind since the times she and her sisters would sneak up when their parents were out; they would open its case and scare each other with talk of the thing coming alive and getting them. She found the battered black cardboard guitar case right where they'd left it. Dust swelled as she lifted it. She made her way down the ladder.

Owny took the guitar case to the kitchen. She placed it on the table, opposite the Soulcatcher, and wiped it with a damp cloth. Pulling in a deep breath, she unlatched the crooked brass buckles and opened the case. The contents were wrapped in an old sheet. Carefully, she lifted the oblong object and removed the white shroud. It was exactly as she remembered it . . . yet somehow different. It wasn't her father's scary ceremonial effigy anymore. Today it was hers. Only now could she acknowledge her relationship with the mask.

This was an authentic transformation mask that dated to the time of the potlatch. Few original masks had survived from those years; most were destroyed during the time of attempted assimilation. Masks symbolized the potlatch and old beliefs that white society felt needed to be suppressed. This one had survived by being hidden, never displayed for decades.

It was carved of cedar and adorned with copper plates above the eyes. It showed the elongated sea serpent face of the Sisiutl. Decorated with faded pigments of red, black, and yellow, the mask was split down the middle; the dancer who wore it could transform it. In the heat of a dance, by the light of the fire, the dancer could manipulate the strings and open the mask to reveal another mask, of a man, inside. The man was the traveller, the invincible warrior. He had that wide-eyed look, his lips rounded and protruding, as if he was saying, "Ooooo." He was the icon of both the spirit world and the world of man. Red-stained dry seagrass was fastened on the top of the head like a plume, and down the front like a beard. The inside surface of the split face was painted like the sea serpent also; when opened it was a complete rendition of the Sisiutl, a man in the middle of two serpent heads. The dancer would open and close the mask, symbolizing the transformation of man into the spirit world and back again.

Owny lifted the mask and looked it over thoroughly. She had never pulled the strings before, so she practised opening and closing the long face. She took another cloth, wetted it, and gently cleaned the inside of the ancient wooden artefact. The surface inside was worn smooth from the foreheads, cheeks, and noses of those who had donned the strange mask in many ceremonies over many generations.

Stoneblanket would recognize this mask. It used to be his. At least he was the caretaker of it for most of his lifetime—like Owny was now. He might be surprised to see his own mask and his own leg bone used together. The combination was strong medicine Owny thought would have enough impact to call Stoneblanket all the way from the spirit world—and send him back there permanently. Fix his wagon for good. Stay away from Patsy. Stay away from her family. She was the *haɫayt* today.

Of course, this could backfire. Maybe Stoneblanket wouldn't respond. Maybe he wasn't real. No, no, he was real. She had seen him. She had seen the light show before. The shitshow, as Ryan had disparagingly called it. She had to get this right.

Feeling sure, she put the mask on, needing to know how it felt, how it worked for the dancer, how to size it for her head, how to dance with it on. She would need to practise. She became anxious; somebody or something wanted that mask on her—now. There in the kitchen, in her bloomers, with the mask on, she moved to the chant that started faintly in her throat. Ancient words came to her. Words she had never used, never known, words that were coming out of her as if they had always been there. A dozen coaches showed her the Ghost Dance.

* * *

Patsy watched from the shadowed hall in utter amazement. Unnoticed by Owny, the Soulcatcher rocked slightly, then rose in the air and hovered a few inches above its bag on the table. A flicker of light came from inside the spiral bone. The little man began to glow faintly and rotate in his marrow channel, eager to make his historic trip.

* * *

Owny became a marionette to the *halayts* of the past. Her arms moved in waves; her head animated the mask convincingly. Her legs rose and fell in slow motion, strong and balanced. She was sure her grandfather was guiding her steps, dancing inside of her. Her voice became more confident and filled the thick air. Distant drums reverberated from the spirit world. Only now did she understand the power of the *halayt*. Only now did she feel the resonance of the chant empower her spirit.

Owny sensed the Soulcatcher's power. It was like a static electrical charge about to snap across the room at her own spirit. She started thinking it would embolden her, solidify her power, but instead it gave her a deep sense of dread.

Owny finished, kneeling on the floor, sitting on her heels. Undoing the ties of the mask, she removed it and turned the face around so she could see it, then placed it on her lap. Instead of feeling drained or scared, she felt confident. She had found her place now, found her voice, her connection to her father, and to his father.

She sensed her grandfather near the Soulcatcher. It settled again on the velvet bag. He hadn't been lifting it as Owny originally sensed, but holding it down. Keeping it in check. It had to be put away. It was too powerful, too strange. She would not use it again; it was beyond her skill and experience.

* * *

Patsy carefully stepped back to her bedroom. She waited a few minutes for her mother to close the ladder to the attic, then she made her way to the bathroom.

She looked at herself in the mirror. In just a few short months, she had gone from a robust young woman to a gaunt spectre staring back at herself. The change in her mother's attitude since hearing the latest prognosis scared her more than the prognosis itself. Stage 3B. What was the *B* for? Bad. *That's it—it stands for bad.* Down deep Patsy knew she wasn't going to improve. Not with the chemo, not with the radiation, not with the lake, not with the exercises she couldn't perform anymore. Not with the smoothies her mother made her. Not with anything. She decided then and there she couldn't live like this. She wanted to go out on her own terms, whatever that meant.

* * *

Gerald returned just before supper, and Aster and Iris came home from the after-school activities at the rec centre. The family sat down to the first normal meal they'd had in a long time—as normal as it could be with a dying family member in the next room.

Immediately after supper, Aster and Iris left the quiet house as usual to get away from the morbid atmosphere their mother couldn't help but manifest.

Gerald spoke from his place at the table after the two younger daughters were gone. "I've been thinking," he said cautiously as he watched Owny gather up the dishes from the dinner table.

Owny just looked at him and nodded and raised her eyebrows, as if the dishes she held were impairing her speech.

"She doesn't like the stretcher idea, or the wheelchair idea, but I think we're on the right track. Maybe we'll get a real doctor from the Jube to support a traditional medicine ceremony? Maybe a nurse would come? Maybe Pastor Michael from town? Maybe we could get some community support that she'd see as a real boost. You could appeal to the band council for support. I'm sure they'd all be willing to do something. It could be a new tradition, or a revival of tradition. What do you think?"

"I think you're right. Maybe something on a grander scale would make her feel special, would show her the whole community is behind her. Get her fighting again. No Pastor Michael, though. Nothing against him, but this isn't a funeral. Not last rites. I don't want her or anybody else getting that idea." Owny was firm. She thought of the reaction of the Soulcatcher to her little dance. Same idea—that thing also had to stay home.

"Okay, yeah. Could be."

"Weekly council meeting the day after tomorrow. I'll bring it up. I feel a little funny since it's our own daughter."

"Don't. Don't feel bad in the least. You're just reaching out for ideas to help a loved one. You'd try to help another council member if they brought something like this up, wouldn't you?"

"Yes, of course."

Chapter 33

The band council was surprised that Owny brought up the idea of a ceremony. Not because they thought it was frivolous. Not because they thought she was pulling rank. Not because it would take effort, and not because it might cost something. No, they were surprised Owny was compelled to do it at all. It meant things were bad, in the final stages, and the family was looking anywhere and everywhere to change the course. The group, who knew each other so well, looked into each other's eyes and felt a sombre cloud fill the boardroom.

Owny continued to speak after she had initially aired her concept. "We'd go to the lake, she and I. Sometimes with Gerald. Right over to where the spring fills the lake—the source, you know. At first she hated it!" Owny felt emotion catch in her throat as she reminisced. "But she would get in and float over to the bubbles. I think it helped. She's not strong enough to go anymore." She looked around the table. "We're just trying to think of a way to show her we're all behind her and hopefully give her a lift. A show of community support to get her fighting again!" Owny, sitting at the head of the table, a position meant to signify strength and respect, blinked away tears. She looked around the group. "Think about it. If anyone has any ideas, please let me know. We just want to help Patsy—with modern medicine, traditional medicine, Eastern medicine, anything. Anything that will help, we're open to trying." She looked down at her clasped hands. "I'm going to go." She suddenly felt emotionally drained. "I need to go and check on Patsy."

The elders around the table nodded and mumbled approval.

After Chief Oneida Wilson left the band council meeting, Tom White, the caretaker at the Old Town dock, spoke up. "I have an idea," he said. "Patsy always loved the canoe . . . *loves* the canoe. More than any kid I ever saw. We could do something with the canoe."

"Like what?" Cecil, the Assistant Chief, asked. "The canoe is at tidewater in Old Town. We need to do something at the lake!"

"I know," Tom said. "I know."

* * *

Nothing on such a grand scale had ever been done before. Tom White had an idea for a ceremony would be a unique and special way for the community to show incredible support for one of their own.

On a chilly morning in early fall, volunteers from the villages assembled at the shore near the docks at Old Town. The large dugout canoe decorated with the Sisiutl motif was beached, and six stout men on each side struggled to pull the heavy craft completely ashore and onto a stabilizing frame that Tom, Gerald, and Willie Dubois had fashioned at the sawmill the day before for the portage to New Town.

If anyone wondered what the point was of bringing the ocean-bound craft up to the lake, they didn't ask. If anyone wondered why they didn't simply trailer the big canoe up to New Town, they didn't bring it up. This was a labour of love. A show of respect. It was a way to gather the spirits. Through travail. Through abnegation. Through the collective focus of mind and muscle, flesh and bone, and the sacrifice of time.

Once the boat was on the gravel shore, Tom lashed poles that extended several feet on each side to the spreader beams in three places. This would give the porters a solid station from which to push the craft. Tom had also amassed about a dozen small logs, each stripped of bark, close to the same diameter, and just over a meter long. These were the rollers the dugout canoe would travel overland on up to the lake. The volunteers lifted the tip of the stabilized canoe up, and Tom jammed the first roller log perpendicular to the frame rails under the canoe. He placed another one on the ground in front of the first log, and another three beyond that. The men then positioned themselves alongside the dugout and heaved it forward onto the rollers. They pushed it until it was completely off the ground and in a position to move atop the short logs. As they pushed it forward, others picked up the rollers from behind the boat and rushed with them to the front.

Once off the beach and onto a level spot, they stopped, cheered, and high-fived each other; the ancient, labour-intensive method of transport was going to work. Tom got two heavy ropes and tied them to the front cross brace of the canoe. Two groups could pull from the ropes, three groups could push from the sides, and two individuals could cycle the log rollers, back to front, as they moved over them.

The canoe started its slow journey up the incline to the top of Old Town. The pitch was relatively steep from the perspective of someone rolling a canoe uphill on a chilly morning. The porters struggled not only for forward motion, but just to keep the boat from rolling back down the hill. They persevered and found a level of exertion and acceptable pace for all.

Once they had rolled the canoe to the top of the hill, they stopped as planned to await the start of the procession, set for two in the afternoon. In some ways the hard part—getting the canoe off the beach, setting it on the frame, figuring out if they could actually roll it, and getting it up the steepest hill—was over. The volunteers went home to await the gathering a few hours hence. Those who had ceremonial garments would be wearing them for the special day. Moving the canoe to the lake would be a formal ritual that would become an annual tradition for the clan.

Owny decided to walk the two and a half kilometers to Old Town for the canoe ceremony. Somehow it just seemed right; driving down and then starting the parade would be too easy. Then someone would have to go back for the vehicle. The walk down made sense, and Gerald and Iris joined the matriarch, also in their capes and traditional rain hats, for the half-hour walk. Aster stayed back to keep Patsy company. Her secret duty was to keep her sister focused and on task, and to support her when the canoe finally came for her, passing through New Town to the lake.

While Owny drove her vehicle down to Old Town several times a month, it had been years since she had walked down to the older settlement. In her younger days she had done it countless times to visit relatives, go fishing, or to party. Those memories flooded back as she walked the tree-lined gravel road to meet the entire community. The alders that grew close to the road were turning yellow, creating a colourful route as the sun illuminated the treetops. Leaves were beginning to drop, softening their footfalls.

It pleased her greatly that the band council had come up with the idea for the ceremony on their own. It confirmed their commitment to the cause and validated their support for her and her family. And while it was something of a strange idea and required a huge effort, the ceremony was a new tradition her people could identify with forever and call their own. The "Grand March of the Canoe" would be led by the Chief every year henceforth. It connected tidewater to freshwater, Old Town to New Town, clansman to clansman, and the world of man to the spirit world.

The Wilsons arrived at the awaiting canoe at the top of the hill overlooking Old Town. Like a small ship, the canoe looked huge when out of the water and on the rollers. Dozens of Owny's people were already there, most in their finest traditional garb, chatting and laughing—not disrespectfully, but just in the way of clan. When they saw Chief Owny and her family approach, the conversations softened and some stood back a little from the large wooden dugout.

Owny stopped in her tracks. The image of the huge canoe on blocks, her people showing up in complete support, the sense of community, and the spirits surrounding them made her heart feel full, and emotion briefly overwhelmed her. She looked at Gerald and Iris, then wiped tears from her face before getting too close to the crowd. She recognized that the congregation around the ceremonial canoe would have looked the same and felt the same if this was a hundred years ago, or a thousand years ago. Maybe that was another reason she'd walked there.

As the top of the hour arrived, Tom White gave quiet instruction to his volunteers, positioning them on the ropes on the sides of the craft; the youngest would be moving the rollers.

Owny reached into the canoe and removed a smudge pot she had arranged to be waiting for her. It was a large abalone shell with three twine ropes tied at the top to suspend it. She removed a bundle of red cedar strips and bark from under her cape. With a lighter she lit one end of the bundle and blew on the glowing end to give it oxygen. She then placed the smoking bundle in the abalone smudge pot and picked it up by the twine. Red cedar was for clarity and health. The smoke set the mood with its aroma. Owny walked forward, swinging the shell not unlike a Catholic priest swinging his incense burner. The entire band council started walking with her, most in traditional raiment, many with hand drums and mallets. They began to chant to the rhythm of the skin drums.

Tom White signalled the volunteers to get on the ropes, and to position themselves to the side of the dugout. On his signal, they grunted, "Hai" on the downbeat to start the boat moving. It barely budged. "Hai," they grunted again on the beat, and this time the boat made it over the first roller. With another "Hai," they covered two more rollers and a young man picked up a log, now useless, from the stern of the craft and rushed it to the front. Five rollers were out. Tom gently ordered another young man to get out in front of them and move any large rocks that lay in their path on the gravel road. These could impede their attempts to roll the canoe.

The entire clan turned out, at least everyone who could walk or wasn't shut in. The band council, with their relatives and close friends, led the way. Others walked alongside the slow-moving boat, while others still pitched in to push; it was already emerging that it was an honour to push the craft, and a distinct honour to be a selected an official porter. The rest of the clan followed behind, fully two hundred souls in all. Owny's smudge cleansed the group as they walked, the wind cooperating by softly sending the smudge over her people, down the channel the road made through the trees. Their drums and chants became more defined, and the Sisiutl canoe began to move at a pace that seemed powered by the chants of the people, the will of the clan, and the draw of the smoke, rather than the physical efforts of the young men who moved the craft. The porters themselves felt the big dugout had become lighter, and the rollers worked better as the road levelled off, the spirit of the clan uniting to smooth the process.

When they had travelled about halfway, Owny signalled to stop for a break. The group ground to a halt; Tom and the porters looked at each other and then back at Owny. They gestured to suggest there was no need to rest, as the vessel was moving with little effort; they were merely keeping it centred on the rollers. It was as if it was somehow moving on its own, like a giant Ouija board planchette, with each person touching it but not influencing its movement or making any concerted effort to create forward motion.

Owny understood the body language from Tom and his crew, yet she continued to signal that she needed to stop. She had to light a second cedar bundle, which she produced from under her garment. She lit it, blew on it, and pushed it in place beside the ashes in the large shell, which she had placed on the ground. Owny nodded and smiled at her success, then gave a big sweep of her arm, as if to say, "Wagons ho," to get everyone moving again.

With very little effort the porters got the large dugout moving across the rollers again. The drums started, the chant renewed, and the group moved apace. Within a few meters, the boat again began to gently move as if on its own. The porters signalled to direct Tom's attention to this phenomenon.

Perplexed, Tom said, "We must be on a bit of a downslope? That must be it. But you sure can't see it. I know roads can sometimes fool you as to whether they're flat or going down a little. I think the leaves are greasing things up a bit too." For several hundred meters the porters never laid a hand on the push poles. The spirits were with them, there to bring Patsy home. Safely.

In less than an hour from the rest stop, the dugout, surrounded by the clan, was turning down the beach road and the lake was in sight. The porters easily skidded the craft ninety degrees on the smooth, wet rollers and pointed the boat toward the water. They continued to place the rollers in front of the craft, now on a distinct slope down to the boat ramp. It was as though it was anxious to return to the water; the caretakers had to hold the thing back. It swerved slightly back and forth over the damp logs, like a giant eager otter wiggling down to its preferred element. Once at the water's edge, Tom removed the push poles, the ropes, and the boards that secured the canoe to the frame, and they pushed it into the lake. Several porters jumped in and paddled it over to the vacant moorage at the New Town docks.

Owny looked around for Aster and Patsy. She only saw Aster, standing on the beach road watching the clan. Aster was in her traditional costume and holding the battered guitar case that held the Sisiutl mask. She looked like an unusual musician waiting for the crowd to settle down. Owny gave her smudge pot to Iris and walked back up the beach to Aster.

"Where's Patsy?" She knew what Aster would say.

"She can't make it. She's too weak, she says."

"She can't make it, or she doesn't *want* to make it?"

"She can't—I'm pretty sure. I think she wants to come. She seems excited. Excited as she can get, I guess . . . under the circumstances."

"Did you try to help her, to walk with her?"

"Yes, Mum, yes. We got just outside the door and down the steps, and she said she was just too weak. She's back inside."

Owny sighed. Maybe this wasn't such a good idea after all. She looked back at the crowd that had assembled for her daughter. She thought of a walker. A wheelchair. She waved at Gerald to come over. They walked away from the group so they could speak privately. The elaborate ceremony with the canoe carrying Patsy across the lake to the source didn't make any sense without Patsy being there.

Down at the beach, Tom and his porters were busy organizing the ritual for the Chief. They started a large fire, and they moved picnic tables and logs into a rough circle back from the flame. Elders could sit and rest from the walk while still watching the ceremony. Gerald tried to call Tom over to where he and Owny were talking. He couldn't get his attention. He opted to call him on his cell phone. Tom answered in the distance. "Tom, we need some help with Patsy. Bring six guys, please. Over to our house."

"Okay, we'll be right there!"

Gerald watched Tom point to a few of his crew, and they started walking up the beach to the road.

* * *

Patsy looked surprised when so many people crowded into her small room. Owny asked her to stand up, and she and Aster took her to the bathroom as the men lifted her bed, then turned it sideways to get it out the first bedroom door, then the front door of the Wilson home. They set it down on the road, positioned the mattress, tucked in the loose bedcovers, and awaited the girls.

Owny came to the door and beckoned to Gerald to come in. After a minute he emerged, carrying his eldest daughter in his arms. She was dressed in the family's traditional bloomers and her mother's button blanket. She turned her face into her father's chest, embarrassed by the spectacle. Patsy didn't weigh much anymore, but he carefully navigated the porch and the few steps down to the gravel. He set her down on the old brown metal-framed single bed. She lay there for a moment, covering her face, turning into the bed, trying to avoid the reality of the moment. When the porters hoisted the bed, even though she must have expected movement, Patsy seemed surprised. She twisted around to grab the bars of the headboard for stability. She managed to wiggle up and sit upright with her back to the headboard. She held on to the bars with both arms outstretched.

"Okay, Patsy, let's go!" Owny tried to sound enthusiastic.

The canoe porters, now Patsy's bed porters, moved down the street a block or so to the beach access. They stopped at the top of the beach, Patsy still aloft.

The crowd turned to see the odd sight of the girl on the bed and was silent for a moment, processing what they were seeing, then cheered heartily. The Wilson family was gratified at the outpouring of support; it confirmed that the strange gathering was indeed the right thing to do.

Incredulous, Patsy couldn't help but smile. Always the shy girl, always the quiet one, the one groomed to be stoic and ready, she managed a laugh and a queen-like wave to the crowd. She had finally embraced the moment after realizing it would be impossible to avoid being the centre of attention today.

The terrain became uneven as the bed carriers stepped off the road. The bed lurched and tipped, but they kept Patsy as level as possible. The crowd parted, and under the guidance of Owny and Tom, the porters set Patsy down a safe distance from the fire, but within the circle of picnic tables and the fluid circle of people surrounding the makeshift site.

Owny had some experience in Indigenous ceremonial matters, but this was unprecedented. She had planned several rituals but struggled with what would be most appropriate. She wanted to ensure this would be a time of inspiration. They needed to tap into historical healing, calling on the people of the present and the past to help Patsy, and maybe her people in general, to a healthier place. She needed to get this right. She didn't want to send any mixed messages or disrespect the traditions. Her practice in the kitchen was effective, but she feared that the coming combination of rituals might miss the mark.

Owny signalled to the rhythm keepers to start a drumbeat, let the tempo stabilize for a few moments, then nodded to the women she had requested earlier to start a female chant. It started discreetly, then developed into something high-pitched and moving. After an appropriate amount of time, Owny stepped into the centre of the circle near the settling fire and waved her arms to get everyone's attention. A small piece of paper in her hand would remind her of her talking points.

The wind settled down; the lake became glass. The fall colours became amplified in the late-afternoon light. Owny looked resplendent in her traditional regalia and was now wearing the traditional Chief's headgear—a high hat with upright eagle feathers and a copper plate relief of a sea otter.

"Thank you," she began. "Thank you all for coming. Thank you all for your support, your understanding, and your positive energy for this important day. Today is a new day for our people. Today is a new day for Patsy!" She paused for cheers from the crowd. Owny had become completely invested in the high stakes ceremony, but tried to suppress her emotions. She told herself to calm down, and to carefully select her words. "Our traditions have power! Our medicines have merit! Our people are united in this cause! And the spirits are with us today!" Cheers resounded. "Thank you to those who helped move the canoe, thank you to the rhythm keepers, thank you to the chanters. Thank you to the dancers we'll see. We'll have an eagle dance from the children, a chant from the men to our ancestors, and then a spirit dance. From there we'll go to the canoe and proceed to the other side of the lake. If you'd like to accompany us in other boats, you're welcome to. Molly?" Owny looked around for the daycare supervisor to start the children's dance.

A frantic little woman pushed her way through the group with about ten children in tow. Their ages ranged from about four to seven. She instructed them to arrange themselves around the fire. A drumbeat started and they walked around the flame, a few starting off in the wrong direction, then correcting themselves. They walked and bobbed around in a circle, looking in the crowd for their parents or a familiar face, smiling and waving at anyone who responded. After several minutes of this, Molly stepped in and stopped the children. The clan clapped and whistled in support of the children's non-dance.

Owny looked to the rhythm keepers to step up, ten positioned themselves around the fire. Then, about twice as many men stood outside their circle, ready to sing. The drumbeat started, then the chant. It was as firm and loud as anyone had ever heard. The volume increased, and the hair stood up on the necks of many supporters. The men reached out and held each other by the shoulders, creating an energy circle with drummers in an inner circle and the fire at the centre. The chanters and drummers became one, their wall of sound extending up to the heavens. Afterwards, many participants said they felt as if they'd left their own bodies and floated above the circle, looking down at the people on the ground, floating like ravens on a thermal updraft created by human emotion.

By then the clan knew something special was happening. They'd had ceremonies before, often several a year, but this was something grand. It evoked strong feelings, with most individuals sensing the connection between their heart and their ancestors. The chanters receded into the crowd, and the drummers also moved back and formed a line. The clan sensed something coming and stood back, creating an opening through to the fire. A mysterious figure skulked into the gap.

It was the Sisiutl. The Sisiutl was coming to the fire. The invincible warrior would transfer his energy to Patsy to make her invincible too. The late-afternoon light dimmed, as if the sun was being eclipsed. The fire created light and shadow. The Sisiutl stopped and was motionless for a moment, gazing into the flame. Most of the people had never seen the mask before, while a few could vaguely remember it from childhood. But all were in awe of it. Most knew it must be Owny in the mask, but she was just a vessel the spirits were inhabiting to do their own dance.

Drums began, slowly at first, then movement. The creature craned its neck and gawked like a bird. With great skill and balance, the Sisiutl moved around the fire, ducking deep on the downbeat, moving to stare into the faces of onlookers, then into the flames. After a couple of revolutions around the fire, the Sisiutl pulled the strings on the mask and opened it slightly. It was a tease—the mask closed quickly. The crowd cheered and called, wanting to see it again. Again, it opened a little, then closed. The children's eyes were as wide as saucers. After more attempts, the Sisiutl finally opened up its mask to expose the inner man. It now looked as though the man's head had wings; the mask was awkward and wide. He wasn't grotesque, but his weird eyes made him look as if he was in awe of the world, having awakened after so much time asleep.

The fire cracked and popped as added cedar mixed with alder and burned into a lively flame. Hot embers jumped out as if the fire itself was expelling any dissenters. Smoke rose straight up like a column to the sky people on the windless evening. The Sisiutl beckoned the spirits, as only he, the conduit between the spirit world and the land of the living, could. He raised his arms to reach for the stars, then stepped around the fire again, opening and closing his mask in a fluid motion that mesmerized the onlookers.

Two other dancers joined the Sisiutl—one a common man, the second a man with dried white clay on his face, representing the spirits. The Sisiutl danced back and forth between the two, symbolizing the movement between two worlds, all the time opening and closing the mask with the strings. The drums pounded harder; the chanting became a throaty call from nearly all of the audience. Then the Sisiutl worked his way through the crowd and away from the fire. The clay-faced ghost followed, leaving only the common man in his own corporeal world. Realizing the dance was over, the group cheered and whistled. They were happy to see such an historical dance and grateful it wouldn't be lost to the mists of time but revitalized, helping to define their culture going forward.

With Gerald's help, Owny quickly removed the mask and placed it in the guitar case. She didn't know if she was exhausted or invigorated. Gerald gave her a hug, and they picked their way through the group to Patsy's bedside. Patsy tried to present a brave smile to her mother.

Owny whispered to her daughter, "How are you feeling. Are you ready to go out in the canoe?"

Patsy shook her head. "No, Mum, I don't think so. I'm just so tired."

From the look of her daughter, Owny had expected the pushback.

"But I *would* like to get to the water. I know that's what this is all about, so maybe just here near the shore?"

"Can we carry you?"

Patsy shook her head.

Seeking Tom White, Owny scanned the faces of those watching them. She spotted him and waved for him to come over. Tom made his way to the Chief.

"Tom, do you think we can get the bed on the canoe? The whole bed, as it is, with Patsy on it?"

Tom seemed taken aback. He raised his conical cedar hat and scratched his head. It had been a very odd day, and it was about to get even odder. "Uh, well, the canoe is very stable. I suppose we could set the bed across the middle and paddle her over like that. Are you sure you want to do that? Is Patsy okay with that?"

"She just has to lie there!" Owny was determined her vision would be realized, and she wanted the maximum benefit for her daughter. "Let's do it before it gets too dark!"

In spite of the incredible request, Tom called on six porters to manhandle the bed again with Patsy on it. Owny watched him explain her idea to them, and they looked at each other in disbelief, then at the occupied bed. On Tom's cue, amid some shrugs and okays, they lifted Patsy and the bed high onto their shoulders in one motion. They made their way toward the dock, and Patsy held on tight as if she were Cleopatra being taken to her Nile barge on a litter.

The crowd cheered as soon as they realized what the plan was. The group set the bed on the wooden dock, then with little difficulty transferred it to the awaiting canoe, the bed sitting high but securely across the beam. All twelve rowers piled into the canoe, ready to paddle to the source. Supporters who had a boat got into their respective vessels, having been previously selected to accompany the canoe on its special trip.

Owny was inspired by the fire dance, so she hastily told Aster to run and get the guitar case so she could once again don the mask. She would stand in the bow of the canoe as the Sisiutl. The image would be a powerful reminder of the past. As she got into character and stepped into the bow, a flotilla formed around them. Many onlookers were taking pictures with their phones. This was something historic. Tom grabbed a small hand drum and tossed it onto the bed for Patsy. He encouraged her to pick it up and give them all the beat to start their paddle strokes. She wanted to please Tom and the crew, so she mustered the strength to tap lightly on the skin. Other rhythm keepers in surrounding boats picked up the beat immediately, and they pushed away from their berth and out onto the calm lake. With a few deep strokes, they were up to speed, the huge canoe with the bed astride it. A half a dozen other small boats struggled to keep up.

Patsy seemed genuinely pleased. She lay on her bed, half propped up on one elbow, the centre of attention in the historic pilgrimage. It was obvious her mother couldn't love her more. Owny took her place as both Chief and her mother, and somehow also as the Sisiutl dancer leading a ceremony that was both ancient and new at the same time.

They neared the source. Owny realized that in the activity and emotion of the day, she had forgotten a life jacket. She very much wanted Patsy in the water, if only briefly. This would take a bit of thinking. Perhaps the porters could lower her down, holding on to her all the time. She was confident that would work. They were there for healing after all, not to sacrifice a virgin. Stoneblanket wanted the latter.

Chapter 34

Owny hadn't consciously excluded Ryan from the events of the day, but it never occurred to her to let him know of the elaborate plan, or to give him a heads-up about the canoe being moved to the lake. This was a family matter, a clan matter, a cultural matter, and it was no concern to him. He was not one of her people. The Chief just focused on the task at hand.

However, as the strange flotilla descended upon the traditional source of healing   , she realized that all this was taking place right in front of Ryan's cabin, and if he was home (and he usually was at this time of day), the spectacle would be quite a surprise. *Oh well,* she thought in her Sisiutl mask, *too late now.* He would likely put two and two together anyway.

* * *

Ryan and Laura had just sat down to an early supper. As they broke bread, Laura looked out through the twilight. A group of boats led by a huge dugout canoe—a bed straddling it—was assembling on the lake.

"Well, you don't see that every day," Laura said in an understated way.

"What's that?" Ryan responded. He followed her gaze out the front window. His eyes widened and his jaw dropped. "Oh. My. God. Oh my God! I-I can't believe this!"

"What's going on?" Laura seemed completely perplexed. "Or *does* this happen every day? Have you been holding out on me?"

"Oh my God. No, this does *not* happen every day. This never happens." Ryan stood up at the table. He took in the view of the familiar carved canoe, the strange sight of a bed perched across it, and the other boats and people attending. They could hear the drums begin. Immediately, he knew what this must be. Ryan had no clue what was happening inside him, and tears sprang to his eyes. Grief flooded his heart and pushed aside all the other thoughts and emotions within him. This was about Patsy. Had to be.

He hadn't seen anyone from the Wilson family for many days, and hadn't seen Patsy come for a dip in many weeks. This was a demonstration of something incredibly special: audacious, absurd, desperate love. They walked to the window for a closer look.

Ryan couldn't help himself; he started to sob. Laura looked at him in complete shock. One moment they had been sitting down to a pleasant meal, and the next he was inconsolable.

"What's going on, Ryan? What's wrong with you? My God, are you okay? What is this? Are you upset about these boats?"

Ryan couldn't find the words. He nodded yes, then shook his head no, then nodded again, further confusing his wife. He sucked in air and shuddered. He wiped his eyes and tried to compose himself. "I'm not positive, but I'm pretty sure this is for Patsy. Remember Patsy, the girl you met at the hospital? And the story about the life preservers and her mum, Owny?"

"How could I forget?"

"Like I said, the kid has cancer. She's the Chief's daughter. I've gotten to know the Chief—Owny—quite well. I told you I first met them when they came here so Patsy could get into the water."

"Yes."

"At first I was pissed off. I just thought they were trespassing, a nuisance. But then I got to know them and started to understand what was going on, why they came to this spot. Got to know the family. She's really a good kid. This is unbelievable. Look at that damn bed. My God." He shook his head and choked up again at the display of unity. He was distressed at knowing what it must have taken for the clan to get to this point. Sadness. Desperation. Solidarity. Creativity. Faith. He picked up his binoculars from the window ledge for a closer look at the occupants of the canoe. Then he focused on New Town across the lake. Dozens of people watched and waited on the other side; he could only just make them out. "Oh my God," he repeated under his breath. "That's got to be the whole clan out there."

"What do you mean?"

"I mean across the lake, waiting, and in the boats. Everyone. Everyone from both villages. Incredible." He scanned the canoe, which had floated broadside to the shore, and focused on the bed. "Yup. It's Patsy. On the bed. Damn it." He viewed the whole group, all in their finest. This was a significant gathering. He saw the strange masked figure in the bow. "I don't want to disturb them, but I want to get closer. Let's go out to the end of the dock."

"You sure?"

"Yeah, I'm sure. I need to get closer. She won't mind. I know her." Ryan was referring to Owny. She had to be there somewhere.

They quietly went down the stairs and out to the dock. They sat down cross-legged to lower their profile, Rosie between them. With a clear view of the group, Ryan saw the person in the bow take the elaborate mask off; it was his friend Owny. She started to speak in the old language and tossed flower petals into the water. Then wood chips, then ashes. The rhythm keepers started in earnest, some in the canoe, some in adjacent boats, keeping a solid, steady beat. Then there was chanting. Owny gestured to Patsy, who was propped up in the bed on her left elbow with her legs to one side. She appeared unable or unwilling to move.

* * *

"Can you, Patsy?" Owny asked her daughter, knowing Patsy understood. "Can we help you?"

Patsy rocked slightly as if trying to dislodge herself.

Owny was in the bow of the boat and out of reach of her daughter. She was relying on the people next to the bed to help. "Patsy?"

Patsy pushed the button blanket cape with her arm, indicating she would move. The chanting was steady and measured. Then she pushed the garment over her head; she was in her white undergarments. She mustered some strength and got to her knees. Wobbly, she stood up.

"No, no, Patsy!" Owny cried. "Don't stand up—they'll lower you down!"

Patsy looked at her mother and shook her head to indicate she didn't need any help. Then she bent down and picked up a long velvet bag from inside her button blanket. She pulled the black sleeve off and wielded the Soulcatcher. Wobbling again, she raised it high above her head.

"No, Patsy!" Owny yelled, panic-stricken as she suddenly realized her daughter's intent. "Stop her!"

The paddlers next to the bed weren't sure what was going on. Not knowing what to do, those close by reached over and held her ankles.

"Don't shake that thing!" Owny cried at the top of her lungs.

Gerald scrambled forward from the stern, clambering over paddlers. He fell between two men. "Don't shake it, Patsy!" he demanded. "Don't let her shake it!" he cried to anyone close.

Patsy raised the Soulcatcher straight up like a lightning rod to the heavens. Then she lowered it slightly and gave it a vigorous shake. The little man clacked back and forth. "Take me home!" she yelled as loud as she could, straining her frail voice. She pointed the Soulcatcher to the sky. "Stoneblanket, take me with you!"

Inky clouds rapidly coalesced above the boats. The wind came up like an emerging tornado. The sky above them twisted and roiled, dark and foreboding. Ryan's shitshow had started. Beams of green "northern lights" emanated from the depths of the grey-brown murk overhead. The lights spun as if attached to a reckless carnival ride. The wind was like a sustained, punishing blow, and garments billowed, cedar hats were sucked into the sky, and boats rocked. The waves formed a circular pattern within the churning wind. Despite the rocking of the canoe, Patsy somehow found the strength to balance herself.

A green-and-gold arc of lightning crackled out of the brooding cauldron of clouds and spinning light. It moved downward like the awkward digit of a demon, seeking the Soulcatcher. It found it quickly, making a solid connection through the antenna, and into Patsy. She convulsed, a wave of contraction starting in her lower back, up through her body, and into her outstretched arm. The lightning got thicker.

The Soulcatcher had been released from her hand and was poised vertically in the air. The air crackled with energy. An intense light came from inside the marrow channel; it was the little man, illuminated to incandescence. He moved up and down inside the Soulcatcher while it hung in the air. Everyone watching was transfixed and immobile. The hot white light spun in the ribbon relief decoration of the Soulcatcher, reflecting with a mirror ball effect on the lake. The Soulcatcher floated for several seconds, then was pulled straight up into the carnival ride. Patsy's spirit, still firmly connected to the arc, became visibly dislodged from her body. It slipped off her like a nightgown coming off for the day and was gently pulled upward by the thick green-and-gold arc of lightning. This retracted into the cloud, taking the young woman's spirit with it. Patsy's body collapsed. She tipped over in slow motion and fell without grace into the water.

Unable to move and with no leverage, the porters holding Patsy's ankles couldn't stop her fall. The others in the boats were stunned, as were Ryan and Laura. Rosie was silent until the lifeless body hit the water. When it did, she let out a vivid bark like a starting gun. Then bedlam ensued. Two porters, then a third, jumped from the canoe into the cold water after Patsy. Then Gerald followed. Others from adjacent boats jumped in.

In shock and despair, Owny flung off her cape and also jumped in. How could she save her daughter? She couldn't swim.

* * *

Seeing Owny jump in, Ryan automatically peeled off his coat, grabbed the orange life preserver, and leaped into the frigid lake. Not to save Patsy—he knew she was gone. Owny wasn't in her right mind and someone needed to save her. She would be lost in the confusion. Rosie followed her master instinctively, as she had done so many times before when enjoying the lake. Bodies flailed and splashed in a panic. Laura stood and stared at the epic scene as if she was in a nightmare.

Gerald and the porters managed to bring Patsy to the surface. Compared to the lake, her body was still warm. Warm from the lightning. Steaming. Near the bow, Owny was sinking in the bubbles, unnoticed by others. Not swimming. Not trying now that Patsy was gone. The Soulcatcher was gone, back to its rightful owner. That could only mean trouble. In her despair, she wanted to join her daughter. Protect her in her afterlife. She had been fooled by her daughter. She had failed her in a Chief's folly, thinking she would heal her.

Ryan dove deep, as she was sinking like a stone. The lateness of the day and dark clouds had robbed the depths of any illumination. He strained to see in the cold water. He had to abandon this first attempt and came up for air, exhaled, and breathed deeply, then dove down again. Using the life preserver as a marker above, he swam straight down, groping the water in the dark. He felt an upright, limp arm. He grabbed onto it, pulled up, and pushed Owny toward the surface. He yanked at her clothing to keep her going. As they broke the surface, he scrambled for the orange ring Patsy had so often used. Ryan put it over Owny's head and managed to get her arms over the ring. She was unresponsive. From the back, Ryan gave her a hard squeeze, his fists under her ribs. Her eyes bulged. At the second squeeze, she coughed out lake water, took in a raspy breath, then coughed some more.

Gerald hadn't seen her go in. He swam over as others pulled Patsy onto the canoe. "My God, woman! What were you doing?" He knew she couldn't answer. He looked at Ryan with a thank you, or a thank God, in his eyes. "I don't want to lose two girls in the same day!" Gerald caressed his wife's cold face.

Chapter 35

To be or not to be? Patsy had answered the question. *Not to be.* She could no longer suffer the slings and arrows of her outrageous fortune.

It was hard for Owny and Gerald to fathom what their daughter had gone through. Maybe she'd felt all along that her destiny was to join her long-dead twin brother, Alan. Survivor's guilt magnified over many years, and then punctuated by the final curtain—cervical cancer. It was meant to be.

Owny took some time to recover. It was days before she could even talk to her family. Eventually, she spoke up. She wanted to burn the canoe with Patsy in it, Viking style. She wanted to burn the ancient mask too, and anything with any semblance to the Sisiutl. In her mind the link had to be broken. The band council refused the idea outright. The canoe was a piece of art. It had been commissioned. It had taken almost a year to carve it. And the mask was a priceless relic. Owny may have been the caretaker of the thing, but she didn't own it. Patsy could be cremated and her ashes spread in the lake, if they wished, but that was it.

Owny was petrified that Stoneblanket, the personification of the Sisiutl, was now too powerful. He had his leg back; he was whole again. He had Patsy, which was a concern. Could Patsy fight him off in the spirit world? Would she have to? Did she want to?

Patsy Wilson's funeral was miserable, in every sense of the word. It rained sideways the whole afternoon. Owny was absolutely stricken. Even though she had a history of being strong, it was hard to watch. The death of her Patsy hit a deep and foul chord within her, rekindling dormant memories of Patsy and Alan at birth. They were together again. The grief was too much.

It looked as if the whole clan was there. Even Ronny Two Livers showed up. At Owny's behest, Halayt Jona Mason came all the way from Alert Bay to perform the main part of the ritual. Pastor Michael was invited and did an excellent job of keeping the white man's version of the funeral relevant. The spreading of the ashes would be a ceremony for some other day.

* * *

The Wilsons had a celebration of life after the formal gathering, and Ryan and Laura lingered for a little while. From the times he'd spent with them at the lake and beyond, Ryan felt a deep connection to Owny and Patsy, as well as to Gerald. They had often adopted Ryan's crazy ideas, and this was a source of pride for him. It linked him to the Wilsons, even the entire clan, in some ways. He wanted Laura to see that connection first-hand. Even Ronny's sideways glances held no power over Ryan that day.

For certain the spirits were present in great numbers at the gathering. Emotions were high for everyone, and the exchanges between them were very laboured.

When the Hansons returned home to their cabin, the rain finally subsided as day turned to twilight. Ryan could hardly look out at the lake anymore. Every time he did, he envisioned the shitshow, Patsy standing upright on her bed, the lightning bolt, the smell of the ionized air, and the girl finally tipping into the water like a porcelain doll.

Laura busied herself making some herbal tea to warm their bones after the damp, dramatic day. Ryan let Rosie out to pee, and a few moments later she started to bark incessantly from the deck. He looked out to investigate. In the dimming light he saw a familiar figure lurking by the sign tree. It looked as if he had just come out of the water. It was him, the psychopomp. The soul trafficker. The escort through the ether. Stoneblanket himself.

Ryan quickly pushed open the door. "Rosie, shut up!" He silenced his dog, his voice straining as he yelled. He walked over to the corner of the deck, his heart fluttering in an unprecedented panic attack. In spite of his fear, his chest twitching, he stared Stoneblanket down. "There's nothing for you here, old man."

Stoneblanket turned at the sound of Ryan's voice. *"Metoken a xolmet. S'loh tem exw ka,"* he said in the old language. An odd voice inside Ryan's head let him understand: *This is my land. These are my special waters.*

"You're dead, old man. Go back to where you came from."

I have, Ryan understood. *That's why I'm here. I'm whole again. I'm born again. This is my world also.*

"Go away! Don't come 'round here no more!"

I've come to check my trapline. You're on my trapline now. Your wife is on my trapline!

"Don't you dare even mention my wife! She has nothing to do with you! You get the hell out of here!" Ryan yelled.

The harbinger of death smiled back at him for the first time. The little man in his leg bone glowed in the waning light. It cycled up and down, almost like a dog wagging its tail, happy with itself.

"Leave us alone!" Ryan bellowed.

Stoneblanket's dirty yellow smile widened. Then the rogue, now made whole again walked away into the night, striding confidently on his own two feet.

Laura stuck her head out the door, oblivious to Stoneblanket. "What are you yelling at?"

Ryan collected himself. "Oh, nothing—just a stray dog."